"I have no doubt that E. E. Knight is going to be a household name in the genre."
—Silver Oak Book Reviews

Praise for the Vampire Earth novels

Tale of the Thunderbolt

"An entertaining romp rife with plausible characters; powerful, frightening villains; suspense; romance; and monsters. Everything good fantasy and science fiction should have."

—SFF World

Choice of the Cat

"I dare you to try to stop reading this exciting tale."

—SF Reviews

"Strong characterization, excellent pacing, [and] believable depth in world-building . . . an entertaining story."

—SFF World

"An impressive follow-up sure to delight all fans of dark fantasy and hair-raising heroic adventure . . . unique and wonderfully entertaining."   —Rambles

"A sequel that surpasses the original."   —SF Reader

continued . . .

Way of the Wolf

"A winner. If you're going to read only one more postapocalyptic novel, make it this one."
— Fred Saberhagen, author of the Berserker series

"Powerful. . . . Readers will want to finish the tale in one sitting because it is so enthralling." — *Midwest Book Review*

"If *The Red Badge of Courage* had been written by H. P. Lovecraft." — Paul Witcover, author of *Waking Beauty*

"Knight's book of dark wonders is a marvel — simultaneously hip and classy, pulpy and profound. Evocative of Richard Matheson as well as Howard Hawks, Knight's terrifying future world is an epic canvas on which he paints a tale of human courage, heroism, and, yes, even love."
— Jay Bonansinga, author of *The Killer's Game*

"This is one of the best books I've read in years. If you like action books (or horror or military or suspense . . .) just buy it."
— Scott Sigler, author of *Earthcore*

"E. E. Knight has managed to create a compelling new world out of the ruins of our existing one. It's a major undertaking for a new author. . . . He does it with style and grace, and I would highly recommend checking out the book as soon as you can."
— Creature Corner

"Valentine is a complex and interesting character, mixing innocence with a coldhearted willingness to kill. . . . Knight brought the setting to vivid life. . . . His world is well constructed and holds together in a believable fashion . . . compelling."
— SF Reader

VALENTINE'S RISING

BOOK FOUR OF *THE VAMPIRE EARTH*

E. E. Knight

A ROC BOOK

ROC
Published by New American Library, a division of
Penguin Group (USA) Inc., 375 Hudson Street,
New York, New York 10014, USA
Penguin Group (Canada), 90 Eglinton Avenue East, Suite 700, Toronto,
Ontario M4P 2Y3, Canada (a division of Pearson Penguin Canada Inc.)
Penguin Books Ltd., 80 Strand, London WC2R 0RL, England
Penguin Ireland, 25 St. Stephen's Green, Dublin 2,
Ireland (a division of Penguin Books Ltd.)
Penguin Group (Australia), 250 Camberwell Road, Camberwell, Victoria 3124,
Australia (a division of Pearson Australia Group Pty. Ltd.)
Penguin Books India Pvt. Ltd., 11 Community Centre, Panchsheel Park,
New Delhi - 110 017, India
Penguin Group (NZ), cnr Airborne and Rosedale Roads, Albany,
Auckland 1310, New Zealand (a division of Pearson New Zealand Ltd.)
Penguin Books (South Africa) (Pty.) Ltd., 24 Sturdee Avenue,
Rosebank, Johannesburg 2196, South Africa

Penguin Books Ltd., Registered Offices:
80 Strand, London WC2R 0RL, England

First published by Roc, an imprint of New American Library,
a division of Penguin Group (USA) Inc.

First Printing, December 2005
10 9 8 7 6 5 4 3 2 1

 REGISTERED TRADEMARK—MARCA REGISTRADA

Printed in the United States of America

To those in uniform, past and present.
Thank you.

All along that singing river
A black mass of men was seen
And above their shining weapons
Hung their own beloved green
Death to every foe and traitor!
Whistle loud the marching tune
And Hurrah! me boys for freedom
'Tis the rising of the moon

The rising of the moon
The rising of the moon
And Hurrah! me boys for freedom
'Tis the rising of the moon

Well they fought for dear old Ireland
And full bitter was their fate
What a glorious pride and sorrow
Fills the name of ninety-eight
Yet thank God while hearts are beating fast
In manhood's burning noon
We will follow in their footsteps
By the rising of the moon

—"The Rising of the Moon" by John Keegan Casey

Chapter One

The Ouachita Forest, Arkansas, December of the forty-eighth year of the Kurian Order: The pines stand, colorless spindles under a winter overcast. The low mountains of the Ouachitas huddle dark all around, just touching the cloud sea. Water beads linger on bough, trunk, leaf and stone as though freshly dropped; the earth beneath the fallen leaves smells like decay. Birds overturn dead leaves and poke about the roots in silence, walking the earth as if too dispirited to fly. Brown ferns lie flat along the streambanks, under patches of frostbitten moss flaking off the rocks like old scabs. Even the wind is listless, seeping rather than blowing through the pines.

Naked outcroppings of stone, etched with lightning strikes of quartz crystal, project every which way from the ground like the work of titans who tried to pull out the mountain by its roots. The strata of the Ouachita slopes are jumbled, pushed up and twisted from a seismic pileup millennia ago. Thanks to the blind runs, box canyons and meandering crest lines of these elderly mountains, the landscape doesn't lend itself to habitation. These hills have been hideouts of liberty-loving Indians, die-hard Confederates, and law-evading brigands — the notorious Younger gang used to hole up here with the James brothers. Between the stands of rock, the ferns' squashed-spider shapes lie in boot tracks and hoofprints forming a trail that suggests a similar hurried flight from authority.

The boot tracks have a source, noisily crunching over the hilltop's still-frozen ground. Six mud-stained figures walk with the oddly stiff motion of men on their last legs, strung out in front of and behind a lone horse pulling an A-frame drag supporting an unconscious man with blood-matted hair. Two dreadlocked men in blue-black uniforms share a blanket as they move, muttering to each other in the patois of the sunny island of Jamaica. Walking alongside the horse is the oldest of the group, a meaty-faced man of six-two, dark brown hair flecked with early gray and a boxer's shovel jaw. His clothing, indeed his whole body, has the look of having just emerged from a threshing machine. An improvised poncho is fixed about his waist with a wide brown belt. Dried blood stains the parts that dirt hasn't touched; bits of rag are knotted around wounds in his left leg and right arm. He moves the horse along with a switch, though the occasional lash does nothing more than send it lurching forward a quick pace and into the man leading it.

The lead shape, seemingly bigger than any two of the others put together, is of another species. So forbidding that one might think he was pried off a cathedral and placed among Arkansas pines as a prank, he moves along leaning toward his right side, one tentpole-length arm supporting his midriff. An even longer gun rides his shoulders, tied there by a bit of leather like an ox's yoke. He has bandages wrapped about the waist, a tight corset of brown-stained cloth that accentuates the width of the meaty, golden-furred shoulders above. The creature's eyes shift, widen, and even go a little wet as he spies a figure far away in the trees, jogging toward the file from ahead.

The young man the apish humanoid sees places his feet deliberately as he trots, for a trail in wet leaves on the hillside could be spotted by experienced eyes as easily as a line of signal flares. He favors his left leg, leading with the right up difficult patches of the hill. His shining black hair and bronze skin mark him as more than a spiritual relative of the Osage who once hunted these hills; he moves like them, flowing from spot to spot with the speed of a summer stream: sometimes fast, sometimes slow, sometimes deceptively still when he stops to examine the ground. He wears a simple black uniform, mud-splotched, set off by a strange bandolier of snake-

skin with oversized loops, as if the sash had been designed to carry hand grenades, and carries a rugged submachine gun fed by a drum magazine.

His right cheek is scarred from the outer edge of his eye down. The wound, like a Prussian dueling scar, traces its pale way along the edge of his face, marring an otherwise handsome frame around brown eyes. The wary, intent gaze of a wild animal patiently reads the woods behind when he pauses to rest and lets the column come to a stop at its own pace. . . .

Have to turn again. The first zig left had been nine hours ago, to avoid a long string of soldiers walking at ten-foot intervals like beaters driving game. Then there'd been another left turn to avoid a watchtower looking over a length of old highway. Now he'd spotted teams of men and dogs combing the banks of an ice-choked stream.

They were boxed in, no doubt about it. Every step the survivors of his Texas column took now brought them closer to the area around Bern Woods, where they'd been ambushed two exhaustingly long days ago. Since then no one in his party of survivors had slept or eaten hot food, and there wasn't much play left in their strings.

His head ached. Fatigue or dehydration. He took a drink from his canteen.

"What passes, my David?" Ahn-Kha said, sliding up to him using his legs and one long arm. The Golden One doesn't look at David Valentine; he keeps his eyes on the forest-cutting road below.

"We're cut off. A picket line. Maybe dropped off from trucks."

The Jamaicans, ex-*Thunderbolt* marines named Striper and Ewenge, dropped to their knees, unconscious atop each other within seconds of the column's halt. The man leading the horse spat a white bubble onto the forest floor. William Post, Valentine's lieutenant since their service together on the old Kurian gunboat *Thunderbolt*, dropped his bloody switch and joined David and Ahn-Kha. The drooping horse blew a mouthful of foam out from either side of its bit.

"How's Tayland?" Valentine asked.

Post glanced back at the wounded man on the dragging A-frame. "Unconscious. Strong pulse still. The horse'll be dead before him."

"We've got maybe twenty minutes, and then a picket line will be on top of us."

"I heard dogs behind," Ahn-Kha said. The Grog was the only one who didn't look dejected. He rubbed a bullet tip on his bandolier with the large thumb particular to the Golden Ones' hands.

"That's it, then," Post said. "We can't get back to Texas."

"Listen up," Valentine said loudly, and his complement of six—as recently as two days ago he'd been leading hundreds—was brought to life by prods from Post, except for Tayland. "We're boxed in. We've got three guns with ammunition still between us"—Valentine still carried his old PPD out of affectation; it was as impotent as one of the quartz-etched rocks jutting from the soil—"and I've not seen a hint of friendly forces."

Jefferson, the Texas drover at the horse's head, asked, "How many are coming after us?"

"More than enough."

He let that sink in for a moment, then went on. "I'm going to have to ask you to trust me. The Quislings love nothing better than taking prisoners."

"You want to surrender?" Post asked.

"Worse," Valentine said. "I want all of you to surrender. We fight it out here and we'll just be dead. Giving up, you have a chance."

"They'll feed us before they'll kill us," Striper said. "I'll hold my hands high, if it means hot tuck and sleep." His mate looked down, blinking at tears.

"I'll follow. I expect they'll take you back to Bern Woods; we've been heading that way for the last two hours, and we know that town is occupied. Perhaps something will turn up."

"I could play that I'm your prisoner," Ahn-Kha said. "They might keep an eye on me, but leave me free."

"No, I'll need you at the town."

"You want to see if there's any Quickwood left?" Ahn-Kha asked.

"I want the rest of our men. The wood will have to wait."

"How about a vote, Captain?" Post asked.

"Sure. Ewenge?"

All Valentine saw was the top of his hat as the man spoke. "Yes, sir. I give up."

"Striper?"

The Jamaican nodded. He took out a small eating knife and tossed it to the ground.

"Slave labor camp's not my style," Jefferson said.

"You're free to try to make it on your own."

"Okay then," Jefferson said. He knelt and relaced his boots.

"Tayland's still out," Post said.

Valentine handed Jefferson his canteen. "That leaves you, Will."

"Wonder if they'll send me back to New Orleans to hang as a renegade?"

"If that happens, I'll surrender and hang with you," Valentine said.

Post shrugged. "Sure. Don't do that though, sir. Just find my wife and tell her what happened on the *Thunderbolt*."

The only other refugee from the column couldn't speak. The horse just shifted a foreleg out and gulped air.

"That's it then," Valentine said. He walked around to the rear of the horse, and opened Tayland's eye. The pupil reacted to the light of the overcast, but the former Texas wagonman showed no sign of regaining consciousness. Valentine nodded to Post, who untied the saplings from the horse's saddle. They lowered the litter to the ground, placing it gently on the winter leaves. Jefferson shook hands with everyone, accepted Post's pistol, received a few words of encouragement and some jerky in wax paper from Striper, and ran southward.

"I couldn't run if the devil himself poked me," Ewenge said, watching him go. Jefferson waved as he disappeared from sight. The Jamaican marine mechanically removed the horse's saddle and wiped the sweat from its back.

"They'll be here soon. Walk around a lot and mess up the tracks," Valentine told Post. "If they ask about me, tell them I took off hours ago."

"What about me?" Ahn-Kha asked.

"You left now. Scared Grog running for tall timber."

"You'll leave tracks just like Jefferson, Captain," Striper said. "Maybe they follow you too."

Valentine nodded to Ahn-Kha, who was, as usual, ahead of his human ally's thoughts in throwing a blanket over his shoulders. Ahn-Kha bent over and Valentine climbed onto his back. He clung there like a baby monkey.

"One set of tracks," Post said. "Good luck, sir. Don't worry about us. Remember to find Gail. Gail Foster, her maiden name was. Tell her . . ."

"You were wrong," Valentine offered.

Post bit his lip. "Just 'I'm sorry.'"

Valentine thought of telling Post that he could tell her himself, but with hope vanished from the Ozarks like the winter sun, he couldn't bring himself to offer an empty lie to a friend.

Ahn-Kha ran, legs pounding like twin piledrivers in countersynch, clutching his long Grog rifle in one hand and Valentine's empty gun in the other. The trees went by in a blur.

They splashed up an icy stream, startling a pair of ducks into flight. If the freezing water hurt the Grog's long-toed feet, he gave no indication.

Valentine heard a distant shot from the direction of Post's group.

"Stop," he told Ahn-Kha.

Ahn-Kha took two more steps, and placed Valentine on a flat-topped rock midstream.

"You need a rest?" Ahn-Kha asked, blowing.

"I heard a shot."

"Maybe a signal?"

"Or something else."

Only the running water, wind and an occasional bird could be heard in the Arkansas pines and hardwoods. Ahn-Kha shivered. Valentine saw a fallen log upstream, felled by erosion so that it lay like a ramp up the riverbank.

"Let's cut back. Carefully."

It was Tayland. His eyes were shut, and he had the strangely peaceful look of the recently dead.

They'd just left him in the woods on his litter, wrapped in blankets that would soon be disturbed by birds or coyotes, a bullet hole dead center in his chest. The tracks said that a group of men and dogs had turned after Jefferson, but no one had bothered to follow the lone Grog.

As he said a few words of prayer over the deceased, Valentine remembered Tayland, wounded as they fled the ambush at Bern Woods, cutting the horse free from the traces of a teammate with a big bowie knife. He rooted around at the man's waist, and freed the knife and its scabbard.

The blade was sticky with its owner's blood.

"Shall we bury him?" Ahn-Kha asked.

"No. They might send a party back to get the body. You never know."

"The tracks lead back to town," Ahn-Kha observed. A wide trail showed that men walked to either side of the short-stepping prisoners. They'd probably put them in shackles.

Valentine nodded into the big, enquiring eyes and the pair turned to follow the trail.

If it weren't for the winter drizzle, the rider would have raised dust. Valentine watched him come into Bern Woods from the north, long coat flapping to the thunderous syncopation of his lathered mount's hooves. He clutched mane and reigns in his right hand, leaning far over his horse's neck so his left could wave a red-and-white-striped gusset above him, hallooing all the way.

Valentine waited and watched the guards in the south-gate tower smoke cigarettes. He felt strangely uneasy in his hiding place, near the foundation of a flattened house outside of town where he stowed his .45 automatic and clothes. He was concealed well enough, under a sheet-sized length of old carpet, planted with mud, leaves and twigs. He had used the carapace to crawl at a turtle's pace from the ruin.

It took only fifteen minutes of the forty or so before sunset for them to ride out again. The messenger trotted a new horse at the head of two clattering diesel pickups, beds loaded with support-weapons men, and tracking dogs riding in baskets tied to the cabin roofs. Behind the oil-burners a column of twos streamed out of Bern Woods, their horses tripping in the winter ruts of the broken road. Then a final figure appeared. Valentine drew an anxious breath. A Reaper. It strode out in a meter-eating quick-march, booted feet a blur under heavy cape and cowl.

The final figure explained his uneasiness while waiting. Something about a Reaper's presence gave him what an old tent-mate from the Wolves had called the "Valentingle." At times it was so bad the hair on the back of his neck stood straight out, or it could manifest as a cold, dead spot in his mind. It was a capricious talent; he'd once walked over a Reaper lying hidden in a basement without a hint of it, but in another time and place he'd felt one on top of a hill a mile away. The Reapers, the praetorian guard doing the bloody work of Earth's Kurian Order that raised, and devoured, his species like cattle, had the ability too. They could sense humans through night and fog, rain or snow. Only through special training could men hide their presence; training that he had started when he was nineteen, seven long years ago. Since the ambush he'd—

Stop it. Since the ambush, regrets about his misjudgments while bringing his convoy home, his eagerness to turn the men and material over to the first Southern Command uniform he saw, had tormented him hourly, and he clenched his fists in frustration until bruises appeared in his palms. Valentine called himself back to the outskirts of Bern Woods and watched the column disappear up the old highway.

Ahn-Kha must have hit the bridge post. They had scouted the blockhouses to either end of the old concrete bridge—it turned out only one was occupied; three soldiers that hardly qualified for a corporal's guard—and Valentine told Ahn-Kha to pick off a man or two from the distance with his Grog gun an hour before sunset, before heading toward Tayland's body. The bridge was only a mile north of Bern Woods; they'd call for help from there.

His part was more of a challenge. After changing clothes in a lonely, recently abandoned farmhouse—he'd found a suitably smelly set of overalls, a knit coat and a shapeless woolen winter cap, and muddied his boots sufficiently so they wouldn't be an instant giveaway—he kept the snakeskin bandolier, wrapping it about his waist beneath the overalls. He wanted to be within the palisade around the old border-town before nightfall. Once in, he would have to evaluate which options were likely, which were possible, and which were madness.

He started a cautious creep toward the wall, down a ditch beside what had once been a short road heading west out of town, still beneath his moldering carapace. Even after he was out of sight of the guard-tower he stayed in the ditch. He abandoned the carpet while still away from the wall, since a patrol would find it more suspicious up close than abandoned in the field.

Boarded-up windows and corrugated aluminum nailed over doors faced him from the backs of what had been the main street of the town. Many of the little roadside towns in the borderlands of the Ozark Free Territory were like this, walling the spaces between buildings with wire-topped timber blocking any ingress other than the gate; what had been a sleepy rural town was now a frontier fort.

It went dark with the suddenness of a clouded winter night. Valentine's night vision took over—another biological modification, courtesy of the Lifeweavers, the ancient enemies and blood relations of Earth's new masters. Colors muted but edge details stood out. The grain of the wall and blades of tired winter grasses formed their delicate patterns on his enhanced retinas. Valentine's nose picked up the town's evening aromas of wood smoke, coal smoke, tobacco, cooking and outdoor toilets. The last was especially noticeable, as his ditch served as an open-air septic tank at the end of a pipe running from under the wall. He slunk up on the sluice that served as the town's sewer from downwind. If a dog patrol came, there was a chance that the odor would mask his.

Valentine examined the sewer-pipe. The PVC plastic was not something he could wiggle through, but rainwater making its way into the ditch had opened a gap under that part of the wall. Child-sized hand- and footprints ringed the gap. He smelled and listened for a moment, then crawled for the break.

If he was lucky—which he hadn't been since leaving the piney woods of Texas, admittedly—the garrison of Bern Woods would be short enough on pairs of eyes that it would be all they could do to keep the gate, prison and tower manned.

Waiting had never gained him much, so he stuck his head under the gap. The sluice stood next to what looked to have been a chicken takeout, the remnants of its friendly red-and-yellow decor incongruous next to the Fort Apache palisade.

He drew Tayland's bowie knife and wiggled through. The fighting knife was the only weapon he carried. Being gunless kept him cautious and alert. It might also buy him a little time if he were captured. The only people allowed to carry guns in the Kurian Zone were those who worked for the regime; a quick harvesting in the grasp of the Reapers was the usual punishment for anyone else found with a firearm.

The town wasn't electrified at the moment. Valentine saw a few lanterns and marked the faint glow of candlelight from the upper stories of the buildings on the main street. He smelled diesel and heard a generator clattering some distance away to the south. Following his ears, he saw drums in a fenced-in enclosure next to a shed behind a stoutly built building.

Valentine got away from the wall as quickly as he could. The town seemed empty. He untied his long hair and mussed it with his fingers so it covered the scar on the side of his face, and pulled the hat down to his eyebrows. He took a slow walk toward the highway cutting the town in two, turning onto the main street at a gas station whose garage now sheltered broken-down horses instead of broken-down cars. He recognized the horse that had been dragging Tayland in an oil-change bay.

In the Kurian Zone you had to walk a fine line between looking like you were busy and drawing attention to yourself. He walked purposefully toward the one building lit with electricity.

A feed store still held feed, by the look of it, but the drug and sundry had been recently boarded up.

The brightly lit building turned out to be the town bank, complete with drive-thru teller, though it had become an antique store sometime before the cataclysm of 2022, judging from an old, rain-washed sign painted where once tellers had stood behind armored glass to service cars. Blue banners, with three gold stars set in a horizontal white stripe, hung from the flagpole next to the door of the bank/antique shop. A painted sign jutting from a pile of whitewashed rocks announced its latest incarnation: Station 46. Red-painted gallows stood just a few steps from the headquarters at what had been an intersection, dominating the central street like a grim plaza statue. There was no trapdoor, just a pair of poles and a crossbeam.

A tall sentry with a forehead that bore an imprint where it might have been kicked by a horse's hoof stood to one side of the door. Another man, proportionally older and rounder, sat in an ornate rocking chair with a shotgun across his lap. His sideburns were russet, but the sparse hair streaming out from under a pisscutter cap was gray. Both wore khaki uniforms with brown leather pads at the knees, shoulders and elbows, though the seated one had lieutenant's bars and a more elaborate uniform.

"Is this Station 46?" Valentine drawled, head tilted to match the poor leveling of the sign's face.

"Goddammit, seems like every day I hear that," the older man screeched. "The friggin' sign is out there, plain as paint, everything but a spotlight on it. But still I hear 'Is this Station 46?' from some shitheel six times a week and twice on Sundays. Never fails."

"So this is Station 46?" Valentine asked.

The aged lieutenant turned even redder. "Yes, dammit! This is Station 46."

"I'm to speak to the commanding officer."

"He ain't here, boy. I mean, that's me, seeing as he's out. Whatever the question is, the answer is 'no.' Now get going before I jail you for breaking curfew, you dunk."

Valentine was happy to swallow the abuse, as long as the lieutenant stayed angry.

"I was told by one of your officers to speak to the commanding officer, Station 46. That's what I'm here to do, sir."

The lieutenant leaned forward in his rocking chair. "What about?"

"My boy's watchin' two pen of hawgs bit north of here, 'round Blocky Swamp. There's a lot less hawgs in those pens thanks to some sergeant with a uniform like yours. He didn't pass any scrips or warrants, just took 'em. He told me if I had a problem with it to speak to the officer commanding, Station 46, Bern Woods. Walked all day, practically, as I do have a problem with someone just takin' my stock."

"What the crap, dunk? Haven't you heard yet? There's been some changes, boy. Southern Command's not riding 'round handing out scrip no more. That's all over and out."

Valentine widened his stance.

"I don't fight these wars, or know about it from nothing, and I keep my boys outta it too. I'm short salt and flour and sugar; thought I'd pick some up and catch up on the news after Christmas. But being short hawgs now too, I thought a trip to town was in order. I want to write on some papers and make a complaint."

"A complaint? A complaint?"

"That's correct, sir."

The old man wavered in perplexity, then looked at Valentine sidelong, under lowered lids, like a bull trying to make up its mind whether to charge or run.

"I'll take your statement," he said. "I don't expect you'll get the answer you're looking for, but I warned ya fair."

"Thanks. Would've saved us both some time if you'd done so in the first place," Valentine said.

The older man snorted and led him inside the command post. He held the door open for Valentine with a grin, and Valentine suddenly liked the aged lieutenant a little better, and hoped it wouldn't come to killing.

Little remnants of both the banking heritage and retail life of the building remained in the form of a vault and stock tables. Valentine looked inside the vault, where arms and boxes of ammunition stood in disarray from the hurried muster he had seen ride out of town. A few footlockers and gun cases with Southern Command notations on them huddled in a corner as though frightened of the new pegs and racks. Opposite the vault a row of rooms held prisoners, confined behind folding metal gates like those used to protect urban merchants' streetside windows from burglars. Valentine counted the men, his heart shrinking three sizes when he recognized their faces. Eleven remaining marines from the *Thunderbolt* sat in the bare, unlit cells—pictures of grubby despair. Post and the two Jamaicans occupied another cell. Two more, in Texan clothes, shared another; Jefferson passed him a hint of a shrug—he had dried blood from a cut lip in his beard. The other was a drover named Wilson. Guilt pulled at him with an iron hook. The marines took in Valentine with darting eyes but said nothing. The surviving teamster ignored him.

Valentine heard a hoot, and turned his head to see a pair of Grogs in loincloths. Simpler, shorter versions of the Golden One known as Grey Ones, they bore brooms and dustpans, cleaning rags and wood oil. They were the last of Ahn-Kha's team, the lucky pair who had made it all the way to Haiti and back. Not bright enough to understand Valentine's disguise, they chattered in excitement at his familiar face. Valentine took a step back.

"Hell, those things give me the creeps. You got them in town?" Valentine asked, feigning fright.

The Grogs gamboled up to him, hooting. Valentine put a long table between him and the excited pair.

"Must be the smell of pigs," the temporary commander mused. He pushed the Grogs off.

"Don't let 'em touch me," Valentine said. The fear in his voice was real enough. If the officer decided to point the shotgun and start asking questions, there wasn't much he could do.

"What's all d'excitement?" a musical voice asked, coming from the hallway behind the Grogs.

Valentine looked down at Narcisse. She was uninjured—assuming one didn't count the missing legs and left hand, old souvenirs of her escape attempts on Santo Domingo—and dressed in her customary colorful rags and bandannas. She "walked" by swinging her body on her handless arm, using the limb as a crutch. An accomplished cook was welcome in any army, and she'd been put to work, judging from the aluminum dish gripped in her good hand. Valentine's sensitive nose detected the aromas of hot peppers and thyme in the steaming mixture of pork and rice. Narcisse looked once at Valentine, and then turned to the officer, pivoting on her left arm like a ballet dancer on pointe.

The Grogs forgot Valentine at the smell of food.

"You ready to eat, Cap'n? Extra spicy, just like you asked."

The older man's nostrils widened. "Sure am." He picked up a yellowed piece of blank paper and a pencil, and handed them to Valentine. "Get lost, boy. Write down your complaint, then give it back to me."

"This isn't official; it doesn't have a seal," Valentine said.

"There's enough for your friend, Cap'n. He looks hungry."

He glowered down on Narcisse. "You're supposed to feed officers first, then the men, and the prisoners long way last. He can try for a meal at the church hall."

"Yes, Cap'n. Sorry, mister, I just do what I'm told. Thank you, Cap'n."

Valentine picked up the pencil. "Can I write this in here where there's light?"

"As long as you shut up and stay out of my way, you can do what you like."

Narcisse filled the officer's plate, and brought out a plastic water jug with a cup rattling on the nozzle. "You want me to take some to the boys in the tower, Cap'n?"

"No, they're on duty. We're short men with the Visor out with the riders."

"Yes, Cap'n. Apple cider?" For someone with only one hand, Narcisse acted the part of a servant with skill.

"There's some left? Sure. This is some fine spicy. I'm from Dallas, and I'll tell you that this is good cooking."

"Thank you, Cap'n."

The officer, who never corrected her when she called him "Cap'n," even ate with the shotgun in his lap. Valentine looked at the service pips on his sleeve, wondering why a man with so many years was just a lieutenant, and a junior one at that. Valentine wrote out his phony story in scraggly block capitals. The wall above him was festooned with wanted posters and poorly reproduced photos, perhaps a hundred in all. "Terrorism" and "Sabotage" looked to be the two most common crimes, though "Speculation" appeared on some. He recognized one face: Brostoff, a hard-drinking lieutenant he had served with six years ago when he ran with the Wolves of Zulu Company. There was a four-year bounty on him. Just beneath Brostoff was a half-familiar face; Valentine had to look a second time to be sure. A handsome young black man looked into the camera with calm, knowing eyes. Frat—listed in the handbill as F. Carlson—had a ten-year bounty on him for assassination and sabotage. Frat would be about twenty now, Valentine calculated. He'd last seen him when he brought Molly back to the Free Territory and reunited her with her family, when the youth was serving his term as an aspirant prior to becoming a Wolf.

Valentine watched Narcisse sneak a few spoonfuls out to the guard on duty, but when she stumped her way over to the men in the cells, the lieutenant growled at her. As she turned away from the prisoners' outstretched arms she gave Valentine a significant wink.

"*Dix minutes,*" Narcisse said, under her breath.

Narcisse had shown her talents before in Haiti and beyond, where her curious mixture of herbalism and *vaudou* rendered surprising results. She had once put a man named Boul to sleep with a mickey in his chicken. He had also seen fevered men recover and be walking around in perfect health a day after one of her infusions. Biochemistry or magic, she performed miracles with food and the contents of her spice bag.

Valentine counted the minutes and continued his scrawled essay on the loss of his fictitious stock, punctuated by plate scrapings and burps from behind. At last he heard the utensils laid down.

"Aww, I'm stuffed," the lieutenant belched. Valentine crossed out a misspelled word and wrote a new one above it with an eye on the lieutenant, occupied exploring one hairy ear with a pinky. The oldster looked thoughtful, then doubtful, and gave a little burp.

The lieutenant stood up so fast his chair fell over backward. He went to the door at a quick walk, picking up the shotgun on the way. "Watch things in here," he ordered the man outside, handing over the pump-action.

The tall younger guard entered, the shotgun looking like a child's toy in his grasp. "He okay?"

"Just finished his meal and left. Shithouse run, I suppose."

The guard sat down and put his feet on the table, shotgun in his lap. Valentine tried to keep his eyes on the paper, rather than the odd crescent-shaped dimple across the man's forehead.

"Oh hell, I got 'em too," the giant said, standing up. "C'mon, can't leave you in here alone," he added, grabbing some keys.

"I'm not—"

"Out, pig-man, or I'll throw you out," the private threatened, his eyes bright with anxiety.

Valentine relented, and the man escorted him out, and turned the key in the lock of the steel door. It looked like the only modification to the outside of the structure in dozens of years.

Valentine stepped aside on the porch. The guard hurried around the corner, undoing his suspenders with the shotgun under his arm.

He heard the lock turn.

"Daveed, I thought you'd never come," Narcisse said, smiling up at him. "Let me show you where they keep the spare keys."

The tall private returned, a little white-faced. His face drained even more when he unlocked the door and found a phalanx of rifles and shotguns pointed at him.

"You want to put the gun down?" Valentine asked from a corner, a tiny .22 automatic he'd found in a box marked "local confiscations" in his hand.

The private's eyelids fluttered and he toppled over in a dead faint.

"Beats shooting him," Wilson said, picking the dropped shotgun off the floor.

"About time we got a break. Andree, Botun, handcuff him and get him in a cell. Jefferson," Valentine said to the other Texas teamster, "keep your gun at his head."

"What did you put in the food?" Valentine asked Narcisse as his men tied the private lying against the bottom bars of a cell. Post was still in the vault, choosing weapons and ammunition for their flight.

"Cascara Buckthorn bark, child. Opens them up good."

They repeated the procedure when the lieutenant staggered back in.

"Fuck me," the old man groaned when he read the situation.

"No thank you," Valentine said, pulling the revolver out of the lieutenant's hip holster. "I'll leave that for the Hoods."

The man put hand to collarbone, as if to ward off the probing tongue snaking its way toward his heart already. "They'll have me."

"Hard luck."

"Like you care."

"Help me get past the gate and I'll let you get a running start for Dallas, Lieutenant. Or wherever. You might have a chance. "

"Seems to me it's my choice of the frying pan or the fire," the old man said.

"A fight is the last thing I want," Valentine said.

"You're the leader of the column, right? Some kinda Indian scout for the commissary wagons? They said he had black hair and a scar."

"You going to trust this turncoat, sir?" Jefferson said. "I say we don't even give the Reapers the satisfaction. Leave the two of them hangin' with greeting cards for when they come back."

The old man stiffened. *Damn, almost had him.*

"Jefferson, make yourself useful in the kitchen, please. Narcisse is packing up, and we need food." He turned to the Quisling. "Look, Lieutenant . . . err . . ."

"M'Daw, mister good cop."

"I'm going to offer you a deal, M'Daw. Help us get away clean. You're a lieutenant; you must have some idea where patrols and so on are out. You get us out of this town without bloodshed, and I'll let you go in a day or two with food and water to walk to safety."

"*Shove, dunk,*" M'Daw said.

"Let me finish. The alternative is we kill every man of your troop in town. There can't be that many of them."

M'Daw said nothing.

"Hard way it is," Valentine said. He beckoned one of his Jamaicans. "Ewenge, keep an eye on this man. Post!"

"Sir?" his lieutenant called from the vault.

"We need to be ready to move in fifteen minutes," he said, removing his boots. He slipped a spare box of .22 shells in his overall pocket and picked up Tayland's bowie knife, then found a towel in the little kitchen atop a twenty-gallon water cask. "I'm going to make sure the streets are clear."

* * *

The streets were clear enough—a Kurian curfew had that effect. After test-firing the pistol a few times in the clattering generator shed—the tiny pop of the .22 could hardly be heard over the buzzing rattle of the generator—Valentine crept along the town wall, listening all the way. Only half the buildings in the little widening-in-the-road town seemed occupied.

He got his first rats at the tower. A Quisling, maybe seventeen and in a coat too big for his shoulders, stood watch in the bullet-scarred gate-tower as faint snores echoed from inside. The muzzle of a mounted machine gun pointed toward the sky, a canvas tube on it to keep the on-again, off-again rain from wetting it. Valentine waited until he moved to another corner, and heard a faint sigh and a heavy step as the kid crossed the sleeping sentry.

Valentine didn't take the ladder to the tower. Instead he jumped from an outhouse and ran along a beam that reinforced the wooden palisade, a six-meter drop to either side.

The boy turned as Valentine swung into the tower. Valentine shot him three times with the .22, wrapped up in an old towel to muffle the shots. He didn't watch the kid go down, tried not to listen to the bubbling of aspirated blood as he used the knife on the sleeping sentry.

He held the knife tucked under his armpit, shoved the gun back in the overalls, felt the warm blood on the floor of the tower with his chilled feet. Deep inside his lizard-brain, the shadowy part of himself, the part of himself that the rest of his soul hated, exulted.

Valentine lifted the beltless machine gun from its mount and went to the other side of the tower, overlooking the gate. The gate guard stood there looking up, perhaps trying to make sense of the strange clicks and clunks from the tower. Valentine threw the machine gun at him, readied the now-bloody knife again and followed the weapon over the side of the tower.

He missed the third rat with his jump. The man saw him leap and ran—Valentine noted that he limped—and as he gave a shout Valentine was on his back, knocking him down with a body blow even as the knife went into the guard's kidney. The man let out a hissing scream as Valentine straddled him, reaching for the .22. He pressed the gun to the back of the guard's neck and pulled the trigger. The .22 cracked like a small firework. Valentine pulled the body into an alley and took its coat off. Once he had the guard's coat and hat on he reloaded his gun, looking up the street. He saw a faint outline in an upstairs window above a former Ozark Shop 'n Swap.

Valentine trotted to the other side of town, keeping in the shadows. He saw another figure, also in a Quisling fatigue coat, moving down the street equally cautiously. Valentine waved him over, but turned his back so he could ostensibly keep watch in the direction he'd come from.

The man took a few cautious steps and stopped—maybe he'd spotted Valentine's lack of boots. Valentine threw himself into a doorway, putting comforting bricks in between himself and the Quisling, and drew his gun. He followed its muzzle out and saw the man dashing across the street to Station 46. Valentine fired one shot on pure instinct—missed—and lowered the gun. Post was waiting within Station 46, and there was plenty of cell space.

The residents of Bern Woods learned what was happening when they saw their neighbors in the street. Valentine posted Ewenge as a lookout, and as he returned from the tower he had thirty people vying for attention, for news, for some sign that the world they had known had been restored. They picked him out as the man in charge despite his mundane and musty clothes.

Valentine had no answers. The shadowy confusion reminded him of another night, in Oklahoma, when he'd had to leave the residents of the Rigyard after smoking out four Reapers. No matter which way he turned, another desperate face, another clutching hand—

"When are our boys coming back?"

"You can't leave us!"

"Reprisals. There'll be reprisals."

"They drained a man last week, right in front of everyone. Over a dozen eggs. A dozen eggs!"

He had no orders, no higher authority to consult. Instead of being a burden, it was liberating. The decision came easily. This time he could give them a running start.

He ordered Jefferson and Wilson to take what riding animals they could and arm the residents from the remaining weapons at Station 46, and then ride for the Texas pines as though the devil were at their heels—a metaphor not far from the truth. Trackers would follow the hoofprints, but the thick pine woods were only a few hours' hard ride, and every mile they went into East Texas would improve their chances of meeting guerillas—perhaps even the well-armed party he'd crossed Texas with.

Jefferson shook his head and showed Valentine a gap-toothed grin. "I left you once, sir. These Dallas brownshirts started a fight, took out three teeth. I want to be around for the finish. Wilson knows stock as well as I do, and any ten-year-old can figure out what direction south is."

The survivors of Valentine's ill-fated wagon train left as soon as they had gathered their necessities. He'd hoped to find some of the precious Quickwood he'd brought back from the Caribbean, but found just a trio of shot-up wagons. Valentine trotted out to the house where he'd hidden his clothes and .45 to retrieve them, but didn't take the time to change out of the overalls. The troops out hunting Ahn-Kha might give up and return at any moment.

He returned to the remains of his command. They were laden with all the food and water they could carry; even a flour barrel slung from a hammock tied to a pair of two-by-fours. The Grogs carried this last, happy to be moving in the company of men they knew. Narcisse rode on a marine's shoulders.

Valentine, pistol held behind the bib of his overalls, fell into pace behind M'Daw; left-right, left-right . . .

They shut the gate again behind them. "What'll it be, M'Daw?"

"I think the healthiest thing to do is tag along with you."

Valentine carefully lowered the hammer on his automatic,

relieved. He had been nerving himself to shove the pistol into the old man's stomach, muffling the gunshot with paunchy flesh. "I'm glad you said that, M'Daw," he said, quite honestly.

Valentine's Cat-eye night vision caught motion at the base of the wall.

A pair of figures ran toward them. Valentine brought up his gun, but marked a woman's long brown hair.

"Sir, you clearing out?" the unknown man said as it began to rain. He had the dried-out look of a man with a lot of outdoor mileage.

"Mister . . . uhhh . . ." the woman put in.

"You can call me Ghost."

"My name's Rich Smalls," the man said. "This is my wife, Tondi. We got to find my boy."

"You'd better find him in a hurry. Mr. Wilson is leaving for Texas right now," Valentine said.

"We want to go," Tondi Smalls said. She was a short woman with straight, black hair below her shoulders, and pretty features marred by worry. Valentine guessed her to be six or seven months pregnant. "You're heading north, right? Our son's watching some horses in pasture. It's in that direction."

"We're going to be moving hard," Valentine said. "You sure you can keep up?"

"Would horses help?" Mr. Smalls said. "There's twenty or more horses in Patchy Pines. They'll be fresh and rested. Been on pasture for weeks."

"We'll need them. Show me, Mr. Smalls. You're a godsend."

"I could say the same about you, mister. It's been a hellacious year."

"I'd like to hear about it. Horses first. No tack, I suppose."

"Just rope, for leads."

"Bareback it is," Valentine said.

Smalls led the way down a bridle track, and fifteen minutes' walk brought them to the pasture.

The meadow circled a little cluster of pines and rocks, and

was in turn surrounded by thicker trees, forming a badly cooked doughnut. The cold rain had faded into a drizzle, which would become snow as soon as the temperature dropped a degree or two more. Valentine, the crisis in town past, felt suddenly exhausted as he led his wet column northeast into the clearing. He heard stamping sounds of nervous horses under the trees as they splashed across a tiny creek swollen from the winter rain.

The meadow was too close to town. Valentine hurried his men toward a fire set under a rock overhang. Old cuts of carpet hanging from the rock made a shelter somewhere between a tent and a shack. Smalls ran ahead.

"Hank, you there? Wake up boy, your mother's here."

"Yes, Pa," a sleepy voice said from under the overhang. Valentine saw a bow and a quiver of arrows hung in the branches of a nearby tree. Joints of meat, cut from an animal that was probably a mule, also hung in the boy's camp.

A blanket-draped boy emerged, looking to be about thirteen years old and in the midst of a growth spurt. He wore brown corduroy pants, topped with a leather-trimmed blue shirt decorated with a gold star, similar to the one on the flag outside Station 46.

"Don't let the uniform bother you, sir," Smalls said, closing up the blanket on the boy's shoulders so it covered the star. "He spends a lot of time out in the woods on his own, and it's better if he's in the Honor Guard."

Valentine didn't have to ask what the Honor Guard was. Most Kurian Zones had it in one form or another; paramilitary training and indoctrination for the youth. A good record for a child usually meant safety for the parents. Valentine had seen a dozen forms of it in his travels under an assumed identity in the Kurian Zone, but he found it obscene here in what had been the Ozark Free Territory, as if his childhood church had been converted into a brothel.

"Hank, these are some Southern Command soldiers," Smalls said. "They're going to take us with them." Mrs. Smalls nodded.

"Uhh, with the horses?" the boy asked.

"Yes. Go and start rounding them up."

"Yessir."

"Just a second. Where'd these joints come from?" Smalls asked.

"Wounded mule. Wandered in two days ago with a wagon team; smelled out the other horses I suppose. I quick hid the wagon and the harnesses, and put 'em with our horses. Some searchers came through and didn't know the difference, so we're up five head for sly-trading."

"You say there was a wagon?" Valentine asked.

"Yessir. It was kinda shot up."

"Did the searchers find it?"

"Sorta. I put her the middle of the field like it'd been parked there when a team was unhitched. There wasn't much in it, just a big load of lumber, so they didn't look twice at it. They asked if I was gonna build a hut out here. I said it was for a smokehouse. I was more worried about them finding the Texas driving rig I'd tossed in the creek, or them noticing new horses missing brands."

"Where?" Valentine asked, so intensely that the boy shrank against his mother in fear.

"Sorry, Hank, is it? My name's David, and I was in charge of those wagons. Where is it?"

"Just the other side of these trees, sir. C'mon, I'll show you."

"Corporal Botun," Valentine ordered. "Keep everyone together here. C'mon, Jefferson, let's see what we can do with this rig."

Valentine followed the boy and Smalls, the tall Texas teamster at his side. At a word from Narcisse, the marine carrying her trailed along. They cut through a mixture of pine and hickory and came to the other side of the meadow ringing the boy's wooded campsite. The wagon stood there, its battered wooden sides dark and wet in the night's gloom. Valentine couldn't restrain himself. He ran and jumped up into the bed of the wagon like a mountain goat leaping to a higher rock.

A load of wooden four-by-four beams, coated with preservative resin, lay in the bed of the wagon. The raindrops beaded up and ran off like flowing tears. Tears that matched those on Valentine's face, concealed by the drizzle. He couldn't do anything about the dead men he'd failed. But now he could do something for those still living. Shaking, he turned to Narcisse.

"Quickwood," Narcisse said, looking into the wagon from atop the marine's shoulders.

"What kinda wood?" Smalls said.

Valentine sank to his knees in the bed of the wagon, running his hands along the beams. "Mister Smalls, I owe your boy a mountain of gratitude."

"Why's that? For finding your wagon?"

"A lot more. Hank might have just saved the Free Territory."

Chapter Two

Pony Hollow, Arkansas, Christmas Eve: One of the winter snowstorms that blows this far south dusts the Ouachitas with tiny pellets of snow. Less painful than hail and less treacherous than freezing rain, the snow taps audibly on the remaining leaves as it falls. The snowstorm provides the only motion in the still of the afternoon as curtains of it ripple across the landscape. Bird and beast seek shelter, leaving the heights of the rounded mountains to the wind and bending bough.

The ridges of the Ouachitas here run east-west, as if a surveyor had laid them out using a compass. But for the pines, the rocky heights of the mountains would look at home in the desert West; the mesalike cliffs rise above a carpet of trees, naked cliffs cutting an occasional grin or frown into the mountainside. Between the ridges creek-filled hollows are the abode of bobcat and turkey, songbird and feral hog. The latter, with their keen senses matched by cunning and surprising stealth, are challenging animals to hunt.

But one of the callous-backed swine has fallen victim to a simple speared deadfall of Grey One design, baited with a sack of corn. After thorough boiling, individual chops sputter in a pair of frying pans within a rambling, abandoned house. The fugitives enjoy a Christmas Eve feast—complete with snowfall. Horses are tethered tightly together in the garage, blocked in by the recovered wagon in what had been the home's gravel driveway.

A single guard watches over the animals from the wagon seat, a horse blanket over his head and shoulders. The hairy mass snags the snow pellets out of the wind as if it were designed to do just that. David Valentine, sitting under his sugar-dusted cape, whittles a spear point out of a piece of

*Quickwood with Tayland's oversized Texas bowie. His dark
eyes look in on the celebrating men and Grogs.*

"Pork chop?" William Post, former lieutenant of the Quisling Costal Marines, asked. He had found enough rags to
complete an outfit of sorts, though the mixture left him looking like an unusually well-stuffed scarecrow. "It's practically
still sizzling."

Valentine reached out with his knife and speared the chop.
The meat was on the tough side, even after being boiled, but
the greasy taste was satisfying.

"Merry Christmas, Val," Post said, his voice flavored with
a hint of a Mississippi drawl. By common consent the for-
malities were dropped when they were alone together.

"Same to you, Will."

"My wife used to make peanut brickle and pecan pies at
Christmas," Post said, his incipient beard catching the snow
as well. There was a pause. Valentine knew that Post's wife
had run away when he became a Quisling officer in New Orleans. "Narcisse is up to something with a pot of rice. I saw
sugar out, too."

"Station 46 had a good larder. Sissy emptied it."

"Wonder what happened to that tall guard," Post said. "He
didn't seem a bad sort."

"Not our problem."

"I know that. Can't help thinking about the poor bastard,
though. I spent more time under them than you did. The
choices are difficult. A lot of them don't cooperate with the
regime as willingly as you think. Every other man's got a
blind eye that he turns if he can get away with it."

"Yes. Those fellows weren't frontline material." Valentine
stared off into the snowfall. "Where do you suppose their
good soldiers are?"

"I think there's still fighting here and there."

"We've got one load of Quickwood left. We should try to
find it."

Post nodded. "The men can't believe you went back for
them, by the way."

"I owed them as much. Stupid of me to drop my guard, just because we were back in what I thought was the Free Territory. The ambush was my fault."

"Done with."

Valentine let it lie. He looked through the narrow windows of the house at the celebrating men. They weren't a fighting force anymore, and wouldn't be for a long time. They were survivors, happy to be warm, fed and resting.

"How's the radio holding up?"

His lieutenant had found a portable radio back at Station 46. "The Grogs love charging it up with the hand crank. I think they like to watch the lights come on. Lots of coded transmissions, or just operators BSing. I've gotten more information out of M'Daw."

"What does he say?"

"The Kurians only sorta run these lands; they're in the hands of a big Quisling Somebody named Consul Solon. Even M'Daw had heard of him. The rest I don't have facts about."

"He know anything about Mountain Home?" Valentine asked. The former capital of the Ozark Free Territory was tucked into the mountains for a reason.

"The president is gone. Don't know if he's dead or hiding. Smalls said the Kurians passed around a rumor that he joined up with them, but he doesn't believe it."

"Can't see Pawls as a turncoat," Valentine said.

"You ever meet him?"

"No. He signed my promotion. Used to be an engineer. He got famous before I even came to the Ozarks, the last time the Kurians let loose a virus. I remember he was lieutenant governor when I came here in '62. He became governor in '65 while I was in Wisconsin."

"Maybe he made a deal. Happened before," Post said. "Like the siege at Jacksonville when I was little."

"I doubt a man who lost his kids to the ravies virus would take to cooperating." Valentine tossed the gnawed pork chop bone to the ground. One of the horses sniffed at it and snorted.

"You coming in for dessert?"

"I'll sit outside a bit. I like the snow. We always had a couple feet by Christmas in the Boundary Waters. Kills the sound, makes everything quiet. I like the peace."

Post shuddered. "You can keep it." His old lieutenant returned to the house.

The Free Territory gone. It was too big an event to get his thoughts around just yet.

The idea of the resourceful, hardworking people having succumbed to the Kurians after all this time was tragic on such a scale that it numbed him. His father had fought to establish this land; Gabriella Cho had died to defend it, hardly knowing the names of thirty of its inhabitants. The risks he ran, his innumerable sins against God and conscience, all were in defense of these hills and mountains—or, more properly, the families living among them.

He kept coming back to the kids. He'd spent enough time on both sides of the unmarked border to know where he was just by a glance at the children. They played differently in the Free Territory, laughed and made faces at soldiers passing through—though they tended to be on the scrawny side. Their better-fed cousins in the plains or on the half-flooded streets of New Orleans or in the cow barns of Wisconsin startled easily and watched strangers, especially those with guns or enclosed vehicles, with anxious eyes.

Valentine preferred laughter and the occasional raspberry. The thought of Hank, turned into one of those painfully quiet adolescents . . .

All fled, all gone, so lift me on the pyre . . .

Defeat had always been a possibility, but the Ozark Free Territory had stood so long, it seemed that it should always stand. This is how the residents in the skyscrapers of Miami must have felt as they saw the '22 surge roll over the hotels of South Beach: *It's been there my whole life, how can it be gone?* There had been invasions in the past, some shallow, some deep. Territory had been lost, or sometimes gained, for years. He'd seen a grim battlefield after a big fight up in Hazlett, Missouri, and heard the tales of the survivors. But the Kurians were by nature a jealous and competitive lot, sometimes at war with each other more than the Free Territory. To coordinate the kind of attack that could roll up the Ozarks would require sacrifices the surrounding principalities weren't willing to make. During his years of Cathood in the Kurian Zone, Valentine had formed a theory that the Ozarks were a useful bogeyman for the brutal regimes. Death and deprivation could always be blamed on "terrorists" in the Ozarks, or the other enclaves scattered around what had been North America.

Had the Free Territory been on the verge of becoming a real threat? A threat that had to be eliminated?

Did the Kurians know about his Quickwood?

No. No; if they had, the Bern Woods ambush would have been carried out by swarms of Reapers, not Quisling red-hands.

Valentine reached into his tunic and put his hand around the little leather pouch hanging from a string about his neck. He felt the peanut-sized seeds of the Quickwood trees, given to him by the Onceler on Haiti, jumbled together with Mali Carrasca's mahjong pieces. Had his mission on the old *Thunderbolt* not been so long delayed—first in New Orleans before the voyage and then later among the islands of the Caribbean—he would have gotten back to the Free Territory with a weapon that might have made a difference. Quickwood was lethal to the Reapers. The wood was a biological silver-bullet against the Frankensteinish death machines, aura-transmitting puppets of their Kurian lords.

Southern Command gone. Better than a hundred thousand men under arms—counting militias—defeated and apparently scattered or destroyed.

Regrets filled his stomach, writhed in there, like a cluster of wintering rattlesnakes clinging together in a ball. How much did the delay in Jamaica while the *Thunderbolt* was being repaired cost Southern Command? He could have pushed harder. He could have driven the chief away from his girlfriend; stood at the dry dock day and night, hurrying the work along. Instead he made love to Malia, rode horses across the green Jamaican fields, and played mahjong with her and her father. Malia . . .

Another if, another snake stirred and bit and he locked his teeth at the inner pain. Perhaps if he hadn't had his mind on the message from Mali about her pregnancy—*I'm going to be a father*, he reminded himself. He shoved the thought aside again as though it were a crime he hated to remember; he should have paid more attention to events after crossing back into what he thought was Free Territory, asked more questions, gotten to a radio. He might have avoided the ambush. . . .

His thoughts were turning in a frustrating circle again. He found he was on the verge of biting the back of his hand like an actor he'd once watched portraying a madman in a New Orleans stage melodrama. He was a fugitive, responsible for a single wagon rather than a train, running for his life with a handful of poorly armed refugees instead of the hundreds who had crossed Texas with him.

But he still had to see his assignment through. While he had never seen the plans, in his days as a Wolf he had been told that contingencies had been drawn up against the eventuality of a successful invasion. Southern Command had stores of weapons, food and medicines in the Boston Mountains, some the most rugged of the Ozarks. It didn't amount to anything other than a hope, but if some vestige of Southern Command existed, it was his duty to get the Quickwood into its hands.

There were obstacles beyond the Kurians. Getting north across the Arkansas River would be difficult. He had his shattered marines, a family with a pregnant woman, a Texas teamster and a Quisling he couldn't be sure of—and the precious wagonload of Quickwood. They were too many to move quietly and too few to be able to fight their way through even a picket line. He didn't know whether luck had gotten them this far into the Ouachitas or just Kurian nonchalance. The mountains were empty, almost strangely so; they had cut a few trails of large numbers of men, but only on old roads. If the Free Territory had fallen, he would expect the mountains to be thick with refugees: old Guard outfits, bands of Wolves, or just men determined to get their families out of the reach of the Kurians. Instead there was little but strings of empty homesteads in the hollows, fields and gardens already run to weed and scrub.

He looked down and discovered that he had finished his spear point. It was conical, and rough as a Neolithic arrowhead. They had no pointed steel caps for a tip of the kind Ahn-Kha had made on Haiti. Getting it through a Reaper's robes would be difficult.

The Jamaicans were singing in the other room. One of them had found a white plastic bucket of the sort Valentine was intimately familiar with from his days gathering fruit in the Labor Regiment, and employed it as an instrument with the aid of wooden-spoon drumsticks. With the backbeat established, the rest of the voices formed, seemingly without effort on their part, a four-part harmony. The rest, military, civilian and Grog, sat around listening to the calypso carols.

Narcisse, in the kitchen with Valentine, scooped some rice pudding onto his plate. She used a high kitchen stool and a chair to substitute for legs, moving form one perch to the other as she cooked.

"I used to have one of these with a turning seat in Boul's kitchen. Got to get me another someday. You'll like this, child. Just rice, sugar and raisins," she explained, when he raised an eyebrow and sniffed at it. "Okay, a touch of rum, too. It's Christmas."

"Rum?"

"I liberated the prisoners held in the officers' liquor cabinet back in town."

"You're a sly one. How did you make it inside that rigged-up jail? More magic?"

Narcisse spooned some more pudding into his cup. "Sissy's old, but she still has her game. Good thing I kept some coffee in my bag; those men back there didn't know a coffee bean from their earlobe. I ground it and brewed it, and before I knew it they had me in their kitchen. Just in case you didn't come back, I had them thinking that the Jamaicans were special farmers who knew how to grow coffee and cocoa and poppies for opiates. Was hoping to save their lives. Those soldiers believed me. Ignorance isn't strength."

"You know your George Orwell," Valentine said.

She shrugged. "Never met him. It was one of Boul's sayings." Boul was the man she cooked for before Valentine had brought her out of Haiti.

"Boul struck me as more the Machiavelli type."

"Daveed, you're troubled. You worried about the baby?"

Valentine was dumfounded. The letter Mali had left him with, with orders not to read it until he reached the Ozarks, had never left the pouch around his chest, where it rested among his precious seeds.

"Did Mali tell you?"

"Oh no, Daveed. I smell the child in her when we left Jamaica. She young and strong, Daveed; your girl'll be fine."

"It's a girl?" Valentine was ready to believe that someone who could smell a pregnancy could also determine the sex of an embryo.

"Daveed, you got to quit being a prisoner of the past. Forget about the future, too. Come back to the here and now; we need you."

Valentine glanced into the other room. Maybe it was the soft Caribbean tone of her voice, a bit like Father Max's. It reminded him he needed to confess. He lowered his voice. "Narcisse, there are people dying because I let them down. You know how that feels?"

Narcisse put down her spoon and joined Valentine at the table. Someone had spent some time varnishing the oak until the grain stood clear and dark—the Free Territory had been filled with craftsmen. The pattern reminded him of grinning demon faces.

"I've never been a soldier, child. Spent a lot of time runnin' from them, but never been one. The men, wherever they're from, even those ape-men . . . they believe in this fight too. They're not as different from you as you think. They don't follow you blind, they follow you because they know that if it comes to a fight, they want to look out for you as much as you want to look out for them."

"Think so? Narcisse, I ran outside of Bern Woods. I got up and ran."

"No. I saw Ahn-Kha dragging you away with my own eyes."

"I still left."

"Dying with them wouldn't have done your people any good. You saved yourself for the next fight. You saved the wood, at least some of it."

"That was an accident. A lucky accident. An officer belongs with his men. If he doesn't share their fate, he hasn't done his duty to them. It's the oldest compact between a leader and the led. Goes back to whatever we had for society before civilization."

Narcisse thought this over. "Was it wrong of them to surrender?"

"Of course not. It was hopeless from the start."

"But you fought, they fought."

"Couldn't help it. It was instinct."

"When you left, Daveed, that was instinct too, no?"

"Not the kind you should give in to."

"The past can't be changed, child. You keep worrying at it, you'll be doing the same thing as you did at the fight. Running away. Don't pick at a scab, or a new one grows in its place. Let the hurt heal. In time, it'll drop off by itself. Better for you, better for the hurt. If there's one thing I know about, child, it's getting over a hurt."

The Vaudouist didn't refer to her injuries often. She answered questions about them to anyone who asked, but Valentine had never heard her use them as a trump card in an argument before. Valentine let her unusual statement hang in the air for a moment.

"Narcisse, it sounds fine, but . . . a bit of me that isn't quite my brain and isn't quite my heart won't be convinced yet."

"That's your conscience talking. He's worth listening to. But he can be wrong . . . sometimes."

* * *

Valentine half dozed in front of the field pack with the headset on. Ahn-Kha snored next to him, curled up like a giant dog. Like most Quisling military equipment, the radio sitting on the table before him was ruggedly functional and almost aggressively ugly. Late at night the Quisling operators became more social, keeping each other company in the after-midnight hours of the quiet watches. Someone had just finished instructions on how to clear a gummed condensation tube on a still. His counterpart was complaining about the quality of the replacements they'd been getting: "Shit may float, but you can't build a riverboat outta it." Valentine twisted the dial back to a scratchier conversation about a pregnant washerwoman.

"So she goes to your CO. So what? She should be happy. She's safe for a couple years now. Over," the advice-giver said.

"She wants housing with the NCO wives. She's already got a three-year-old. She wants me to marry her so they can move in. Over," the advice-seeker explained.

"That's an old story. She's in it for the ration book, bro. Look, if a piece of ass pisses you off, threaten to have her tossed off-Station. That'll shut her up. Better yet, just do it. Sounds to me like she's—"

Valentine turned the dial again.

". . . fight in Pine Bluff. Put me down for twenty coin on Jebro. He'll take Meredith like a sapper popping an old woman. Over."

"Sure thing. You want any of the prefight action? Couple of convicts. It's a blood-match; the loser goes to the Slits. Over."

Valentine had heard the term "Slits" used by rivermen on the Mississippi. It referred to the Reapers' slit-pupiled eyes, or perhaps the narrow wounds their stabbing tongues left above the breastbone.

"No, haven't seen 'em. I'd be wasting my money. Over."

Valentine heard a horse snort and jump outside the cracked window, the way an equine startled out of sleep readies all four feet for flight. The sound brought him awake in a flash. A pair of alarmed whinnies cut the night air.

Ahn-Kha came awake, nostrils flared and batlike ears up and alert.

"Arms! Quietly now, arms!" Valentine said to the sleeping men, huddled against the walls in the warm room where they had enjoyed dinner. He snatched up his pistol and worked the slide.

Ahn-Kha followed. How so much mass moved with such speed and stealth—

"What is it, my David?" Ahn-Kha breathed, his rubbery lips barely forming the words.

"Something is spooking the horses. Watch the front of the house. Post," Valentine said to his lieutenant, who had appeared in his trousers and boots, pulling on a jacket. "Get the Smalls and M'Daw into the cellar, please. Stay down there with them."

Valentine waved to the wagon sentry, Jefferson, but the man's eyes searched elsewhere. Jefferson had his rifle up and ready. Two of the horses reared, and he stood to see over them.

Three Reapers hurtled out of the snow, black-edged mouths open, bounding on spring-steel legs. Three! He and all his people would be dead inside two minutes.

"Reapers!" Valentine bellowed, bringing up his pistol in a two-handed grip. As he centered the front sight on one he noticed it was naked, but so dirt-covered that it looked clothed. A torn cloth collar was all that remained of whatever it had been wearing. He fired three times; the .45 barked deafeningly in the enclosed space.

At the sound of the shots his men moved even faster. Two marines scrambled to the window and stuck their rifles out of the loophole-sized slats in the shutters.

A Reaper leapt toward Jefferson, whose gun snapped impotently, and Valentine reached for his machete as he braced himself for the sight of the Texan's bloody disassembly. Perhaps he could get it in the back as it killed Jefferson. But it didn't land on the sentry. The naked avatar came down on top of a horse; on the balls of its feet, like a circus rider. It reached for the animal's neck, got a good grip—Valentine almost heard the snap as the horse suddenly toppled. The Reaper's snake-hinged jaw opened wide as it straddled the fallen animal to feed.

The other two, robeless like the first and running naked in the snowstorm, also ignored Jefferson, chasing the horses instead. The Jamaicans' rifles fired in unison when one came around the cart and into the open, but the only effect Valentine saw was a bullet striking into a mount's rump. The horse dropped sideways with a Reaper on top of it. Some instinct made the wounded animal roll its heavy body across the spider-thin form and came to its feet, kicking. As the Reaper reached for the tail a pair of hooves caught it across the back, sending it flying against the cart. It lurched off into the darkness, clutching its chest and making a wheezing sound.

The third disappeared into the snowstorm, chasing a terrified bay.

"Stay with the others," he said to Ahn-Kha, who stood ready with a Quickwood spear point. He threw open the door—and held up his hands when Jefferson whirled and pointed the rifle at him, muzzle seemingly aimed right between his eyes. The gun snapped again.

Valentine almost flew to the feeding Reaper. It heard him and raised its head from the horse, the syringelike tongue still connected to the twitching animal. It lashed out. Valentine slipped away from the raking claw. The momentum of the Reaper's strike turned its shoulder, and Valentine buried his knife in its neck, forcing it facedown in the snow as the tongue retracted, flinging hot liquid like a bloody sprinkler. He ground the bowie into the Reaper, hearing its feet scrabble for purchase on the snowy ground. It tried to shrug him off. Valentine brought up a knee, pressed on the blade . . .

The Reaper twitched as nerve tissue parted. In five seconds it was limp.

A blur—Jefferson's rifle butt came down on the back of the Reaper's head so that Valentine felt the wind pass his nose. Jefferson raised the gun up again.

"It's done," Valentine said.

Valentine pulled his knife from the Reaper's corpse, and Jefferson clubbed it again. "Jefferson, calm down. You might try loading your weapon. It's deadlier from the other end."

"Sorry, Captain. Sorry—"

Valentine ignored him and listened with hard ears all around the woods. Years ago, when he'd learned the Way of the Wolf, a Lifeweaver had enhanced his senses. When he concentrated on his senses—hardening them, in the slang of the Wolves—he could pick up sounds others would miss. He heard branches breaking in the snow somewhere, in the direction of the Reaper who had been kicked and then run. Valentine tried to make sense of the behavior. They had attacked randomly and hit the biggest targets they could see. Evidently they were masterless; their Kurian had probably been killed or had fled out of control range and they were acting on pure instinct. The severed-necked Reaper gave a twitch of an arm, and Jefferson jumped a good two feet in the air.

"Just a reflex," Valentine said.

"Should we burn it or something?"

"Get inside. Don't worry about the horses for now."

The Texan backed into the house. Valentine put a new magazine in his gun and took a few more steps around the yard, still listening and smelling. Nothing. Not even the cold feeling he usually got when Reapers were around, but his ears were still ringing from the gunshots inside, and the snow was killing odors.

He rapped on the door and backed into the house, still covering the Quickwood.

"Anything out back?" he called, eyes never leaving the trees.

"Nothing, sir," Botun said.

He heard a horse scream in the distance. The Reaper had caught up with the bay.

"Post," Valentine shouted.

"Sir?" he heard through the cellar floor.

"I'm going out after them. Two blasts on my whistle when I come back in. Don't let anyone shoot me." Valentine caught

Jefferson's eye and winked. The Texan shook his head in return.

"Yessir," Post answered.

Valentine tore off a peeling strip of wallpaper and wiped the resinlike Reaper blood off the bowie. He considered bringing a Quickwood spear, but decided to hunt it with just pistol and blade: It would be vulnerable after a feed. He nodded to the Jamaicans and opened the front door. After a long listen, he dashed past a tree and into the brush of the forest.

A nervous horse from the other team nickered at him. He moved from tree to tree, following the tracks.

Valentine dried his hand on his pant leg and took a better grip on his bowie. He sniffed the ground with his Wolf's nose, picking up horse blood in the breeze now. He instinctively broke into his old loping run, broken like a horse's canter by his stiff leg, following the scent. He came upon the corpse of the bay, blood staining the snow around its neck. He turned and followed the footprints.

He didn't have far to travel. After a run that verged on a climb up a steep incline, he came to the Reaper's resting spot. Water flowing down the limestone had created a crevice cave under the rocky overhang. An old Cat named Everready used to say that Reapers got "dopey" after a feed, that with a belly full of blood they often slept like drunkards. This one had hardly gotten out of sight of the horse before succumbing to the need for sleep. He saw its pale foot, black toenails sharp against the ash-colored skin, sticking out of a pile of leaves.

Valentine heard whistling respiration. He put his hand on his pistol and decided to risk a single shot. He drew and sighted on the source of the breathing.

The shot tossed leaves into the air. The Reaper came to its feet like a rousted drunk, crashing its skull against the overhang. A black wound crossed its scraggly hairline. It went down to its hands and knees, shaking its head. Valentine sighted on a slit pupil in a bilious yellow iris.

"Anyone at the other end?" Valentine asked, looking into the eye. The thing looked back, animal pain and confusion in its eyes. It scuttled to the side, shrinking away from him.

Valentine tracked the pupil with his gun. "What are you doing out here?"

Harrrruk! it spat.

It exploded out of the overhang.

Valentine fired, catching it in the chest. The bullet's impact rolled it back into the cave, but it came out again in its inhuman, crabwise crawl, trying to escape up the hill.

It moved fast. As fast as a wide-awake Reaper, despite its recent feeding.

Valentine shot again . . . again . . . again. Black flowers blossomed on the thing's skin at the wet slap of each slug's impact. It fled beneath a deadfall, slithering like a snake, trying to avoid the hurtful bullets. Valentine leapt over the trunk after it, bowie ready. He pinned it, driving the knee of his good leg into the small of its back, wishing he hadn't been so cocksure, that he'd brought Quickwood to finish it. He raised the blade high and brought it down on the back of its neck, the power of the blow driving it into the monster's spine. He tried to pull it back for another blow, but the black blood had already sealed the blade into the wound.

It continued to crawl, only half of its body now working.

Valentine stood up, and drove his booted heel onto the blade. If he couldn't pull it out, he could get it in farther. He stomped again, almost dancing on the back of the blade. The Reaper ceased its crawl, but the head still thrashed.

Urrack . . . shhhar, it hissed.

Valentine put a new magazine in his gun. It was beyond being a threat to anything but an earthworm or a beetle now, but he wouldn't let it suffer. He brought the muzzle to the earhole, angling it so the bullet wouldn't bounce off the bony baffle just behind the ear. He didn't want to risk the jaws without a couple of men with crowbars to pry the mouth open and a pliers to rip the stabbing tongue out.

He heard a sliding footfall behind, and turned, the foresight of the pistol leading the way.

It was the other Reaper, blood covering its face but cruel interest in its eyes. It squatted to spring. It had possessed instinct enough to approach from downwind.

Valentine emptied the magazine into it, knocking it over backward. Then he ran. Downhill. Fast.

It followed. Faster.

Valentine listened to it gain on him in three awful seconds, its footsteps beating a snare-drum tattoo. The footfalls stopped, and Valentine flung himself into the dirt in a bone-jarring shoulder roll.

It passed overhead, a dervish of raking claws and kicking legs. As he rolled back to his feet, he saw it fly face-first into a thick-boled hickory with a *thunk* Valentine felt through the ground.

Valentine had never felt less like laughing in his life. He continued his run downhill, blowing the whistle for his life, as the Reaper picked itself up.

He saw the house, and Post with the marines at the window. Jefferson, terror written on his face, pointed his rifle right at him.

Valentine dived face-first into the snow, sliding the last few feet down the hill.

Jefferson fired, not at him but over. More shots rang out, bright muzzle flashes reflecting off the dusting of Christmas snow like photoflashes.

The Reaper behind him went over backward. Valentine rolled over, pistol aimed in a shaking hand. Someone must have got in with a luck shot, for it lay thrashing, trying to rise. Failing.

"Hold your fire," Valentine panted. "Post, give me your spear."

"I'll do it, sir," Jefferson said, opening the bolt on his rifle and setting it down carefully. He reached behind the door and came out with a pick. "This is how we finish 'em in the Rangers."

"Careful now, Jefferson," Post said. "It might be playing possum."

Jefferson approached it, pick raised high. Valentine stood aside with his Quickwood stake. Jefferson needed this, after his fright earlier.

"Okay, dickless. Time to see what happens when you steal a Texan's horses."

"Damn, that fella right. That *bomba* doesn't have one," Botun said over the sights on his rifle.

Jefferson grunted, and swung the pick down. The Reaper brought up a limb to ward off the blow but the pick went home through its face and into the ground beneath. It stiffened into immobility.

Valentine turned to the marines at the windows. "Thank you, Post. Good shooting, men. Six shots, four hits. That's outstanding for a running Reaper." Valentine hoped the light-hearted tone didn't sound forced.

"On Jamaica bullets are rare, sir," a marine named Andree said.

He turned to look at the private. "In the Ozarks, men who can shoot like you are even rarer."

Chapter Three

Magazine Mountain, Arkansas, January of the forty-ninth year of the Kurian Order: A Southern Command Station Post once stood here, huts and wooden cabins placed to take advantage of folds in the ground and the canopy of trees for concealment and defensibilty.

Servicemen walking about on their duties added life and color to the camouflaged buildings. The Guards, the common soldiers in their neat charcoal gray uniforms and regimental kepis, would march past files of scarecrow-lean Wolves in fringed buckskins. The Wolves, rifles cradled in tanned fingers, assorted pistols and knives shoved in belts and boots, and no two hats alike, struck one as sloppy-looking when compared to the disciplined Guards. A Cat might be sleeping beneath an oak, head pillowed on rolled coat and Reaper-killing sword, exhausted after two months spying in the Kurian Zone, but still coming to full wakefulness at a gentle tap. Everyone from cur dog to colonel of the Guards would make room when teams of Bears entered the post. Southern Command's shock troops, wearing uniforms of patched-together Grog hide and bullet-ablative Reaper cloak, the latter's black teeth hanging from neck or ear, were people one instinctively avoided. Perhaps it was the forbidding war paint, or the scalps of Grogs and even Quislings dangling from belt and rifle sheath, or the thousand-yard stare, but whatever the source the Bears had an aura about them demanding a wide berth. Then there were the others in camp, the logistics commandos: scroungers who went into the Kurian Zone to steal or trade for what Southern Command couldn't make for itself, driving their wagons to the commissary yards and yelling at women to get their children

*out of their mule team's path. There were always civilians in
camp, families of the soldiery or refugees waiting on transportation to other parts of the Freehold. There would be pack
traders and mail-riders, gunsmiths, charcoal sellers with
black hands, hunters trading in game for more bullets and
farmers selling vegetables for government buckchits. It was
chaos, but chaos that somehow kept the soldiery fed and
equipped, the civilians prosperous (by the standards of the
Free Territory) and, most importantly, the Ozarks free of the
Reapers.*

  But that was before.

  *By that dark, wet winter of '71, the base of Magazine
Mountain had only rats and raccoons standing sentry over
burned huts or nosing through old field kitchens that
smelled of rancid cooking oil. Bats huddled together for
warmth in SCPO mailboxes, and the carts and pickup trucks
rested wheelless on the ground, stripped like slaughtered
cattle.*

  *Heavy equipment rendered inoperable had a large red X
painted on it. The same might be done with maps depicting
the Ozark Free Territory.*

  "Goddammit, another fallen tree ahead," Post called
from a rise in the road. He turned his horse and looked at
Valentine for orders. One of Ahn-Kha's scouting Grogs
squatted to rest.

  "We might do better off the trail," Narcisse said to Valentine from her perch in the Quickwood wagon. Joints of
horsemeat hung from a frame Jefferson had added to the
wagon bed. It was too cool for flies. "These roads are almost
as bad."

  Smalls' son took the opportunity to put a taconite pellet
in his wrist-rocket, a surgical tubing sling that he used to
bring down squirrels. The boy ventured into the trees while
Valentine thought. David looked at Ahn-Kha, who was
sniffing the wintry air.

  "Rain soon," Ahn-Kha said.

"The Magazine Mountain Station can't be far," Valentine said to Post. "Let's pull off the trail and camp."

There had been no more Reapers since leaving the house. The refugees Valentine led made agonizingly slow progress through the ridges of the Ouachitas, with occasional halts to hide at the sound of distant engines. They had seen no living human—though they had come across a Reaper-drained skeleton lodged in the crotch of a tree, giving Mrs. Smalls a warmer coat once it was pulled off the corpse and cleaned. A pack of stranger-shy dogs tailed them, exploring the surroundings of the campfire and digging up the camp's sanitary holes in search of choice snacks. Valentine had tried to tempt them closer with fresher food than something that had already passed through the human digestive system, but the dogs would have none of it. Every now and then he saw a wary, furry face appear on the road behind, proving that they were still being tailed. Valentine wanted the dogs with them. Dogs hated Reapers—or feared them—and usually whined or bayed an alarm if one was near.

Valentine waved Ahn-Kha and Post over.

"Sir?" Post asked.

Valentine looked up at the flat-topped loom of Magazine Mountain. "Post, we're near one of the big camps of Southern Command. I'm going to take Ahn-Kha and see what, if anything, is left. Pull off out of sight of the road, cover your tracks and camp. We'll go on foot; give the horses a rest."

"Chances are that fort's in Kurian hands."

"I know. That's why I'm bringing Ahn-Kha. Having a Grog along might confuse them long enough for me to talk my way loose, or get the jump on a patrol."

"How long you figure on being gone?"

"Less than a day. If twenty-four hours go by and you don't hear from us, act as you will. I'd say the Boston Mountains are your best chance, on the other side of the Arkansas River. If there's anything left of Southern Command, it should be there. Get the Quickwood to them. Don't forget the seeds."

Post fingered the pouch around his neck, identical to

Valentine's, though it didn't contain any mahjong pieces. "I'll see it through, Val."

"Thank you. I'll probably be back in time for horsemeat and flatbread."

He took Ahn-Kha over to the supply wagon. They each threw a bag made out of old long-sleeved shirts over their shoulders. The shirt-sacks contained bread. Mr. Smalls rose from where he squatted next to his wife.

"Everything all right with you two?" Valentine asked them.

"Just a little tired, Mr. Ghost," Mrs. Smalls said, her belly prominent through the opening in the coat.

"We're stopping for a day or two. Fix yourselves up under the bed of the wagon. Looks like we might get some rain."

"Hank's been picking up sharp quartz crystals; there's lots of them in these hills," Mr. Smalls said. "If we attach 'em to the front of those wooden spear points, they might serve you a little better." He reached into his shoulder bag and pulled out a spear point.

Valentine looked at it. The boy had set a piece of quartz into the front, carving the wood into four prongs, like a gem-holder on a ring. Valentine tested the point on the quartz. It was sharp enough. "How'd he fix the quartz in so tight?"

"He soaked the wood after he carved it," Mrs. Smalls said proudly. "When it dried, it shrank down on the crystal."

"Good thinking," Valentine replied, handing it to Ahn-Kha for his opinion. The Golden Ones were accomplished craftsmen in their own right.

"This is fine work," Ahn-Kha agreed, fingering the point.

"Have him make some more, if he can," Valentine said.

Smalls nodded, and Valentine led Ahn-Kha off. They watched the Smalls boy search the tree limbs, but the squirrels were making themselves scarce. "Smart kid. In the Wolves we used to take boys on patrols, called them 'aspirants.' That spear point alone would have got him a place with my company."

"He thinks quickly. Remember what he did with the wagon."

"We could use another sharp set of eyes," Valentine said. "Want to bring him along?"

"He'd have a better chance at a squirrel with us," Ahn-Kha replied, his long ears twisting this way and that.

"Settled," Valentine said. He put two fingers in his mouth and whistled. "Hey, Hank, come over here."

The boy ran up to them. "Yes, Mr. Ghost?"

"We're going out on an all-night scout. You want to come?"

"Yes, sir!" Hank answered, his voice breaking with excitement.

"Go on, ask your parents. If it's okay with them, catch up to us."

"Thanks, Mr. Ghost," the boy said, and ran off toward the wagon.

Valentine and Ahn-Kha moved off into the woods. After a hundred yards, Valentine touched Ahn-Kha's shoulder.

"Time for his first lesson," Valentine said. "Keep going."

Valentine held his sheathed knife in his hand and waited next to the trail. Ahn-Kha disappeared into the brush, leaving a Grog-wide trail. Soon he heard the boy's footsteps as Hank ran to catch up with Ahn-Kha's furry back.

As Hank passed, Valentine stepped out from behind the tree. Quick as a Reaper, he got the slim youth in the fold of his left arm and put the sheathed knife to the boy's throat. Hank let out a squeal of fear.

"Just me, Hank," Valentine said, releasing him. "Don't pass so close to trees big enough to hide somebody."

"You didn't have to grab me!" Hank said.

"Your heart beating hard?" Valentine asked.

"Yeah. I don't like being grabbed."

"Then move a little more carefully when you're going through the woods. Long time ago, over on the other side of Arkansas, some friends and I weren't. They're both dead. The Hood stepped right out from behind the tree and grabbed

Gil, as easily as you'd pick up a rabbit knocked out with your slingshot."

"Hood? That's another word for a Reaper, right? We were supposed to call them Visors."

"Do you know how it all works, Hank?"

"I know the Vis—the Reapers drink blood."

"A Reaper's like a puppet. There's another person pulling the strings. We call them Kurians because they're from another world, a planet called Kur. They use the Reapers to feed because it's less dangerous for them when they get the energy. The donor puts up a fight."

"That energy they get, it's something in us, right? Like our souls?" Hank said.

Valentine felt as if the boy had kicked him in the stomach. He thought back to the graves of his parents, brother and sister who fell in Minnesota when he was eleven. He had asked Father Max if their souls had been eaten. "Nobody knows. Yes, it's something humans have more of than other creatures. The man who raised me called it an 'aura.' There's more aura in an intelligent being than there is in a dog or something. That's why they feed on us."

"We walked past a Reaper once on an Honor Guard march. They had us out burning down houses. It didn't move. Just looked at us dead cold. Reminded me of a snake sitting on a rock."

"Dead cold, all right," Valentine agreed.

"So that's why everyone's scared all the time now. They're afraid the Reapers will get them."

"That's why people cooperate with them. The people who serve them get badges, or cards, or pieces of jewelry that mean the Reapers can't touch them."

Hank nodded. "Yeah, we heard some of that in Honor Guard. Our Top Guardian had some sorta certificate that signified his family was too important to reassign. I hated him, Dallas trash if ever there was one."

"You grew up here in the Ozarks, right?"

"Yes, in the borders. My pa would go out into Texas and steal, or trade for horses. He sorta worked for Southern

Command; at least they gave him stuff when he brought horses in."

"You remember what the Free Territory used to be like, right?"

"Yes, it all happened last spring, or last summer, really. I heard a lot of fighting. Then there were new people in charge. My pa was in Texas at the time; when he got back he said we had to do what they say for a while."

"You liked it better before they came, right?"

"Yes. Momma was happier. She hated it when Pa was in Texas though."

"I was gone for a couple of years myself. Now that I'm back I'm trying to find if there's any Free Territory left."

"Are we going to live there? Is there anywhere safe now?"

"I hope so, Hank. If there is, we'll find it."

They were refilling their water skins at a trickle when Ahn-Kha came back from his scout of the old camp.

"Everything's burnt out, my David. Picked clean. Lots of holes in the ground. If there were buried weapons, I'd say they've been dug up."

"No one there?"

"Tracks. I smelled urine."

"You speak really well, for a big stoop," Hank said.

Ahn-Kha stood straight, towering over the boy. "We call ourselves the Golden Ones. I grew up trading with men in Omaha. I translated for my people when I was David's age."

"What's old for a stoop?"

Ahn-Kha's ears folded flat against his head.

"About forty years older than you're going to get if you call him a 'stoop' again," Valentine said.

"You can call me Ahn-Kha, or Uncle, if that's too hard for you to pronounce."

"Uncle? My ma would smack me if I called a . . . Golder Ones my uncle."

Valentine decided to change the subject. "Hank," he asked, "what kind of scrounger are you?"

"Haven't had many chances. We'd just burn when we'd go out on the Honor Guard sweeps."

Valentine picked up a stick and put three parallel scores in the ground. He added a fourth, under them and perpendicular to the other three. "That's a mark for a cache. You know what a cache is?"

"Ummm . . ."

"It's a hiding spot. The mark would be on a tree or a rock. See if you can find one as we walk. Chances are it would be out at the edge of the camp. We're all going to go in and have a look around."

The crossed a series of gullies and came upon the camp, folded into the base of the mountain in the broken ground there.

The camp was in ruins, inhabited only by the memories in Valentine's mind. The Quonset huts were gone, the shacks and cabins burned to the ground. The smaller branches of many of the trees in camp were black-barked where the flames had caught them. Valentine saw again the old faces of his platoon, remembering the smiles of his men over mugs of beer in the canteen and Sergeant Gator's slow, easy laugh. He was a Ghost haunting a Southern Command graveyard, and in a few more years there wouldn't be anything left to mark a place where legends lived.

Ahn-Kha picked up a handful of dirt at one of the burned cabins and let it trickle through his hands, sniffing it. "Jellied gasoline," the Grog said. "Bad way to die."

Valentine kept an eye on Hank, who was examining tree bark.

"Is there a good death?"

"Among my people's warriors, we have a saying. 'A good death can come through battle, at a place that is remembered. A better death can come through heroism, sacrificing yourself in the saving of others. The best death comes late, after seeing grandchildren born, for then you've also had a life.' "

"There's a lot to admire in Golden One wisdom. Beats *dulce et decorum est, pro patria mori.*"

"What is that?"

"A phrase from Latin: 'It is a sweet and proper thing, to die for one's country.' That kind of death's neither sweet nor proper. Just ugly. Necessary sometimes, but not sweet and proper."

The allies stood in silence for a moment.

"It will be dark soon," Ahn-Kha offered as a change in subject.

"I don't want to sleep here. Let's make a camp farther up on the mountain. Somewhere we can hear."

"We could make it back to the wagon if we hurried."

Valentine found Hank's footsteps with hard ears. "I don't want to travel with the boy at night. I can hide my lifesign, and you don't show as human. Hank might get sensed if there are any more of those loose Hoods around."

"That was odd, to run across three masterless ones. Do you suppose that many Kurians died when they fought here last summer?"

"I hope so."

Valentine was getting tired of hoping. Ever since returning to the Ozarks, his hopes had been vanishing from his mental horizon like a series of desert mirages. Hopes that his Quickwood would make a difference in the war. Hopes that he might be able to return to the Caribbean, where Mali Carrasca was carrying his child—or daughter, according to Narcisse. Hopes that they'd find some vestige of Southern Command still in these hills. But if there was still hope to be found, it wasn't at Magazine Mountain.

Valentine ate his flavorless bread, and tried not to think of the plentiful fruits and vegetables of the Caribbean. Ahn-Kha was occupying Hank with the story of the Golden Ones' battle against the General in Omaha.

"They would have rolled over us. But our Ghost found the railroad cars filled with the men who were operating the Reaper soldiers. He blew up some, burned the others where they were parked. The Reapers didn't go wild, like the ones with the horses; they just dropped in their tracks. Took the heart out of the rest of the General's men; they were used to having the Reapers at the front of the fight. In the confusion my brothers broke their chains and rose against them. But if it weren't for David, wounded twice—"

Valentine tossed a pebble at the Golden One. "Don't leave out the other details. Be sure to tell him how I almost had my head shot off," Valentine said, rubbing his aching leg. He pointed to the scar on his face. "An inch closer and the bullet would have taken the side of my face with it. Don't leave out the part where you found me in an interrogation cell, with my pants full of shit and a gun to my head. Ahn-Kha was the one who killed the General, Hank. I had a pair of handcuffs on at the time."

"Just wanted to know how you became friends," Hank said. "The sto—the Grogs I've seen don't mix with men."

"Grog is a word that covers a lot of territory, Hank. It's a term for the beings the Kurians brought to our world. Or maybe made, nobody knows, though the guys at the Miskatonic have some interesting theories. Technically you, a dog, and an oyster are all animals, but your similarities pretty much end there. Same with the Grogs. Some are as smart as Ahn-Kha, who's smarter than most men I know, but some aren't any brighter than a catfish. I think you're talking about the Grey Ones, like the Lucky Pair."

"Your ape things with thick ol' hides? They're called Grey Ones?"

"In my tongue, yes," Ahn-Kha said.

"The ones the Kurians use carry long guns. Fifty calibers," Valentine said.

"'They'll take your head off at a thousand yards with 'em too, if you're fool enough to show yourself and not be movin',' a voice called from the darkness. "That's what Sergeant Samuels used to say, anyway."

Valentine came to his feet, hand on his pistol. He looked up to see a shaggy man in buckskins, coonskin cap on his head and a sheathed rifle cradled in his arms. Valentine noticed his hand was inside the sheath, though, gripping it so he could get at the trigger easily. Nearly half of the man's face was covered with a stiff leather patch, but the remaining eye was familiar.

"Finner?" Valentine asked. "Jess Finner?" Valentine suddenly felt like a sore-footed recruit again; he almost came to attention with chest thrown out.

Finner's eye took in the whole campsite, not resting on any one spot for more than a fraction of a second. "Yep. Was Sergeant Finner, Tango Company, up to a few months ago. Last time I saw you, Valentine, you were eating a watermelon the size of an anker of rum in Missouri. Heard you got a commission in Zulu Company under Captain LeHavre. He still alive, I hope?"

"I don't know. I'm no longer a Wolf. You look hungry, Jess. You want to come down and have a bite?"

"Maybe. If I do, know that you've got three rifles on each of you."

"Stand down, Sergeant," Valentine said. "I don't want an accidental shooting."

"Been watching your little procession for the better part of a day. Recognized you by the hair, at first. Limp's new. Saw you break off and thought it was time for a chat. I'm a bit curious about what you're doing out in the woods with a Grog, Valentine. What kind of rig are you wearing? That's not a Guard uniform."

"Its mostly a Coastal Marine uniform, dyed black. The bandolier is from a snake."

"Must have been some snake. Be more impressed if you had some friendly insignia, Valentine."

"Technically I'm a captain now, Sergeant, though you'll have to go on faith for that. I couldn't prove it any better to you than I could prove why I'm out here with a Grog. His name's Ahn-Kha, and he also outranks you. I've been out of the Free Territory for better than two years. Sort of a Logistics Commando operation."

"The boy?"

"Just a refugee. None of us are out here for fun. I'm trying to find any kind of Southern Command organization. If you can turn us over to one, I'd be obliged."

Finner took his hand out of the sheath. "No longer a Wolf, eh? Ain't no such thing, Valentine. Once you've looked into the eyes of Father Wolf, you're one until the day you die." He pushed the cap back on his head, revealing a greasy forehead. "Hell, whatever you are, it's good to see you again, Captain, sir," Finner said, holding up his hand palm outward in the Wolf salute. "I'm running with what's left of Southern Command here in the Ouachitas. If you want to meet the boys, just say so. They're only a couple hilltops away."

"I'll say so," Valentine said. "Ahn-Kha, take Hank and find the others. Tell them to camp quietly for another day, and wait for me. This should be the end of our trail."

"How did it happen, Jess?" Valentine said, as they walked in the loom of Magazine Mountain. The radio antennae Valentine remembered atop the rock-faced cliffs were gone.

Finner must have answered the question before to other fragments of Southern Command, searching for higher command like children looking for a missing parent. The words came out in a practiced, steady beat.

"Not sure. I was recruiting up in the Northwoods. Wisconsin this time, same's I do every year since you met me. It was August. Hottest one I can remember in a while, even up there. We had a little temporary camp south of La Crosse, where we picked up some food courtesy of the underground, and the boatmen said there'd been barges full of men brought across the Mississippi. Our lieutenant thought we'd better not try for the Free Territory until we knew which path was safe. He sent out scouts. Only one came back, and he said the riverbank south of St. Louis was crawling with Grogs. Captain Dorn finally showed up, and he left it up to us. We could scatter up north, or try to get through to the Ozarks. Most tried, a few recruits even. Well, they were right, the hills were crawling. We got picked up by some of those flying shit-eaters, and the harpies put the big ones on us. Legworms barreling through the brush like tanks with Grogs picking us off right and left as we ran. It was a massacre. No other word for it. I made it out, running south. Came across a week-old battlefield on the Crowley Ridge; our men were hanging in trees everywhere, getting picked at by crows. 'Round there I think I got some bad water, picked up a bug. Woke up in a hayloft; some farmers had found me wandering. Said I had a fever, babbled. I was about twenty pounds thinner. This family said the Kurians were running the show now, but they'd heard there was still fighting in the Ouachitas down by Hot Springs. Let's take a break."

Finner sat down and Valentine joined him, rubbing his tired left leg. Finner passed him a little stainless-steel flask. Valentine smelled the contents and shook his head, handing it back.

"I'd lost my blade and my gun while I was sick. When I felt well enough to move on they gave me a bagful of food and made me promise to say I got it in another village if I got caught. I ran into three deserters trying to make their way to the mountains in Kentucky, they said it was all over for the Ozarks. We'd been hit from everywhere—including up. They flew over at the beginning, dropping wild Reapers. Called 'em 'sappers.' I guess there were hundreds of 'em loose at one point."

"I've seen them. They're still running these hills."

Finner wiped his brow. "Southern Command had to send out teams of Wolves and Bears to deal with the sappers. Not enough reserves when the real attack came, though they tell me it wouldn't have made a difference."

"So when did you reach the Ouachitas?"

"Last summer. Gotta warn you, we're an ad hoc unit. Every man's there because he wants to be there; no parades or drill or courts-martial. Not enough supply to do anything but keep us alive. The fighting we do is purely to keep from getting captured. I wouldn't throw that 'captain' title around; the General wouldn't like it, unless he puts you on his staff."

"General who?" Valentine disliked it when someone was known only by the title "General." It reminded him of the leader of the Twisted Cross.

"Martinez. Twelfth Guards, formerly."

"Don't know him."

Valentine felt the darkness coming on. The air took on a wet chill.

"He wasn't a general before. He was colonel of the Twelfth."

"They had the tiger-striped kepis. Orange and black, usually stationed in the Arkansas Gap."

"Yup. Got the hell knocked out of them by troops coming in from Texas. That's who's running the Fort Scott area and the Ouachitas. Texans and Oklahomans. They must've stripped the Dallas Corridor bare; they say the invasion was over a hundred thousand men."

"How are they feeding them? Aren't guerillas hitting the supply lines? When I was in Zulu that was supposed to be our catastrophe assignment."

"Can't say. I spend my time scavenging, not on ops or recon. I've seen low-draft barges coming up the Arkansas. Cattle and rice."

"I came through northeast Texas. I thought the patrols looked slim."

"Yeah, the Ks in Texas think big. They're supposed to get a chunk of the Ouachitas. But there's some new bigshot organizing things out of the ruins in Little Rock. That's who's really running things hereabouts now. A man, if you can believe it. Ol' Satan and his gang of Kurians."

"Satan?"

"Solon. Consul Solon, his papers say."

Valentine's nose told him they were approaching the camp before they came across the lookouts. Latrine discipline wasn't a priority for this particular remnant of Southern Command.

"So this is what defeat smells like," Valentine said.

"It's not that bad. You get used to it. Hush, now, we're coming up on the pickets."

They were still in uniform, more or less. Mottled camouflage pants and gray winter-uniform tunics, many with hunt-

ing vests thrown over them; scarves and gloves made out of
scrap cloth. Similarities ended at the extremities; there were
a variety of hats, gloves and boots. Some of the men had re-
sorted to cobbled-together shoes or sheepskin moccasins. A
boy with a hunting bow whistled from atop a rock, and four
men drew beads on them.

"It's Finner with a new 'un," one of the men said.

"Found a stray in the hills," Finner said. "Wolf, I know
him personally, I'll vouch to the captain." Valentine wondered why he didn't mention Ahn-Kha or Hank.

"Then report to him," the one who recognized him said.

They passed the pickets, who dispersed again as soon as
they moved up the hillside for the camp. Valentine's nose
added other camp smells to the list headed by men shitting
in the woods: smoke, tobacco, open-pit cooking and pigs.
He heard a guitar playing somewhere; it drifted softly
through the trees like a woman's laugh. To Valentine it
seemed forever since last fall's wagon train, when he'd enjoyed the music of the Texans under the stars.

"Why didn't you mention the others?" Valentine asked.

"Didn't want your Grog friend hunted down. Standing
orders, no alien prisoners."

"He's not a prisoner, he's an ally. He's worth those four
pickets, and another six like them."

"All the more reason to keep him alive. Quislings we
bury, but dead Grogs get stewed down to pig feed."

They topped a flat little rise, thickly wooded like most of
the Ouachita Mountains, overshadowed by another hill
whose summit was scarred with limestone on the face toward the camp hill. Valentine saw watch posts under camouflage netting among the trees of the taller hill. Tents were
everywhere, interspersed with hammocks and stacked
stones to hold supplies and equipment clear of the wet
ground, along with little shacks and huts put together from
everything from camper tops to bass boats. Evil-smelling
trash filled the bottom of every ravine. There was no sign-
age, no evidence of any kind of unit groupings. It reminded
Valentine of some of the shantytowns he'd seen in the

Caribbean, minus the cheerful coloring and kids playing. The men sat in little groups of four to ten, trying to get in a last game of cards by firelight. Valentine passed a still every sixty paces, or so it seemed, all bubbling away and emitting sharp resinous smells, tended by men filling squared-off glass bottles.

"Welcome home, Captain Valentine," Finner said.

This wasn't home. Not nearly. It looked more like an oversize, drunken snipe hunt. "Thanks."

"If you want some companionship, just look for one of the gal's tents with a paper lantern out front. They get food, washwater and protection as long as they're willing to share the bed once in a while. Sort of a fringe benefit of this outfit."

"Does this 'outfit' ever fight a battle?"

"We do a lot of raiding. General has us grab the new currency they're using here; we use it to buy some of the stuff we need from smugglers."

"Sounds more like banditry. Do you get overflown?"

"If the gargoyles come overhead, they only see a few fires. We don't try'n knock 'em out of the sky. We figure they just think there're refugees up here. We're far enough from Fort Scott so's they don't care, and the folks on the east side of the mountains have enough to do just controlling the flatlands."

"Many refugees?"

"No, unless they're Southern Command we send 'em elsewhere."

"Where's that?"

"Anywhere but here. That's part of what we were doing when I came across you and the boy and the Grog, keeping an eye out for runaways to warn 'em off. We got these higher hills around to cut the lifesign, but you never know when a Reaper'll be trailing along behind some broke-dicks to see where they're headed."

Voices rose to an excited roar from an opening in the trees, and Valentine's hand went to his pistol.

"Get him, Greggins!" someone shouted.

Finner shrugged. "Sounds like a fight. Interested?"

Valentine scowled and followed Finner downhill to a ring of men. Someone came running with a burning firework. In its blue-white glare he saw forty or fifty men in a circle, expanding and contracting around the action in the center like a sphincter. Valentine heard thudding fists, punctuated by roars from the crowd when an especially good blow was struck. He saw a few women among the men, some on top of the men's shoulders angling for a better view.

Instincts took over, even in the unknown camp. He elbowed his way through the press. "Make a hole!" he growled, then realized that Coastal Marine slang didn't mean much in the Ozarks. The crowd surged back around him and Valentine found himself with the back of one of the combatants sagging against him.

"No fair, that guy's holding him up," someone shouted.

A bloody-browed Guard corporal looked at Valentine over his scuffed knuckles. "Pull off, mister, otherwise he can't go down."

Valentine turned the soldier sagging against him, saw the bruised ruin of a face, then let go his grip. The man sagged to his knees, mumbling something in Spanish.

"Knees ain't down. Finish him, Greggins!"

The corporal stepped forward, corded muscles bulging from his rolled-up sleeves.

Valentine held up a hand. "It's over, Corporal. I'd say you won."

"What're you, his manager? Fight's not over until he's flat. He questioned my authority."

Valentine looked at the beaten man's uniform. "I see sergeant's stripes on him, *Corporal*. If I were you I'd be worried about a court-martial for striking your superior. Even if he were a private, a fistfight isn't the way we keep discipline."

Something in Valentine's voice made the man lower his fists.

"Now help him to his feet and get him to a medic. Better have him look at you as well. That eye doesn't look good."

The corporal took a step forward, then lashed out with a roundhouse. Valentine was ready for it, and slipped under the blow. He brought a driving knee up into the corporal's off-balance stance, and hammered him in the kidney with an elbow as the corporal doubled over. The corporal dropped, his mouth open in a silent scream.

Valentine looked at the circled men, not quite sure what they had seen in the blur of motion. "This how you do things now? Is there a sergeant in this circus?"

A man with a handlebar mustache stepped forward. "I'm a captain, Eighteenth Guards, East Texas Heavy Weapons. Who are you?"

"He's logistics, just come outta Texas, Randolph," Finner said.

"Don't see a uniform."

"I find my duties in the Kurian Zone easier to perform if I don't wear a Southern Command uniform, Captain." Valentine said, and a few of the men chuckled.

"I don't care for spies," Randolph said.

Valentine got the feeling Randolph wanted to see if he could be provoked into another exchange of blows. He reduced lifesign—the old mental technique that also did wonders for his temper.

"I know him, sir," Finner said. "Good man. Wolf officer."

"Disperse, damn you," Randolph said, rounding on the men. "Fight's over. Get some sleep." He turned back to Valentine. "Is that so? We'd better get you to the General, *Captain*, so he can decide what to do with you. We shoot spies trying to penetrate the camp, you know."

The men helped the brawlers to their feet. Randolph jerked his chin and put his hand on his pistol holster. Valentine walked off in the indicated direction, and the captain drew his gun. He didn't point it at Valentine, but the muzzle could be brought to bear easily enough.

Finner trailed along behind as they walked. Only Valentine had ears good enough to hear him click the safety off inside his rifle sheath.

*   *   *

"The General keeps late hours," Randolph said as they approached a vintage twentieth-century house. Lights burned inside and sentries stood on the porch. Where a swing had once stood, piled sandbags and a machine-gun post dominated the parked vehicles in the yard in front of the house. Valentine smelled a barbecue pit in the backyard.

"We've got a LC just in from Texas to see the General," Randolph said to the lieutenant who appeared at the other side of the screen door. "Or so he says."

"I brought him in," Finner added.

"Thank you, Sergeant, that'll be all," Randolph said.

"Let them in, boys," the lieutenant said. He had golden, braided hair and bare arms protruding through a Reaper-cloak vest hung with pistols and hand grenades. Four red diamonds stood out on the meat of his forearm. Valentine suspected he was a Bear. The lieutenant looked Valentine up and down. "I think I've seen your face. Can't place where though."

"Red River raid, sixty-five. You Bears hit the power plant and armory while two companies of Wolves raided some of the plantations. I was the junior in Zulu Company. Never got your name though."

"Nail's the handle. I was in Team Able. We had a hell of a skedaddle out of Louisiana on that one, as I remember, Captain . . . ."

"Ghost is what goes down on the paperwork for me," Valentine said.

Nail held out his hand. "Paperwork. That's rich." They shook. "Nice to see you alive, Ghost. Zulu got caught up in a fight on the Mississippi when all this started. I don't—"

"We can catch up later, Lieutenant," Randoph interjected. "I'm sure the General would like to hear this man's report. Colorful as the conversation is with all the Hunter code names." He turned to Valentine. "I take it you're a . . . hmmm . . . Cat?"

Valentine said nothing.

"Lots of us have family, beg your pardon, sir," Nail said. "It keeps them safe."

Randolph ignored the Bear and waved over an adjutant. Valentine's gaze followed the adjutant into the dining room of the house, where a long table piled with files and a sideboard covered with half-eaten trays of food and liquor bottles stood under dirty walls. Under a candelabra's light a man in red-striped trousers sat, a coat heavy with chicken guts draped over the chair next to him. He had a massive body and a small, balding head on a thin neck; the odd proportions made Valentine think of a turtle. General Martinez rose and threw on his uniform coat.

"Distractions, nothing but distractions," the General grumbled. He had the most perfectly trimmed Van Dyke Valentine had ever seen, as if he made up for the lack of hair on his head with extra attention to that on his face.

"Sorry to add to them, sir," Valentine said. "I'm looking for Southern Command."

"You're talking to a piece of what's left."

"My name is David Valentine, Cat codename Ghost, on independent assignment. I just came out of the KZ in Texas, sir. There wouldn't be a Lifeweaver associated with your command, would there?"

"They've gone to the tall timber, Cat. They're hunted even more than we are."

"I got jumped just across the Red coming out of Texas. I've got close to twenty mouths to feed and have no idea of what to do with them. Fifteen are trained soldiers, including some Grog scout-snipers. The others are refugees."

"Grogs? What unit has Grogs?"

"*Thunderbolt* Ad Hoc Rifles," Valentine said. It was near enough to the truth and saved explanations.

"Never heard of them. Still armed?"

General Martinez wasn't curious about what he was bringing in from Texas. Which was just as well. Valentine wasn't ready to trust him with his precious Quickwood. While they wouldn't use it to fuel the stills, it wouldn't be used to hunt Reapers, either. "Yes, sir."

"You said you came out of Texas?"

"Yes, sir."

"Well, Cat, we could have used a little more warning about what was building."

"I was further south. I only got to Texas—"

Martinez cut him off. "You'd be better off back there. Seems like every Gulag gun's here stamping out the embers."

Doesn't just look like a turtle, Valentine thought. *Snaps like one too*. Then he felt guilty for the thought. He'd been operating outside the military hierarchy for too long: his superior deserved his respect.

"Couldn't make it, sir. I've got some horses that need shoes, and my wagon could use a new team. I was hoping to draw from your commissary. Food and clothing and camp equipment would be helpful."

"None of which I can spare just now," General Martinez said. He paused in thought. "Let's have your team here. You can draw rations from the common pool for now. You'll have to lose the civilians. I've got a militia regiment I'm trying to turn into regulars; you and your veterans'd be a help with them."

"We'll keep heading north, sir. Can someone on your staff show me—"

"No, Valentine. I need every man who can shoulder a gun. We're bringing you in, that's an order. You'll be safer with us."

"I'm responsible for the civilians—I gave my word."

"Fine, we'll provide for them for a few days while we sort this out. I could attach them to a labor company, I suppose." He reached up and rubbed his beard with his knuckles, stroking first one side of it, then the other, making him less of a turtle and more of a cat sizing up a cornered mouse. "Randolph, take your light platoon and bring them in. I'm sorry I can't give you more time, Valentine, but other matters demand my attention. We'll talk again tomorrow. You know what to do, Captain Randolph?"

"Yes, sir," Randolph said, saluting and executing a neat about-face.

Faced with a direct order, Valentine could do little but

obey. He saluted and left with Randolph. They descended the steps and joined Finner. "I feel like I've just been shanghaied," Valentine said.

Finner grinned, with the *schadenfreude* of a fox who has lost his tail seeing another fox lose his. "No, you've just been incorporated into the Bitter Enders. What's left they want to make sure stays till the bitter end. They've been shooting deserters."

"In other words, if the enemy doesn't kill you, we will," Randolph added. "Hate that it's come to that, but there you are. Six-bullet sentencing."

"How does that look stitched on a brigade flag?" Valentine asked.

Randolph let out a harrumphing noise that was half squawk and half bark. "Don't question us unless you've lived what we've been through. Valentine, the more I see of you the less I like you as an officer."

Randolph's light platoon was light on experience. Valentine doubted any of the soldiers were much over eighteen; beneath the dirt the majority looked like they should still be in school. They moved over the hills with youthful energy, however, and came upon Post's camp before noon the next day. Finner rejoined his Wolves, who appeared and disappeared in wary silence. Hank spotted the approaching column first, and when he saw Valentine he took off his straw hat and waved it.

"We've been ordered to rejoin Southern Command," Valentine said to Post as the two groups eyed each other. "These kids are here to make sure we do it." Ahn-Kha rose from a squat behind a wagon and some of the light platoon grabbed at their rifles.

"What are you doing with Grogs?" Randolph asked, hand on the butt of his pistol.

"As I explained to General Martinez, they're on our side and they're trained. They helped us in the KZ, and I expect them to be treated with the respect due any other soldier in Southern Command," Valentine said.

"And we speak," Ahn-Kha added. "Have those children take more care with their rifles."

"Seems suspicious, you coming out of the Zone with Grogs."

M'Daw rose from the campfire. "Mister—"

"Quiet, M'Daw," Valentine said. Then, to Randolph: "He escaped the ambush in his underwear, Captain, and the only clothes we could find that would fit him were Quisling. We don't have any dye, so I'd appreciate some, or a change in uniform for him. I don't want him shot by accident on standing orders."

M'Daw sat back down and huddled under a blanket in such a way that his stitched-on name didn't show.

"Let's load up, Post," Valentine said. "Ditch the lumber; we won't need to build shelters after all, and there's no point hauling it up that hill. Let's make Mrs. Smalls' journey as comfortable as possible."

"Yes, sir."

Valentine, Ahn-Kha, and the two Grogs unloaded the Quickwood while Post put the marines and the civilians in marching order. Valentine marked the spot, triangulating off of the peak of Magazine Mountain.

"Something wrong, my David?" Ahn-Kha asked as they threw another beam on the pile.

"I don't like the way this outfit we're joining is being run. I have no business challenging a lawful superior's methods, but . . . hell, I've seen groups of Chicago hookers that are better organized. I didn't come all this way to hand over the Quickwood to a bunch of outlaws."

"Do we have an option?"

"Southern Command is finished, if this is representative of what's left. I'm thinking we might be better off with your people in Omaha, or maybe mine in Minnesota. In six more months this crew is going to be robbing towns and trains to feed themselves, with the meanest knife fighter calling the shots. I want to see M'Daw and the Smalls safe, then we'll talk about taking off."

Ahn-Kha's ears sagged. "Better do it quickly. If they break the marines up into other units—"

"Randolph is coming," Valentine whispered. Ahn-Kha's ears pivoted to the sound of footsteps.

"Why's everyone got wooden spears along with their rifles?" Randolph asked.

Ahn-Kha growled an order, and led the Grogs back up to the wagon.

"For the feral pigs in these hills. Those are boar spears."

"One of your men said it was for killing Reapers. That black cripple said the same thing."

"Have to tell them something or they just run at the sight of one. They think it's got big medicine. But so far they've just been used on pigs."

"Hope you boiled the meat good. I've seen men die eating wild pig. You might want to have your men check their shit. Our doc has a great remedy for worms. Just tell him you need to be sluiced out."

"Thanks for the tip. Is there contact with any other pockets of resistance?"

"General Martinez gets his orders through special channels. When it's time to move we'll hear it from him. There's talk of a counteroffensive next fall, when the Kurians think the Ozarks are pacified."

"Seems to me they're pacified already. How many do you lose each week?"

"You won't get far questioning the General, Valentine. The men love him. He's daddy and Santa Claus and Moses all in one. Have patience, the Promised Land is there."

"The Promised Land is occupied. We don't have forty years. We shouldn't be acting like we have forty days. Inertia and illness are going to kill your General's army; the Quislings and the Kurians are just going to be buzzards feeding off the corpse."

"Look, Valentine, I'm liking you less and less by the minute. You ever talk to me like that again and I'll deck you. You weren't here when it was raining Reapers, or when we got blown out of Fort Scott by so many guns you'd think they had enough to land a shell every six feet. Martinez took five thousand beat-up men who were ready to surrender and pulled us back together. Southern Command put him in charge of the central Ouachitas after that. He's keeping us fed and armed without any help from a rear that plain vanished on us. Quit questioning him, or I'll turn you in as a traitor."

"In the Free Territory that trained me two officers speaking in private could criticize anyone without the word treason being thrown around. You swing on me anytime you like, as long as the men aren't watching. If you do it where they can see I'll have you up on charges for striking a fellow officer, Captain. Write up a report if you want. I'll be happy to repeat everything I've said word for word to the General."

They returned to the wagon, both simmering. Post had Narcisse and Mrs. Smalls in the wagon and everyone else lined up behind it. Randolph's platoon had been dispersed to form a screen. When all was ready, they hitched the team to the wagon and set off. Valentine elected to walk beside Ahn-Kha and the Grogs, picking the way southeast and ready to chop a path through the growth blocking the hill road if necessary. They forded a river and rested the team after the crossing.

"Why did you leave the Quickwood, Daveed?" Narcisse asked as they rested. Valentine was inspecting a wobbling wheel on the wagon, wondering if it would make it the rest of the trip.

Valentine glanced around, and found himself gritting his teeth at the gesture. He was used to looking over his shoulder in the Kurian Zone, but here, in the middle of titular comrades, the precaution grated.

"The boys we're joining up with, they're one rung on the ladder over the bandits on the borders between the Kurian Zones and the Freeholds. For all I know this General is getting set to go Quisling. He's keeping a lot of men who might be useful elsewhere liquored up and lazy. Their camp's in a state any junior lieutenant in a militia company wouldn't allow, but that doesn't stop them all from talking like they're the last hope of the Ozarks."

Mrs. Smalls rubbed her lumbar while her husband went to get her a drink from the river. "Some sergeant tried to disarm your funny-talkin' island men while you were with the Grogs. Mr. Post put a stop to it."

"I'm liking this Captain Randoph less and less," Valentine said.

"Whoo-hoo boys, horsemeat coming in!" a voice called from beside the road.

Valentine saw machine-gun nests set to cover the bend in the road running up against the taller hill of the camp. They'd been set up while there were still leaves on the trees and now looked naked against the hillside.

"We're here," Randolph said from the saddle of what had been Valentine's horse. The column had made good time; it was barely afternoon of the second day since setting out from the shadow of Magazine Mountain.

"This isn't much of a road, but it's obliging of the others not to patrol it," Post said.

Randolph's platoon led them up the hill, the Grogs and marines sweating to help the wagon up the incline.

"Damn, they got them ape-men with 'em," one of the idlers said, pointing with the stained stem of a pipe.

"Prisoners? I thought we were getting a new company," the other said. "It's not even a sergeant's platoon. *Thunderbolt Ad Hoc Rifles*—bah."

Word spread through camp and men gathered, hoping to see familiar faces. The Jamaicans, in their strange blue uniforms, excited some comment among the men with dashed hopes.

"Can I speak to a supply officer?" Valentine asked. "I have to feed and billet my men."

Valentine heard a buzz at the back of the assembled men. General Martinez strode through. There was something of Moses in him after all; the men parted like the Red Sea at his presence. Some removed their hats or wiped their eyeglasses clean as he passed, gorgeous in his braided uniform coat, Van Dyke aligned like a plumb line.

"Welcome back to the Free Territory, Captain Valentine," Martinez said. "Those rifles your men have; Dallas Armory, aren't they?"

"Yes, sir, we took them off the post at Bern Woods. Those were the ones who ambushed us coming back across the Red."

"Every man counts here. Every man is important," the General said, loudly enough for all to hear. "The Grogs are another story. They'll run back to their buddies as soon as they see 'em. Sergeant Rivers, shoot the Grogs."

A man with stripes sloppily inked on the arm of a long trenchcoat pulled up a shotgun.

"Sir, no!" Valentine said. "They're my men. Let me—"

"Shoot, Sergeant," Martinez ordered. The gun went off. A Grog fell backward, his chest planted with red buckshot holes, his legs kicking in the air.

Ahn-Kha ran from the back of the column, knocking aside Valentine's old marines as he burst through them.

"David!" Ahn-Kha shouted.

"*Druk*?" the other Grog said, looking from the kicking corpse to the sergeant with the shotgun. Its confused eyes turned to Valentine as the gun fired again.

Everything slowed down. The Grog wavered like a redwood with its trunk severed, then crashed to the ground. Valentine heard his own heart, louder in his ears than the gunshots, beating in time to Ahn-Kha's footfalls as the Golden One ran to his Grogs with arms outstretched. The smoking shotgun muzzle swiveled to Ahn-Kha as the red shell casing spun through the air. Valentine's hand went to his belt.

Valentine moved. Faster than he had in his encounter with the corporal the other night.

"Rivers," Valentine said, stepping behind the General with his .45 pressed to the back of Martinez's ear, "you shoot again and I'll kill him, then you."

"Valentine, have you gone—-awwwk," Martinez started to say as Valentine grabbed a handful of goldenrod shoulder braid in his left hand and whipped it around the General's neck.

"Everyone calm down," Valentine said. "I don't want any more shooting. Post, don't draw that."

"Valentine!" Randolph shouted, pointing his pistol at Valentine's head in turn. "Let him go, right now."

"Men!" Valentine roared at the assembly. "General Martinez is under arrest for ordering the murder of soldiers of Southern Command. Randolph, you heard me tell him that the Grogs were part of Southern Command, under my authority. Twice. Uniform Code says no soldier of Southern Command can be executed without trial and unanimous verdict of three officers." Valentine decided not to add that the penalty for summary execution was a bullet in the back of the head.

"Southern Command is gone," General Martinez gasped. "There's no Uniform Code anymore."

"Then it's law of the jungle, Martinez. You're not a general, you're just some bastard who killed two of my friends. Last words?" Valentine thumbed back the hammer on the automatic.

"Shoot these bastards! Every one of them!" Martinez yelled.

"Guns down! Guns down! Keep order, there," a female voice shouted from the crowd.

Valentine looked across the heads of the crowd and saw men being pushed aside, before returning his eyes to the men around him. A stocky woman elbowed her way to the front. No, not stocky; short and powerful. She wore the cleanest uniform Valentine had seen yet in Martinez's camp, her muscular shoulders filling the Southern Command jacket in a way that would do credit to a Labor Regiment veteran fresh from six months of earth moving. Near white-blond hair disappeared up into a fatigue hat. The captain's bars on her collar were joined by an angled crossbar, forming a shortened *Z*.

The crossbar meant she was in the Hunters. Perhaps staff,

but part of the organization that encompassed the Wolves, Cats, and Bears.

"You two," she called to Valentine's marines, "open the bolts on those rifles. Sergeant Rivers, lay down the shotgun." The men, even those who had never seen her before, obeyed. She looked over the situation, smelled the cordite in the air, and shook her head at the dead Grogs Ahn-Kha knelt beside. She turned to Valentine.

"Captain, you can put up the gun. I saw what happened from up the hill. General Martinez, it's my duty to place you under arrest for murder."

"I bet you're just loving this, aren't you, Styachowski," Martinez said. "I wouldn't fall asleep for the next week or so, if I were you. These men know their duty."

Styachowski's pallid features showed no sign of even hearing the threat, though her face had gone so white that Valentine wondered if she was about to faint at the sight of the bodies. Valentine released Martinez, carefully brought down the gun's hammer, and offered the pistol to Styachowski.

"Keep it, Captain Valentine. You're not under arrest. Neither are you, Rivers," she called over her shoulder. "But don't count on keeping those stripes, or the shotgun. You'll do your fighting for the next year with a shovel."

"Men!" Martinez roared. "Handcuff and gag this little bitch. Two-step promotion to any man—"

"The General's no longer in a position to give orders; he's relieved of command pending trial," Styachowski countershouted. Valentine couldn't help but be impressed by the volume she put into her roar. She coughed as she got her wind back. Perhaps she was ill; that might account for her pallor. "Corporal Juarez, I need you and your men to escort General Martinez to his quarters. Sergeant Calloway, have *Private* Rivers grab a shovel and start digging graves for the Grogs."

"But Grog bodies go—"

"Soldiers' bodies get buried on Watch Hill. That's where they'll go, right with our men."

Martinez glared at them from between two nervous soldiers. "Good luck finding three officers to convict, Styachowski. You and this other mutineer here both arrested me. You can't serve as judge and accusing officer. After I'm acquitted I'll try and hang you both for mutiny."

"Captain Randolph, find a place for Captain Valentine's people, please," Styachowski said. She nodded at Valentine, then turned and followed the corporal's guard up the hill.

"Post, have the men make litters for the Grogs. I'm sorry, Ahn-Kha," Valentine said.

Ahn-Kha looked up. Golden Ones cried; in that they were like humans. He held one of each of his Grog's hands in his own. "Nothing seems to change, my David. Always expendable."

"Ahn-Kha, I'll try and prove you wrong someday. First I want to see some justice done for the Lucky Pair."

The irony of the nickname tasted bitter, like hemlock in his mouth.

Valentine's only look at the trial came when he gave evidence, and he didn't like what he saw. The crisis in command required prompt action. The trial was held, without a preliminary inquiry, the next day in the old brick ranch-style home that served as a guardhouse. Perhaps it had once been a vacation home, or a quiet retirement spot at the end of a winding, mountainside road. The owner liked his architecture low and spacious: wide porches, wide doors, wide windows. Inside, a great brick wall bisected the house into a huge living area and smaller bedrooms, which now served as cells, thanks to the limestone blocks of the walls.

Tables and chairs were arranged, nearly filling the big living room, with the three judges pressed up against the longest wall and facing the prosecution, the defense and a witness chair between the two. The temporary commander of the camp, Colonel Abraham, had excused himself from the trial, as traditionally no officer who stood to replace an accused superior could serve as a judge. The next senior officer in the shattered chain of command was a colonel named Meadows, who presided over the trial. At other times he might have been a good officer, but all Valentine saw was a nervous man seated between Randolph and a lieutenant colonel who smelled, to Valentine's sensitive nose, of marijuana.

Meadows had only one finger to accompany the thumb on his right hand, which clutched a handkerchief used every fifteen seconds on his sweating brow. A throng of men outside, given no duties by officers sympathetic to Martinez, listened through open windows as best they could and added boos and cheers accordingly. Captain Moira Styachowski— Valentine learned her first name when she took his statement—acted as prosecuting officer. She performed admirably under the circumstances, which at one point included a rifle bullet coming through a window and whizzing past her ear. Court adjourned to the floor.

The rifle was eventually found, dropped in a stand of bramble, but not the shooter.

After the missed shot Valentine swore to himself that he'd get his charges out of the camp. This bit of Southern Command was turning into a madhouse of angry, well-armed drunkards. But how far could they get on foot with a pregnant woman, old M'Daw and a boy, with a grudge-holding General following?

Valentine told his story, and answered five questions from Styachowski, stressing that he had told General Martinez at the evening meeting the nature of his command and his use of the Grogs. He tried to keep his voice even as he told of the summary execution of the Grogs, simple but skilled creatures with whom he'd served for a year.

"Did it occur to you, Captain, that General Martinez and his men had been fighting those very creatures for years?" the officer acting as defense counsel asked, leaning down to put his face close to Valentine's, probably in an effort to intimidate. Both the defense counsel and the General had been drinking during the previous night as they talked over the coming trial, according to Styachowski, and his breath made

Valentine turn his face toward the triumvirate of judges to avoid the fumes.

"He's been fighting Quislings, too. Does that mean he kills every man who comes into the camp?"

"Answer the question, Valentine," Randolph said.

"I've fought Grogs myself."

"That's still not an answer," Randolph said.

"I took it for granted that he's fought them."

The defense counsel nodded to Randolph. "Then why didn't you make it clear that they were Southern Command soldiers and not prisoners? Why didn't you give them uniforms?"

"I identified them repeatedly. I didn't have any uniforms to issue, and even if I had, they served as scouts in the Kurian Zone much of the time. That's what made them so useful. Putting them in our uniforms would have detracted from that. Even if they were naked, it shouldn't have made a difference because—"

Loud boos and catcalls came through the windows.

"You'll answer the questions asked, Valentine," Randolph said. "No more. You run on again and I'll have you arrested for contempt."

The men outside cheered that.

"I'm giving evidence; I'm not an official of the court," Valentine said. "You don't have that power."

"Don't go tentpole-lawyering with me," Randolph said, "or as soon as you get off the stand you'll be brought to a cell." The men outside cheered him.

Styachowski stood up, her lower lip swollen from her biting it. "Sir, can we close those windows and shutters? The circus outside—"

"Is of your own making. The camp is in disarray. This isn't a Star Chamber. The men have a right to know what's going on."

Valentine looked at Martinez's face. The General ran his knuckles down each side of his beard. Triumph shone in his bloodshot eyes.

*   *   *

So it was with trepidation that Valentine stepped away from the courtroom and went out onto the wide porch. An egg overshot his forehead and smacked the door's lintel, releasing a sulfurous reek.

"Next person throws anything deals with me," Nail said, stepping up and putting his thin frame in front of Valentine. The Bear was sunken-chested, but his tattooed arms were solid muscle and tendon. Perhaps it was just the aggressive stance, but his blond braids seemed to bristle. Men in Southern Command with regard for the integrity of their skeletal systems listened when a Bear made a threat; the catcalls quieted.

He escorted Valentine through the crowd using his elbows, an icebreaker smashing room for the larger ship behind. They made their way through the dirty camp. Nail found one of the squared-off green bottles, sniffed the mouthful that still remained inside and drained it.

"Goddamn that's vile, Captain." Nail sent the bottle spinning down the hillside, and after a faint, tinkling crash led Valentine uphill a short way on a trail. Valentine smelled more cannabis smoke from a cluster of men in a hollow.

"How long have you been in this zoo?"

"Long enough to know it's falling to pieces. If you ask me, a couple regiments of Quisling militia could sweep us off this hill. With slingshots."

"You can see it. Why can't the others?"

"The General got them out of a tight spot outside Fort Scott. These Guard brigades were the only ones to make it out of that pocket more or less intact, considering. Every time they thought they had us cornered, we got away. There's been some desertions, but no bad casualties since he took over. Food, light duties, wine, women and song. Everything a soldier could ask for, as long as they don't ask for a victory. Whatever else you want to say about the General, he knows how to slip out of a noose."

"I think he'll slip out of Styachowski's."

"You stepped into a private war, Valentine. Word around the campfire is Martinez tried to pull her pants off using his rank, if you follow." They crossed a narrow gully using a log bridge, with a rope strung as a handhold.

"When you say tried you mean—"

Nail winked. "Failed."

"He's been making her life hell ever since?"

"More like the other way around. She came out of Mountain Home GHQ, one of these invisible staff types that suddenly show up to fix screwups. Really sharp. Martinez made her his intelligence chief, but she quit. She landed in the quartermaster tents. If the men are well fed, I'd say it's because of her. The only ones to leave these hills are her scavenger patrols. Funny ideas, though."

"What do you mean?"

"She said she was a Bear."

Valentine raked his memory over. "I never met a woman Bear—but then I don't know many in your caste."

Finner shrugged. "No such thing. If she is one she's the only one I've ever met, too. I heard they tried it on a few women, but they died from whatever that goop is that the Lifeweavers pass out to the Bears at Invocation."

"We lost one when I became a Wolf."

"Yeah. Bears, too. But it's a hundred percent failure with women."

Valentine smelled a mass of humanity ahead, even upwind. "Now who are these?"

"You'll find out in about five seconds."

They passed down into a dimple in the hillside where Post had pitched their camp's tents. The tents were surrounded by a sea of uniforms. Guards, Bears, Wolves, even militia with inked insignia; all rose to their feet as Valentine and Nail crested the hill.

"It started at the Grog burial this morning," Post said, coming up to them. Ahn-Kha followed behind.

"I would have liked to have been there, but my testimony was required this morning," Valentine said.

"At first it was just the marines," Post said. "Then Finner and some Wolves came up, and others just kind of followed. Before the holes were finished it was in the hundreds. They

had their guns; for a second it looked like a lynch mob. Then
Ahn-Kha said something in his tongue—"

"The Third Lament, for the unjustly killed," Ahn-Kha
added. "I practiced saying it so often in Omaha, I could re-
cite it backward."

"When Ahn-Kha spoke everyone bowed their heads,"
Post continued. "When he finished, we all looked at each
other. Like we'd all agreed."

"We're ready to come or go at your order, Captain," Nail
said. "Every man here's had it with Martinez. We're ready
for a change."

Valentine looked at the expectant faces, from old friends
like Jess Finnner to strangers and back again. His stomach
went tight and sour. The death of the Grogs and his actions
had polarized the camp; if he stayed there would be open
feuding.

He'd had enough of the torn bodies of friends and fol-
lowers. A weary part of him had decided to vanish with what
was left of the *Thunderbolt*'s complement. All he wanted to
do was find a safe valley somewhere, then perhaps try for
Denver in the summer. But he had to tell the gathering
something.

"I'm glad you're here, all of you. I think . . . I know what
happened to Ahn-Kha's Grogs was wrong. Right now in that
cabin they're deciding if there's going to be a change, but
even if there is, General Martinez will just be replaced by
his Colonel Abraham."

"He's worthless!" a woman's voice opined from the
crowd.

"Look what he's letting go on outside the guardhouse,"
another called.

"Enough. He's your superior officer, and mine too, for
that matter. If this camp divides, it'll be destroyed. If you're
unhappy about something, you're free . . . you're expected
to bring it to the attention of your superior. I know you have
the best intentions, but let's not give even the appearance of
mutiny. The soldiery of Southern Command I see gathered
here is better than that. The trial is being conducted accord-

ing to the Uniform Code. Whatever happens is going to be legal, and it'll be our duty to accept the court's justice."

"They're breaking now," a boy called from the window, where he was listening to the voices in the guardhouse.

A restive mass of men, including Valentine, Ahn-Kha and those who had gathered at his camp, stood in the dark around the guardhouse, listening to the boy summarize the events inside. Colonel Abraham had placed a group of mounted soldiers around the court, putting them between the guardhouse and the men of any opinion. A massed fistfight had broken out when someone threw a rock at Ahn-Kha, and shouted, "You're next, stoop," but it ended when the horses waded into the fray.

Valentine waited, rolling and unrolling a piece of paper run off by the camp's primitive printing press. He had found it discarded in the camp.

SOLDIERS!

I write you from a cell, knowing the unjustness of the charges against me and sustained by your presence. I put my trust in the hands of God, for he is the final arbiter and whatever the outcome of my trial I can face him content that I have done right for you and for our Cause. I trust you to behave as the Loyal Hearts I know you are in this the darkest hour of our struggle. Carry yourselves as men of honor and obey until I am restored to command.

P. Martinez, General

Valentine reread the page-filling type. He admired the wording, equivocal enough to show Southern Command that he had asked the men of his command to keep order and obey those who had arrested and tried him, but he wondered if there wasn't an implicit threat in the final sentence. One interpretation of "Until I am restored to command" simply meant that he was confident of exoneration. A darker possibility could be that he was telling his loyalists that if he wasn't restored to command, he didn't expect them to obey those who had removed him.

Styachowski had been brilliant at the end, at least from what Valentine heard passed via the boy. The defense argued that it wasn't murder to shoot a Grog any more than it was to put down a mule, and that rules that protected a Southern Command soldier simply didn't apply to this case. After some back and forth the judges demanded that Styachowski give evidence that a Grog enjoyed the same rights as a Southern Command soldier.

After a pause—during which Nail predicted that they were sunk—Styachowski began a recitation of the court-martial of a sergeant in charge of a Grog labor detail recruited from the ranks of prisoners. One of the Grogs hadn't moved quickly enough to suit the sergeant; he shot the laggard as an example to the others. The wounded Grog died, leading to the sergeant being brought up on charges of murder by the Grog's keeper, a Mississippian named Steiner. Steiner pushed the case through both military and civilian officials, and testimony provided by Grog experts from the Miskatonic affirmed that the Grogs reasoned, felt emotions, formed attachments, created art, created tools and the tools to make more tools; indeed everything humans did. Because of the landmark nature of the case the sergeant, though found guilty, had his sentence reduced: even when he shot the Grog he did so in the leg, trying to wound rather than kill. The case was affirmed a year later when a barroom brawl between a Grog janitor and a riverboatman resulted in the death of the Grog and manslaughter charges against the sailor, who ended up serving a long sentence.

Martinez's consul ended its defense with an argument that Grogs were often summarily executed when taken prisoner, and the General was simply following a standard practice.

The three judges, having no chambers to retire to, went out to the old garage of the guardhouse to discuss the verdict. They could just be seen in the gloom within through a single window in the back door. Valentine's ears picked up

Randolph's raised voice again and again. "Just Grogs . . . emergency . . . situation requires . . . indespensible."

Soldiers in the General's camp lit torches. The numbers had swelled in the darkness as others came off duty.

Finally, the front door opened.

The crowd quieted. Had Valentine been in a better mood, he would have smiled at the first display of discipline by the men since his arrival at the camp. He was finally able to hear voices from within the guardhouse, thanks to his Lifeweaver-sharpened ears.

"Bring him out of his cell," Meadows said. Valentine thought he heard Styachowski gasp, but he couldn't be sure.

There were footsteps, followed by the sound of chairs scraping.

"They're bringing him in!" the boy at the window shouted. The crowd froze; only the crackle of torches and the horses shifting weight from hoof to hoof came from the assembly.

"General Martinez," Meadows began, "this court recognizes your service to Southern Command. Every man here owes you a debt that cannot be repaid. However, the Uniform Code gives us little room for interpretation. As the code now stands, a guilty verdict in a willful murder case carries with it automatic penalties that cannot be suspended or commuted by this court in any way. Indeed, the only leeway given with a guilty verdict is life imprisonment instead of hanging, and as matters now stand there is no possibility of commutation from an executive authority since the governor cannot be reached.

"Though the charges are of willful murder, this court, in cooperation with the prosecution, has decided to find you guilty only of simple murder, which gives us the leeway to—"

"Guilty!" the boy shouted.

Martinez's supporters roared out in anger; Valentine heard no more. The mob threw two torches at the guardhouse. One sputtered out as it flew; the second landed on the timber roof, alight. Soldiers shot in the air, the muzzle flashes giving brief illumination to the mass of contorted, shouting faces. The most violent ran for the porch, gripping their guns like clubs to smash at the shutters and door. The guards ran inside, slamming the door behind them.

Nail barked an order and a triangle of men formed around Valentine, backs to him. They were Bears, big-shouldered giants who closed around him in a wall of muscle and attitude. Valentine, at six feet two inches, had to shift his head to see events around the guardhouse.

"Nail, can we get closer?" Valentine shouted.

"We can try."

"Ahn-Kha, let's get to the door," Valentine said.

Ahn-Kha's ears went back flat—the Golden One's equivalent of a man rolling up his sleeves—and he went down on all fours, using his two-ax-handle shoulders to clear a path like a bulldozer going through brush. The Bears followed, surrounding Valentine in a muscular cocoon. The horsemen were having no luck keeping the mob back; a few of the crowd had even been vaulted onto the roof. They extinguished the incipent fire, then continued stamping hard on the wooden eaves. Others kicked at the posts holding up the porch.

"They'll tear it down in a minute," Valentine said to Nail.

The door swung open. General Martinez appeared on the wide porch, holding his hands up for quiet. The men broke into cheers and whistles.

Martinez's small round eyes were sorrowful. He was sweating, even in the cool of the winter night. "Soldiers, soldiers! Quiet, men, quiet," he said, still moving his arms as if giving a benediction.

Even the men stomping on the roof stopped and waited for him to speak.

"I convinced them to let me speak to you. This madness has to stop. The camp is tearing itself apart because of these charges and this trial. As you have heard, the court-martial has found me guilty—"

Boos drowned him out until he held up his hands again. Valentine saw a self-indulgent smile cross his face, as if he found the whole proceedings to be a poorly executed practical joke.

"Yes, guilty, for doing my duty to the best of my ability. They are trying to destroy our army, the last, best hope for freedom for this land. Therefore I declare my emergency powers to be in effect, and these proceedings voided. This camp is in a state of martial law; the judges, Captain Styachowski, Captain Valentine, and any who helped them are under arrest for treason."

Valentine and Nail exchanged incredulous looks. The legalistic gibberish made no sense to them, as technically the soldiery of Southern Command had always been under martial law, from the moment they raised their right hands to be sworn in. A general in Southern Command had no emergency powers over his troops to invoke, any more than he had wings to fly. But the words sounded fine to the men, at least to the more stirred-up among them. Martinez stood aside while a dirty flood of them poured into the guardhouse. Valentine heard fighting, a pained cry. A man flew backward out of the front window and lay on the porch, folded like a clasp knife, cradling his solar plexus and gasping for air. In a few seconds Styachowski was dragged out, held aloft by the mob with a soldier at each limb, followed by the judges, guns to their backs.

"General, sir, I've been on your side the whole trial," Randolph said, his mustache black against his fear-paled face.

"I'll make my mind up about you later, Randolph."

"None of the General's orders are legal," Styachowski shouted, held aloft by the mob. Blood ran from her nose as she turned to bite at a hand pulling her hair. "He's no longer in command. He can't—"

"Take her shirt off," someone shouted. Others cheered and whistled. Valentine heard cloth tearing.

"General Martinez," Valentine boomed, stepping up beside Ahn-Kha. "I started this. I arrested you. I held a gun to your head."

The mob quieted at this; the men wanted to hear the exchange between their idol and his usurper.

Valentine felt a hard hand on his shoulder. "What the hell are you—" Nail began.

"I'm the one responsible," Valentine continued, shrugging off the Bear. "Nobody had a choice once I arrested you; there had to be proceedings from that point on. This is still Southern Command. I'm the only one you should charge with treason."

"Randolph, here's a chance to redeem yourself," Martinez said. "Shoot that mutinous bastard right now. Here, in front of his pet Grog."

"Auuugh!" Styachowski shouted, still writhing atop her holders. "This is insane! Don't be an idiot, Randolph. Put me down, now!"

Valentine saw the desperation in her upside-down eyes.

"You'll be on the ground, all right," Martinez said.

Valentine stepped forward. "What's the matter, Martinez? Afraid to do a summary execution yourself? How come somebody else has to pull the trigger for you? You never been blooded?"

"Somebody shoot—" Martinez began. Randolph reached for his holster.

Ahn-Kha chambered a round in his long Grog rifle, and Martinez looked down the barrel of .50 caliber of death sighted on his chest.

Nail and his Bears came forward, again surrounding Valentine. "No," Nail said, slowly and clearly. A short submachine gun appeared like magic in his hands. "Anyone shoots, Martinez, and my team comes up on that porch. After you. We won't leave enough of you to fill a shoebox. Then we start killing everyone with a hand on Styachowski. Then everyone who tried to interfere with either of those jobs. How many of y'all do you think we'll get before we go down. Twenty? Forty?"

"Whose side are you on, *Lieutenant?*" Martinez said, making the rank sound like an epitheth. "Sounds like you boys are getting set to do the Kurians' work for them."

"That's so, General," the largest of the Bears said. He had the smooth, rounded accent of the rolling Kentucky hills, rather than the trans-Mississippi twang of Nail. He pulled a knife from his belt, tossed it in the air and in the second before he caught it again drew a tomahawk with his left hand. "But only if you start it. My finishers are out. Any blood spills, they won't go back in again without your guts strung on 'em."

"He's not a general, Rain," another Bear said. "Not anymore."

"Martinez is right," Valentine said. "Let's not do the Kurians' work for them. What'll it be, Martinez? A bloodbath?"

The Bears and Ahn-Kha must have made an impression. The crowd shrank away, perhaps not wanting to be the first to be tomahawked on Rain's way to the General.

"Name your terms, Valentine," Martinez said.

"First, nobody gets arrested for treason. Second, Styachowski and the judges walk out of camp with us. Somehow I think there'd be reprisals if any of us stayed. Third, you let anyone who wants to go with us leave. Peaceably."

"This is mutiny, Valentine."

"You have to have military organization to mutiny against. Your command is that of a warlord, maybe, but not armed service as Southern Command defines it."

"Then it's to the warlord to give his terms to those he's defeated. You and your men can leave. You may take personal possessions only. No Southern Command weapons, food, or equipment. You walk out of here as civilians, and I'll be sure to let my superiors know why that's the case. We won't be sorry to see you go; my men don't want to breathe the same air as traitors."

"He's awful free with that word," the Bear called Rain muttered.

"Try to get our guns. We'll walk out over—" Nail began.

"Wait, Lieutenant," Valentine said, putting a hand on his shoulder. "Nobody gets killed, that's good enough."

"Is this a surrender, my David?" Ahn-Kha asked in his ear.

"A tactical retreat, old horse," he said. Then louder: "You have it, Martinez. We walk out with just our possessions. Now let Captain Styachowski go. We'll be gone in twenty-four hours."

"This looks like a conference of war," Finner said the next day, as Ahn-Kha opened the tent flap. Styachowski, Post, Nail and, strangely enough, Colonel Meadows all sat around a folding camp table spread with maps.

"An informal one. Jess, they tell me you know the mountains east of here better than anyone. What are our chances of getting seven hundred people to the Arkansas River without using any Kurian-patrolled roads?"

"I don't see anyone smiling, so I guess this isn't a practical joke. Seven hundred?"

"That's what the numbers packing up look like," Colonel Meadows said. "Some are good soldiers, sick of hiding in the hills. Some are afraid that the General's gone loco." Meadows tapped his chest with the hand missing the fingers for emphasis.

"Styachowski says the hills are our only hope for moving that many without being noticed," Valentine added. "The Quislings stay out of the mountains because of those feral Reapers, except for big truck patrols. We'd hear those coming."

Finner looked at the maps. One, covered with a sheet of clear plastic, had a cryptic mark over where Valentine's refugees had been camping when the General added them to his command. "I was coming here to tell you that we've got two platoons of Wolves ready to go out with us. With them screening we might be able to do it. The lifesign will be horrendous. We'll draw trouble like a nightlight does bugs."

"And we'll be short, very short, on weapons," Post said. "It makes the route even more critical."

"How are you going to feed everyone, sir?" Finner asked.

"Working on it," Meadows said, with a glance at Stya-chowski. She looked tired.

"That's been most of the conversation. We'll take live-stock. Like the myriads out of Egypt, we'll go with our flocks," Valentine said.

"What happens at the Arkansas? The river's watched and patrolled. I'd have trouble getting across with a platoon."

"Just get us there, Lieutenant," Valentine said.

"Sergeant, sir."

"You're going to be in charge of two platoons of Wolves. That's a lieutenant's command," Meadows said.

Finner looked nonplussed. "Any chance of turning down this promotion?"

"We get back to Southern Command, and I'll fill out the rank reduction paperwork myself," Valentine promised. "Let's give Finner some time alone with the maps."

"Don't need 'em, sir," the new lieutenant said.

"You'll at least need to know where we're starting. First waypoint is the old campsite where we dumped that load of lumber."

"Captain Styachowski, a word," Valentine said as they left the tent.

"Yes, Captain?"

"You still have friends on the old intelligence staff?"

"Staff? Friends? I had one nearsighted military analyst. She's coming with us; she doesn't like this moonshine brew-ery any more than I."

"I need everything you have on enemy organization on the Arkansas River."

"That's a lot of data. The river's their backbone running up the Ozarks."

"You've got to find us a way across."

"Short of stealing some flatboats or swimming the whole column, I don't see how we do it. Only bridges up are in Lit-tle Rock, and that's their new headquarters."

"Think about it for me."

Styachowski's eyes narrowed, but she spoke with a

cheerful bounce to her voice. "I can't count on the waters parting, can I?"

"Sorry."

"Ah, well. When a Saint came marching into camp, I had hope—"

Valentine laughed. "What's the crossbar for?

"Hunter staff. I'm a Bear. Never made it on a combat team, though. Always some excuse."

"What did they invoke you for, then?"

"Didn't. I was sort of born into it. Only action I've seen was Hazlett, and that was in a mortar team."

"I was up that way. Didn't see the fighting, just the cleanup," Valentine said.

"Lucky. But it was a picnic compared to the last few months."

"One more thing. You had a rough time, at the trial and after. Are you okay?"

Her eyes narrowed. "What do you mean?"

"You don't look well. Have you been sleeping enough?"

She ran her hand through her hair and rubbed the back of her neck at the end of the gesture. "I always look like a slice of fresh death. Don't worry."

"I mean the fight at the trial. Hell of a thing to go through."

"I'm a bit numb still. I'm glad we have a lot to do . . . I'll just work till I drop tonight. Be better tomorrow."

"Don't short yourself sleep. Just makes everything worse." Valentine spoke from experience. "Sometimes a drink helps."

"I've had three drinks my whole life, Captain. Two of them were last night, after all that. Didn't help. Thanks for hearing me out about the Bear stuff. Lieutenant Nail just laughed. Our good General said I had too good a brain for fighting, and too tight an ass for uniform pants. I hope you'll give me a chance to prove myself."

"You proved yourself when you stepping in at the Grog shooting."

"I should have taken action before then. Been watching

and waiting too long, should have followed my gut a long time ago. When he started letting the gargoyles overfly us without so much as a shot . . ."

She left the last to hang for a moment, and Valentine wondered at her absent stare into the distance. Then she swallowed and threw her muscular shoulders back. "Okay, time to round up some livestock and then sit down with a map. If you'll excuse me, I have a lot to do."

Colonel Meadows put himself between Valentine and Martinez as the column made ready to leave.

"You've nothing to fear from me, Meadows," Martinez said. He glanced up to Randolph, perched on a rock above. Randolph had decided to stay, and sat atop the rock, rifle in his lap, looking out at the assembled "mutineers."

"That whole farce was my fault," Meadows said. "You should have been tried from your cell in the guardhouse. You're a disgrace, but I'm the bigger disgrace for letting it happen."

Valentine looked out on the road, filled with files of people in their assortment of Southern Command uniforms, rain ponchos, coats and hats. Perhaps six hundred soldiers were interspersed with a handful of tagalong civilian specialists. Packhorses and mules, leashed pigs, chickens and geese in baskets, and a total of four wagons added to the noise and smell. Squads of Guard soldiers were relieving the men of Southern Command rifles, while others poked in the packhorse loads. A cold wind coursed through the hollow.

"None of the animals have a Southern Command brand," Valentine said, continuing the argument Meadows had interrupted. Ahn-Kha wandered up the file, cradling his long Grog rifle.

Out of Martinez's hearing, Valentine heard Ahn-Kha make an aside to Post.

"How'd you get a captured gun?" Ahn-Kha asked, touching Post's holstered .45. It was a duplicate of Valentine's; Post had given him one while they served together on the *Thunderbolt*.

"It's not Southern Command issue."

"Letter of the law," Ahn-Kha said. "A few dozen guns between all of us."

"For a column a half mile long."

Valentine turned his attention back to Martinez, still arguing with Meadows. "You think you can move this many through the hills? You're throwing away the lives of everyone here. I'll offer an amnesty. We can bring the command back together."

Meadows unhooked his pistol belt and handed it over to Martinez. "That 9mm is Southern Command issue. Wouldn't want to set a bad example." He looked at the men holding the horse teams. "Five minutes!" he shouted. "We get going in five minutes!"

"Don't be a fool, Colonel," Martinez said. "We need you. And these good men." His beady eyes glanced up and down the files of men. It seemed that those who still shaved and cleaned their uniforms were all lined up with Valentine.

"Martinez," Valentine said, "you don't have a command. You have a mob. They way things are going in this camp, you won't even have a mob much longer."

Martinez sneered. "Think so? I'll give you a prediction in return. We'll outlast you."

Chapter Four

The Eastern Ouachitas, Arkansas, February: In the decade before the Overthrow, the interstate between Little Rock and Hot Springs enjoyed a high-tech growth spurt. With key computer networks in prominent cities worldwide challenged by everything from terrorism to extended power outages, backup locations became the focus of a substantial slice of investment. In America's heartland, in the basements of nondescript office parks, fiberoptic lines connected servers waiting to cut into action should the need arise without the slightest interruption in data flow; "transparent redundancy," in the phrase of the times.

Southwest of the blasted ruins of Little Rock, off of one of the feeder highways to the old interstate, a chocolate-colored three-story with bands of black windows once housed claim and policy-holder records for one of the world's top ten insurance companies. In 2022 the building nestled in the Ouachita foothills looked a little like a giant slice of devil's food cake amidst its landscaping and parking lots. Now the lots are meadows, and saplings grow on its roof as birds fly in and out of paneless top-story windows; just another unraveled piece of the commercial fabric of a rich nation. The lowest floor shows some sign of recent renovation. Plywood has been nailed up over broken windows and horses graze behind the building in a paddock made from downed power-line towers. A few camouflage-painted pickups sit parked outside a barbed-wire festooned gas station between the highway and the office building. The battered office building looks peaceful behind a sign reading STATION 26.

Except for the three bodies rotting in the noonday sun.

All male, all naked and all covered in a black mixture of

rotting flesh and pitch, visited only by crows, they swing from a pylon that once held four lights above the parking lot next to the gas station. An uprooted stop sign stands in the parking-lot meadow between the bodies and the entrance road, redone in whitewash and black lettering — the two colors have run together in the hasty paint job — reading SABOTER'S REWARD.

"Bullfrog's been at it again," Finner said. "Sumbitch never could spell." He and Valentine crouched in the thick bush bordering the improvised horse pasture, examining the bodies from a stand of wintering lilac bushes, the western wind blowing the stench the other way. The rest of the column sheltered in the deeper woods a kilometer away, eating the midday meal out of their packs. The screening Wolves had been exploring the more open ground around the old office park and came across what looked like an inhabited office building. When they found the bodies they had summoned Valentine.

"Bullfrog?" Valentine asked.

"Sergeant Bill Frum. Top sergeant in the Guards, or so the men in his old unit say."

"A guerilla?"

"In a manner. He and his men joined up with Solon's crew in Little Rock and they gave him a commission. Only he's playing double agent or whatever you want to call it. He's got twenty or thirty diehards, twice that in part-time guerillas in the farms east of here, and about two hundred men scattered around who are supposed to be hunting guerillas. What they mostly do is look the other way."

Valentine reread the block letters on the sign. "So what about the bodies?"

"Camouflage."

"What's that mean?"

"His guerillas aren't really going up against the KZ forces. More like sneaking around and hitting the folks who cooperate. That burned-out farm we passed yesterday; I bet that was his work."

The scouts had reported bodies in the ruins, Valentine remembered.

"He's a good source of intelligence about the roads between the Rock and Hot Springs, for all that. Sometimes he sends a messenger, trades information or supplies he's been issued. In the last swap he told us they'd open the rail line south from the Rock again."

"He went to some effort to preserve the bodies. I wonder why?" Valentine asked.

"Shows any inspection groups that he's killing guerillas. I know he shoots deserters trying to get back home to Texas or Oklahoma. Picks off an occasional wildcatter come in from Illinois or Tenesseee to set up shop, and then burns down an empty house or two in fake 'reprisals.' Bullfrog likes a good bonfire. He burns anything used to trade with the enemy—from a cart to a farm, and buries locals who join up and are carrying arms."

"Buries?"

"Buries alive, in a coffin with an airhole of old pipe, so they have time to think about what they did. Then claims the guerillas did it. That's what Major Rojo used to say, anyway."

Valentine found himself feeling less contemptuous toward General Martinez and his moonshine-sotted camp. He'd rather have his men drunk and disorderly than burying people alive. Valentine squatted and crept away from the bodies through the new grass. Finner and his patrol rested among the newly mature trees that had sprung up in old landscaping.

"You said this is was pretty quiet area, Jess."

"Quiet's relative, Val," Finner said.

"Let's visit this setup," Valentine said.

"What, everyone?"

"No. Keep the column hidden in the hills. I want to visit this Bullfrog's lily pad and find out for sure which side he's hopped on."

*   *   *

Valentine crouched alongside a wrecked pickup covered in kudzu, and moved his hand as though he were throwing a dart three times. He could hear Styachowski's quick breaths behind. She'd vouched for the authenticity of Bullfrog's intelligence; as far as she knew his information had never led to the capture or destruction of Southern Command forces. Nail, looking back at him from twenty meters ahead, whipped his wiry arm in a wheeling motion forward and his Bears rose out of the ditch in front of the chocolate-colored office building—Valentine guessed it had once held a decorative pond—and entered, two remaining behind to cover. At another wave from Nail in the doorway, they ran in after him.

His old Wolf senses took over and he listened to the footsteps, the low calls, the crash of something heavy overturning.

"Blue Tick! Blue Tick! Blue Tick!" Nail called. The Bears had reached the door of the office building. Some boarded-over windows had STATION 26 stencilled on them.

"Running! They're running," Nail shouted.

Valentine rose and another thirty men rose with him. They trotted inside the swept-up but still water-damaged reception foyer; it stretched up through the building's three stories to paneless skylights, and dispersed to cover all sides of the building. Years' worth of plant life had established itself on the floors above so that roots and old extension cords and recent phone lines shared space on the wall. Valentine and Styachowski followed a pointing Bear named Ritter down a flight of stairs. Finner waited for them at the bottom. The landing was cluttered with suspiciously fresh blown leaves.

They stepped down an electric-lit corridor just in time to see Nail fling himself at a vaultlike door that was being closed.

"Open up, Sergeant Frum," Nail called. "Southern Command. Operations verification Squeak-Three."

"That's out of date," Styachowski said, coughing after the run.

Valentine examined the cinderblock walls. Heavy girders supported a concrete ceiling above. This Bullfrog had chosen his panic room, or hideout, or bomb shelter well.

"Southern Command hasn't set a new code for this year," Nail said. "It's the last effective password." Then, to the door: "C'mon, Sergeant, Squeak-Three. This is Lieutenant Harold Nail, Volmer's Bears."

Valentine pressed his ear to the cool metal and listened. If anyone stood on the other side of the door, he or she remained silent.

Finner pounded on the door. "Jess Finner here. For chrissakes, Bullfrog, gimme a break and open up. These Bears is just gonna blow you out otherwise. I'm not shitting you, ol' buddy."

Valentine heard an authoritative click from the door and breathed a sigh of relief. They had no explosives to make good Finner's threat.

The door opened and a brilliant beam of light filled the corridor. It hit Valentine's eyes like a knife, giving him an instant headache. Valentine could just make out light-frosted outlines of heads and gun barrels.

"Whoa there!" he said, holding out his hands. "Friends, okay? I'm codename Ghost, Cat of Southern Command."

"No Southern Command no more," argued a deep voice, smooth as buttermilk being poured.

"You call me 'sir,' Sergeant, and get that light off."

"Just making sure." The light went out and Valentine could see a dozen hard faces, guns ready, set against nondescript gray-green office décor.

"Just making sure, sir," Valentine corrected.

"I'm not blowing your head off, and I'm not calling you 'sir.' I might change my mind about one. Like I said, no Southern Command to say 'sir' to. They sold us out, just like they did my granddaddy in '22." A man proportioned a little like Ahn-Kha stepped forward, filling the doorway, and held up his hand, palm out. "Howdy, Jess. Had to make sure there wasn't a gun to your head. I'm Bill Frum. What can I do for you boys?"

*   *   *

It turned out Bullfrog was willing to do almost nothing.

Valentine sat among silent machines in the dusty basement room. A single candle made more shadows than light. He stared at the six dark boxes. Each about the size of an up-ended footlocker, the old computers—netservers, or so the tiny chrome letters next to the main power button said— stood like a squad of soldiers on parade. Bullfrog's men avoided this small, stuffy corner room, like Visigoths afraid to enter the heart of a Roman temple, fearing ancient, half-understood wrath. A little dusting and some power, and it would be hard to tell the past half century had even happened—

Except for some long-ago philosopher who'd written THE JOKE IS ON US on the wall, using a permanent marker to form the two-foot block letters.

He had to think.

His command was divided; the rest of the column was resting in the woods just under a mile away, while the team that penetrated the old office building stayed and mixed with Bullfrog's men, with orders not to reaveal anything about their numbers.

Bullfrog had taken the handful of guests on a tour of his domain, made cozy by gear plucked from the dead organs of Southern Command or issued by the Kurians. Crates of supplies covered with stenciled letters were stacked floor to ceiling along with guns, leather goods, bolts of cloth, camp gear, cooking pots, and medical and commissary supplies. The sergeant organized his command with a professional NCO's eye to detail and a mind for long-term operations. His men were clad in a variant of the old Louisiana Regular outfits Valentine had an intimate knowledge of from his days posing as a Kurian Coastal Marine in the Gulf.

Bullfrog wouldn't part with any of it, orders or no. He was overgenerous with what was lying around on the mess room tables and counters, offering the guests canned peanut paste smeared on heartroot, jerky, creamed corn, even root beer.

"No Southern Command no more," Bullfrog said each

and every time the subject came up. "Just patriots and collaborators, mister, patriots and collaborators. We've gone underground. Literally. I got arsenals hidden all over the place for my Night Watch."

"You're guerillas."

"Yes," Bullfrog said, smiling so that his face seemed mostly made up of teeth. "Helluva war I got going here. I'm running both sides of it."

"And what do the Kurians get out of it?"

"A bunch of 'somedays,'" Bullfrog said. "I'm supposed to be recruiting. They're broke-dick on troops, not getting as much cooperation out of Ozark folks as they expected, and the troops that took down Southern Command are heading home. They got soldiers running the lights and phones, driving trucks, running switches on the railroad. Most locals won't do anything unless you've got a soldier poking them along with a bayonet."

"What do you do with the ones who cooperate?"

"They get a warning. The Night Watch beats the hell out of 'em. After that—" He passed an index finger across his throat.

"We could really use some of those guns I saw in your armory."

"Can't. Strict inventory. Those are for the forces I'm supposed to be recruiting. They watch guns and gas like Jew accountants. There's never a pistol missing or a drop short. That's why they keep me as honcho hearabout. Figure if I'm honest about the small stuff, I'll be honest about the big stuff too."

Valentine felt hot and restless. He wanted to swing his arms and kick with his legs. Seeing the hoarded supplies appear and then vanish like a desert mirage frustrated him. If he could draw on Sergeant Bill "Bullfrog" Frum's stores in a substantial way his column might be able to make it the rest of the way to the Boston Mountains. They were already short of food; seven hundred people on the march couldn't live on the local rabbits and wild onions. Frum's obstinacy might mean the destruction of his column.

He needed release. An hour chopping wood might clear his buffers. What did that expression mean, anyway?

"Hell, sir, you look like a Bear warming up for a fight," a voice from the other side of the Arkansas broke in.

"What's that?" Valentine temporized, bringing himself back to the room with the dead servers.

Nail stood in the doorway, scratching the afternoon's growth on his face. The Bear officer put a half-eaten lasagna MRE on one of the old computers and crossed his arms as though he were wrapped in a straightjacket, pulled his heels together and rocked on them. Valentine realized that Nail was aping his pose. "You look like a stomped-down spring."

"About to go 'boing,' huh?" Valentine forced his body to relax. "I'll give you a warning before I snap."

"I've worked with Bears for six year, Captain. I'm used to it. It was more the staring-at-nothing look in your eye. You smell action in the wind?"

"No. I should get back to Post and Meadows."

"You know, sir, we've got enough men to empty this joint. Lots of stuff here we could use. Ol' Frum could say his headquarters got attacked unexpectedly."

"The sergeant's worked hard on his setup. I don't want to give the Kurians a reason to replace him."

"Still like to see Bullfrog taken down a notch. He's been the biggest buck of these woods too long; thinks he makes right and wrong. I don't like making war on civilians, ours or theirs."

Valentine felt a better warmth at those words. He saw a crack of light from Frum's locked-off door. "Neither do I. Follow me, would you?"

Valentine traced a line with his index finger under the THE JOKE IS ON US graffiti as he left. He nodded at one of Bullfrog's guerillas, dripping wet with a towel around his waist as he came back from the improvised bath—Bullfrog had turned an old janitorial closet into a one-man shower—and followed his ears to the canteen, where Bullfrog was shooting the breeze with Finner about the last few months.

"Troop trains heading back south and west lately," Valentine heard as he approached. "Borrowed troops heading home with boxcars of booty and prisoners. As long as the Night Watch keeps out of Little Rock and away from the lines, these hills stay quiet. If I touch the railroads I get a flying regiment sent—"

"Bullfrog, I'm taking over," Valentine said, cutting off the storytelling.

Bullfrog had one leg up on the table, the worn waffle pattern in the boot turned toward him, like a religious icon shifted to ward off evil.

"Taking over what?"

Valentine's heart tripped when he saw Bullfrog's hand fall to his holster.

Valentine stuck his thumbs in his belt. "Your unit. They'll be taking orders from me, until I depart."

"Doubt it. They answer to me."

"Never said otherwise. I outrank you. I'll give the orders to you, then you'll amplify, organize and carry out. Way it always worked in Southern Command."

Bullfrog sighed. "That again. I told you before, I don't—"

"You will, or I'll knock you into next week."

The sergeant stood up. Valentine's leveled stare hit Bullfrog just below the collarbone. "You think you can whip me?"

"If you won't take my word for it."

"If you're dead set on an ass-kicking, I'll oblige, Valentine."

"You've been around the Kurians too long. You're not the local demigod. Time to put you back in the chain of command, since you can't handle the responsibility." Bullfrog turned an intriguing shade of purple, took a breath— "I'm going to use these stores. And another thing. I won't stand for any more reprisals against civilians," Valentine finished, delaying whatever was coming.

Bullfrog's rapid-fire laughter filled the mess room and echoed like a string of firecrackers going off: heh-ha-heh-ha-heh-ha. "I fight with my fists, not paper."

"That's your prerogative. I'm not filing a Jagger complaint."

Bullfrog wasted no time. He led Valentine outside. Word passed around among the men via the mysterious network that exists in any organization, always faster and more effective than any communications flowchart. As they walked out the thick steel door and up the stairs, everyone from Nail's Bears to Bullfrog's own headquarters staff followed.

Valentine took off his tunic as he exited the plant-cluttered office building. The cool air felt good as it licked across his hot ears. The sky had become overcast again; the late-winter rains looked to be building again. Meadows, guided by a pair of Wolves, was crossing the parking lot.

"Valentine," Meadows hallooed. "Since we're resting I wanted to—"

"Sorry, sir, busy," Valentine said.

Meadows' forehead wrinkled as Bullfrog removed his own jacket. "That you, Fa—no, Frum. Sergeant Frum?"

"Colonel Meadows," Bullfrog said, not bothering to salute.

"What's all this?" Meadows turned in a circle as he looked at the mixed contingent of men, some throwing suspenders over their shoulders or still pulling on boots as they emerged from the office building.

Valentine ignored him, but the remoter, calmer quarters of his brain filed away Bullfrog's familiarity with Meadows. "Men!" he said, not having to try too hard to sound fighting-mad. "An exchange of blows between officers of Southern Command is considered a court-martial offense by the Uniform Code, especially if there is a difference in rank. I picked this quarrel with Sergeant Frum; he's to be held blameless." Valentine spat into each palm and formed his hands into tight fists. "Sergeant Frum, do you hold me blameless under the Uniform Code?"

Bullfrog planted his feet. "You can count on it, Valentine."

"Tell the men, and Colonel Meadows, so he's a witness. I don't want to hang with those others."

Bullfrog somehow managed to shout using the side of his mouth, keeping his vision locked on Valentine. "He's blameless too, under the Uniform Code."

Valentine lowered his fists. "Sergeant, the Southern Command's Uniform Code isn't a buffet. You can't pick and choose which rules apply. You either operate under it or you don't. You've just accepted its protection, and with its protection goes—"

"Bullshit!" Bullfrog shouted. "Tricks won't—"

He charged, arms up and reaching for Valentine's throat.

But Bullfrog was just big, and Valentine was a Cat. He sidestepped the rush, reached out and grabbed a handful of Quisling-issue collar, whipped his legs up and got them around Bullfrog's waist. They both went down, Bullfrog using his weight and strength to hammer Valentine into the ground.

Valentine got his forearm under Bullfrog's chin, an old wrestling move he'd learned—the hard way—from his old top sergeant in Zulu Company.

Bullfrog croaked in what Patel called his "hangman."

The sergeant gave one terrific shrug and spun, bringing Valentine sideways into the ground, but Valentine clung, battered and smashed by Bullfrog's weight, with the same tenacity as Rikki-Tikki-Tavi with his teeth locked in Nag the Cobra's neck. For the honor of his family Rikki wanted to be found dead with his teeth locked in the enemy, and for the honor of Zulu Company's champion wrestler Valentine clung to his choke hold despite the red-yellow-red flashes of pain from his ribs. Then Bullfrog went limp.

Valentine suspected a trick until he felt, and smelled, warm urine on his leg.

"He's done," Valentine said, getting to shaky legs and brushing himself off.

Bullfrog groaned.

"Somebody get the sergeant a towel," Valentine said, breathing into the pain.

"Enough of that, Captain," Meadows barked. He hooked Valentine with his good hand and his thumb and finger, pulling the Cat up. "You men, help the sergeant inside. Captain, you'd better have Narcisse look at those ribs. The rest of you, pay off your bets and get inside. Sun's going down."

Valentine's eyes rose to the tarred bodies hanging from the lamppost. Meadows nodded in understanding.

"Lieutenant Nail, take a detail and get those bodies down. Anyone else feels like fistfighting can work off their aggressions digging six feet down."

"You come back from a beating like no man I ever knew," Narcisse said the next morning, applying cool, water-soaked towels to Valentine's battered frame. Unfortunately, Bullfrog's substantial inventory didn't include an ice machine.

Valentine looked at his reflection in the washroom mirror. A great blue-and-purple mark on his chin was just beginning to show a hint of yellow through the skin. The right side of his rib cage looked like van Gogh's *Starry Night.*

"I've never broken a bone before," he said, feeling around at the soft spot.

Narcisse rapped him across the probing knuckles with her handless arm. "Leave it be, and it'll heal. Just a rib. Count yourself lucky; your lung stayed airy and you got lots of stuff holding that rib in place."

A heavy tread sounded in the basement corridor, and Ahn-Kha's bent-over frame appeared. There was now enough of a mixture of Valentine's column and the guerillas that Styachowski had judged it safe for Ahn-Kha to make an appearance. The Golden One bore a contraption that looked a little like a corset made of tube steel. He'd put it together using the frames of a stack of office chairs he found and leather scraps.

"I adjusted it, my David. Try it now."

Ahn-Kha could be as gentle as a cooing dove when he chose to be. The great arms, thick as well-fed pythons, wrapped themselves around Valentine and then worked the buckles on the brace. Valentine had always had good posture; constant insistence from first his parents, and then the more recently departed Father Max had given him an instinctive, erect carriage, but with the brace on he felt like a heroically posed statue, elbows slightly out. But he could breathe this time, unlike the preliminary fitting.

"Thanks, old horse."

He tottered out into the hallway, walking a bit like a drunk trying to conceal the extent of his load. He couldn't favor his bad leg, the way he usually strode. He made for Meadows, who stood at the far end of the hall, checking off supplies as they were distributed to Valentine's column. A somewhat subdued Sergeant—now Lieutenant, Valentine corrected himself—Frum stood just beside him, the bruise under his chin looking like a hangman's beard.

Colonel Meadows and Bullfrog were comfortable enough with each other that Valentine had suggested that Meadows stay at the hideout with whoever felt unfit for a try at the Boston Mountains. Bullfrog could find jobs for them as guerillas or in some of the settlements under his command. Meadows accepted, and with the help of a staff captain had begun to sort through the horde of Quisling supplies. Everyone seemed happier for it, like tired horses back in familiar stalls.

"All this stuff missing; it'll go against me at the next inspection," Bullfrog said.

"You'll be able to justify it."

"How's that?"

"You were doing your job. Recruiting and equipping warm bodies."

Bullfrog scratched his head, and Valentine turned to Meadows.

"Colonel, I think I'm fit enough to talk to the men. Could you get them together, please, sir?"

The men who couldn't fit underground had to be dispersed every night in case of a prowling Reaper, looking for lifesign where it wasn't supposed to be. Once the sun was well up they usually gathered for meals and news. There had been plenty of the first and not much of the latter lately, though everyone was looking better for a few days' rest.

Styachowski popped up, dabbing a coffee mustache from her lips and showing her old snap-to-it briskness. She'd spent the past day combing through Quisling paperwork with the help of a corporal on Bullfrog's quasi-Quisling staff.

"I'll pass word around as soon as the morning patrol comes in," she said.

"Lieutenant Frum, you think you could send out your men as sentry? I'd hate to have a convoy come by for refueling and spot the whole bunch of us."

Bullfrog nodded. "Sure, Captain."

"Anything overnight?"

"Another train, pulling south; men returning to Texas and Louisiana, looked like," Frum said.

"The Ozarks seem good and pacified," Meadows said. "We're beat and they know it."

"Always interesting times, the pause between conquest and exploitation. I wonder if they're as organized as they think they are," Styachowski said. Valentine's selection of documentation from Bullfrog's files had given her quick mind enough to make a guess as to what the column's next move would be.

"Or if we're as beat as they think we are," Valentine added.

Valentine stood at one of the glassless windows above the entrance to the office building, on the second floor. Bullfrog hadn't gotten around to reclaiming this floor of the building yet. Birds flitted in one side of the building and out the other, zipping over low cubicles and around offices.

Creeper and broken glass crunched underfoot as he tottered to the window, glad that the men hadn't seen Ahn-Kha half carry him upstairs. The men and women who had followed him out of General Martinez's camp sat around the door of the lot and in the notch leading toward the main entrance; unformed, unranked, a mass of faces and variegated uniforms—some still damp, Valentine noted, from a quick wash. Some elbowed others at Valentine's appearance, and faces turned up toward them. The chatter stilled.

The silence of their anticipation made Valentine oddly uncomfortable.

Valentine inflated his lungs, ignored the pain in his rib. "You all know about the Cats, am I right?"

"Yes, sir," a few answered back. Valentine thought about making them all holler a response back at him, but he wanted an honest conversation with the men, not an oration filled with theatrical tricks.

"They work behind the Kurian line," Valentine said. "Sometimes in their uniform. I've done it on more than one occasion."

He let that sink in for a moment before continuing. "We're making for what's left of Southern Command in the Boston Mountains. But if we keep going as we are, snaking back and forth, backtracking and sidestepping, we'll only show up sick, hungry, unarmed and tired—if we make it at all. If you men are willing, I know a way we can ride instead of walk, and join our comrades with rifles in our hands and ammunition in our cartridge cases."

They perked up at this. Even the jokers and snoozers in every informal assembly of personnel shut their mouths and fixed eyes on him.

"There'll be risks," Valentine continued. "But the risk of getting across the Arkansas River and through the lines with an unarmed column this big is about the same, by my calculations.

"So we have to balance the likely risks with the possible rewards. Anyone who isn't up for it, anyone who wants out of the game, can stay here with Colonel Meadows and Lieutenant Frum. Guerrilla service is just as honorable, just as important. But I have to make it to the Boston Mountains for reasons of my own. Anyone who wants to follow me, meet at the hollow where Lieutenant Post and and the Wolves are guarding the wagons."

"Then what?" Styachowski asked from among the audience. Just as they'd arranged when Valentine went over his prepared speech with her.

"Then we shave, strip and sew."

Chapter Five

The Ruins of Little Rock, Arkansas, February: The city never recovered from the nuclear blast inflicted on it in the death throes of the Old World. Though the fires went out and the radiation dispersed, the only life to return permanently was nonhuman. Pine Bluff, closer to the breadbasket of southeastern Arkansas, replaced it as a transportation hub; Mountain Home and Fort Scott surpassed it as government and military centers. At the height of the Ozark Free Territory's progress, it could boast of little more than a dock and a ferry in a cleared-out patch of rubble, though even that was based on the north side of the river; the south-bank heart of the city was avoided as if it were cursed earth.

The new rulers have a grander vision of a rail, road, and river traffic hub built on the decayed remnants of the old. The Rocks, as the locals call them, buzz with activity. The new human constructs have an anthill quality to them; low buildings made out of the blasted components of pre-2022 architecture. Some are already smoothed over by fresh concrete and white paint, and a more traveled eye might think of a little Greek town between hill and Aegean. The pilings and ruined bridges prevent barges from going farther up the river—only small boat traffic goes west to Fort Scott—so Little Rock is an amphibian marshaling yard. Warehouses and tents under the New Order's supply officers support the final mopping up and reorganization of the Ozarks. The river hums with traffic, and trucks and horse wagons fill transport pools as Consul Solon builds his capital.

One building stands apart from the others, avoided by all but a few humans who work on its exterior and still-unfinished upper floors. It is a Kurian Tower, home of one

of the new masters of what had been the Ozark Free Ter-
ritory. Other towers like it are going up in Pine Bluff,
Mountain Home, Hot Springs, and a dozen other, smaller
towns. Only Consul Solon has seen them all.

Consul Solon. Little is known of him, save that he came
from somewhere on the eastern seaboard. The name makes
Quisling captains break a sweat. Children are hushed with
warnings that Consul Solon will hear about misbehavior. An
argument can be stopped with a threat to take the matter to
him—a turn of events that might mean doom to both sides.
Consul Solon is the man responsible for keeping human
order in the various provinces of what was the Free Terri-
tory. He answers only to his Masters who have carved up the
region: the dark princes of Fort Scott and Crowley's Ridge,
the Springs, the Plateau, the Southern Marches, the Corri-
dor . . . and other regions. Unlike much of the Kurian Zone,
Solon is trusted to ensure the defense of all with a common
force, rather than dozens of private armies in the hands of
each overlord. Each Kurian has a Reaper representative at
Solon's temporary headquarters at Fort Scott, the Consul's
nerve center until the grander Consular Palace is built on
the north bank of the Arkansas near Little Rock.

"Get out of the way of the trucks, like obedient little
Quislings," Valentine ordered over his shoulder to Post, who
signaled with an arm to pull the files off the paved road.
Valentine leaned against the base of an old traffic signal pole
on the outskirts of Little Rock and waved first to a motorcycle, then to the trucks as they passed on southward. Only
ten feet of the pole remained; the rest of it lay in an over-
grown ditch atop an engine block. But ample enough for
leaning.

Valentine pulled off his helmet and rubbed his newly bald
skull as he surveyed the column. The fuzzy-headed troops
looked good enough in their Quisling uniforms, though they
marched poorly. They were all shorn of their hair, and even
the elaborate mustaches and beards—the pride and joy of

many of the soldiers of Southern Command—had been left on the dead leaves in the woods near Bullfrog's station.

He had organized his footsore charges into three parts after leaving seventy-odd men and women tired of the trail or unwilling to face the risks of operating in the enemy's uniform. At the lead were Finner's Wolves, bereft of their beloved buckskins. They now wore the uniforms of the TMMP, an acronym for the Trans-Mississippi Mounted Patrol—the military police of Solon's newborn empire, entrusted with everything from guarding rail bridges to directing traffic. He, his officers, the Bears and the Jamaicans wore the simple, shapeless uniforms of recruits newly incorporated into the Quisling AOT—Army of the Trans-Mississippi.

At the center of the column, teams of four "recruits" each carried a Quickwood beam on their shoulders, faking exercises under the shouted direction of their NCOs. Mrs. Smalls rode in one of the wagons with the camp equipment; her husband and son led teams carrying the sick. The family had insisted on coming along, so that Mrs. Smalls could have her baby in the hospital reported to be in Little Rock. Valentine thought she stuck out like a cardinal in a coven.

Valentine watched the southbound trucks kick up gravel from the potholes with hungry eyes. In his days with the Wolves, a lightly armed convoy of six trucks falling into his lap would have been cause for celebration. He would have waited for signals from the observation scouts, then pitched into the convoy if his scouts flashed the all clear. The Quislings were sure of themselves if they were sending trucks with nothing more than a motorcycle and sidecar leading the way down the long road to Hot Springs. General Martinez must not have been too aggressive in the eastern Ouachitas over the winter, and Bullfrog only attacked the occasional Quisling target at night.

When the way cleared he got his column up and moving again. He stayed by his signal post, watching the men's faces as they walked toward Little Rock. A few looked excited, even eager to play the game, but others wore their fear like lead overcoats. They moved with the deliberative plod of men too tired and hungry to hope.

"Let's step out a little more, Calgary," Valentine called to a former Guard shuffling down the road with a hangdog expression. "We're having a hot meal tonight."

Calgary picked up the pace and smacked his lips, pleased for some reason to be recognized. Valentine felt better too. The weeks of starts and stops, double-backs, circling, hunger and cold in the hills, and soggy, fireless camps, keeping seven hundred men out of the way of Quisling patrols, were over. They were right where Valentine had placed his finger on the map at the conference the night they left Colonel Meadows and Bullfrog, and his column had all solemnly shaved their heads—starting with Ahn-Kha's destruction of Valentine's shoulder-length locks. At first it had been play, learning the AOT and TMPP ranks, working on their imaginary stories as mercenary recruits in Arkansas, or up from the swamps of Louisiana or the woods of East Texas, looking to seek their fortune in the new empire Solon was raising.

When they emerged from the hills and turned up the road for the old state capital, the men grew more and more anxious as the task became real, rather than just an imagined challenge in the future. At a rest halt, Valentine gathered the men and spoke to them as best as he could, relaying details of a plan he had kept from all save Ahn-Kha, though he suspected Styachowski had an inkling. When the time came to speak to them he had the men unharness the wagons and rest on a hillside, making a natural amphitheater.

"You all know I'm a Cat," he finished, booming the words out so all could hear. "As of today, you're all Cats too. We're going to pretend we're Quislings recruits. Lieutenant Frum has phoned in to headquarters here the happy news that he's finally met, indeed overfilled, his recruitment quota. We've got faked documents requisitioning us food, new clothing, shoes and weapons. You've all suffered because of shortages of those things. The Quislings in the Ruins have plenty, and we're going to trick them out of them, get across the river and rejoin Southern Command. Just keep your mouths shut. One loose tongue could do us all in."

So as they approached the Ruins, Valentine needed something to get their minds off their situation. Most of the men were worried they were walking right into a prison yard, the intermediate holding place leading to the inevitable Reaper embrace.

"How about a song, Jefferson. An old marching tune. 'Yellow Rose of Texas,' anyone?"

"Huh?" Jefferson said, looking down from his wagon.

"Narcisse, I've heard your singing. Give us a song," Valentine said.

"One everyone can sing?"

"If you can think of one."

Narcisse ran her tongue beneath her lips. "Lesseee . . .

"Mine eyes have seen the glory of the coming of the Lord:
   He is trampling out the vintage where the grapes of
      wrath are stored;
He hath loosed the fateful lightening of His terrible, swift
      sword:
   His truth is marching on."

The men took up the march with a will. They began stepping out in time; some, used to singing hymns or just musically inclined, added harmonies. Even the Jamaicans knew the words.

While the song lasted Finner fell in beside him.

"Captain, you sure about what you're doing?"

Valentine considered telling him to shut his mouth and obey orders, but the man who'd brought him south from Minnesota deserved better. "Commanding one of the worst marches in Ozark history. I'll let Consul Solon take care of transport from now on."

"But from the Ruins? Why not grab some boats and just cross at some quiet bend upriver? From a distance we'll look like a training march."

"Styachowski says the AOT is scraping men from every border station. Little Rock is a supply depot. New formations are brought there now, to be equipped before being sent elsewhere."

"If I had a suspicious mind I might be worried that you were marching everyone into a prison yard. That'd rate a brass ring and an estate in Iowa. If I had a suspicious mind, that is."

"Would it make you feel better to know that I'm keeping your Wolves outside the wire?"

"It'd make me feel better. Don't know about the rest of these lunks. How far outside?"

"About seven miles. I want you to camp around Mt. Summit. We won't be in Little Rock for more than three or four days, I expect. If this turns bad we'll make for you if we can. You've got a good view of the old Highway 10 from there. If I need to talk to you and I can't come myself, I'll send Ahn-Kha or Post. Just a nice ride in the country. We'll have one of these red bandannas tied on our heads."

"Red bandannas. Okay."

"One more thing." Valentine reached into his AOT officer's winter coat, a hanging mass of leather and canvas covered with bellows pockets. "Here's a report . . . well, several reports. Send a couple of good, and I mean real good, Wolves out to the Boston Mountains. They're to find whoever's in charge there and hand them over. A Lifeweaver would be ideal."

"I've got eight men who've run courier for Martinez up north. They know where to go."

"Keep those uniforms handy. You may need them again."

"Very well, sir."

"More responsibility than you wanted, I'm sure."

Finner rocked back and forth on his heels, keeping time to the music, fighting a smile. "I'm getting used to it. I think I'm better at this than I thought. Hope you didn't think I was accusing . . ." Finner let the sentence trail off.

"No. Stay suspicious, Finner. If I'd been more suspicious when we hit the Free Territory—oh, never mind. I want to pay this Consul Solon back with some of his own coin."

*   *   *

Finner and his Wolves left them while they were still in the hills. The road sloped down into the Ruins. It began to rain again. Valentine put an old green towel over his shaven head so the ends hung down like a bloodhound's ears and seated an old Kevlar helmet over it.

"This cover my scar?" he asked Post. "I'm worried I've made Solon's Most Wanted."

"Pretty much, " Post said, tilting his head to see the thin white line descending Valentine's right cheek. "It's shaded off, anyway. You can still see the bit by your eye. It's the haircut that makes the real difference."

"That wasn't a haircut, that was clear-cutting."

"Your teeth could use some coffee stains to complete the disguise. I've never known anyone who spends so much time brushing his teeth in the field."

"Every meal, the way my momma taught me." That memory caused a brief stab: the last time he'd seen them in Minnesota he was eleven and she'd—*stop it*. "If you'd ever seen a nice, runny oral infection you'd join me," he finished, a little lamely.

The column passed shells of buildings. Empty gas stations, strip malls with their glass fronts blasted out, foundations of homes that had burned and died grew closer and closer together as they came into the city limits. Gutted two-story structures gave way to piles of rubble, though the highway they walked on had been cleared. The debris lined either side of the road like snowdrifts.

The column sighted a guard post.

"Okay, Post, I'm going to talk to them. They'll probably take me to the CO of this scrapheap. If I'm not back in two hours, or if you hear shooting, just fade into the hills. Split up if you have to."

"Told me that, sir."

"I'm repeating it. Nobody, not even Ahn-Kha, goes in after me. We want them confused; fighting will unconfuse them faster than anything."

A sergeant with a corporal trailing behind like a heeled dog stepped from a little shelter at the spectacle of a quarter mile of humanity waking down the road toward his post. They wore tiger-striped cammies, with AOT yellow insignia at the shoulder. Valentine kicked his horse on and trotted forward. Ahn-Kha stepped in front of his horse and took the reigns.

"I heard you speaking to Post. If this turns, we're not to go in after you?"

"Not even you, old horse."

"If I can't go in after you, my David, I'm coming in with you."

"Post will need you if—"

"You'll need me more."

Ahn-Kha's ears went flat and the Grog took a stance a little wider than a riverside oak, four hundred pounds of road-block.

"You'll be my bodyguard then," Valentine said, knowing when he was beaten, and not wanting to look like there was a crisis in his command.

They approached the guard station. Valentine hailed the sergeant from horseback.

"We're a day late, I know. Bad weather," Valentine said.

"A day late for what?" the sergeant said. He looked more at Ahn-Kha than at either Valentine or the unarmed column far behind. Valentine was suddenly glad Ahn-Kha had insisted on accompanying him.

Valentine glared, and turned his chin so the three pips on his collar showed.

"Colonel," the sergeant added, saluting.

"For outfit and transport, Sergeant. Recruits up from Station 26, District Commander Frum's HQ."

The corporal checked a nearly blank clipboard. "You're Colonel Le Sain."

"From Louisiana," Valentine said, opening a satchel. He passed down a wad of paperwork in an expandable water-proof envelope. "Route Orders are near the top. You'll see supply, transport, OI for each recruit and the roster's in the back, not that you need to concern yourself with the rest. Don't think you have to check off every name that passes;

my officers are responsible for everyone getting on the barge. I take the heat if anyone deserts."

The sergeant took another look at the ID card dangling from Valentine's breast pocket. "Didn't they have transport for you on the road, uhhh, Colonel Le Sain?"

"Too cheap. Besides, it toughens 'em up."

"I'll let the general know you've arrived."

"When you do, mention that weather held us up. Hell, I'd better come along in case they have questions."

"Yes, sir. Corp, let the colonel and his stoop pass." The sergeant disappeared into his guardhouse.

Valentine dismounted and stepped over the chain hung between two concrete dragon's teeth blocking the road. "Up from Louisiana, sir? I used to serve in Texas, myself. Can't wait to get back." The corporal's face showed curiosity, not suspicion.

"I'm here permanently."

The guardhouse consisted of the remains of some concrete-and-steel professional building. Men in loose dungarees were rebuilding exterior walls from the rubble, fitting together more or less intact cinder blocks around electrical conduit already laid. Others worked on a superstructure to the building, building something that looked like a miniature aircraft control tower. The workers all had bright orange zipper pockets sewn on the breasts of their overalls.

"Forced labor?" Valentine asked the corporal.

"You know it, sir. At first it was lots of force and not much labor, but they've settled down."

"Good."

Valentine smelled the wet cement and waited while the sergeant passed responsibility up to lieutenant, and lieutenant to a radio. The lieutenant, a thirtyish man missing an earlobe, hung up the field phone and approached Valentine.

The Cat tried not to look relieved when he saluted. "Howdy, sir," he said, revealing a mouth full of black-rimmed teeth. "I apologize for taking so long. I'm sorry, but there's some confusion. They know about the men, but

Brigadier Xray-Tango doesn't know you, sir." Valentine felt a cold sweat emerge on his back.

"I got my orders a month ago. Only thing to happen since then was a last-minute change; they had me set out from Fort Scott instead of Hot Springs. That got countermanded the next day; turned out they wanted me at Station 26 to command these recruits."

"Looks like when you got switched back, someone didn't follow up, sir."

"Order, Counter-Order, Disorder. Hot Springs had some confusion, too."

The lieutenant shrugged. He looked as if he was going to say something to Ahn-Kha, and thought better of it. "Brigadier Xray-Tango wants to see you and your orders before your men get billeted, sir. I suppose your Grog can go with you."

"Excuse me, son. 'Xray-Tango?' That an acronym you use up here?"

"No, it's a name. He's CO for this whole New Columbia area. He's new, too."

"I see. Wish they'd tell me these things."

"If you'll follow me, sir."

Valentine smiled. "I look forward to meeting the brigadier."

Little Rock's collection of warehouses and piers was Station 3, according to the sign over the entrance. Station 3 also had a motto: "Crossroads of the Future." Or so Valentine read as he stepped up the stairs and under a pre-2022 post and lintel in the neoclassical style. The rest of the headquarters building was a cobbled-together mix of wood floors, brick walls and beam roof. Communications passed from the radio room upstairs through old-fashioned air-pressure tubes. There was an audible *shoomp* as a new message arrived at the desk of an officer. Another wrote outgoing messages in block letters on square-lined paper and sent them shooting back upstairs.

"The general will see you now, sir; your assistant can

wait outside," a corporal said. He had the self-assured look of a ranker who was used to having officers at his beck and call. Ahn-Kha waited for a nod from Valentine, then went back outside.

The brigadier general had a corner office with narrow windows filled with the first unbroken glass Valentine had seen in the Ruins. What wall space wasn't taken up by windows had maps and bulletin boards on it. A liquor sideboard held trophies of figures in various martial arts poses instead of bottles. The desk smelled of recently applied varnish.

"Coffee?" Brigadier Xray-Tango asked. He had a neat uniform, with the same yellow star on the shoulder, and a hearty manner, under a haircut so close it resembled peach fuzz. Friendly but harassed eyes looked out from under bushy brows. There was something wrong with the face, though, and it took Valentine a moment to see it. Xray-Tango's left eye was open wider than the right; it wasn't that the right was squinting, it was more that the left lid stayed a little farther open. Valentine liked to look at a man's hands after his face, and as he poured the coffee Valentine looked at the work-roughened fingers. The nails were rimmed with a stain that matched that on the new desk, which was topped by a stenciled desk plate that read BGDR GENERAL S. XRAY-TANGO.

"Thank you, sir." Valentine sniffed the aroma from the thermos. "The real thing?"

"Privileges of rank."

"What's all the hardware for? Boxing?"

"Some. Ever heard of Tae Kwon Do?"

"That's like kickboxing, right?"

"A little. It's a martial art. I fought for my old brigade out west. Retired undefeated." He held out his left hand; on the finger next to a wedding ring Valentine saw a ruby red championship ring with "S X T" engraved beneath the "Single Combat Champion" title. "Can I see your orders, Colonel?"

Valentine sorted them and placed them in three piles on his desk. "Marching orders. Supply requisitions. Organization Inventory for the recruits. Y'all like your paperwork up here."

"That's a weak-looking OI," Xray-Tango said, glancing through the pages.

"Farm kids and men in from the borderland boonies. But they're good woodsmen. They know about moving through country and shooting."

"That territory organized?"

"Not as well as it should be. Most of them are the usual assortment of malcontents who chose carrying a gun over using a shovel in a labor camp."

General Xray-Tango's left eye twitched; a quick three-blink spasm, the third slower than the first two.

"You're moving kind of stiff, Colonel. Injury?"

"I came off a horse a couple weeks ago and broke a rib. I just got the cast off."

The eye twitched again and Xray-Tango took in Ahn-Kha's formidable frame.

"Why the bodyguard?" he asked Valentine.

"The Grog? SOP down there for anyone above captain, sir. Bodyguard. Master-at-arms. I don't know what you'd call it up here. He shakes up soldier and civilian alike."

"Kind of like your own personal Hood, eh? Not sure if I like that. A good leader shouldn't have to dole out summary justice. How often you use it?"

"I lost one on the way. I had to shoot a deserter. Just a homesick kid. I didn't know what kind of paperwork I had to fill out so I just made a report, countersigned by my second in command and the dead man's sergeant. We don't have dog tags but his work card's attached. That's how we did things in Natchez."

"That's the least of my worries, Le Sain."

"Why's that, sir?"

"To be honest, we've no record of you coming here. By Kur, I need you, that's for sure. All this rain with the spring thaw; I've got a command and a bunch of warehouses that might be underwater in a day or two. Consul Solon has zero, and I mean zero, tolerance for wheeling and dealing. So I'm going to have to do some checking. No offense to how they do things in Louisiana." The eye twitched again; *blink-blink-bliiink*.

"Don't follow your meaning, sir."

"I started out in the Okalahoma High Plains, Colonel. Not the most exciting place for duty. We had a captain out there, got bored with his duties and got himself a transfer to Lake Meredith. And when I say got himself a transfer, I mean he wrote one up, signed it and moved his troops a hundred miles just for a change of scenery. He figured he'd earned it after a lot of dusty years watching railways and cattle wallows. So happens he was a good officer and the Higher Ups let him get away with it. We've been after Frum at Post 26 for months to meet his recruitment quota for the year—and all of the sudden he's not just met it, he's overfilled it, with a Louisiana colonel to boot."

Valentine sipped his coffee, straining to keep his hand steady. The story was so close to his own that he listened for men moving in behind to put him under arrest, but all he heard from outside the office was typing.

"Now, could be you heard, down in your Louisiana boonies, that with the Ozarks getting pacified there'd be opportunity under the Consul's new system. Could be you decided that the way to a general's star would be to make yourself useful up here. Could be you knew there were fifty-seven brass rings given out over the last year, since we went in once and for all. Not just to generals either, but we got our share."

Xray-Tango opened his shirt, and there, hung from a golden chain, was a brass ring. *Blink-blink- bliiink*.

Valentine thought it odd. The brass ring–types he'd met usually displayed them on their right ring finger. The token indicated special favor in the Kurian Order. A wearer and his family would never be at risk of being sent to the Reapers.

"It happens that I like a man with ambition. I like an officer with initiative. I also like to hear the truth. I've got a way of knowing when someone's spoon-feeding me horseshit and telling me it's applesauce. Leaves a bad taste in my mouth. So fess up. The orders for you to come up here didn't go through Fort Scott, or Hot Springs, did they?"

Valentine's bowels had turned to liquid as he sat in the chair, as if Narcisse had spiked the coffee with her emetic, and he decided to admit to as much as possible. "You're close to the truth, sir, but I don't want to say much more. I had some help along the way and I don't want people who've covered for me to get into trouble. Least of all anyone under me. My men, except for some of the new ones, trust me. I'm responsible for them, and if someone has to go to a Hood because of this, it should be me. It's my idea." Valentine felt strangely relieved with his confession—but would a partial truth set him partially free?

"No reason for it to go that far. I've just had over five hundred strong backs fall into my lap; I should be shaking your hand and buying you a bottle of Old Kentucky MM. You're in Little Rock—err, New Columbia, now, and I'm the lead longhorn in these parts. If your friends in Louisiana start asking about you, we'll play dumb. But I expect you to fit into the system here, or you'll wish you'd stayed in the swamp. Here's my command."

Xray-Tango stepped over to a map on the wall. It was a copy of an old Free Territory map, redrawn to take into account the realities of the new world. "This rockheap used to be the center of Arkansas. It will be again. We're at the crossroads of the river traffic and the road artery running the eastern side of the mountains, here. Makes an 'X,' as you can see. Within a year we'll have two new rail lines, one running down from Memphis over to Tulsa, the other down from St. Louis to Dallas. So there's a new 'X' going to be laid over the first. A line branching down from Kansas City to Fort Scott, and Fort Scott connecting Tulsa and points south and west is already running; Consul Solon had us working three shifts till that was done. But Fort Scott was promised to the Higher Ups in Oklahoma in return for their help with this. The new capital will be right here, at the intersection of all those Xs. This'll be the nerve center of the Trans-Mississippi Confederation."

"How many smaller states are there? I see a lot of borders."

"Twenty-six in all. Each one has its Higher Ups. Most just have one running the show. In this system Consul Solon's got rigged, we're supposed to call them 'governors.' But as you know, it's really Solon's land. Who's obeying who remains to be seen. He's keeping the peace between them, Kur knows how. He's even planning to set up some kind of court to work out disputes between them. You ever heard the like?"

"No. Natchez was—"

"I've heard it's a snake pit."

"I wouldn't say. But there were feuds all the time with the New Orleans Kur. They could use a court down there, too."

"Out on the High Plains I spent more time fighting with the boys out of Santa Fe than guerillas and saboteurs."

"I've been bushwhacked myself for scavenging in the wrong place at the wronger time, " Valentine said.

"Can't say how you'll figure into this just yet, Le Sain. Right now I need disciplined labor more than anything, with the river rising. These hillbillies who used to be here weren't much on civil engineering; they didn't care if a bunch of ruins flooded. I've got two regiments of infantry and a fair amount of artillery, but it's on the other side of the river; there's still fighting in the Boston Mountains, and that's Solon's reserve. I don't dare use them. Over on this side I've got a few companies of reserves, my engineers, hospital and headquarters, and I'm hip-deep in quartermasters getting the river traffic where it's supposed to go. There are military police for the prisoners working on the river banks, and I'm trying my damnedest to get more."

"I'll put my men to work right away. I have a few with engineering experience. Sooner the job's done, the sooner we get activated."

"You *want* a combat command?"

"You bet."

Xray-Tango's droopy eye narrowed. "We'll see, Colonel. I'll have a lieutenant show you to a clear spot. You'll be in tents for a while, but I can get you running water and some gas stoves. If your men want better quarters, you'll be building them. You'll have more water than you can imagine, shortly. Now you get to spend the rest of your day filling out paperwork. This time it'll get stamped by me."

"Any chance of getting north of the river and seeing some action, sir?"

Xray-Tango smiled, triggering his eye again. "You are eager, aren't you?"

"Want one of those rings. You could give another brigade a break, sir. If they've been in the mountains all winter they'd appreciate time to refit."

Blink-blink-bliiink. "Let me run my command, Le Sain. You'll get your chance."

"Of course, sir."

"What kind of action have you seen?"

"Small-scale stuff, General. Skirmishes here and there. I've done a lot of ambushes and guerilla hunting. I've only heard cannon fired in training."

"Let's take it one step at a time. According to your OI, most of your command is green. Or is that falsified too?"

"They're a mixed bag, but I have some good NCOs. The men can shoot. You'd be surprised."

"I'll look forward to finding out what you can do, when the river's back under control. One more push when spring comes and things will be over with. It'll just be a matter of smoking out the remnants. I'm a busy man, otherwise I'd pour you another cup of coffee and warm it up with a touch of bourbon. I'd like to hear stories about life in the swamp. Do you have any questions?"

"Not a military one, sir. Your name, sir. It's—"

"Different, isn't it? My mother was a POW when she had me. I got put in an orphanage in Amarillo. There were a fair amount of us. The orphanage was run military-style, it even had a military name. 'Youth Recovery Center Four' was where I spent my salad days. They used the initials of our mothers. So I was always Xray-Tango. I never found out if I had been given a first name."

"The 'S'?"

The general's eyebrow trembled, but only for a second. "My wife used to call me 'Scotty.' She said I looked like one. The dog, I mean."

"Used to, sir? I apologize, sir. That's personal."

"It was quick. Heart attack. That's why I transferred to Solon's command. Couldn't take the flats out there anymore." *Blink-blink-bliiink.* "Too much empty."

An adjutant entered with a clipboard full of flimsies of radio communiqués. Valentine resisted the urge to glance at the top one as the soldier passed.

"That'll be all, Le Sain." General Xray-Tango lifted an order off his desk and dashed off a signature, then stamped it. "Corporal, give this to Lieutenant Greer.

"Oh, Le Sain. Good thing you were honest with me and I liked the shape of your shadow. I had two orders on how to deal with you sitting on my desk. The one going to Lieutenant Greer says he's to feed and uniform you and your command. The other said to shoot you and your officers. It's staying in my desk, just in case."

Lieutenant Greer was a sandy-haired monosyllabalist with the intent features of an owl. Though a young man, he was hard of hearing.

"Still lots of junk near the river at your camp, sir," Greer said. He spoke accentless English as though it were a foreign tongue. He walked beside Valentine, leading the column through the Ruins. Structural steel beams and plumbing fixtures poked out from the debris like leaning crucifixes in an old frontier cemetery. "Not all bad. Flat ground, good drainage. Old sewers, too."

They passed what must have once been multistory office buildings at the heart of the old downtown. One remaining spindle of girders had been left, and most of a tower clung around its central support. The spiral minaret reminded Valentine of the long, pointy shells of turret snails he'd seen on the beaches of the Caribbean. Laborers walked up the endless stairs winding around the structure, bearing bricks to the top.

"What's that suppose to be?" Valentine asked.

"The Residence," Greer said. "Eleven floors."

"Of"—Valentine paused and glanced around—"the governor?"

Greer averted his eyes and hunched his shoulders as they passed wide of the building. Valentine saw armored cars parked before it, covering the cleared streets outside the beginnings of a wall. A Kurian Tower, sticking there like a knife in the heart of the Free Territory. Valentine's throat went dry.

Greer murmered something so quietly Valentine thought he was talking to himself. "Two in the city. Brothers, or maybe cousins. Don't know names. Eight and five." Valentine guessed this last to be the number of Reapers each controlled, respectively. Reapers that needed feeding.

"Thirteen. Unlucky," Valentine commented.

"Don't worry now. Still plenty of prisoners. Much work to do. For now, they take only hurt and bad sick. This big state. I come from Indianapolis. Six years ago, bad drought, many farms die. Other Bloodmen from hills in south came, stole people. Then they fed on us in army."

"That's a hard piece of luck. This is a sweeter situation. That's why I came."

"Yes, sir. Duty with a future, here."

They continued north, almost to a little finger of a hill separating river from city, and reached their camp. It was a former city block now called "Dunkin Do," according to the old sign propped up among the rubble. The street had not even been cleared yet, and among the bulldozer tracks there were little piles of debris in hummocks, but it was still preferable to the mountains of shattered concrete elsewhere in the city. The block was circled by nine-foot posts, and rolls of barbed wire had been left out to rust in the rain.

"Was to be prison camp, sir," Greer said. "For after last push this year. But you can use."

Valentine wondered if this wasn't another warning from Xray-Tango that any nonsense would convert him and his men from allies to inmates in short order. He and Post trailed Greer around as he pointed out the water taps, already flowing, and the sewer outlets.

"Provisions tonight, sir, uniforms tomorrow, maybe stoves and fuel day after," Greer said. "Here's paperwork, sir. I fill some, you do rest, please, sir. Mostly just signatures. Officers can billet in garage, or stay in tents with men, up to you."

"Garage?" Post asked.

"You see soon. Underground parking. Like bunker, you know? Meet others. Good food, good times."

"We'll drop by," Valentine said. "Let us know when happy hour starts."

Greer's owlish eyes rolled skyward. "Happy hour, sir?"

"Never mind. I'll be here tonight, getting the men settled in."

They watched the men file into the camp, followed by the wobble-wheeled wagons. Jefferson cursed a blue streak, trying to get his team around a clump of reinforced concrete, its rods threatening horse leg and spoke alike.

"Questions, sir?"

"Who's in charge of supplying us?"

"Commissary Sergeant Major Tucker, in Quonset hut behind headquarters. Good man. Answer all questions. Usually answer is 'yes.'"

Tucker was more than just a good man. He appeared that evening like a horn of plenty, playing a sprited version of Beethoven's "Ode To Joy" on a silver concert flute. He showed up in the shotgun seat of a roofless, antiquated Hummer, interrupting the men as they were setting up their tents in military rows.

"General's orders," Tucker shouted, pointing with his flute at his cargo. "Fresh bread, fruit and veggies just up from the Gulf. Spring potatoes, winter cabbage, first peas and even apples. We've got beer in cask, but before I can issue that, we need to see what kind of workers you are."

The men forgot they were in the heart of an enemy camp enough to start cheering as he handed out the bounty. Cured side meat lay in baskets revealed as eager hands took the food.

"Whee-ooh, y'all need the showers rigged pronto, boys," Tucker said. "Ever heard of field hygiene?"

"We've been on the road for three days," Valentine said, stepping forward to help hand out the foodstuffs.

"You're up from Louisiana, they tell me."

"Sergeant Tucker, the smell's unfortunate, I know. They need some washtubs and soap more than anything."

"Coming tomorrow, sir."

"I'm only about half armed as well. I'd like to see that rectified."

"Guns are a problem, sir. You'll get a few for marksmanship, to familiarize yourselves with our models, but we don't have enough to arm all your men at the moment."

"That's unfortunate. Suppose there's an emergency and the camp has to turn out to defend itself?"

"We have contingency plans, sir. When y'all are properly integrated into the general's command, you'll be outfitted, but there's too much work to do here for now. You'll be in reserve a few months at least . . ."

"Months! I thought the fight was coming sooner than that."

"I can't say, sir. Those were the general's orders; he was specific about it."

Valentine recovered his mental equilibrium. "I haven't been fully briefed yet."

"Sorry you had to hear it from me, sir. But be glad for it; you'll have a better time back here. Those boys up north are dug in like ticks on a bear; burning them off isn't going to be a summer picnic. If you saw the hospital you wouldn't be so willful about it."

*　　　*　　　*

Months. Valentine spent two hours trying to fall asleep, staring at the silhouette of the Quickwood center pole in his tent. Using Quickwood to form their tents seemed as good a way as any to hide the material in plain sight.

Such a small thing, the Quickwood beam. But it was the source of all Valentine's hopes. He saw some of the men touching it as they passed, some with a reverence that brought to mind odd bits of mental flotsam about medieval pilgrims and alleged pieces of the True Cross, others caressing it as though it were a lover in passing. Even Post, who'd never shown any other signs of superstition, would give the tent-pole a double rap with his knuckles whenever he passed it in Valentine's tent.

The ruse might last six days, but more than a few weeks was out of the question. Sooner or later some fool would let something slip, a face would be recognized despite the shorn heads, an assumed identity would be dropped. There would be questions, and then, when he didn't have answers, more questions. From what he'd seen of the docks and warehouses, they were well guarded against any attack he could mount, armed as he was, even with his Bears. The Quickwood had to make it to Southern Command, where it would be used to kill Reapers instead of hold up waterproofed canvas. But if he simply decamped and marched across the river, his chances of ever seeing the Boston Mountains were negligible.

Realizing sleep was impossible, he rose, dressed and found an ax. He wandered around the camp, nodding to the men on firewatch, until he found piled cords of firewood. David Valentine split fulls into quarters and quarters into kindling until he could drop into his bunk, body soaked with sweat even in the cold night air, muscles aflame, fretful thoughts finally beaten into numbness.

Chapter Six

The Arkansas River, February of the forty-eighth year of the Kurian Order: Part of the defense strategy of the Free Territory was simple inaccessibility. Southern Command tore up railroads leading into the Ozarks, broke roadbeds down, wrecked bridges, let forests grow over airstrips, and flooded bayous long since drained by the Corps of Engineers. As part of this strategy Southern Command rendered the Arkansas River unnavigable by destroying locks, sinking snags and pulling down levees, blocking invasion by water east from the Mississippi and west from the old river port on the Verdegris east of Tulsa. Four hundred feet of elevation from the Mississippi to Fort Smith were made impassible to anything other than shallow-draft traffic, thanks to the sand-clogged river and vigilant Guards at Arkansas Post and Fort Gibson. While both strongpoints changed hands several times over the course of the Free Territory's star-crossed history, they were always eventually won back.

Until now.

In their months of occupation the Kurians have opened the river to some traffic between Little Rock and the Mississippi; small barges are again making the ascent to supply the armies still fighting in the mountains. But Nature takes her part in the conflict as well: a wet winter, early spring and heavy rains have raised waters to levels not matched since the floods of the nineteen twenties. The last controls, hydroelectric dams at the Jed Taylor and Dardanelle Lock & Dams, were destroyed as Southern Command fled to the mountains, leaving the river open to flooding. Only the fact that the levees were destroyed years ago, siphoning some of the water

away in secondary floods, has saved the new masters of the
Ruins so far.
   But the river is rising.

   The irony of the situation was not lost on David Valentine.
He drove his men, enlisted and officers alike, in an exhausting war against the swelling Arkansas River. A wall of sand-
bags was the battle line. On the one side of the miles of
sandbags, pumps and drainage ditches were the war materials
of Consul Solon's military millstone, now grinding Southern
Command into chicken feed. On the other side swelled a
God-given natural disaster waiting to strike a blow for their
Cause potentially more damaging than even batteries of
heavy artillery with the town in their sights could hope to do.
   Nonetheless he threw his men's bodies against the river.
Even Ahn-Kha stood waist-deep in cold water, hardly stopping to eat, plunging his long arms again and again into the
base of the levee, digging sluices for the pumps.
   The endless labor inured his men to living hearth-to-hearth
with the Quislings. When Tucker and his men handed out new
AOT uniforms—a mottle of sea greens and browns, some
with the look of reclaimed and redyed clothing about them—
Post brought them in groups before Narcisse, who marked
their foreheads in a *vaudou* version of the anointing of the
ashes. She smeared them with a red paste and flicked them
about the head and neck with a powdered white feather,
chanting in her Haitian Creole. Even Styachowski submitted
to it in good humor, after Narcisse explained to her and Valentine that it was just for show: The paste was winterberry with
a touch of poison sumac to give it a tingle. Narcisse promised
the men that the ritual would help them fool the enemy, guard
their tongues and curse any who deliberately gave away their
true allegiance so that any reward given by the Kurians would
turn to ash and their hearts' blood to sand. Valentine watched
M'Daw's face as he underwent the anointing; there would be
a brass ring for him and land of his choosing if he were to go
over to his old masters, and it would be so easy. So very easy.
Just a word or two in the right ear at the wrong moment. The

healthy respect for Narcisse's powers M'Daw had gained when she changed the old Quisling's bowels to the biological equivalent of a fire hose showed itself when he jumped at her touch as though she carried electrical current.

Valentine had considered assigning someone unobtrusive but reliable, like the Texan drover Jefferson, to keep an eye on M'Daw, but the old Quisling had been as willing as any on the march, and complained not at all. Valentine was inclined to trust him. Keeping track of worries in the current predicament was like following individual ants pouring from a kicked-open hill.

Mrs. Smalls was the only one excepted from the ceremony, though Narcisse ministered to the pregnant woman as midwife and cook. She and her husband were confined to their tent. The baby had dropped, and they were expecting it to be born any day.

Valentine had Mrs. Smalls on his mind as he paced back and forth at the drainage ditch, watching the next two truckloads of sand and bags make their way to the waiting shovel-wielding prisoners.

"Your shift was over a half hour ago, sir," Styachowski said. She passed him a hot cup of roasted chicory coffee, sweetened to a syrup with molasses. The mixture had been passed around as the closest thing to real coffee they could make in quantity.

Valentine gulped and looked through the steam at Styachowski. Even dripping wet she managed to look neat, though there were circles under her eyes, made worse by pallid skin and close-cropped hair. Styachowski had been tireless at the riverbank, still working when men twice her size dropped in exhaustion.

"I can go a couple more hours. Do two more dry in your bunk, Styachowski."

"I can—"

He swiveled his gaze to the prisoners. "Hey, you two there, don't pack 'em like sausages, or they'll burst under pressure."

"Sorry, sir," the prisoner with the shovel replied. He wore

a faded Guard uniform with POW stenciled in orange across his back and down his pant leg.

"Sorry, Styachowski, you were saying?

"Nothing, sir."

"Then move along. I'll cover your duty."

"Neither of you ever quit," Styachowski said, looking down at Ahn-Kha. The Grog grasped a seventy-pound sandbag in each hand and stuffed them at the bottom of the levee. "He's like a machine; I don't worry about him. You, on the other hand—"

"Can take care of myself. As you said, I spend my time shouting, not moving earth."

"Then why do you have mud up to your neck?"

"Clumsiness."

"I've seen you walk across a two-strand rope bridge without breaking stride. I doubt it."

"You'll spend eight hours in your bunk, Styachowski. That's an order."

She lifted her chin and opened her mouth—her cropped hair would have bristled were it not wet—but no sound came out for a second. "Yes, sir," she finally said. She waited to turn; Post and a corporal were trotting along the rim of the drainage ditch.

"Sir," Post said excitedly. "We've got a big bulge up next to where it's reinforced on that old park bench. "It looks like it'll give way any minute."

"Take Rodger's squad and shore it up," Valentine said, leaning around the wide shoulders of his lieutenant to take a look.

"It's in Captain Urfurt's section," Post added quietly, referring to the Quisling responsible for the length east of Valentine's. "He's dealing with a broken pump, hasn't noticed it and none of his prisoners are anxious to bring it to his attention. Know what I mean?"

"Shore it up, Will."

"But—"

"I'm not used to giving orders twice," Valentine said, his voice not a shout, but not conversational either. He'd never raised his voice to Post before, outside the din of battle. He rounded on Styachowski like a bar brawler who's felled one opponent and is looking to loosen some teeth in another. "Speaking of which, why aren't you in your bunk, Styachowski?"

"Sir," they both chirped, backing away to obey.

Valentine raised his mug. Some artist had painted a yellow star on it, and added "We Build New Columbia: Crossroads of the Future" in neat brushstrokes before glazing it. The incessant rain had already chilled the coffee. It tasted like dry leaves and old gum.

A whooping shout of joy came from his section of levee. Valentine saw two bedraggled men—the one with a hat belonged to his group, the other had the orange POW stenciling. Both men had skin the color of milk chocolate, long, handsome faces and similar silhouettes as they embraced.

Valentine had feared a moment like this. "Ahn-Kha," he said as he trotted over to the pair.

"Lord bless, Dake, I knew you made it out of the pocket. What gives, slick?" the one in the POW fatigues said.

Valentine thought his soldier's name might be Abica. Dake Abica sounded right in his head.

He heard Ahn-Kha's squelching footsteps behind. "You there, Abica," he shouted, as a sergeant hurried to interpose. "Come over here."

Abica put a hand on the arm of his relative—

"Alone!" Valentine shouted. "Ahn-Kha, keep an eye on that man."

"Be cool, Clip," Abica said. He approached Valentine.

The sergeant, a former supply clerk named Roybesson, joined him, instinctively placing herself facing both Valentine and Abica.

"Sorry, sir," Abica said. "That's my brother Cli—Clipton. Third Cavalry regiment, light artillery. He's smart and—"

"I don't need his Q file, Abica," Valentine said. "Roybesson, if those two speak again, you'll wish you'd been bit with Ravies Six. Got me?"

She blanched but answered quickly enough. "Yes, sir."

"Sir, we could—" Abica began.

"Private, we're going to talk to your brother in my tent.

You, me and Ahn-Kha. If you don't do exactly as I say, Ahn-Kha'll kill your brother and you'll spend the rest of our time here in a tiger cage. Near the dike, so if it breaks we'll get a nice loud warning before you drown."

Abica's eyes flamed, and Valentine stared until Abica dropped his gaze to his feet.

"We go about this right, your brother will be in your tent with you tonight."

The private and his sergeant both unclenched their legs at that. Valentine forced a friendly smile. "We'll need some playacting out of you first, Abica."

The form read:

LIMITED PARDON

This document grants provisional immunity for any and all previous offenses against the Kurian Order. By signing it the pardon applicant renounces, completely and irrevocably, its former affiliations, begs forgiveness for its crimes, and asks for the privileges and benefits of fellowship in the human community.

I, _____,
seek a place within and protection of the Trans-Mississippi Extended District. I agree to obey the orders of my lawful superiors who will take my life forfeit if I violate this oath.

Sworn this (day)_____ of (month)_____, (year)_____.

Signed:_____

Witnessed: _____

Recorded and sealed:_____

A lined-off empty space in the lower right-hand corner waited for a cheap foil seal.

Valentine sat at his field desk, a slightly warped office table resting unsteadily on the plywood floor of his tent, hat-ing himself for what he was about to do. This bit of playacting was the only alternative, and if it went wrong—

Cross that bridge when you come to it. The form, placed with a dozen others like it on a clipboard complete with tied-on ballpoint pen, rested next to an oversized shot glass.

The POW, his eyes shaded from the single bulb by his thick brow, stood before him. Abica stood behind, his sergeant just outside the tent. Ahn-Kha rested on his knuckles, a little stooped over in the confines of the wood frame and canvas. The drizzle outside grew heavier and lighter in fits, reminding Valentine of the sound of gentle surf on the Texas coast.

"Scotch?" Valentine asked, pouring some amber fluid from an unmarked bottle. He'd been told it was his whiskey ration, the designation just sounded better. "Cold work out there."

"You signed this?" Clipton Abica asked his brother. The skin was tight against his face, and Valentine saw his brow twitch.

"Had to. It was that or the boxcars, and I wasn't getting shipped to Dallas on a last ride. This is good duty, bro. Food's better—"

Valentine tapped the clipboard. "Son, the war's over here. We're reorganizing. It's better to be reorganizing than reorganized. I'm at full complement, but your brother asked very nicely. He's a smart man, and I always have room for another smart man."

Clipton Abica shook his head, looking at his brother rather than Valentine.

"Six years in and you'll get an allotment if you want. I'm about to make your brother a corporal, and I'm sure you'd rise too. Find a nice gal, or you can have your pick out of the pens waiting to go. It's hard but it's life. Any POWs we don't assimilate—" Valentine waved his hand out at the dripping water.

Abica broke in on the rain. "Do it, bro. Don't forget about Ma and Sinse and our cousins. They're caught up in this somewhere. Us being dead won't help them."

Clipton Abica picked up the brimming shot glass and

smelled the whiskey appreciatively. "Better than strained brake fluid."

"You know it," Abica said.

The parolee tipped it into his mouth, put down the glass next to the clipboard, then with a lunge spat it at his brother and Valentine. He sent the clipboard skittering across the table at Valentine, who blocked it with his palm.

"Fuck both of you! Throw me—"

Ahn-Kha grabbed the man in a bear hug and dragged him out of the tent screaming and kicking. Valentine heard a few faint obscenities as Roybesson put him in handcuffs.

Abica looked out at the sight of his brother thrust into the mud, Ahn-Kha's sheep-sized thigh pressing into the small of his brother's back.

Ahn-Kha and Roybesson dragged him off.

"Why didn't we just tell him—"

"The truth?" Valentine asked. He refilled the glass and pushed it toward Abica. "We could have. But your brother's doing more for us back behind barbed wire."

"How's that?"

"They have spies among the prisoners. I'm sure of it. Your brother talking about what a rotten, traitorous, son of a bitch he's related to backs up all our stories."

Abica smelled the whiskey, looking more morose than his brother. Valentine thought he'd be sprayed a second time, but Abica drank it with a grimace. He shook his head. "I'm proud of Clip, sir. I'm proud of him. Dunno if I'd've done the same. I'm damn proud."

"How do you feel about yourself?"

"Like a shit."

"Welcome to the Cats, Abica."

"You don't owe me an explanation, sir," Post said later, in Valentine's tent. Valentine sighed, exhausted and wrung out. The faint smell of his whiskey shower made him feel like a barfly at last call. "But why didn't you just let the levee breach?"

The river was under control; the water level had stabilized.

Reports from upriver said within a day it should fall. The rest of the struggle would be a holding action. Valentine wanted to be on his back in his bunk, but he couldn't be that discourteous to a subordinate, friend or no. He sat on the edge of his cot, rubbing the prickly growth on his skull. Ahn-Kha made a clattering noise outside as he fashioned an oil-drum cook-stove that could double as a water heater.

"We're being watched. No, it's not one of my feelings, it's logic. It may be Xray-Tango, or the bat-winged bastards in the tower. I don't know if they're suspicious, or just trying to figure out what kind of officer I am. But I had to go above and beyond. Xray-Tango said he liked initiative; he's getting it. Not that I'm going to cry another river if the levee falls; it's just not going to happen on my watch, or in my view."

Post looked out the tent flap. The drizzle had finally stopped. "Back on the old *Thunderbolt* I swore I'd never wear their uniform, or help them, again. But I'm killing myself to save racks of shells so they can be fired on my new side. It gets stuck in my craw, Val."

"Have the men said anything?"

"Not even jokes, at least in my hearing. They're scared of giving anything away. I would be too, surrounded by an army and minus a gun."

"They're working as hard as they would have if they'd been captured and put in a labor camp."

"They're better fed. I've been over to the prison camp."

Valentine shot a glance up at Post, who looked like someone had just stepped on his corns. "When were you there?"

"Day after we got here. I asked for a review of female prisoners."

Post was easier to read than a billboard at ten feet. "Your wife?"

"I always figured she headed here. It was the nearest Freehold to Mississippi."

"Will, you'll drive yourself crazy if you start searching every face for her. I've had a . . . person in my life. Was in my life. She's caught up in this somewhere, but if I start thinking about her, I won't be able to concentrate. I have responsibilities now."

Post looked at him sidelong. "Where was she last?"

"A village called Weening, just west of Crowley's . . ." Valentine stopped.

"Only human to hope," Post said.

"Being human is a luxury, at least these days. Feelings. Attachments. They stop you from doing what's . . . what's necessary. Someone called Amu told me I wouldn't be one anymore when I became a Wolf. I must have misunderstood what he was talking about."

"How long have we known each other, Val?"

"What, a year and a half? Since I came on board the *Thunderbolt*."

"You're the most human person I've known since my wife. Except when you do what's 'necessary.'" Post meant by this the wild night when the Reapers came up from the old Kurian submarine, and after sinking it Valentine had shot the submarines sailors struggling in the oily water. His emotions turned gray and cold whenever he remembered.

Valentine wondered if he could unburden himself. Confessing to not just the things he'd done, but worse, that he'd enjoyed, even reveled in—

"Colonel! Colonel!"

The shout even overcame Ahn-Kha's metalwork.

Valentine cast a regretful look at his bunk.

"Come in. What is it, Lieutenant Purcel?"

The company officer saluted, gasping. "Overheard on the radio, sir . . . Blue Mountain dam's gone."

"Oh, Christ," Post said.

"Guerillas blow it?" Valentine asked.

"Just went."

"Mr. Post, get everyone up. I don't care if they've just spent twelve hours shoring sandbags. Everyone to the levee. If Mrs. Smalls's had her baby, I want her holding sandbags open. If it's a boy, I want him shoveling. Mr. Purcell, if the general doesn't know it, pass the word along. I respectfully suggest that he empty the prison compound, and get those buckets of lard at the wire—wait, strike the last."

"Pass the word to the general—" Purcell began.

"Don't bother, Mister Purcell. Just run."

Valentine looked around the little tent, touching the leather sack at his chest. *It might as well all be swept away, but what about the Quickwood?*

"Ahn-Kha," he called, pulling on his tunic.

"Yes, my David?"

"Have the men bring the Quickwood to the levy. We'll use it to shore up. If it gives way, have everyone grab on."

Valentine and Ahn-Kha raced up and down the camp, gathering the men and deflating the tents by pulling out the Quickwood center poles. He and the men ran to the levy, carrying the four-by-four beams in earnest rather than for exercise.

Styachowski was already putting the men to work. At other parts of the levee men were gathering, and Valentine walked the length, giving orders regardless of whose section it was. Farther back General Xray-Tango was organizing troops and prisoners alike, directing the flow of manpower to the dike.

The levee was already a sandbag sieve. Even Hank stood in the water, helping maneuver shoring timber against the sandbag wall. Farther down the levee a camouflage-painted bulldozer growled as it battled with the river, pushing walls of dirt against the drainage channel.

Valentine's men worked for hours, taking only handfuls of cold water from the river for refreshment. It was a blur of sandbagging and shoring for Valentine, all the while watching the debris-filled river as he slogged through the water on the other side of the levee. Darkness came, and still the river ran mad. Men began to drop to their knees in the water in exhaustion.

"We're losing it," Post said, watching Styachowski, up to her waist in water, direct shoring efforts. "I think it's going to go."

Valentine felt a personal animosity toward the river. It was like a living thing, determined to overcome him no matter how hard he drove himself and his men. "We're not beat yet."

Shouts and a scream. He spun to see a crowd jumping back from the levee, where part of a sandbag wall had collapsed.

"Get the bulldozer over here," Post yelled.

Valentine rushed to the site, Ahn-Kha joining him from the other side of the breach. A waterfall was coming through a notch in the levee; something had given way at the bottom and it had subsided.

"She's trapped, sir," one of the Jamaicans shouted. "It caught her on the legs as she fell."

"Who?" Valentine shouted.

"Styachowski," another said, forgetting to use her false name. "Captain Styachowski."

"It started to bulge and she jumped in with a shoring timber," Smalls said. "She was trying to place it—"

Valentine plunged into the swirling waters at the base of the fall, and began to feel around for her. He submerged. Under the water he felt a frantic hand grasp his. He pulled, but her body didn't yield. He felt around, and touched her face. Keeping a grip on her hand, he surfaced. Through cascading water, he looked up at the worried faces.

"Christ, get some of these bags away. I can feel her down there."

"That'll open the breach," a Quisling sergeant said.

"It's already opening."

Ahn-Kha plunged in next to him as Valentine shifted his back to protect Styachowski from the sandbags sliding off the pile. He felt her hand spasm in his.

The Golden One tore into the pile, hurling sandbags right and left. Others jumped in beside.

"No, Warren, more to your right, she's under here. Ahn-Kha, pull away just above my elbow. Watch your feet, you!"

The bulldozer approached, digging in and pushing a wall of dirt toward the rescuers.

"Hold that machine, dammit, I've got a man trapped!"

"Out of the way, sir, or when the breach caves you'll be trapped too," the Quisling sergeant shouted.

Valentine felt Styachowski's hand go limp in his. He screamed through the water falling all around him.

"What's going on?" Xray-Tango called, coming around the mound of dirt pushed by the bulldozer."

"She's trapped," Ahn-Kha said. "Officer Wagner," he added, remembering to use her false name.

"How long's she been under?" *Blink-blink-bliiink.*

"Five minutes, maybe," someone said.

"She's dead then," the Quisling sergeant said. "Bring that bulldozer forward."

"No! I've got her hand."

"Wait, Sergeant," Xray-Tango said. Valentine met his eyes, pleading with him. Xray-Tango shifted his gaze to the bulldozer, held up a hand. Then to Valentine: "Hurry, Le Sain."

Ahn-Kha plunged into the water and found the shoring timber Styachowski had been maneuvering. Valentine watched the Grog's back, matted fur shedding water, and saw muscles heave. The pile shifted. Knotted shoulders breached, and Ahn-Kha took a breath.

"Help me, you bastards," Ahn-Kha gasped. Valentine felt something give.

Valentine heaved at the lifeless hand, terribly limp in his. She began to move. He prayed she didn't have compound fractures in her trapped legs; she'd end up looking like Narcisse, even if she wasn't paralyzed.

Anxious arms helped him bring her up out of the water. Valentine laid her out on the mound of dirt pushed up by the bulldozer.

"Work the breach, back to work," Xray-Tango shouted. The men and a smattering of prisoners started relaying sandbags. The bulldozer backed off and approached again from a new direction, digging into the ground.

Valentine saw none of it. There was just Styachowski, pale and limp beneath him, blue-faced and mottle-cheeked. He cleaned the froth from her mouth.

"Push on her legs and get the water out of her lungs," someone suggested.

Ahn-Kha knelt next to Styachowski, panting, water streaming from his body.

Valentine lifted his ear from Styachowski's chest. "That doesn't work," Valentine said, bending back her head. "Get a blanket, a dry one." He turned her head up, explored her mouth with a finger, and put his lips to hers. He forced air into her lungs.

"Get a medic, too," Xray-Tango shouted at the soldier going for a blanket.

"Ahn-Kha, push on her chest, here," Valentine said, indicating a spot. "Don't be gentle about it." He pressed his lips to her cold mouth again.

The Golden One worked her heart.

"Should we rub her hands and feet?" Xray-Tango asked.

"No," Valentine said between breaths. He was too busy to explain that it would draw blood away to the skin. She needed it in her brain, not her limbs.

Minutes in the wet dark passed, or perhaps just seconds. Hours? The only thing that mattered to Valentine were breaths, air into Styachowski's flooded lungs. Whatever time it took to run and get blankets had passed; the soldier returned with an armload.

Her eyes fluttered and opened. She coughed and heaved. Valentine rolled her on her side, and a mass of water and vomit came up. He held Styachowski through a series of wracking coughs, pulling blankets around her.

"Styachowski?" Valentine said as the coughing ebbed. Behind him the bulldozer was pushing the mountain of sandbags back into place. Valentine heard a beam snap and winced—he hoped that wasn't one of the Quickwood supports smashed.

Styachowski turned her face to see who was holding her. "God, Val—" she began. Valentine pressed his lips to hers, shutting her up. Xray-Tango turned away, perhaps embarrassed, and began to shout orders to the men helping the bulldozer. Valentine released her from the kiss.

"Dreams," Styachowski said.

"What's that?"

"Dreams," she said, and gathered herself. She burped, and

glanced up at Valentine apologetically. "The wall fell on me, and I had dreams, or something. It was warm and pleasant, like I was being held by my mother as a baby. Then I woke up and you were there. Except my legs hurt."

A medic knelt at her feet. He ran his hands up her right leg, gently rolling it. He repeated with the left, and Styachowski cried out.

"There's a break. I don't think it's bad. Simple fracture; I don't feel any protrusions. We've got to get her on a stretcher."

"*Hsssssssssss!*" Styachowski sucked in air, closing her eyes. "It's throbbing. Am I bleeding?"

The medic splinted her. "It's the fibula, I think. Her knee's tore up, too. Abrasions."

"No, you're wet, you're not bleeding," Valentine said after looking at her legs. "Not badly. Bring the stretcher here."

The medic finished fixing the splint. Valentine took her shoulders and the medic her legs, and lifted her onto the stretcher.

"The infirmary at headquarters," the medic said to the men who took up the handles. "There's no hurry. Don't jog her."

"You can go too, Le Sain," Xray-Tango said, appearing at his shoulder. "Your captain there has things in hand."

"The breach?"

"God knows."

"Then I'll stay."

Like a close-fought battle, or a football match where the lead changes hands, the issue hung in doubt until the next morning, when once again the water stabilized. Then it fell, at a pace that could almost be measured with the naked eye.

"I wonder if something gave way farther down the river?" Post said, eating bread and cheese with dirty fingers as they sat together on a ready pile of sandbags.

"Some old Corps of Engineers dike," Valentine said. "Or Pine Bluff landing is underwater now." He was too tired to care about the whys; all that mattered were the whats. And the big what was that the water was going down.

The men were asleep in the mud all around, heads cushioned on sandbags or backpacks. The scattered groups of prisoners slept in huddles, like wallows full of pigs.

"You going to check on Styachowski, sir?"

"We should see about reorganizing the men. Work out some shifts. Wish we'd get some fresh bodies from the other side of the river."

Post stretched his arms and yawned. "They have problems of their own. The River Rats are flooded out."

"River Rats? I've heard that before, somewhere."

"The boatmen who work the barges and small craft. They've got a little town over there, from what they tell me. A couple of bars, music and girls included, a slop-house. Bona fide red-light district, sounds like. Some of the other soldiers go across for a good time, or to do a little black-market trading. They smuggle, too, of course."

"The soldiers or the River Rats?"

"Both, I suppose."

"I was wondering where Xray-Tango got his coffee," Valentine said. "Being in the Caribbean spoiled me. I've got a taste for the stuff, now."

"I'm ready to go back," Post said. "You're probably right. I'll never find her."

"Southern Command's not dead yet. There's Styachowski to think of, too."

"Go check on her, if you like. Ahn-Kha and I'll hold the dike."

Styachowski was asleep, her leg already in a cast, and after speaking to a nurse about her Valentine made himself comfortable. She was the only one occupying a bed in the infirmary; the real field hospital was on the other side of the river, in the old library. The nurses were keeping busy bandaging bashed fingers and wrapping sprains. A ruptured man groaned as the doctor probed his crotch.

Valentine made the mistake of putting his feet on her bed. The next thing he knew he was being kicked in the leg.

"Colonel," Styachowski said. "You're snoring."

He massaged the bridge of his nose until his eyes felt like focusing again. "Is it light out? How's the pain?"

"Better. They gave me a shot and I went out like a light. Codeine or morphine, I think. It's morning now. We're still in the dispensary, so I guess the levee held."

"The water was receding last night."

"New Columbia lives."

His stomach growled. "Aren't they going to feed you something? Wait, I'll go myself."

After retrieving bread, honey, and some kind of cooked cereal from the headquarters kitchen, he returned to Styachowski.

"You broke a leg once, sir?"

"No. It wasn't for lack of trying."

"You limp. I thought maybe—"

"An old wound. Line of duty."

Styachowski nodded. "You'll have to tell the story someday."

"When you're better."

"That'll be the day. I'm always down with something. If it's not a cold I've got a fever.

There was a long pause in the conversation while they ate. Valentine had never shared a meal in silence with a woman before. She probably needed to sleep again. "Can I get you anything before I go, Wagner?"

She shook her head, and Valentine relaxed a little, seeing her respond to her assumed name even under the influence of the painkiller. "No, thank you, sir. There is one thing though."

"What's that."

Styachowski glanced around the infirmary. "What's the policy here? Do they shoot the crippled horses, or send them . . . somewhere else?"

"Don't be silly. You're not getting out of my outfit that easy. I'm not going to let anything happen to anyone in my command. Especially to someone hurt doing her duty. The battalion's not going anywhere without you."

She sank back into her pillow. "Thanks, Colonel."

"I'll see if I can get you put back in your tent. You'd be more comfortable there, I think."

"Thank you, sir. But not just for that."

Valentine arched an eyebrow; she blushed and buried her face in her mush bowl.

"You wanted to see me, General?" Valentine asked

Xray-Tango thrust a curious, umbrellalike apparatus into the ground. It was a five-foot pole with four arms projecting from the top. At the end of each arm hung a string with a washer tied to the end. The spear end, currently buried in the dirt of what had been an underpass, was tipped with metal.

Styachowski was back in the tent she shared with a female sergeant. The ground had dried up, and the river was down feet, not just inches. Mrs. Smalls was expected to deliver within hours. Men still worked the levee, but life was returning to what passed for normal in Consul Solon's Trans-Mississippi KZ.

Xray-Tango smiled. "I hope this isn't a bad time. I'll try not to keep you too long. Technically, I'm off duty. I keep what used to be called 'business hours.' "

"Curtiz said that, but he told me that I could find you here right now. I'm used to coming immediately when sent for. I'll be in first thing tomorrow, if you'd rather, General."

"No need. Unless you had plans for the evening."

"Maybe a trip to the screen center."

The south side of the river had two common rooms with projector screens, one for officers and the other for enlisted ranks. The soldiers lounged on everything from club chairs to old sofas watching the impossibly vivid colors on the pull-down screen. Valentine had put in an appearance at the officers' screen center and learned about the designer of a new riot bus, a biography of a woman who had produced an astonishing sixteen children, then an inspirational speech by a colonel who had won a brass ring in the rugged mountains in what had been West Virginia. He left to walk past Xray-Tango's headquarters and poked his head in the enlisted room, where a video of dancing showgirls on a Memphis stage had the packed soldiers drooling. An advertisement for a reenlistment bonus all-expense-paid trip to Memphis played immediately following. He hadn't gone back since and didn't intend to.

"Give the popcorn a miss. I think the butter is reclaimed machine oil."

"If you don't mind me asking," Valentine said, "what are you doing?"

"I started out as a section chief on the railroad. I still like to survey. You do anything to clear your head, Le Sain?"

"I swing an ax. To cut wood. I like turning big ones into little ones."

"I would have guessed music. Something artistic. There's a look in your eyes that makes me think you're the creative type. For Christ's sake, at ease, Le Sain. This is a chat, not an ass-chewing."

"Music's a good guess, sir. My mother used to sing. I had a little . . . recorder, that's what it was called. A recorder I'd play. Since you said this is just a chat, can I ask what that thing is, sir?"

"It's called a *groma*. It's an old Roman surveying tool. They used it to make straight lines. Works good for corners, too, but it's best for staking out roads." He leaned over, hands on thighs, to eyeball the lines strung with washers at the end, comparing them with the shaft. When he was satisfied that it was level, he sighted down the *groma* and waved a private holding a flag over a step to the right.

"No fancy optics," Xray-Tango went on. "The Romans built their roads straight, using that doohickey."

"They were great road builders, weren't they?"

"Yes. The old United States interstate system only built about half the miles that the old Roman network had. If you leave total lanes out of account, I imagine. They would have caught up, if they'd lasted as long as the Romans."

"Kur took care of that," Valentine said, keeping his voice carefully neutral.

Xray-Tango waited for another twitch to pass, then signaled to his private to place the little red-flagged stake. "You've had the usual indoctrination, I suppose."

"It varies from place to place."

"What's your wrist-cuff crib on it?"

Valentine had heard the Kurian catechism so often he was able to repeat it without thinking, half believing it. It had been drilled into him, twice weekly, at the community center meetings and Universal Church lectures in his time in the Zone. "Our planet was dying. War. Overpopulation. Pollution. Disease out of control. Mother Earth had a cancer called the human race. They came in and restored balance, brought order to the chaos. Kur did for us what we couldn't do for ourselves. Over half the population has proper food, shelter and health care now; everyone in care has access to the doctor. There are even dentists in a lot of places. New Orleans, for example. In Natchez we had to go to a plumber to get a tooth taken out."

"You know the words. You ever think about it?"

Valentine looked around to see if they were being overheard. "I think history gets written by the winners. The Old Regime had its problems, but they made some beautiful stuff. How many engines they built fifty or sixty years ago still run? Lots. If Kur makes anything that wonderful, they're keeping it to themselves. What's made now is clumsy by comparison, even when it works."

"The terrorists? The renegades?"

"They're right about them. Most of them are just misled. They don't know the Reapers are like white blood cells in an organism. If a piece of the body isn't working right, if it doesn't belong, if it's dead wood, it gets taken out to keep the rest of the system healthy."

"So you don't have problems with the system." He waved his assistant farther away to plant another stake.

Valentine's dancing heart missed a step. He'd found that among people who disliked the Kurians, they put a little extra stress on the phrase "the system" as a way of sounding out others who might share unorthodox opinions.

I've been running my mouth again. Is this a trap? Does he

want to see how far I'll step into the noose? The problem was, he liked Xray-Tango for some reason, and when he liked someone, the dam on his garrulousness broke. This time, a breach could cost every man in his command his life. He needed to stuff a sandbag in his mouth, block it up like the river, before his tongue hung them all.

"I've done well under it," Valentine said, after a pause he hoped didn't betray him as thinking about his answer too much.

"Nothing's perfect under the sun. Come to think of it, even the sun up there isn't quite round. It's a bubbling sphere. Sends out some long arms of superheated gas now and then, if you look at it close. But the governors and their Reapers are in the here and now, not millions of miles away. When you're close to them, just like with the sun, sometimes you see the flaws. But we're a stronger civilization, thanks to them. Even if the system's ugly at times, doesn't work as fairly as it should."

"Are you saying something's wrong with the system, General?"

"I suppose I am, in a roundabout way. Thing is, if something doesn't work right, you either throw it away or you fix it. The poor bastards who used to live in this part of the country, they tried to get rid of it. It got rid of them, instead. I'm sure you've noticed as you get higher in the ranks it becomes more seductive. You know who Nietzsche was?"

"Ummm . . ." Valentine knew, but he wanted to let Xray-Tango talk.

"He talked about supermen, beyond old concepts of good or evil. You get to feel that way after a while. Beyond law, because there really isn't one, except don't cross the Kurians. Beyond morality, since there's no one to censure you—and as long as you do your job right the Higher Ups won't."

Valentine felt his admiration for Xray-Tango ebb. He'd heard too many upper ranks in New Orleans talk this way. *The supermen rise, and decide who shall rise behind them. The others have to die.* "Freedom," Valentine said.

"Yes, it's damn near perfect freedom. I've got a brass ring, so I know what I'm talking about. But you know what? While most use their freedom to put on airs, or lose themselves in drink, or vice—hell, I know a colonel who screws little boys and girls—some of us use it to improve things. You can improve the system. Not all at once, and maybe not outside where you hold whatever authority you've climbed to, but you can make a difference. Tell you the truth, Le Sain, it's pretty satisfying, helping those who don't have a choice about anything."

Valentine stood silently, until it became clear Xray-Tango expected him to say something. "I'm not going to argue with anything you've said, sir. But why are you telling me this, General?"

Xray-Tango turned. He accidentally bumped his *groma* and, before it fell, caught it up again in a blur of motion. Valentine hadn't seen anyone move like that, anyone who wasn't tuned up by the Lifeweavers, that is. Now he knew how Xray-Tango won all those trophies. He wondered if he was looking into the mismatched eyes of a Cat, deep undercover.

"I'm telling you this, Le Sain, because I've taken a shine to you. You're a good officer. I've decided I want you in my command. You'll have an enviable place in New Columbia— in the new Trans-Mississippi, one day. I want to put men in place who think like I do. Maybe together, we can build something worthwhile. Consul Solon's got the vision, he just needs men who can help him carry it out."

"Thank you, sir. But I've promised my command a chance to distinguish themselves, at least doing something other than hunting down the moonshiners."

"Are they that eager, or is their commander?"

"Action means promotion," Valentine said.

"You may get your chance soon. We're going to activate your brigade, refit them as light infantry. Once we've gotten through the final push up those mountains, we'll be in a position to promote you. Maybe even get you the ring you're sparking on."

"Thank you, sir."

"It's not quite as easy as that. You still need to speak to someone before you formally join AOT Combat Corps. Trust me, you'll come through with flying colors. You're intelligent, and you've already proven yourself where it counts. He might test you some more, but don't worry; I passed it and I'm sure you can, too."

Xray-Tango shouted to his assistant, "Sun's dying, son. Let's call it a day. We'll finish laying out the quad tomorrow." He picked up his Roman surveyor and shouldered it. "Hungry, Colonel?"

"I could eat."

"Good. Maybe our little meeting would go better over dinner."

Had Consul Solon slipped in early? The rumor, spread up and down the slop-pail lines, was that Solon was due in New Columbia, to check on plans for construction of his new capital city and especially his Consular Residence on the north bank of the Arkansas. He'd heard grumbling from the engineering officers, who were still clearing rubble with a single bulldozer while Solon's engineers had a crane, backhoe, cement mixer, and "the good dozers" up on his hilltop west of town. Supposedly, plans for the final push against the remnants of Southern Command were to be outlined, giving the generals in the field time to work out the details once the general strategy was handed down. Boats were already ferrying men from the hospital to clear bed space.

The worst cases went to the seashell-like tower still under construction. Some said that afterward their bones ended up in the cement mortar.

As they walked back to Xray-Tango's headquarters, Valentine marshaled his arguments to petition for a role in the offensive; he wanted all the operational knowledge he could get. The fact that Xray-Tango had offered to arm and activate his men could mean that the battalion was to take part.

The general led him past his sentries. His headquarters still buzzed with activity, though there were fewer present to be busy. Instead of taking Valentine to his corner office the general led him down a set of stairs, along a whitewashed warren of corridors, and around a corner to another sentry. This one had a different uniform than the other rough-and-ready soldiers in the general's command. He wore a dark, crisp uniform that was a cross between old Marine Corps dress blues and an SS ceremonial uniform. A bullpup assault rifle came to present as the general rapped on the door and opened it.

So Consul Solon's got his own version of the Praetorian Guard, Valentine thought as he passed in. He readied his mind for the interview with the new administrator of the Trans-Mississippi.

Then he stopped. This was an interrogation room. Complete with mirror at one end, a desk and a waiting chair.

Sitting behind the table in the bare little semicell was a Reaper.

Chapter Seven

New Columbia, March of the forty-eighth year of the Kurian Order: The Reapers.

For the residents of any Kurian Zone, fear of the Reapers is as natural an instinct as hunger, thirst, need for sleep or sexual desire. The Reapers come and go as they please, the eyes, ears, mouth and appetite of their vampire masters from Kur. Pale-skinned, yellow-eyed and black-fanged, one might think they had been designed to inspire dread; death incarnate, as painted with the fearful symmetry of Bosch. And one would be right. The Reapers are designed and grown by Kur to be their avatars among the human race, for the process of extracting the vital auras the Kurians use to extend their lifespan into immortality. When animating one of their Reapers, the Reaper is the Kurian and the Kurian a Reaper, the ultimate version of a puppet. The symbiotes consume humans—the Reaper feeding off of blood, and the Kurians restoring themselves through the energy created by all sentient beings. Even a plant gives off vital aura, though in such minuscule quantities that only one Kurian Valentine had ever heard of managed to exist off of it, and even that was at the cost of lassitude and an addict's pangs. Like their brother Lifeweavers, divided millennia ago by the great schism over immortality gained through consuming sentients, a Kurian can appear to humans in many forms, but even this is not sufficient to protect their precious lives—all the more valuable thanks to their belief that they've cheated entropy. So for the dangerous work of mingling with, and feeding off, humans, they employ a team of Reapers, going from consciousness to consciousness and place to place the way a pre-2022 human might flip cable channels.

The Reapers are instruments built to last. Cablelike muscles are fixed to a skeleton as light as ceramic and strong as high-tensile steel. They're strong enough to take apart a car without tools, and can run faster than a horse from the time the sun goes down to dawn. They wear heavy robes and cowls of bullet-absorbing material. Daylight is not deadly to either them or the Kurians, though it interferes with the link between puppet and master, and obscures lifesign, the ethereal emanations created by vital aura that the avatars use to home in on prey. So the Reapers restrict their dark purposes to the sunless hours.

Like the night David Valentine came in for his interview with a vampire.

"*have a seat, mr. knox le sain,*" the Reaper hissed. It had a dry, menacing voice, like old bones grinding against each other. Its skin had all the life and animation of a rubber mask; its heavy robes had a faint mustiness, but a sharper smell—like hospital disinfectant—came from the sleeve holes and cowl. Piss-colored eyes, as cold and unblinking as a lizard's, fixed on him. The Reaper's gaze escorted him into the room.

"Colonel Knox Le Sain, my lord," Valentine corrected, sitting in the armless chair across from evil. The presence of a Reaper made the everyday motion into a fall. It was poised, still, and every instinct in Valentine's gut told him that it would spring into action, a praying mantis going after an unwary fly. He wondered how many fearful tells could be read on his face, and tried to assume the complacency of one who is used to conversation with a Reaper.

"*that remains to be decided. do you know to whom you are speaking?*" The Reaper's face had all the expression of an Easter Island monolith.

"I haven't had the privilege of your lordship's acquaintance."

"I can handle introductions," Xray-Tango broke in. "Le Sain, you're in the presence of the governor of New Columbia, Lord Mu-Kur-Ri. You understand how this"—*blink-blink-bliiink*—"errr, works?"

"I know I'm speaking to his lordship's vehicle for inter-acting with us. At least that's how it was explained to me."

"you're nervous, le sain." The Reaper used a quiet monotone, so Valentine wasn't sure if it was a question or a statement.

"Put yourself in my shoes. Wouldn't you be?"

"we are beyond emotion. you need not be frightened. we simply wish to thank you for your service in our recent flooding. had the warehouses and their stores been lost, our preparations would have been delayed. it is time for this territory to be pacified, once and for all. it has already taken far too long. one concern remains."

Sometimes the Kurians liked to toy with their food. Valentine wondered if the ax was just slow to fall in this case, or if the creature was speaking the truth.

"What concern?" Valentine asked. He tried to lower his lifesign, worried that the Kurians could use it as a lie detector of some sort. He imagined jamming all his fear into a blue bag he could reduce to the size of a marble that he could carry about in his pocket.

"the origins of your ghost commission. our cousins in louisiana do not care to cooperate with us in tracing you. certain inconsistencies need to be explained."

Valentine tried not to react at the word "ghost," his code name. "Guilty. I'm not a colonel. I was a captain once, but I got busted back to the ranks. Got involved with the wrong man's daughter. I heard you needed men fast. Figured it would be a chance at a new start, fresh ground."

"Sort of a Foreign Legion, Le Sain?" Xray-Tango said. "Not a bad idea. They've got one of those on the Mexican border with California. From what I hear it's a success."

"the aztlan rangers do not concern us in the trans-mississippi, general. tell me, le sain, how are you at following orders? do you put your ambition ahead of your lord's trust?"

"My main ambition was to get out of the swamp. Then

find a position where there was a chance of promotion. Done and done. You've already shown yourself hell-and-gone better than their lordships in Louisiana and Natchez. Food and uniforms are both an improvement up here. You said something about a reward?"

"we shall get to that. but where are my manners, colonel? general, have some food brought in."

Xray-Tango left. *"he is an efficient officer,"* Mu-Kur-Ri's caped mouthpiece said. *"he carries out orders intelligently. you would do wise to learn from him, in all things save one. he is a blade lacking an edge."*

"Meaning?"

"he is shy of the hard decisions that come with a man of his position and responsibilities. at times, to keep a machine running smoothly, worn-out parts must be replaced. do you think you could do better?"

Valentine shook his head. "No. I've shot a few men in the back, but I'm not much at stabbing them there. Running a command of this size isn't in the cards; I don't have the know-how." Valentine smiled. "At least, not now."

"then you have the spine to do what is necessary in our service?"

"Try me," Valentine said.

A soldier knocked and entered, bearing a tray of sandwiches and milk, carefully averting his eyes. Xray-Tango followed him in, carrying a coffeepot and a bottle filled with amber fluid.

"Sandwiches are all we keep handy here, Le Sain. I thought a toast might be in order, to welcome him to our command."

"we too wish to join your repast."

The soldier set down the tray, almost bowling Xray-Tango out of the way in his hurry to make it out the door. He mumbled an apology under his breath and a promise to look for dessert.

"Yes, my lord?" Xray-Tango said.

"le sain, a woman in your camp has just given birth. the squalling morsels are most delectable when new and slip-

pery. go to your camp and retrieve it at once. general, go with him, and impress upon him our need."

Valentine rose from the seat on shaking legs.

"Come along, son," Xray-Tango said. "Let's not keep his lordship waiting."

They went through the headquarters, grim-faced and silent. Only when they were out in the darkness of the rubble-lined streets did they speak again.

Xray-Tango's eye twitched as quickly as an experienced operator could tap out Morse. "I didn't know that was coming, Le Sain. I figured they'd test you somehow. Had no idea that would be it."

"I've turned people in to them before, sir. But never an infant."

"Trust me, Le Sain. Don't think about it, just do it. Dealing with it beforehand just causes problems. Deal with it afterward."

"Voice of experience, sir?" Valentine asked, bitterness creeping into his voice despite himself.

"Just keep walking."

Valentine felt like sticking a knife into the general. He'd grown to respect the man; Xray-Tango was the first Quisling superior he'd ever met who inspired anything other than contempt and loathing. To see him so blasé about turning a newborn over to a Reaper . . . Perhaps he could stick him with words. "You might like to know he probed me about replacing you."

"I know. I asked his lordship to bring the subject up. How did you respond?"

"I said I wasn't up to it. At least right now."

"Le Sain, we're just sounding you out. There's ambition, and then there's ambition. If it drives you to be your best, that's great. If it drives you to try and undermine your superiors, well, I've still got that order in my desk."

"Sign it. I'm not handing that child over to him."

"Keep walking. I told you to shut up and trust me. Look, I didn't just have him ask you about that to see if you were the kind of person to supplant me, given the opportunity.

I've got my ring now. I'm thinking about getting a piece of land and leaving all this someday. Not until we're established here, and not until I think I've got someone in place who thinks like me. Just trust me."

Valentine subsided into silence. He was sick of these conversations in the Kurian Zones, the questions and interviews with a purpose under a motive wrapped up in a trap. He missed the easier days of his service in Southern Command, surrounded by men he knew to be his friends, when every word out of his mouth didn't have to be parsed and weighed.

The Smalls had a little shell of a tent next to the hut Narcisse was turning into a larder. Mr. Smalls had been posing as a camp tinkerer, mending everything from boots to cots for the men. Valentine had thought they would escape notice, just part of the flotsam and jetsam every camp accumulated, civilians who begged a living doing odd jobs the ranks didn't wish to be troubled with. Candles burned within.

"Wait out here, please, sir," Valentine said. Xray-Tango's eye blinked, and he turned up his collar against the chill night air. Valentine turned to the tent. "It's Colonel Le Sain. May I come in?"

"We've got a healthy baby girl in here, sir," Narcisse called.

Valentine entered. "My respects, Mr. Smalls, Mrs. Smalls. Hank."

"This is the thirtieth baby I've brought into this world, Colonel. But this one's the most beautiful I've ever seen. Isn't she something?" Narcisse said. "She's just perfect."

Valentine looked at the little red thing, puffy and sqinteyed. "Mrs. Smalls is the one deserving of the applause," he said. Mrs. Smalls, sweat-soaked and red, managed a smile.

Valentine foreed the next words out. "I came myself because I was worried that if a nurse and some soldiers showed up, you'd be frightened. But every new baby needs its footprints taken, its name and place of birth recorded. It's the rules here. I thought I'd handle it myself, so I could expedite the paperwork and get your baby back to you as soon as possible."

Judas Iscariot, meet your spiritual scion, David Stuart Valentine, he thought to himself.

"That's nice of you, sir, but does it have to be tonight?" Mr. Smalls asked.

"Afraid so. It's to your advantage; as soon as the baby's recorded, you get the extra rations."

"Strikey!" Hank said. A growing teen's appetite was hard to reconcile with ration coupons.

Valentine knelt at the bedside. Though perhaps "bedside" wasn't the correct word, since little Mrs. Smalls lay on the floor, atop a mixture of old rugs and blankets, reinforced with pillows and cushions.

Valentine had to find a way to avoid Narcisse's eyes. "Did you see the birth, Hank?"

"No. My dad said I'd be in the way. Ahn-Kha helped me make a crutch for Styachowski."

"For who?" Valentine said. *Was the general listening to the conversation?*

"Captain Wagner," Hank corrected himself.

"That's more like it, Hank."

Mrs. Smalls bit her lip as Valentine pulled the baby from her breast. Narcisse had put the newborn in a cocoon.

"I should go along," Mr. Smalls said.

"Sorry, Mr. Smalls, it's past curfew for civilians. Don't forget, your status here is sort of informal. I don't want any more questions asked than the absolute minimum."

"Keep her out of the wind. Let me wrap her some more," Narcisse said, her voice quavering.

"I'll take good care of her," Valentine said. The bland lies were coming easier now. He took the blanket from Narcisse and together they put the infant under another layer. He got up and turned for the tent flap. The sooner he was away from Narcisse's eyes the better.

"Don't you need to know her name?" Mrs. Smalls said. Doubt crept up her face and seated itself between her eyes like a biting centipede.

Valentine felt like slapping himself. "Oh, yes, I do. I don't imagine you want to call her Jane Doe for the next sixteen years." The newborn began to make mewing noises.

"We've settled on Caroline," Mr. Smalls said.

"Okay, baby Caroline it is," Valentine said. "Back as soon as I can." He fled the tent.

General Xray-Tango had to double-time to keep up with him. "You're a helluva liar, Le Sain."

"I come from a long line of liars. We've gotten good at it over the last two thousand years."

The general either didn't understand the veiled New Testament reference or chose to ignore it. "Take it easy, Le Sain. It'll all be over soon. Then we'll get busy outfitting your command. Better days are ahead."

The baby was crying now: a tiny, coughing sound. She was so light! Valentine felt like he was carrying a loaf of bread in the blankets. Chances were he'd never get to hold his own daughter—if it was a daughter—and he wondered if she'd be as active as Caroline, who at the moment seemed to be fighting some internal discomfort. An impossibly tiny hand waved at him.

"For you and me. What about Caroline here?"

"Don't think about that now. Think about that tomorrow. You're following orders, remember that."

Following orders. The old out. But did he have a choice at this moment? He didn't so much as have his sidearm; wearing weapons was discouraged in camp for everyone not on police detail. It led to questions. He had a clasp knife in his pocket; he could kill the general and get his camp up. But how far would they get, unarmed, with a Reaper expecting him back? He sensed another one somewhere near the general's headquarters, aboveground and moving. For all he knew he was being watched at this moment. Maybe a dash west to Finner's Wolves—

No. It would be death for his command, and at the moment he was too rubber-legged with the thought of it to even run. He had to weigh his men's lives against that of the featherweight newborn. It came with the responsibility he'd first shouldered in Captain Le Havre's sitting room over a cool beer. If by some magic he were able to go back in time to that moment, he'd have turned him down and shouldered a rifle as a plain Wolf with Zulu Company. No decisions to make, just orders to follow. But wasn't that the same cop-out that had begun this line of thought? All he could manage was to plod next to Xray-Tango.

As his mind came full circle, he and Xray-Tango returned to the headquarters building.

"Steady now, Colonel. I've told you it'll be all right," Xray-Tango said, as they stood at the stairs leading down to the lower level. Valentine distracted himself by looking at the pattern of the cinder blocks in the walls. This was pre-2022 construction, certainly. There were conduits and plumbing fixtures going deeper into the earth. The Quislings, while clearing rubble above, were making use of the infrastructure below that survived the nuclear blast.

The Reaper had not moved since they left. It might have been a wax figure, sitting with palms flat on the table and head tilted slightly back, were it not for the eyes that opened at their entrance.

"give us the child, and let us fill our need," Mu-Kur-Ri's avatar said. The yellow eyes locked on Valentine. He felt a weightless, falling sensation, as though the slit-pupiled eyes were turning into canyons, the veins leading to them rivers, the yellow irises burning deserts. He was falling toward them, into them. The only thing he could put between his eyes and the Reaper's was the child. He held it out, breaking whatever hypnotic conduit drew him.

The Reaper took the baby. Gravity returned to the floor; Valentine's mind was his own again.

"There, you've got your answer, my lord—" Xray-Tango began, before choking on his words when the Reaper's hinged jaw went wide, like a snake preparing to eat an egg. It ripped away the swaddling clothes with a hand, opening the tiny girl's chest. The newborn had time for one brief cry, stifled instantly as the Reaper buried its face in the baby.

Valentine heard a soft suckling sound. He held himself up with the table.

Xray-Tango went white as a sheet. "Je—" he began, before staggering back against the wall. He slid down it as though he'd been shot.

The feeding didn't take long. Valentine counted vein pulses in the Reaper's pallid hand, held against the dead baby's bottom. After seven it lowered the child and closed its blood-smeared mouth. The yellow eyes were no longer dangerous, just drunken.

"most exquisite. when fresh there is a blend, a residual of the mother's full, mature body overlain with the delicate new energy. it sparkles, it sparkles. . . ." The Kurian lord favored Valentine with a grin.

Death discussed as one would a wine tasting left Valentine cold and nauseated. "If your lordship has no—" Valentine began.

"It wasn't supposed to be like that," Xray-Tango said, trying to stand on his feet but failing. He sat with his back to the wall, arm around a wastebasket.

"general, the idea of you setting conditions on my actions . . . it's just impossible. i hope you do not need a further lesson."

"But you agreed, this was just a test, the baby wasn't to be hurt."

"it didn't suffer," the thing said, approaching Xray-Tango. It dropped the drained newborn into the wastebasket with a empty, wet *thunk*. *"if, after all this time, you haven't learned that we take what we want, when we want it, per-*
•*haps—"*

The Reaper grabbed Xray-Tango by the scruff of the neck and lifted him like a kitten.

"No, I've got my ring, you can't!"

"i wasn't going to," it hissed. *"stop the games, general. this shell game you play with the pows, it stops from this moment. be grateful for them, otherwise we'd be more rigorous in looking for sustenance elsewhere."*

"It's for your lordship to say, of course. But in Texas and

Oklahoma, you took so few. I thought that's all you required."

"we limited ourselves out of necessity. better times are here; we will enjoy the fat years as we made do during the lean ones. more prisoners, general. if you want to keep us happy, and keep your ring, you'll gather more prisoners. the lives are up in the mountains. go up and bring us them to fill our need."

"I've made everything ready here. Logistics aren't holding us up anymore; it's the wet."

The Reaper turned to Valentine. *"le sain, we are told you hunger for combat command. distinguish yourself, bring the remainder out of the mountains, and you'll have a ring too."*

At last, a chance at honesty. "I'm ready to fight," Valentine said. Some of the warmth returned to his stomach. "Give us the guns. We'll show you what we can do."

"Consul Solon will deliver the Trans-Mississippi as promised, my lord. This isn't a riot, or a collective farm that's grabbed a truckload of rifles. Those are trained soldiers in those mountains, and damn tough ones, man-for-man. If you want those troops alive and functional at the end of this, we have to go about it properly."

"we are weary of reasons not to fight. general, it is our will that the colonel be transferred to a combat corps, as soon as his men can be readied. you will turn your fat clerks into riflemen, your construction engineers into artillerists. consul solon allows too much haft and not enough point on this spear he has forged; the terrorists should have been subdued long before now. there is disorder in texas. our cousins in illinois look across the great river with hungry eyes. new orleans hopes for us to hollow ourselves so they may fill the void should we collapse. the campaign must be brought to a conclusion, or even those with rings will be held accountable. now go and consider how you will do this."

Valentine wanted nothing more than to return to his cot and sleep. Sleep would bring oblivion. No more memories of the wriggling infant in his arms, or the blood being flicked from the tongue of the Reaper as it returned to its mouth.

Xray-Tango wouldn't let him out of the office. The general stood, holding himself up on his trophy sideboard, fish-mouthing as though he were about to vomit on his awards.

"I swear to you, Knox, on my mother's grave, I didn't know he was going to do that to the baby. We thought it up as just a test. See if you'd do it. If I'd known he really wanted it, I would have taken it myself. I can't let someone else do something like that. God, I've served them for twenty-three years. That's the worst thing I've ever seen."

Valentine looked out the window and saw Solon's banner on the pole in front of the entrance. In the distance, across the graded rubble, the bone white Kurian Tower shone in the glare of spotlights.

"Then you haven't seen much, sir."

"Well, maybe it was the worst thing I'd seen happen. We came across some bodies once—jeez, that's no conversation for a night like this. C'mon and have a drink. Steady our nerves."

"I've got to go see the parents. Want to come along and explain how it was all a mistake, sir?"

Valentine's icy tone stiffened the general. "You don't have to say anything to them. If they start anything, the MPs can—"

"No, I've got to do it myself."

"You're the opposite of my other officers, Le Sain. You avoid the pleasurable, and you take on the worst jobs yourself."

" 'If you want to prosper, do the difficult.' "

"Who said that?"

"My father."

He left Xray-Tango, passed through the wooden Indians in the headquarters manning late-night communications desks, and walked back to the battalion's camp. Dogs barked at each other in the distance as he crossed the scored scab on the old earth that was Little Rock.

He entered his "battalion" camp. He took no pride in the condition of the tents, the cleanliness and order, or even the painted river rocks along the pathway, markers his old marine contingent had made.

Candles still glowed within the tent. Valentine heard the regular breathing of Hank, and Mr. Smalls' soft snores.

"Ahem. Mrs. Smalls, may I come in?"

"How is she? That wasn't too long," the mother's voice answered. "Please come in."

Valentine let her absence from his arms speak as he entered.

"Mr. and Mrs. Smalls, I'm sorry. It's Caroline. There was a terrible accident. I was going down some stairs to the . . ."

The scream from Mrs. Smalls woke Hank and brought Mr. Smalls to his feet.

"It's a lie! It's a lie! Where is she?" Mrs. Smalls cried.

"God's sake, what happened? Tell us the truth," her husband said, while she still spoke.

Valentine had to turn his face partly away, as if he were facing a strong wind. "It's as I said. I slipped, it's my fault. You can't know how sorry—she never felt anything, her neck broke—"

Mrs. Smalls broke into wracking sobs. Hank looked from his grief-stricken parents to Valentine, and back again.

"Where's the body?" Mr. Smalls said. Valentine wished he'd get up and take a swing at him, anything was preferable to the bitterness in his voice.

"It's at the infirmary. Rules. Cholera because of the flooding . . . won't get it," Valentine muttered.

"Should've known. It didn't sound right," Tondi Smalls sobbed, clutching at her husband as though dangling from a precipice. Valentine met her gaze, begged her to stop with his eyes. There were no more lies willing to come out of his mouth.

"It was planned!" she went on. "What did you get for it? What did they give you? I hope it was worth it. I hope it was worth my baby! My baby!"

Valentine backed out of the tent, but her words pursued him.

"What was it? What was in it for you? What's my baby gone for? What for?" Her voice broke up against her grief and sank into hysterical sobs.

Twenty-four hours later. Dawn was far away. Empty hours until he had an excuse to do something stretched before him. He should be asleep. God knew he was tired . . . He'd spent the day on a borrowed horse, in a long fruitless ride along old state route 10, looking for Finner and the Wolves, and hadn't returned until dark. The lonely hours alone on horseback had given him too much time alone with his conscience. He'd eaten a few bites of food before retiring to his tent, but sleep was impossible. Eventually he just sat up and went to work with his pistol.

By the light of a single bulb—the Kurians were efficient at getting the camp electrified—Valentine sat cross-legged on his cot and looked into the open action of his .45. The classic gun was a fine weapon, in the right hands, and Valentine took care of it. He'd taken it apart, cleaned the action, lubricated the slide, then put it back together and wiped it down, rubbing the protective oil into the gun like a masseur.

He picked up a bullet and rolled it around between his fingers. The brass was pitted here and there, scratched. A reload. But the Texas outfitter who'd given him the box of ammunition knew his business with the lead. The nose was a perfect oval, like the narrower end of an egg. Valentine took a tiny file he kept with his gun-cleaning bag and made a tiny X across the tip of the bullet. The shell was a man-stopper, but the channels would help the lead flatten out, or even fragment, and churn through flesh like a buzz saw. When he was satisfied with the modification, it joined the others next to his leg.

The last was trickier. A private joke between him and his conscience. He went to work on it. It took him almost fifteen minutes to do it to his satisfaction, but in the end there was a little horseshoe. A symbol of luck. He regarded it for a mo-

ment, smelling the lead filings on the tips of his fingers. He
took the horseshoe and added little lines on the ends of the
arms of the horseshoe. Now it was an omega. The last letter
of the Greek alphabet. The End. Also, oddly enough, an
electrical icon indicating resistance. Perfect.

He picked up the empty pistol magazine, examined it,
and set it firmly between his legs, open end up.

The eight completed bullets felt good in his hand.

Of course, a piece of him would live on, barring compli-
cations with Malia's pregnancy. Valentine couldn't decide if
this made ending it easier or harder.

"The Valentine family," he said, feeding the one with the
omega on it against the spring. First in would be last out.

"Dorian Helm, Gil, Selby, Poulos, Gator . . . Caroline
Smalls," he finished, as reverently as if he'd been saying the
rosary, kneeling in his room next to Father Max. He put the
magazine in the gun and worked the slide, chambering Caroline. He extracted the magazine again, and took the last
bullet. There was space for it now.

"Gabriella Cho," he said. "Thought I'd forgotten you,
didn't you?" He blinked the moisture out of his eyes. The
magazine slid back into the gun and he checked the safety.
Handling the automatic with a shell chambered could be
dangerous. He set the weapon down, admiring its simple
lines. Then he placed it back in his holster. The holster was
an ugly thing: canvas-covered something that felt like plastic within, TMCC stenciled on the exterior.

Valentine put out the light. Time passed, then Ahn-Kha
was at the door.

"My David. The men are waking up. The review is in two
hours. It would be best if we ate now."

"Coming."

Valentine put on the pistol belt. Ahn-Kha's ears went up
in surprise when Valentine opened the tent flap.

"You still haven't shaved, my David? It's not like you."

"You're right, old horse. Let's hit the sink before breakfast."

Post was up already, shaving in a basin. Valentine took

one just like it, filled it at the spigot and went to one of the shards of some greater mirror that the men looked into when cleaning their teeth or shaving. Valentine soaked his head for a moment to clear the cobwebs, and then shaved his face and skull.

"My David, is all well?"

"Right as rain, my friend."

"You've nothing to regret," Ahn-Kha said. "What happened was out of your control. Narcisse has spoken to the Smalls. They understood."

Post watched them for a moment before abandoning the officers' washroom. Valentine was glad of it; he was in no mood for his pity.

Ahn-Kha checked to see the room was empty before continuing. "You haven't been sleeping well. You're hardly eating."

"We have a review this morning. Let's look the part, old horse. Put a tent or something around you. I don't want to present one of my best men in just a loincloth."

"Tell me what holds your mind in such a grip."

"Hell, Ahn-Kha, things are looking up. The men are armed. Clean clothes, good food, they're getting healthier every day. All courtesy of Consul Solon. There's talk that in a few weeks we'll be transferred across the river. Once we're in the front lines . . ." He left the rest unvoiced.

"You have another agenda."

"Nothing for you to worry about."

He brought Styachowski her breakfast as the men turned out, sergeants checking the polish on their weapons and the state of their shoes. She'd been making herself useful in her tent with paperwork, since she could not move without aid of her crutch for weeks yet. Her cast was one blue-black smear of signatures and well wishes.

"Think you can hobble out for the review?" Valentine asked.

"I suppose."

"I want to introduce you as my second in command."

She frowned. "I've never been a line officer. The only command action I've ever seen was on the big bugout."

"Technically, you outrank Post and you're known better around here. You're familiar with the Ozarks. He isn't."

"Does he know you've decided this?"

"He's the one who suggested it. He wanted you in front of the troops, too."

"Well, the number-one uniform they gave me has never been worn. I didn't want to spoil the pant leg with the cast. Want to get busy with a scissors?"

Getting Styachowski dressed was something of a comic opera. Valentine tried to ignore the graceful shape of her small breasts under the white cotton T-shirt as he forced the leg of her pants up and over her cast. All at once the material slid over in a rush; he stopped himself from pitching head-first into her belly by grabbing her thigh.

"Sorry," he said.

"That's all right. Thanks, sir, I can finish the rest."

He turned his back as she hiked her buttocks off the cot to pull her pants up the rest of the way, and tuck her shirt in.

"The review is at nine-thirty. Looks like it's going to be nice spring weather. After it the men have a free day. See if the scroungers can set up a bar and some music. I have to go to a meeting."

"Xray-Tango going to have yet another bull session on finding a new crane and a road grader?"

"Solon's brought down some other Combat Command generals. There's going to be a discussion of the endgame for the Ozarks."

"You're invited?"

"Xray-Tango got me in. Our brigade figures in on the plans, somehow, so it's important enough for me to be there."

"Lucky you."

"Exactly what I was thinking."

The men were laid out before their tents along one of the cleared roads, six neat companies dressed according to height, in the wood-bark camouflage of AOT Combat Corps Light Infantry. Then there was Ahn-Kha's scout-sniper platoon in boonie hats, scoped rifles slung. The other men wore coal-scuttle Kevlar helmets and trousers bloused into new boots. Finally, the headquarters and support company, larger than any of the others, badges on their shoulders indicating each soldier's specialty. Nail's Bears were among them in a hulking cluster, assault engineer patches on their shoulders.

He had to hand it to the men running the AOT. What was requisitioned showed up, promptly and in the correct quantity. Very different from Southern Command, where if one put in a request for thirty assault rifles, in a month or two you might get a dozen rebuilt M-16s sharing space with a collection of deer rifles and Mini-14s with folding stocks.

Valentine had already been trained on the guns they'd be issued. The cases of rifles were now waiting to have the Cosmoline cleaned from them. The arms-smith who'd briefed him and his senior NCOs on the long blue-black guns introduced them as "Atlanta Gunworks Type Three Battle Rifles." The principal virtue of the "three-in-one" was its simplicity, but two features intrigued Valentine. With the addition of a bipod and a box magazine to replace the thirty-round magazine, they could do duty as a light machine gun. The interchangeable air-cooled barrel was a little nose-heavy, but the arms-smith showed him how veterans would balance it by adding a sandbag sleeve to the stock that also cushioned the shooter's shoulder against the weapon's kick. By swapping the regular barrel out for a match-grade version with flare suppressor, and adding a telescopic sight and adjustable stock, it made a formidable sniping rifle, throwing its 7.62mm bullet 1200 meters or more. He watched the arms-smith knock three 155mm shell casings off three posts at a thousand meters with three shots as a way of proving his point.

Valentine stood in front of the men, with Styachowski on her crutches to the right, Post to the left. A pair of motorcycles came around the corner from the direction of the headquarters, followed by an enormous black something, as wide as a Hummer but higher. Valentine had never seen a prewar sport-utility vehicle in such good condition before. Another truck followed, this one roofless, various subordinate officers arranged in the open seating. A diesel pickup rigged with benches in the bed brought up the rear.

The miniature column pulled up before Valentine's battalion. The cyclists lowered their kickstands. Valentine tried to look into the restored black behemoth, but the windows were darkened to the point that nothing could be seen from the side. The passenger door opened, and a man hopped out.

"Attend! Consul Solon is present."

A speaker on top of the SUV blared out an overamplified version of "Hail to the Chief" and Valentine stood at attention. The soldiers behind followed his example.

There was something childlike about the Consul, though he had the lined skin of a man in his fifties. He had the delicate features of someone who has survived extreme malnourishment, or even starvation, as a child. Overwide eyes, sparse brown hair, and rather thin lips looked out from a fleshless face bobbing on a scarecrow frame wrapped in a heavy coat and muffler despite the warmth of the spring morning. Valentine had not seen many movies in his life, but there had been a theater in Pine Bluff that showed old pre-2022 films on some kind of projector, and Consul Solon reminded him of a character in an old Bogart picture called *Casablanca*. There was a wariness to the eyes that reminded Valentine of the black-and-white image of Peter Lorre looking around the café.

Valentine took a single step forward, and Xray-Tango got out of the rear of the SUV. He trotted to join the little big man.

"Consul Solon, this is Colonel Knox Le Sain. You'll remember he and his troops were a godsend during the flood."

"Yes," Solon said with a nod to Valentine. None of the other officers were saluting the civilian coat, so Valentine didn't either. "The new battalion. You left the bayous for a healthier climate, as I hear it, Colonel. I like officers with initiative, Le Sain. I trust you'll restrict yours in the future to carrying out orders, rather than inventing your own." The Consul had a clipped manner of speaking, biting off the words. Solon's retinue carried out a small portable microphone, and strung a wire from the SUV to power it.

"Yes, sir," Valentine said.

He began introductions. Solon shook hands with Styachowski, thanking her for her injury sustained in saving the new capital of the Trans-Mississippi. He was polite with Post, but cut the interview short when Post hemmed and hawed out his respects. The lieutenants of each company stepped forward to meet him. Only one forgot himself so far as to salute Solon, but the Consul returned it in good humor.

As Valentine walked him back to the mike, Solon raised an eyebrow. "You have a big Grog there, Colonel."

"He's a good officer, Consul. Smart as a fox, and he tracks like a bloodhound. The men follow his orders."

"I'm not a fan of Grogs, Colonel. Putting them in any kind of position of responsibility, well, it's like Caligula putting his horse into the Senate."

"He's not like the gargoyles or the gray apes. He reads, writes and beats me at chess."

"Indulge yourself, then. But don't allow him to issue orders. The Grogs have no place in the Trans-Mississippi. There's already trouble with them further north."

He stepped to the microphone and faced the men. Post returned to his place in front of the infantry companies, and Styachowski her spot before the headquarters company, Valentine halfway between the two.

"Men of the Light Infantry Battalion, Third Division, Army of the Trans-Mississipi Combat Corps. Your comrades in arms welcome you. The civilized order you are part of thanks you. But before you can call yourself soldiers, with the pride and honor that title entails, you are required to take an oath to the Order I represent. Together we'll build a happier and more hopeful world. Please raise your right hands and repeat after me—"

Solon waited until he saw the hands in the air before continuing. Valentine spoke the empty words, listening to Ahn-

Kha's booming voice behind him. "I do now solemnly swear allegiance to the Articles of the Consular Law of the Trans-Mississipi Confederation, to guard its integrity, to obey the orders of those officers placed above me, and to hold it above my life and those of its foes, foreign or domestic, or all I am and hold will be forfeit, until I am released from duty or am parted from service in death."

Solon spoke the words well. "Congratulations, soldiers, and welcome to the privileges of your new position. General?"

Another man stepped forward, part of Consul Solon's entourage. Solon handed him the microphone. He had streaming gray hair tied in a loose ponytail, and the same blue-black uniform as the guard Valentine had seen outside the Reaper's door, though his legs from polished boot-top to knee were wrapped in black puttees. The thinness of his legs and clear, hard eyes made Valentine think of some kind of predatory bird.".

"Officers and men of the light infantry," the man said. "I'm General Hamm, of the Third Division. I'm your new commanding officer. We're the best division in the Trans-Mississippi, both now and once we're through mopping up that hillbilly rabble." Valentine wondered briefly how his hillbilly rabble felt about that choice of words. "You'll find I expect a great deal, but when this is all over, you'll get a great deal in return. In my old grounds in Texas, those who served me well in war found security in peace.

"Élan, right down to the company level, is important to me. Especially in my light infantry. You'll move fast and fight hard, grabbing ground and holding it until supports arrive. As a sign of your special bravery you'll carry a symbol, your bolo knife."

He looked over his shoulder. The diesel ground forward and stopped before Valentine. Hamm hopped up into the bed. "Help me, will you, Colonel? I like to hand these out personally."

There were long green crates within, like footlockers. Valentine lifted the hinged lid on one. Rows of sheathed machetes rested within. General Hamm picked one out and handed it to him. "Yours, Colonel. A handy little tool. Got the idea from those blades some of the 'Wolf' guerillas carry. You'll find I've improved the design."

"All the troops carry these, General?"

"No, just you lights. The heavy infantry get flak jackets and masked helmets. Consider yourselves saved a heart attack. That armor's Pennsylvania-built; it's hotter than hell down here."

Valentine unsheathed a blade. It was long and rectangular, a blade on one edge and saw teeth on the other. It widened slightly near the handle, which had a wire cutter built into the guard just above the blade. The metal was coated with a dark finish for night use.

Solon had retired to his SUV. Valentine, with the help of a corporal, handed up knife after knife to the general, who passed them out, each with a little word of commendation to the files of men brought forward to receive them. They returned to their company positions. The general took up a blade as well.

"You've got your blades. Your bolos. It was an old war cry, and soon you'll be shouting it again, when we go up into the mountains and get the poor bastards unlucky enough to be facing you. Let's try it out, shall we?

"Bolo!" he shouted, then lifted his hands to the men.

"Bolo," they shouted back.

"Not good enough!" Hamm said. "Booolo!"

"Bolo!" the men screamed back. "Boooloooo!"

"Louder!" the general bellowed. He unsheathed the blade, brandishing it in the air. "BOLO!"

"BOLO!" it came back to him, a wall of noise. Valentine joined in, the scream so long repressed escaping. With it went some of his pain. He looked out at the thicket of waving, blackened steel. The general was right. He wouldn't care to be up against them either.

The next item on Solon's itinerary was a train ride. They took the ferry across to the north side of the river. Above them workmen and prisoners fixed I-beams to the pilings of the old bridge. Xray-Tango was rebuilding the railroad bridge first; the road bridge would come later. They stepped out of the ferry and took the short walk to the old rail yard.

The officers, a mélange of three generals, eleven colonels—including Valentine—and an assortment of accessory captains and lieutenants, ate a buffet served on the platform before boarding the flag-festooned train for its inaugural ride. The beginnings of the line to run, once again, west from the Little Rock area to Fort Scott had only been cleared a few miles northwest, but in those few miles it went to a station near Solon's prospective Residence, even now being constructed on a hill thick with trees, where once a golf course, lakes and the houses of the well-to-do stood. The nukes had flattened and burned house and bole alike, but a grander estate would rise from the ashes.

Valentine tried to keep his hand off his holster as he exchanged pleasantries with the braided Quislings. Solon was a gracious host, and introduced him to a few others as "Colonel Le Sain, a protégé of Xray-Tango." Xray-Tango introduced him to others as an officer nominated to command by Consul Solon himself. As the new officer in the coterie, Valentine received a sort of reserved attention. The generals nodded to him, the colonels seemed suspicious of him, and the lesser officers watched him. One lieutenant in particular pursued him, popping up at his elbow and clinging to him like a wart.

"Your Colonelcy would care for some more wine?" the unctuous lieutenant, a man named Dalton, asked.

"I'm fine, Lieutenant."

The man looked at the turned backs all around them, and lowered his voice. "A man in your position deserves a few comforts to forget the hardships of command. Ask anyone; I'm the sort that can make good things happen. I can make bad things disappear. *Pfsssht.*" He punctuated his conversation with sound effects. "You'd find me good company, and I'm looking for a good billet."

Valentine had already brushed off one captain angling for

a staff position; he didn't want a Quisling with aspirations toward pimphood hanging around his camp. He asked Xray-Tango about it when they got a moment together on the train.

"Solon's at fault for it, really," Xray-Tango said. "He hands out promotions like a parade marshal throwing candy. They join his military advisor's staff until he can fob them off on someone. A lot of them are sons of important men in Dallas, or Tulsa, or Memphis. Anyone who helped him. Some of the officers had trouble fitting in back home, but they've done good service to the Higher Ups, so here they are. We've got generals who are illiterate, colonels who are pederasts; you get the picture."

"They should have gone down to New Orleans, then. They'd've fit right in." Valentine looked out the window as the train crawled west, blowing its whistle every minute on the crawling, festive trip. The official one. Another train with construction supplies had gone out on a test run a few days before.

"The bad ones have an unerring instinct for not getting themselves killed, have you ever noticed it? Colonel Forester took a bullet in the ear on the banks of the Black. General Cruz was sharing a foxhole with three men when a 120mm mortar round paid them a visit. Three privates got a helluva funeral, we had to bury them together because we couldn't tell who was who. Hamm's predecessor, General Patrick O'Connel, our best division commander last summer, had a birthday party and someone decided signal flares would really set off the cake. Six officers died when the house burned down."

"Idiots. But six? Fumes get them?"

"The fire spread fast. There were a lot of papers in there; they tried to fight it to save them. The general traveled with his own supply of gasoline. They locked it up good. Too good—no ventilation. *Whoof.*"

"The fire took a house full of people?"

"One or two made it. The general had an eye for the ladies. They traveled with him. He had this redhead. A real saddlebred—a little on the bony side, but pretty. She got passed on to Hamm like it was in the will."

"Privileges of rank," Valentine said, trying to sound as nonchalant. *Ali?* A fire would be just like her. But the rest didn't fit. Pillow recon, as Alessa Duvalier used to call it, wasn't her style.

The train swung and jerked as it crawled along the points. The track needed some work.

"What's Hamm like?"

"Third Division is a hell of an outfit, though they've really caught it since O'Connel died. They're scattered on the north side of the river now, refitting for the big push."

Valentine looked out the window. Ali would understand, if he could just talk to her. She'd been a Cat almost since puberty, had seen and done things that would turn a tough man's hair gray. He had been planning to put Gabriella Cho's bullet between General Hamm's eyes, right after removing Solon's head with Caroline Smalls', but now he was having second thoughts. After turning them over in his mind, he discarded his hopes. It was wishful thinking, to expect Alessa Duvalier to be wandering almost the same camp he was, even if she was a Cat.

The train finished its short run at a notch in the hills above what had been North Little Rock. Solon's party disembarked, more trucks—this time, hosed-down pickups—met them to take everyone up the steep grade to the estate grounds. Judging from the roadside placement of the posts marking where the fence would be, Solon had great plans for the grounds, if sheer acreage was any indication. A marble block the size of a crypt already bore the words STATION ONE—CONSULAR RESIDENCE in meter-high letters.

The hill flattened out as they rode to the top, and Valentine got his first view of the foundations of Solon's Residence. The vigorous young scrub forest that had been claiming the hillside lay in windrows up the gentle hill and at the top. A cluster of Quonset huts next to a pond housed the builders. The construction site, situated for a perfect view of the river valley to the west and the distant Ouachitas beyond, dominated a chunky, freshly cleared vista. As they drove closer Valentine got a better view of the future center of Trans-Mississippi power. There were basements, foundations and churned-up earth all around something that looked like it once was a college, or perhaps just a sturdy building that had survived the '22 devastation. A new roof had been put on it, surmounted by a cupola. The "college" formed the base of a great *U* of future buildings, some of which had the floors of the second story built along with the beginnings of walls. Georgian-style arched windows, minus the glass, were in place on the lower levels. It was reminiscent of the old Federal White House, expanded into a palace-sized villa.

The surroundings were just as impressive. The tallest hump of Big Rock Mountain, still forested, dominated the villa's "backyard."

Solon gathered his entourage at what would be the turn-around of his drive, in front of the new arched doors. Valentine angled his way through the press of officers to see Solon pointing out highlights. "There'll be a Grecian temple on top of the hill, one day. But that's the sort of finishing touch I'm saving until the masons are done with the important work down here. It'll be the finest view in the Trans-Mississippi, one day. Right now I call it the Lookout. I'll hike up there later, if anyone wants to join me."

He ushered the officers into the central hall. The interior had been gutted and turned into a grand entrance hall, branching off to the right and left to the rest of the villa. The entire back wall was missing, save for a balcony framework and supports for glass.

"This is going to open up on the inner patio. There'll be a pool and a greenhouse but, as you can see, it's just a big hole at the moment. At first I was going to get rid of this building. Old army construction, though the bricks were attractive. They'd turned the basement into some kind of hospital or dormitory. Come down, and see what I've done with it."

He led the party past a worker, who made haste to clear

the way for the officers. "This is the Situation Room. There'll be a conference center and offices, and below, in the subbasement, a communications room and security bunker. The fixtures are in, but it's still missing some equipment." Solon led them into the conference center, separated by glass walls—complete with drapes for security—but as yet unfurnished.

"Now a brief meeting," Solon said, as his aides brought up a pair of easels.

Because of the lack of chairs, only the generals and colonels were allowed to sit for the meeting, and after it was over Valentine was grateful for the chance to walk again. After three hours of maps, orders, questions and arguments, he needed a break. Solon stopped for a meal, with a promise to answer question individually afterward. Access to the flush toilet was by rank, so Valentine grabbed a paper plate full of sandwiches and went up into the clean air and used the workers' outhouse.

He found an empty sawhorse and leaned against it, watching a bulldozer move earth. The sunshine made him feel even more enervated. He'd keyed himself up for nothing, as it turned out.

Two or three times during the meeting he'd rested his hand on his pistol. It would have been easy to draw it and kill five or six of the assembled senior officers. But as he came to the critical moment, the murder-suicide he'd been thinking about seemed more and more like an empty gesture as the emotionally frozen gears of his mind began turning again. A few deaths would not matter. The Kurians would have a hard time replacing someone as manifestly gifted as Solon, but the rest of the officers were easily switched cogs in the military machine. Or perhaps, when it came down to the sticking point, he lacked the courage to go open-eyed to his death.

Through the series of disasters—like falling dominoes he'd raced to stay ahead of—he'd been caught up in, he found himself in a unique situation. All the mistakes and misfortune had placed him in the enemy headquarters, handing him priceless information on the Quisling plans to finish off Southern Command. And his role in the operation couldn't have been better if he'd written the orders himself. His light infantry was assigned to probe the passes into the western Boston Mountains, looking for a lightly guarded route that he could seize so the rest of Hamm's division could put itself into the heart of what was left of the Free Territory's forces in their mountain redoubts. He could get what Quickwood he had where it was needed most, courtesy of the trucks of the TMCC.

The most tantalizing piece of information wasn't stated explicitly; Valentine had to put it together based on the questions from Quisling commanders from Tennessee, Okalahoma, Kansas and, especially, Texas. Solon was a strange cross between a venture capitalist and a military genius: he'd gotten command of large numbers of Quisling troops from all around the Ozarks, but the terms of the agreements were expiring. He'd made another set of deals, like a debtor trying to extend the due date of a loan for a few more months by promising interest greater than had been paid for the previous two years. He had until the end of summer to put paid to the loan, to conquer the Free Territory, before he lost eighty percent of his men. If he could clean up Southern Command's holdouts this spring and summer, he'd have enough to garrison his Trans-Mississippi with the help of the leaders of his Kurian substates, and send captives and prisoners off to the hungry neighboring Kurians, their bodies paying off his debts.

Valentine even found himself admiring his fellow officers. They asked intelligent questions, wrote notes in their order journals with smooth, elegant hands, and offered imaginative suggestions. There was efficiency, yes, but a certain amount of coldness, too, like greyhounds eager for the release of the rabbit, all eyes on the prize and not a thought for the men in uniform around them. A similar group of Southern Command officers would be more informal; there would be jokes and jibes and a good deal of smoke blowing.

"He's seeing everyone individually next," Xray-Tango said, breaking into his thoughts. The general gave a pine door-post an experimental rap. Valentine looked at the twitching eye and knew that Xray-Tango had received orders he hadn't liked.

"Did he give you what for about the bridge, General? Or getting the locks rebuilt?"

"No, nothing like that. That'd be sensible. He wants his house finished, so he can transfer his governement out of Fort Scott. The Twenty-three Representatives will be here soon."

"Twenty-three more Reapers? That won't be pleasant."

"These aren't so bad. I've seen them, all sitting around the conference table. They're more like zombies than anything; they just sit in their chairs until they need to see, hear and speak for the Higher Up at the other end. He feeds them pig blood, not people. Something about the distance, I dunno, they can't be animated right from so far away, and the ones closer have too much else to do."

"Then what's the matter, sir? You seem upset."

"I asked to retire after the big push. I'm feeling my age, Le Sain. Getting sick of making decisions for idiots who had the exact same decision put to them the day before. Then there's the . . . the stuff like the other night. It wears a man down."

"He turned you down?"

"He said he needed five more years to get the groundwork for New Columbia built. Promised me I could leave then. Bridges, highways, roads, factories, housing; he's even talking about an airport. The Kurians don't like anything bigger than bush planes in the air, but he's got this idea for a Trans-Mississippi air force burning in his brain. I'm just worried that after five more years, they'll want another five before I get my estate, and I've got my reasons for thinking that. You see, Le Sain, he promised me that when Southern Command was finished off, I'd be able to retire. I don't like a man who plays me like a fish. Can't stand people who are more convincing at making promises than keeping them."

"I'll go get my talking-to," Valentine said.

"You coming for the party later?"

"What party is that, sir?"

"You've been keeping to yourself lately. We're having a little celebration in the Blue Dome. You been in there yet?"

"No, there was the flood, sir. Since then I've been too busy fitting out."

"You owe it to yourself to live a little, Le Sain. Young man like you. Come along and have some fun."

"Odd you should say that, sir. I've told myself that just today. I thought there'd be some fun with this trip." He hooked a thumb in his gunbelt. "The day's not over yet."

There was only one miserable-looking captain still waiting when an aide shook Valentine awake. Valentine had pretended to snooze as he idled while Solon met with each officer; exhaustion turned his pretense into reality.

"The Consul will see you now," the aide said. He was ushered into Solon's underground office. The teal walls still smelled faintly of fresh paint. There was an oriental panel on the wall, three pictures, each in its own frame, separate works of art but forming a greater work together. The largest figure was of a warrior carrying a bow. Valentine looked in the corner of the office, where a recurved bow and a quiver of arrows had been placed.

"Colonel Le Sain," Solon said, looking up from his paperwork. "Our ambitious young newcomer. Please sit down."

"Thank you, sir," Valentine said, sitting in the club chair opposite Solon's desk. The Consul had shortened the legs on it, giving Solon a height advantage he didn't have when standing.

"I saw you admiring my bow."

"It's a handsome one, sir. Beautiful wood."

"My quiet center. I go away with the bow when I need to think. Or rather, not think, at least consciously. I'll take you out and show you, when we're less pressed by duty. Did you get caught up at the presentation?"

"Yes, sir. It was thorough, I'll give you that. There's only a little mopping up to do south of the Arkansas. North of it, it looks like you've got what's left of the opposition boxed in."

"They're more like a treed tiger. Properly prodded, they'll

jump down. Unpleasant for whoever happens to be under them, but it'll be the end of the tiger."

"Could be dangerous for whoever goes up the tree to do the prodding, too."

"You understand your role, then. You wanted your shot at glory; I've granted your wish."

"They must be pretty hungry by now. Why not wait?" Valentine said.

Consul Solon's hangdog face tightened. "Evidently they'd prepared for years for this eventuality. Food and supplies deep in caves, mines ready in all the critical road junctures. And of course you're aware that our borrowed forces have to return home more or less intact."

"I caught that, sir."

"So headlong assault wasn't an option. It's our own fault. We didn't pursue promptly enough when they collapsed. It must have been some civil defense plan, to have so much put away for civilians, even. You know we've captured livestock up in the hills? I was tempted to take back some rings if my generals allowed them to get away with their chickens and sheep. Hopeless incompetence, but then what do you expect of forces that have been doing nothing but glorified police work and putting down uprisings for decades. They're gun-shy."

"Why not use Grogs?"

"The Grogs have their own concerns. The St. Louis ones only go to war for land; I'm not about to give up an inch of the Trans-Mississippi. Quite the contrary. Once we've got things under control here, we'll expand north. The whole Missouri Valley is crawling with them from St. Louis to Omaha; that'll change."

"The Higher Ups gave them that land in return for—"

"Don't be stupid, Colonel. That was a deal settled long ago. It wasn't with the Trans-Mississippi Confederation, either. I've spoken to the Twenty-three, and they're in agreement. You're seeing only the planting of a seed that will one day flower in the headwaters of the Mississippi, the Tenesseee, the Missouri, the Arkansas, yes, even the Ohio.

That's why I came west, Le Sain. Elbow room. My days of sweating out strategies to control four more counties in Virginia or a town in Maryland are over."

"You're from the East, sir? I've always wanted to see it."

"No you don't. It's chaos."

"So you left? How did you manage that, if you don't mind me asking, sir?"

"You're a kindred spirit, Le Sain," Solon said, a twinkle coming to his basset-hound eyes. "If you don't like a place, your role in it, you get yourself out. I did the same, did you know that? My father was a senator in the old United States government. He didn't survive '22. I barely remember him. My mother struck up a relationship with a general who'd been useful to the Kurians. His lordship held a few towns around the Potomac in northern Virgina. I got my start as a courier; eventually I was running everything for miles around Harper's Ferry. The Kurians are such children in a way; if you're useful in getting them their candy, you can train them like Pavlov's dogs. I learned the art of politics. There must be generational memory in the land, for the whole area around what used to be the District of Columbia is home to the most backbiting, infighting group of Kurians you can imagine, all holding court in their little monuments around the Mall. A woman named Rudland, I believe she was from New York, organized them into a 'committee,' to cut down on the blood feuds. I'd help plead my lordship's cases before the committee, and if that didn't work, bribe a powerful member. Then a deal went wrong, and I had to—let's just say I left in a hurry.

"Not that it's been any easier out here. The soldiers I was originally going to use to flush out these backwoods killers suffered a setback when their Grogs revolted. Grogs are more trouble than they're worth; I've said it enough, you'd think someone would be listening by now. Those fools on the Missouri. It'll be a generation before that particular plan can be brought again to fruition. I'm not the first person to learn that if you want something done right, do it yourself, so I made deals to get the forces I needed. Though I haven't sought a reputation in the cannon's mouth, far from it. I earned my ring

with words and ideas, not with bullets. They're more powerful in the long run."

"I'm still looking for mine."

"I'll tell you something an aging U.S. federal judge once
told me. He had it on a plaque:

Vision without will fades like a dream.
Will without vision grows into a nightmare.

"The Kur are rich in will. I've never seen vision to go with
it, so I'm supplying my own. As to will—well, you've seen
what's being built in New Columbia. It'll be good. I'd like to
think you'd stay out of desire to help me build here. But stay
you will. Do you understand?" Solon curved his finger down-
ward and tapped his desk to accentuate his words. "Stay. You.
Will."

"Yes, sir."

"You've got an ambitious look about you, Colonel. I saw
you at the meeting, looking around, wondering which of your
fellow officers you could rise above. You're still a young
man, and I'll indulge young men in that. At this rate you'll be
one of my leading generals in a few years. Then you'll have
it all: an estate, women, wealth. You're present at the founding of a country. Someday we'll mint coins. Maybe your face
will be on one, if you distinguish yourself."

"I hope so. Did you have all this in mind when you came
west?"

"New Columbia will be another Washington, another London, another Rome. Only better than Rome. Our temples will
have real deities who give real rewards for an appropriate sacrifice. They will be Temples of Meaning instead of houses of
superstition."

Valentine sickened at the thought of more white towers rising in the green Ozarks like that abomination across the hill,
each one asking for its share of Carolines. His mother had
been raped and killed again, and once again he trotted home
just in time to see the horror. He couldn't keep the words in:
"As long as we follow orders."

Solon looked at him with sad understanding—but then,

with those basset-hound eyes, he had a face custom-built for the expression.

"Le Sain, if you've studied the history of China, you know it's been conquered many times. From the Mongols to the British. But in a generation or two, somehow it was China again. This land is the same way. We'll absorb the Kurians; when this fighting gets done with, we'll rebuild. They'll be powerful figures, certainly, like heads of corporations or governors. The real power was always in a set of oligarchs. They just happen to be Kurian now. But the rewards will go to the integrators, the ones who make it all work. Another constitutional government will rise, we'll have legislatures and courts, taxes and tollways."

"They'd let us have all that?"

"Why not?"

"Due process and all that might cut down on the flow of aura."

Solon leaned forward, steepled his fingers under his chin, and lowered his voice. "What makes you think I'd want that?"

"I'm not sure I follow you, sir."

"Every society has is share of drones: the uneducable, the lazy, the unproductive, the crippled, the sick. Then there are the criminals. Civilization has always paid some kind of price for their upkeep. With the Kurians in charge, they'll be fed into that furnace in the place of the talented. Only instead of the haphazard and arbitrary methods of today, it will be smoother, determined by courts and elected officials instead of this random slaughter. The robber barons will still take their toll, but it won't be at random anymore, they'll simply be a surgical instrument keeping the body politic healthy. Evolution did that for millennia, weeded out the unfit, but with our civilization the weeds were allowed to grow as well as the flowers. It's time to replant the garden of Eden. But first, we have to separate wheat from chaff. Every generation produces its share of each."

"I see."

"Do you? That unpleasantness with the baby the other night—yes, I heard about it. It upset you. If you want to be part of my bright future, you'll have to become used to that. Wheat and chaff, Le Sain. Wheat and chaff."

"You're a man of vision, sir. But sometimes the 'unfit' have hidden talents. Wasn't there a brilliant physicist named Hawking who only had use of his mouth? Van Gogh was crazy, Einstein's teachers thought he was retarded."

"You're well read for a bayou woodsman."

"I grew up in an old library, sir. Sort of a private collection. It started out with picture books and took off from there."

"You haven't been listening, Colonel. I've got the answers, so quit worrying about the questions. You see, we'll have courts, appeals. We'll control the flow. The Kurians won't care how the plumbing works as long as the water keeps flowing. In the end, we'll have the real power."

Valentine left the Consul's office, hazy and flattened beneath a steamroller of a headache. He felt pressed flat by fatigue, as though the fading sun could pass through him as if he were a blood-smeared microscope slide. Consul Solon was persuasive. Valentine had to allow him that. He was also quite possibly a megalomaniac. It was a formidable psychological combination. No wonder Solon had come so far, so fast, in his quest for a federated empire of Kurian "states."

But like many ambitious conquerors, Solon had a problem. Would-be empire builders historically had two moments when even the smallest successful show of resistance might bring collapse. One was at the empire's birth, and the other was when it quit growing. Valentine doubted he'd live long enough to see the expansion stop.

That left turning Solon's Trans-Mississippi into a stillbirth.

Chapter Eight

New Columbia, March of the forty-eighth year of the Kurian Order: The Quislings and the Rats. Perhaps history has been overly unkind to Major Vidkun A. L. Quisling. He certainly loved his native Norway, but not so much that he let it get in the way of his ambition for political power through selling his good name and country to the Nazis. In that, at least, he is as dishonorable as his conscienceless namesakes. In the vocabulary of opprobrium against the Kurians, "Quisling" is considered perhaps the most obscene, for they thrive in the service of humanity's conquerers.

For those who spend time in the Kurian Zone, it is hard to be as bitter about the lower ranks. Armed service under the Kurians ensures life for the Quisling soldier and his family. It is hard to begrudge parents decent food to feed their children, a warm house and a few diversions. But some acquire a taste for the luxuries power brings and seek higher rank. They amass property, or gather art, or indulge their physical desires. Some become killers or sadists, exploring the freedom to taste that which is forbidden to others.

To the aid of the great ones with the power and money, there are always those willing to acquire their desires, legally or no. In New Columbia, those fulfilling, and profiting in, that service are the Rats. Not quite Quislings, but somewhere above the unfortunates living under the shadow of Kur, they live on the fringes of the law, their river boats giving them a freedom of movement and privacy that allows them to engage in lucrative smuggling. They have a strip on the north side of the Arkansas avoided by all save the river thugs, or those with the money to pay for a night in the dubious haunts of the riverfront. Most of them are

*clapped-together wooden establishments, already redolent
of the unsavory activities taking place within. But there are
a few substantial, finished buildings, complete with a touch
of landscaping or a colorful coat of paint and expensive
ironwork. Of all these, the most notorious—and expensive—
is the Blue Dome.*

As daylight faded Valentine hitched a ride into town with
a pickup full of workmen, ignoring a pair of lieutenants who
were waiting for more suitable transport. As the truck shuddered into second gear, one pulled a leather flask from within
his shirt, passed it to a buddy, and with a practiced squirt shot
a stream of the concoction within into his mouth before
handing it back to the owner. He held it out to Valentine.

The Cat was tempted. After several sleepless nights, he'd
spent the day keying himself up to kill a hatful of high-
ranking Quislings, and then perhaps himself, only to find the
moment, or his nerve, failing to live up to his destructive
plan.

"What is it?"

"Joy-juice," the bearded laborer who'd produced the sack
said. "Little wine, little homemade brandy, some fruit
squeezings. Go on, Colonel, it's good stuff. Ain't blinded
us yet."

Valentine shot some of the mixture into his throat, but
didn't have the knack for stopping the stream yet. It
splashed across his dress uniform shirt. He gulped it down.
He'd had worse.

By the time the truck passed the markers at the bottom of
the estate hill, they'd all had a round.

"How do you like working on the Residence?" Valentine
asked.

"Good work," the man said, a few stray gray hairs on his
head standing out against the black of his face and beard.
"Ration book, and cash besides. No way I'm going back
across the Missisisippi. There'll be good work for years. I
can do electricity, plumbing, carpentry . . ."

Valentine felt for Xray-Tango across the river, trying to

build New Columbia using captured Free Territory men, while the skilled workers, imported at God-knows-what expense, went to Solon's Residence.

"You don't live on the site?"

"Naw. Town's more fun. We all got a real house, even a couple of Tex-Mex women in residence for the chores and such. It's a sweet setup, Colonel. There's a diner in town, bars. They're talking about getting a movie-house going."

"I'm due at a party tonight. What's good to eat at the Blue Dome?"

The laborer smiled at Valentine with tobacco-stained teeth. "Shiiit, Colonel, what do you take me for? Only time I seen the inside of that place was getting the toilets running. Most of us do odd jobs at night, and old Dom, he pays well. But if I tried to walk in as a customer . . ."

"Exclusive?"

"Strictly for you officer-types and the rat-boat captains. What passes for society in these parts. But don't you worry; they'll treat you right, and the food'll stay down."

Valentine thought regretfully of the cigar box full of "Solon Scrip" back at his tent. He hadn't expected the day to end with dinner and drinks, so he'd left that morning with only a dollar or two tip money in his identification pouch.

The truck dropped him off next to a pyramid of rubble with a watch post atop it.

"Follow this street down to the river, Colonel," the workman said. "You'll see the Ragbag, a clothing-swap warehouse that'll still be open. Just to the right is the Blue Dome. No windows and only one entrance. It's got a neon sign with an arrow; you can't miss it."

"Thanks for the drink," Valentine said, after a second squirt from the leather flask. He offered two dollars in scrip. The laborer refused.

"It comes with the ride. Watch your money at the card table, and when you draw a flush, think of me."

The pickup bucked into gear and Valentine waved goodbye. He walked to the new riverfront of the north side of the Arkansas, at the edge of a little slope above the river proper, and thus safe from flooding. There were tent bars playing music, street vendors with food in carts, and everywhere men in deck shoes and woolen coats and sweaters, wearing knit caps or baseball-style ones with ship names sewn into the crown. A trio of muscular rivermen drinking behind a bar glanced at him, but shifted their eyes apologetically when they took in the uniform.

Valentine peered into the Ragbag's single window. The rest were still boarded up. Long tables and racks of recovered clothing were piled everywhere, and there was a cobbler in the corner tearing apart old shoes to recover the soles. He looked up the lively street and saw that a neon sign advertising the Blue Dome hummed from its position hanging out over the sidewalk. The joy-juice had assuaged his headache and left him sleepy.

The Blue Dome was a squatty block of masonry, better fitted together than most of the antheaps on the south side of the shallow Arkansas bisecting New Columbia, and painted to boot. There were no windows on the first story, and only shuttered, tiny slit ones on the second. Atop the building he could see the awning of something he guessed to be a penthouse; someone had gone to the trouble to hang basketed plants. From the alley between the Ragbag and the Blue Dome he heard the hum of ventilation fans and picked up the charred smell of meat on the grill. Valentine realized he was hungry.

Oddly enough, the Blue Dome's entrance was in the alley rather than on the main street. The aged stairs were pre-2022; he descended them to a new wooden door, which opened even before he knocked.

"Pri—oh, excuse me, sir, come right in," the burly doorman said, moving aside. Valentine stepped inside and halted, awestruck.

He felt as though he'd opened a worm-eaten wooden box only to find a Fabergé egg enclosed. Stuccoed walls opened up on an elegant room. Ensconced lighting behind delicate glass seashells drew his eyes upward to the glow of the Dome.

It stretched above a parquet wooden dance floor and stage to the right of the entrance. The concave surface was painted with some kind of luminescent blue material, which glowed in the reflected light of what Valentine guessed to be hundreds of small, low-wattage bulbs, giving the effect of a cloudless sky at twilight. Opposite him stood a massive wooden bar with polished silver fittings, a solid wall of liquor bottles behind it, and a bartender in a crisp white shirt and black tie standing ready. Between the bar and the stage, an elevated corner platform held a seated knot of musicians playing a quiet variety of jazz. The undomed part of the room stretched off to Valentine's left. Uniformed members of the TMCC sat around linen-topped tables. They stood on staggered burgundy-carpeted levels under the subdued blue light from what looked to be fifty miles of fiber-optic cable artfully wound into the ceiling and structural pillars. Around the edges of the room velvet-curtained alcoves were more brightly lit; Valentine could just make out green-topped gaming tables behind heavy burgundy curtains.

"Quite a basement," Valentine said to the doorman.

A man wearing the first true tuxedo Valentine had ever seen glided over to him. He had the coconut brown features of the subcontinent, and teeth as brilliantly white as his eyes. "Welcome, Colonel. I've been told of you and the service you did in the floods. Your first time here, yes?"

Valentine nodded.

"It was just a murky basement when I came here a year ago."

"You got in early."

"I'm an acquaintance of the good Consul's from back east. He's building a land of opportunity; when I heard his operations were a success, I was on the next train out of Baltimore. My name is Dom, and I'm pleased to meet you, Colonel. You are hungry, yes?"

"Yes," Valentine said. "You must have been building this place while they were still fighting."

"It is a principle of commerce as well as combat to get in first with the most. I'd like to think I've managed that. Your fellow officers wouldn't think of going anywhere else for an evening out, or a celebration."

"I can see why."

Dom bowed, then turned to a screened-off corner to Valentine's right. "Arsie, show Colonel Le Sain to General Hamm's table, would you? You're in luck, Colonel, you've got the best view of the floor from the whole restaurant. Enjoy your meal. If you wish to visit the gaming tables, they'll close for an hour at nine for the show, then they'll re-open."

A tall woman, all chestnut hair and silken skin in a cocktail dress that complemented the décor, appeared at Dom's side. Valentine saw a little tattoo of a faerie with heavy black eyeliner and lipstick winking out at him from her upper breast.

"Er, Dom, I haven't—"

"None of that, Colonel. Everything but your table stakes and bar charges tonight are courtesy of Consul Solon; your liquor is being picked up by General Hamm. Convenient, yes? That just leaves gambling money, and your name is good here; just show your identification to the cashier, last alcove on the left. It's as we're welcoming you to the Combat Corps tonight. I understand your battalion was formally recognized this morning. Congratulations, Colonel. 'Glory on your name, beauty on your arm, and a ring on your finger,' as they say. Speaking of beauty, Colonel Le Sain, I'd like you to meet Arsie, who'll be your escort this evening."

Valentine had sense enough, and joy-juice enough, to offer his arm. She was just an inch below Valentine's six-two. The soberer part of him wondered if Dom paired the officers according to rank or height. "Nice to meet you, Arsie."

"Congratulations, Colonel," she said, taking him across the dance floor to a long table set so it had a central view of the stage. A few other officers and men, some escorted by Blue Dome girls, sat and stood around the finger food on trays there.

"There's got to be a story behind your name, if you'll pardon the phrase."

"Ar Cee. Initials. RC."

"Which is short for?"

"I don't know. They said when I was a baby I was found in an old Royal Crown cola truck. You can say 'Arsie' if you like, Colonel."

"Call me Knox, please."

It was hard to tell just how false her smile was, but it did look a bit like the tattoo. "Thank you, Knox. Oh, you've got a stain on your shirt. Let me get some soda water," she said, hurrying off to the bar.

"Colonel Le Sain, welcome," General Hamm said, sitting at the end of the table with his boots up, stretching his stork-like legs. A purring, well-proportioned blonde was draped around his shoulders like a stole. "Old Extasy said you'd be coming. Welcome to the fun side of the Hard-Assed Third." He introduced Valentine to a uniformed blur of colonels and majors; some he'd met that morning, and others were new faces. There was a civilian in the mix, a sleepy-eyed man in an open-necked white shirt and black trousers. Hamm introduced him as Captain Mantilla. "Mantilla is a good man to know, Colonel. He's good at showing up where he's needed with what's needed. French wine, Italian clothing, Cuban tobacco, Mexican cabinetry, Belgian chocolate . . . he gets it all through connections down in New Orleans."

"I supply the liquor for the Blue Dome," Mantilla added, by way of proving his *bona fides*. He had fine whiskey lines about his hard eyes. "Unless you're well connected down in Nawlins, you'd have to go to Chicago or LA to get a decent single malt or cognac. We've got it right on the other side of that bar."

RC showed up with the soda water. She did what she could, using a table napkin Valentine wished he could use for bed linen, but the joy-juice resisted her efforts.

"Just stand close to me when we dance," Valentine suggested.

"Of course," she said.

"You're from around Natchez?" Hamm asked.

"I've done time in New Orleans, too." Valentine hoped any questions would fix on the latter; his year in the Quisling Coastal Marines would allow him to be conversant about its restaurants, bars and theaters.

"Don't much care for bayou types," Hamm said. "They don't stick in a fight. Not like Texans or Sooners. But I'm prepared to wait and see, seeing as you've got some Indian in you."

"Arsie's got a shot at getting some Indian in her tonight," a major guffawed.

RC waggled her eyebrows, and even Valentine had to laugh.

More food and drink arrived, and Valentine tore into pieces of steak served on thin iron spears, interspersed with vegetables on a bed of rice.

"The rice is native to your Trans-Mississippi," Dom said, visiting the table to see that the party was progressing and noticing Valentine's enthusiasm for the cuisine. "The vegetables come in from Missisisippi, since my usual sources in Texas are pricing themselves out of my reach at the moment. A tragedy, yes? The filet is from a friend's estate in Iowa. He feeds his cattle on a mash of corn and beer, swears by it."

"It is tender," Valentine said. He finished a mouthful and RC wiped grease from his mouth with a napkin.

"You'll need something to wash that down with, Colonel," a colonel named Reeves said. "You still haven't been initiated by the Division Cup."

"By Kur, you're right!" Hamm thundered. "The Division Cup! I brought it all the way here and forgot! Dom, brim it with hero's brandy, would you?"

"Of course, General, but the show—"

"Hold the show, damn you."

"Of course, yes, General."

The Blue Dome's owner returned with a silver two-handled loving cup. He presented it to the general, who took a sip, smacked his lips in approval, then passed it over to Valentine. Valentine looked at the cup, holding what looked to be a quart or so of liquor. The divisional insignia, a sneering, snorting donkey face with "Kickin' Ass!" emblazoned beneath, was etched into the side.

"It's not all brandy; there's sweetwater mixed in," Reeves assured him. "And a tab of Horny, to make sure you're up for the evening."

"You dosed it with Horny?" RC said. "I think I'm insulted, sir."

Not just his fellow divisional officers, but also others looked at him expectantly. There was nothing to do but attempt it, New Order aphrodisiacs or no. He lifted the cup to his lips and drank. And drank. And drank. He felt it running out the sides of his mouth and joining the stains on his uniform shirt and tunic. The men began to pound on the table, chanting, "Kick . . . ass . . . kick . . . ass . . . kick . . . ass."

It was empty. He crashed the cup back to the table hard enough to flip silverware over. The other officers applauded and cheered.

"Outstanding, Le Sain. Well done!"

The accolades whirled around his head as his stomach burbled its outrage. For a moment he was worried it would come back out faster than it went in, but through concentrated effort he kept it down.

RC kissed him on the earlobe. "Well done, Knox."

Valentine sat stupidly, staring at the band, which struck up a tattoo as a man in a red blazer appeared. His heart sounded louder than the big drum on the bandstand.

"Knox?" she said again, before Valentine realized she was talking to him. He tried to focus on her. "Knoooox!?"

"Yes?"

The man in the blazer must have told a joke; everyone was laughing. The band riffed.

"If you need to . . . hit the head, or whatever . . . it's—"

"No, I'm fine," Valentine said, fighting to make coherent conversation. "Warm in here, isn't it?"

"If you need to cool off I've got good air on . . ."

The band drowned her out with a flourish, and two pairs of female dancers each stepped out from either side of the stage. They wore what Valentine guessed were once called biking shorts and sports bras. They started a hip-hop dance number to pre-2022 techno that seemed designed to make Valentine's head throb. Valentine lapsed into silence and watched the girls through their routine, then some kind of magician came on stage and levitated a pair of them into a variety of pseudoerotic poses. RC gave the inside of his leg an exploratory squeeze.

"Ladies and gentlemen," Dom said, taking the microphone from the blazered master of ceremonies when the magician and the girls had gone off stage and the hooting faded. "We've come to the highlight of our show. Returning to our stage, after a too-long absence, is someone I'm sure you all remember well. She needs no introduction, so just let me say . . . Miss Tanny Bright!"

The jazz band exploded into noise again.

A woman marched out onto the stage, smiling and confident, basking in the cheers, applause and wolf whistles from everyone but David Valentine.

He'd even forgotten the witch's brew bubbling in his stomach in the shock of recognition.

Alessa Duvalier wore a stripper's version of the TMCC uniform. A peaked hat was perched on her glorious red hair, tipped so far over it must have been held on with hair pins. Thick layers of stage makeup covered her freckles. She wore a choker with some kind of medal on it, and a sleeveless fatigue shirt cut away to reveal her midriff, held closed by two buttons struggling against her upthrust bosom. A uniform skirt, which ended about where her thighs began, was cut up each side to the web belt. Her stocking-clad legs and patent-leather shoes made the most of her toned limbs. She carried two sheets of flimsies in her hand.

"Oh, how I miss him," she said, pretending to read the pieces of paper in her hands. "All I can think of is the last time we were together."

She looked across the faces in the audience, found General Hamm's eyes, and winked at him theatrically. The men guffawed, and Valentine heard twenty variants of "lucky bastard" muttered. She pretended to finish the letter. "And he's coming home! To me!"

The trumpeter in the band let loose with something that sounded like a bugle call. Duvalier planted her fishnetted legs wide, held the papers to her bosom, and broke into a dome-raising song, set to a marching beat.

> *"My sweetheart's slung his rifle*
> *And marched away from me,*
> *For duty sounds beyond my door*
> *A call to destiny.*
> *Waited true these lonely days*
> *Until his letter came.*
> *I saw the words: 'My darling,*
> *We'll soon be one again!'"*

It was a cheerful, upbeat song, and Duvalier marched across the dance floor, stepping high with her legs, swinging her arms in parody of a dress parade, touching and bouncing from man to man at the edge of the dance floor like a pool ball ricocheting across a billiard table. She ran her fingers up the arm of one, pressed her barely covered derriere against another, brushed a third's hair with her breasts.

Valentine felt the Blue Dome grow warmer, brandy and lust heating his blood.

The other dancers came out on the stage for the chorus, costumed in variants of Duvalier's getup. As they sang, she pretended to wipe the sweat from an officer's brow with the fake letter crumpled in her hand.

She lingered at Valentine's table, tousling the hair of each man as she continued the song. She sat on one's lap and sang into his face, then moved on to Valentine. She wrapped her arms around him and nipped him on the ear as she thrust her hands into his tunic, unbuttoned by RC in her efforts to clean his shirt. Valentine noticed, when her arms came back out, that she only had one sheet of paper in her hand. She kicked up a leg and planted a foot on the table, and all eyes went to her as Valentine buttoned his tunic over the note.

She finished the last chorus of the song at General

Hamm's side, singing it to him. She hopped up on the table before him, feet planted wide to either side of his plate, joining the other dancers for the last chorus.

> *"Wait at the station*
> *For the victory train.*
> *We'll run from the siding,*
> *Dance up lovers' lane,*
> *Stroll along the river*
> *Where first you became mine,*
> *Lose all our worries*
> *In my ring's golden shine!*

The general helped her down and gave her a lip-smacking kiss. Valentine winced, feeling like a man who has just come across his sister in a brothel. Jealousy and disgust, infinitely fouler and more upsetting than the brandy and sweetwater, swirled and bubbled within him.

She looked around the table. "Good evening, Captain Mantilla . . . who's the new face?"

"Colonel Knox Le Sain."

"You don't like oldies, Colonel?"

"A bump and grind on top of my dinner puts me off my feed, funbunny," Valentine said.

"Colonel," Hamm growled. "I won't have you talking about Tanny like that."

"I'll give him funbunny," Duvalier said, reaching for a fork.

RC leaned forward. "The colonel just finished off the brandy in the Third Division Cup—and a tab of Horny. Cut him some slack, Ty."

Valentine's former mentor sat back down on Hamm's lap. She didn't flinch as Hamm rested his hand across her shoulder, fingertips touching her breast. Valentine looked away and back at the stage, nauseated.

"You're in for a messy night," Duvalier said, looking at RC.

"You never know," Valentine's escort answered.

"I am feeling a little—" Valentine began.

"I'll get you some air," RC said, as Valentine rose from his chair.

"No, I'm all right . . . or maybe not." Valentine hurried for the exit. The furniture and décor were an unearthly primary swirl around him. He staggered past the doorman and up the stairs. . . .

When the paroxysm passed he found he was resting against a Dumpster, sweating like a pig and feeling like a small rubber duck floating in a very big lake. He looked around, and reached into his tunic to retrieve the handwritten note. By the blue light of the neon sign, he read Ali's block-capital scrawl.

> Must See You AM Good
> Will be here one day more then to AFB
> Love the (lack of) Hair
>   Meeyao
>   T

Apart from her creative spelling of "meow" it was pure Ali; short, to the point and equivocal in case it ended up in someone else's hands. Much of his education in operating in the Kurian Zone had been from her; though she was just under his age, she had twice his experience as a Hunter. While he wondered if she really was good, he was certain the "AM" referred to A.M. AFB probably meant the old air force base to the north as her destination. Hamm had his headquarters there for the refit; Valentine had been told his battalion was to move north and join him in another week or so. Xray-Tango had promised him more time on the range to practice with the new rifles.

For Valentine, it could not come soon enough. He wanted out of the Kurian Zone; Southern Command needed the Quickwood.

"Feeling better, Knox?" a female voice asked from somewhere across the Missouri line. He dropped the note into the Dumpster, startling a rat sniffing at the vomitus within.

He turned, half expecting to see Ali, but it was RC, holding a hurricane glass full of bubbling water.

"I brought you some more soda. It's good for more than just stains."

"You always this nice?"

"Inside there? Yes."

Valentine accepted the glass and took a mouthful. He spat it into the alley, then drank the rest.

"Better," he said, handing it back to her.

"Is the air helping?"

"Yes. Sorry I'm not conversational. I need sleep."

He couldn't take his eyes from the shadowy vertical line between her breasts. *Her chest was lovely, dark, and deep, but I have promises to keep, and miles to go . . .*

She put a hand on his forearm and drew it from the Dumpster. "My room's just around the corner. We could go up the back stairs."

"Nice of you, but I just need to sleep." If anything, she was more desirable in the muted light of the alley, every turning curve of skin a promise.

"Fine with me, Colonel. If I'm with you, I don't have to make nice in there."

Valentine looked at her, wondering if this was yet another Kurian Zone test or trap. *What the hell.*

"Lead on," he said, holding out his hand.

She took him down the alley and around the corner to the back of the Blue Dome. They went up a wooden stairway, the timbers of which were bolted onto the building like an afterthought. She walked him down a long common balcony.

"Yes, oh man, oh baby, oh my, yes, do it!" A female voice drifted through one of the windows.

"I prefer 'yes, do it, oh my, oh baby, yes,' myself," RC said, turning a knob on a windowless door.

"She gets good marks for volume," Valentine said.

"You wouldn't say that if you lived next to her."

It wasn't so much a room as it was a long closet. There

was a double bed, with a single mounted above in such a way that it formed a half-canopy, a table, two closets . . .

"And a john, for the johns," she said, opening a narrow door. "There's even a shower. If we want a bath, there's a tub down the hall."

"You share the room?"

RC removed her shoes, frowning. "A dancer. Her name's Melanie. If the deadbolt's closed, she knows not to come in. There's a mattress in their dressing room, so she can sleep there tonight."

Valentine collapsed on the double bed, focusing on the ticking pattern on the mattress.

"Bedspins?" RC said, sitting down beside him.

"No. Just really, really, tired."

"Why's your gun off safety?" she asked, examining the gun he'd dropped beside him.

"Old habit, when I sleep in a strange place."

"Tricky with a .45. Don't worry, you're safe. The scuzzies might hit the boats, or the warehouses across the river. Never here."

"I see. You know your guns."

"Basic training starts at eleven for a girl in Dallas. The boys start at eight."

"Louisiana starts at fifteen."

"You don't talk like swamp trash."

"I grew up in New Orleans." Valentine thought he'd better get off the subject in a hurry. "Why'd you leave Big D?"

"You really want to talk, after a tab of Horny?"

"You're beautiful, RC, but I'm about to leave New Columbia. Still a little curious about you. You're authentically nice."

"Authentically nice. I'll take it."

"What's Dallas like?"

"I was on my back at twelve. You invest the capital you're given. I was pretty slender; the guys with a taste for . . . younger stuff . . . dug me until I was over eighteen. My face and hair didn't hurt. But once I passed twenty and had a kid, well, I wasn't worth much to my boss. Dom and Garrett, the doorman, were hunting up girls on the cheap. Dom bought me out for next to nothing, and taught me to talk better and do my eyes right while he was building the joint."

"Where's your—"

"Son, they told me. New Universal Church youth center. Never even got a good look at him."

"Fresh start, huh?"

"Yes. Wasn't a real change, just on the outside. I'm still doing soldiers, still wondering if the penicillin they're giving me is the good stuff or not. I just wear a nicer dress is all. Appearances can be deceiving."

"Yes," Valentine said, drifting off to sleep.

"You ever wanted to change who you are?"

"Constantly."

RC might have been saying something else, just above a whisper, but he sank into an exhausted slumber.

Molly was moving beneath him in the darkness of the little basement room. He felt her bucking beneath him, clawing at his back, but the pain only made him thrust harder. Her eyes screwed up tight in orgasm, then opened as she screamed in passion.

Her slit pupils widened in their yellow irises as her tongue shot toward his breastbone . . .

Valentine woke, the sheets wet against his back, a rancid taste in his mouth as though someone had wiped his mouth with a discarded diaper.

"What's going on?" he whispered. There were thumps and a shout or two from below.

RC turned against him. "Eyuuhh? I don't hear anything."

Valentine felt a Reaper, somewhere below. Its presence pulsed with cold energy. He heard the crash of a table overturning.

"It's two in the morning," RC yawned. "They're just closing up downstairs. Sometimes they have to drag people out."

The Reaper moved into the street as RC spoke. He heard an engine start.

"They took someone out," Valentine agreed. He could picture the scene downstairs. The Reaper arriving, possibly with a human goon or two, and shaking someone awake. The horrible realization that they probably had less than an hour to live as they looked under the hood at the pale, emotionless face. Handcuffs, a waiting vehicle. "The Meet Wagons," they used to call them in New Orleans. Then the final struggle against its embrace: the last dance.

"God, your heart is pounding," RC said, pressing her palm to his chest. "That always happens when you wake up?" She was a shadowy presence beside him, nude, her long hair tied up for sleep. He felt her skin against his leg, softer than the sheets, save for the tickling tangle of hair between her legs.

"I startle easy," Valentine said. The Reaper was gone. He collapsed back on the bed.

Her hand moved lower. "Do you always get a gun when you're startled?"

Valentine's hand had moved to his gunbelt hung on the corner of the bed when he woke, but her attention was fixed on flesh, not steel.

"A gun?"

RC turned up the corner of her mouth as her hand explored him, tugged at his pubes, tested his shaft, cupped his testicles. "That's what I've always called them. Men take a lot of pride in them. Wave them around. They can be dangerous if mishandled." Something of a Texas twang came into her voice. "They shoot. Hell, you've got a real rifle, Knox." She began to stroke him, gently, before turning on the bed. Her nipple left a long, electric trail across his stomach. Her mouth met her hand, and he swelled in excitement. "Big game," she giggled, a string of saliva linking them.

He lay there, enjoying himself, until it occurred to him that Malia Carrasca's baby—his baby, their baby, was due soon. His orgasm, while apparently thrilling to RC, was just an empty series of physical sensations.

* * *

Valentine was on his third glass of water and was reaching for the pitcher again when he heard a knock.

RC rose and slipped a robe on her slight shoulders. "Melanie probably wants the room back. Don't worry, you don't have to leave until you feel like."

"I should be off anyway," Valentine said.

"Mel, gimme a break, woul—" she said to the door as she opened it. Duvalier stood there, her hair tucked in some kind of bag and a mask of creamy mud on her face. "Oh, Ty, hi . . . I've got company."

"I know, RC. Can I talk to him, in private? I need him to do something so I can surprise the Number One on his birthday."

"Umm, yeah . . . I guess."

"Just five minutes, sweetie."

RC looked at Valentine, hurriedly pulling up his trousers. "Knox, you remember Ty?"

"The singer from last night? Check her for forks," he said. "I'm sorry. I was a little drunk last night, Miss, uhhh, Bright. I didn't even know the general's birthday was coming."

"Thanks, sweetie," Ali said. She put a finger to her lips. "Shhhhh, okay? Secret mission."

"My lips are sealed," RC said, grabbing a basket of towels and soap and moving into the hall.

"Not hardly," Duvalier said, closing the door and shooting the lock.

"Tanny Bright?" Valentine said, after sweeping the balcony and the hall with hard ears. It was early morning, still; all he heard were RC's footfalls.

"I told him my real name is Ronny McDonalds, which he thought was even funnier. You missed my second number. Was she worth it?"

"I didn't know you could sing."

"Since this shit started I've sung in three different clubs. I'll let you in on a trade secret: The less she wears, the worse her voice can be. You look a bit green this morning."

Valentine poured himself more water, and offered his fellow Cat a glass, but she shook her head. "The 'hero's brandy' wasn't agreeing with me. I didn't even try to keep it down. My stomach generally knows best. Are we going to talk about anything important?"

She lowered her voice until it made no more noise than the breeze through the shutters. "God yes. I'm still active, under Mantilla. Are you in his contact group too?"

"I understand you're active under Hamm." He used sign language for this, the motions coming slowly thanks to brain-fog.

She switched over to hands as well. "Don't go there, Valentine. I thought you wanted to talk shop."

"You're right. Sorry, whatever you're doing is for the Cause. No, I'm not active. I was delayed getting back from Texas. I didn't return until just before Christmas. It's been nothing but disaster ever since."

Her hands again: "I just found out about you being here when I hit town. Southern Command got the report you sent with Finner. The overrun was already in full swing when I came up from New Orleans. I got the women and kids from your crew out. It's a story I don't have time for. They're safe down at Steiner Station."

"Steiner? Hal Steiner? Lots of rice paddies and a little fortified town?"

"That's the last place I was before this assignment. Steiner's place . . . it's grown. He's trying to feed and hide thousands of refugees in those swamps, plus a chunk of what's left of Southern Command. Got it all phonied up to took like a little Kurian Province. It won't last forever."

"I know," Valentine audibilized this time, though he kept his voice down. "I've got the newest battalion in Hamm's division."

Her hands fluttered like fighting birds; she'd always been better than he at signing. "You say it like it's your fault. It's not. Being mistress to not one, but two, count 'em, two generals and an oily restaurateur wasn't in my plans when I got tasked with infiltration. Mantilla's one of us, too. Not a Cat, but he reports directly to the Lifeweavers. I haven't had the chance to tell him about you."

"You said you have orders from Southern Command?" he signed.

"From the Lifeweavers. They're in hiding, naturally. No sign of Ryu, but your old man Amu's been passing stuff back and forth to me through some Wolves and Mantilla."

"Anything for me?"

She rested her hands for a moment. "Yes, I've got orders. They want you to raise a ruckus behind the lines once the offensive gets under way. Theirs or ours, whichever comes first. Cut the north-south line through Little Rock so they can't shift their forces south quickly. Tie down as many of them as you can for as long as you can."

"If they can hold out a few more months, it'll be a different story. Consul Solon's about to send more of his army back to where they borrowed it. Texas, mostly."

"I've thought they seemed in a big hurry. This is just a guess, but I think something's in the works, Val. Southern Command's going to strike back somewhere unexpected, at least I hope so. If you can gum things up here—"

"I'll see what I can do. What's my line of retreat? Back west to the Ouachitas?"

"I've got nothing for you about that. They said just cause as much trouble as you can, for as long as you can."

With no orders where and when to run? Sorry, Valentine, right place, right time. You're a pawn in a good spot to tie down the King and Queen until they maneuver to take you.

"Who's my superior?" Valentine asked.

"I've no idea. I don't think Southern Command knows much more than that you're in here with some men. They're leaving it up to you."

"Well, there's more. I brought back something, something that kills Reapers. I put that in the report that went out with Finner."

"If you've got something that kills Reapers, start using it. Mantilla might be able to get some to the rest of Southern Command."

"It's just wood. It's some kind of catalyst, acts on the thickening agent in their blood. They seize up and die."

Duvalier pursed her lips in thought. "Wood isn't much help against artillery and armored cars. Speaking of Reapers, that's the second thing I've got to tell you. They arrested a captain on Hamm's staff. I've been stealing papers and I planted some on him to string this out a little more. I think Hamm's getting set to get rid of me. He used to bring his briefcase and what have you when we were together. No more. Kur knows there's a spy in his division. He's taking precautions."

"Good. I'm the new guy; they'll look at me."

"I doubt it. It's gone on since Hamm's predecessor, and they know it. I took him out, by the way. It was business and pleasure. He tried to pass me around like a party favor."

"That house fire. I heard the sad story. Sounded like your handiwork, Smoke."

She smiled and said in a whisper, "That's better than 'funbunny.' You know I wouldn't do the pillow recon if it wasn't for all this shit. The next incendiary device is going down Hamm's pants, then I'm blowing town."

"I'll try to light a fire of my own."

"Be careful."

"Sounds like the orders are to be destructive. That doesn't always go along with being careful."

"Well—"

"Ali, there's something you could do for me. Sort of a last request."

"Still Hornied up?" she said, incredulity written in block capitals on her forehead. "I thought that tall drink of water took care of you. Dream on."

He went back to sign language: "Get me whatever you can on Xray-Tango. He used to serve on the plains. He might even be semifriendly."

"That'll be tricky," she signed back. "I don't even know who's got the intelligence archives."

"Anything you can get me would help," he said.

"I'll see if I can get a message out. Maybe some Wolf can find you with the answer. How important is this?"

"It's important to me. He's got some strange qualities. Makes me think a parent of his might have been a Hunter. Sometimes things get passed down."

"I'll do what I can."

Valentine stood up. "That's always more than enough."

"Thanks, Ghost."

"Keep it safe, Smoke."

She gave him a quick hug and a peck on the cheek. "I've missed working with you, Val," she breathed in his ear. "You're one of the good ones."

Without further explanation, she left.

Valentine picked up his clothes, and looked around RC's shared room. There was a tiny stuffed bear sitting on a shelf in the closet above where the silk cocktail dress hung. He wondered about the little girl it had once belonged to.

He realized he was whistling as he descended the stairs, strangely buoyant. There was sunshine above New Columbia, though the clouds were building as they crept in from the west, but something more than the sun cheered him. RC had brought him an egg-and-toast breakfast after her bath, returning to the half-servant, half-girlfriend manners of the previous night. The taste of fresh eggs and butter wasn't it either. Perhaps it was just the knowledge that Ali was alive and well, and around to help. Despite the hangover he felt as though a door had been thrown open inside him; the world was giving him another day and another chance.

It crossed his mind that it could be the prospect of action. He'd been nervous and breathless since Duvalier's update; plans began to form in his head immediately, and with that momentum his mind shifted to a higher gear. He felt damnably close to precognitive, like a gambler pushing all his winnings onto the green double zero on the roulette table knowing the ball would fall to that slot on the next spin.

Raise a ruckus . . . raise a ruckus . . . Duvalier's words ran through his head like the trumpet's flourish in her rollicking song from last night. He realized where the tune he was whistling had come from.

He made his way through the alley, past the rat-infested Dumpster, and out into the spring sunshine. General Hamm, Reeves and a few of his other officers were enjoying a café breakfast outdoors.

"Coffee's hot, Le Sain, join us," Hamm called.

Valentine grabbed an empty chair. "Thank you. Just one cup, though. I've got to get across the river, General. The battalion is probably wondering what happened to me."

"They'll survive a few more hours. We had some funny business in the night, Le Sain. You've got some mud on your collar, by the way." Hamm stared at the stain for a moment, then continued. "One of my officers was taken away, and I don't like it. Williams. You remember him?"

"I met him last night," Valentine said, remembering the vigorous young officer, exchanging jibes with the rest of the table, frightened only by the bar tab he was running up. "But he wasn't on the trip out to the Consul's Residence."

"No. No, he wasn't. Apparently he went rooting through my papers while I was away."

"He had access to them?"

"He was my chief of staff's assistant," Hamm said, eyes leveled like firing squad muzzles at Reeves. Reeves looked a little pale in the morning sunshine.

Valentine tucked his collar under his tunic, hiding Ali's pasty smear.

"Who came—"

"The usual," Hamm cut him off. "By the time they woke me, he was gone, or I'd have asked some questions. I can't figure out why someone with access to my office would steal everyday correspondence. Something from the safe, yes, that'd be valuable to those crackers. But why steal letters about the state of the transport system in northern Arkansas . . . err, the Upper Trans-Mississippi? We're supposed to stop with the old state designations, by the way, Le Sain. Solon's orders."

"Because he wasn't a spy, someone wanted him to look

like one?" Valentine said, feeling that it was a rhetorical question due out of Hamm's mouth within about five seconds.

Hamm leaned closer to him. "It's looking like there's a spy in my headquarters, Knox. We got royally raped last October, and I think it's because someone knew the hour and date we were pulling out of the line and sidling."

"Ask Solon for different orders for the offensive, or to move up the date, and keep them to yourself until the last minute, is my suggestion, sir. That or get a bigger safe."

"I'm wondering if I need a new chief of staff. I get the feeling you can organize and think for yourself. I need to replace Williams. You want the job? Staff work's a lot nicer than line duty."

"Sir, your offer is tempting, but I have to stay with my men—at least until all this is over. I want to see them blooded."

"Thought you were looking for promotion, responsibility. That'd come with a staff position. They make general more often than not."

"I am, sir, but responsibility is like water. It flows better from the top down."

Hamm murmured Valentine's words, trying them out on his tongue. "Hey, I like that. Mind if I use it in my next speech to the division?"

"I'd be honored, sir. But I need to get back across the river—oh, speaking of the river, where can I find Captain Mantilla? I'd like to put in an order."

"His tug's tied up at the wharf right now. It's battleship gray, with big blue letters on it. OGL. You need something, son?"

"Bourbon and tobacco. Not for me, for my officers."

"I like your style, Le Sain. I'm glad you're in my division."

The barge was even uglier than the old *Thunderbolt*. It looked like a couple of aluminum mobile homes piled on a raft, and needed a lot of rust-stripping before another coat of gray. Sure enough, gigantic letters stood out on the side just below the carbon-coated stack, OGL.

The anchor watch was asleep. A fleshy man, bald as Valentine and bronze-skinned by birth and sun, slept in the sun at the end of the gangway. An iodine-colored bottle rested between his legs.

"Excuse me, boatman?" Valentine said, venturing up the gangplank. He still felt as though there was an inch of air between his feet and the ground—and he couldn't stop looking at the bridge over the Arkansas River, and Solon's Residence hill beyond.

If anything, the snoring grew louder.

"Sir?"

Valentine came closer. The man was a dedicated napper, so much so that he sacrificed shaving and bathing in its pursuit.

Valentine flicked his fingernail against the bottle, eliciting a *ting*. "Closing time. Last call," Valentine tried, a little more loudly.

"Hrumph . . . umpfh . . . umpfh . . . double me up again, good buddy," the anchor watch said, coming awake in eye-blinking confusion.

"Did I guess the password?"

"Sorry there, sir. I was resting my eyes, didn't see you come up."

"They're still pretty red, friend. Eight more hours oughta do it. Can I find Captain Mantilla on board?"

"Engine room, I expect. He's usually there when we're not hauling." The anchor watch stood up and gave his belt a lift. "Follow the blue streak."

Sure enough, Valentine picked up a steady stream of grumbles and curses in English, Spanish, French and what he guessed to be Russian or Polish.

"C'mon, *panoche*. Loosen up, you bitch. *Kurva*, what's the matter with you this morning, you old *putain*."

"Cap, this ol' boy's come aboard askin' for you," the boatman called down the hatch. "Wearin' a TMCC pisscutter and a turkey on his collar."

"*Merde*. Just a moment, Chief." Valentine heard tools being put down, and then someone coming up the ladder.

Mantilla's face appeared in the sun, smeared with grease like Comanche war paint. He furrowed his brows. "Morning, Colonel. Saw you last night but damned if I can remember your name."

"Le Sain, *mon frere*. I want to talk about getting a little extra cargo up here, the next time you come up the Arkansas."

"Thanks, Jim Bob, I'll take it from here." As the sailor moved back to his shady rest, Mantilla pulled out a cigarette and sat on the edge of the hatch. "What can I get you, Colonel?"

"I'm an old friend of Miss Bright's. You've done a few favors for her, and I need something similar. She sent me."

Mantilla took a sidelong look at him and blew out a lungful of carcinogens. "You stick your head in the noose first, Le Sain."

"When you talk to her faraway friends, you probably referr to her as Smoke. If you speak to the same people, call me Ghost."

"Pleased to meet you. How can I help?"

"I need something brought to Southern Command."

"Fair enough. I have to tell you plain, sir, that's getting trickier by the month. I can't guarantee anything. What is it, people, papers, photos?"

"Some wood. Just a few dozen four-by-four beams."

"You're shitting me."

"It's not really the wood, it's what's in the wood."

"Gold? Platinum?"

"If you don't know, you can't tell anyone. I just want to know if you can get them into the Boston Mountains."

"Boston Mountains? You're misinformed. That's just a screen. The Ozark high command's hiding out in the bayous in the southwest. Big Hal Steiner's got them hidden."

"Really?"

"Easier to feed them from the swamps and rivers. He's got rice up the wazoo, too. The part of your army that's holding out up north, it's mostways teams of your Bears and Wolves wearing Guard uniforms. The invaders got so busy blocking up the mountains they didn't catch the evacuation south. They think the whole southeastern corner of Arkansas is a Kurian backwater. All those Grogs Steiner has around the place has them confused."

"I've been there. You could hide an army there."

"They won't be hiding there much longer."

Valentine, already excited, hooked a thumb in his belt near his .45's holster. "When?"

"Soon. Within weeks."

"You a Cat, or what?"

Mantilla bristled. "Look, Colonel, let me have my secrets, too. We're on the same team, isn't that enough?"

"When you're on a team it's nice to know if you're talking to a quarterback or the towel guy."

"I'm more like the towel guy, Colonel. I'm due downriver yesterday. Can you get me your beams in double time?"

"How's tonight?"

"Tonight's excellent," Mantilla said, nodding approvingly and relaxing again.

"How you want to work it?"

"There's lots of shallows on the south bank, just downstream of the pilings from the first bridge. I'll ground her. I'll splash ashore and your men will rock me off using the wood as levers. That okay with you? Don't want to break open the Quickwood and have a bunch of gold fall out."

Valentine came to his feet. "Quickwood? How the hell do you know it's called Quickwood?"

"From you."

"How's that?"

"Call it intuition. Specific intuition."

"I thought only the Lifeweavers did tricks like that."

The enigmatic captain scratched an itch between his eyes. "Lifeweavers and us towel boys."

"Can you get me some bourbon and cigars? I told Hamm I was here to see you about that."

"Popular items. I keep them in stock. I'll drop them off tomorrow."

Valentine held out his hand. "Until tonight, then, Captain."

"Until tonight."

Valentine looked at the traffic waiting for the ferry and decided to hazard the footbridge for the railroad workers. The span was complete, track had been laid to both ends of the bridge and the wood-and-iron construct, Xray-Tango's first priority, would be ready to carry regular trains in another day or two once the sidings were coordinated. There had been a pontoon bridge, but it had been lost to the flood and never replaced. A few of the floats that weren't swept away were still pulled up on the riverbank.

He ascended the bank—one day there would be stairs, according to some wooden stakes pounded into the riverbank dirt. The trusswork was admirable; many of the top beams were recovered and straightened from the structural steel of Little Rock's former skyscrapers. Piled up ties waited for the crews to come and fix the rails to them. When finished, there would be a single track and a footpath wide enough for three men to walk abreast across the river, or a truck in an emergency. But the footpath would be finished last. For now, the workers had to either walk from tie to tie or walk across on the fixtures at the base of the trusses. Valentine chose the latter.

Valentine liked bridges. The engineering appealed to the mathematic, rational part of him, and their suspended airiness gratified his artistic side. He paused in the center and looked around New Columbia, from the northward bend in the river to the northwest, where Solon had his Residence on the steep-sided hill rising three hundred feet above the river, mirroring the wider Pulaski Heights opposite, then across the antheap where his soldiers had their camp, to the swampy flats of the former airport to the southeast.

Raise a ruckus.

He examined the south-side river wharf, where a barge offloaded trucks, a few artillery pieces and little tracked carries that reminded him of beetles. The cargo had probably come from one of the factories on the Ohio—he'd heard the Kurians had opened the river to barges all the way to the Mississippi. It made sense; cargo could be moved more easily on the water than by any other method. The guns were probably 105s, a cheap, simple gun his fellow TMCCers called "use 'em and lose 'ems." The Kurians, in their efforts to keep weaponry—and therefore humanity—at a pre–First World War level to prevent "the human predilection for self-slaughter" as the New Universal Church put it, frowned on most weapons greater than small arms or armored cars. Artillery was brought to a campaign, used and then destroyed when the fighting was over.

Logistics.

He'd heard a lecture in Pine Bluff from a Guard general, who'd modified Napoleon's dictum that "any lieutenant can plan a campaign, but it takes an unusual sort of soldier to carry one out." This general's version was that any lieutenant could fight their troops, but it took professionals to train and supply them so they'd be ready for a fight. Valentine was inclined to agree; in his days with the Wolves it seemed his days were filled with acquisition and distribution of food, water, bullets, bandages, boots, hats, antiseptic, salt . . . If they were lucky, there was only a shortage of one or two items on this long list of requirements for men in the field.

New Columbia was a tribute to the complexities of logistics. Solon was shifting his base from Hot Springs to his new capital, and Xray-Tango's brush hair was going gray in the general's efforts to keep up with the needs of the troops concentrated to the north and scattered to already-conquered stations west and south. Southern Command's factories were so much scorched earth. What had been the Free Territory was in chaos, and the scattered settlements were being concentrated into collective farms; they'd not be contributing to the TMCC bread-bags until fall, if then. Every other day flat-bottomed barges were pulling up to the wharf and offloading, and soon the southern rail line back into Texas would be running more up from Hot Springs.

> *Wait at the station*
> *For the victory train*
> *We'll run from the siding . . .*

Whistling again, in syncopation with his footfalls, Valentine crossed the bridge.

The delivery of much of his Quickwood had gone off without a hitch; Mantilla's tug showed up where and when arranged. He told Mantilla to ask Southern Command to strike as soon as possible, explaining what he had in mind. Time was critical, and they had to move while Consul Solon was still arranging his formations for the closeout moves in his bid to pacify the Ozarks.

"I can put the word in the Lifeweaver's ear, but whether Southern Command'll listen . . ." Mantilla said, shrugging. The night made his eyesockets black wells, unfathomable.

"One more thing, please."

"How can I refuse anything to the Cat who would dare challenge such a lion in his own den? What is it, *mon frere*?"

"I won't ask, but if you have contacts further downriver, especially near Pine Bluff, tell them to be ready to hit hard when I move. Civilian and militia uprising."

"Such an order can only be given by Southern Command's General Staff."

"Then Southern Command's General Staff can take it up with me."

"If you live. It is a forlorn hope, my friend."

"You know my orders; you passed them on to Smoke. 'Raise a ruckus.' The more widespread it is, the better."

"You are exceeding your orders, I think."

Valentine looked at the lights strung on the bridge like holiday decorations. "I think so too. It's still the right thing to do."

"We've got our orders to pack up and join the rest of the division," Valentine said to his assembled officers the next night.

The meeting was held in his NCO bar and recreation

room, formerly a basement gym in one of Little Rock's office buildings. The crowd of sergeants, lieutenants, Bears and company officers kept Narcisse busy at the coffee urn. Everyone was eating dinner off of trays around a Ping-Pong table. The green surface was thick with three colors of chalk.

Nail and Ahn-Kha were lounging in wooden chairs outside the club, charged with preventing any interruptions for three hours. Post, the other officer with detailed knowledge of Valentine's plan, at least since last night when he'd gone over it with his select circle, was keeping an eye on things along with Hanson, the gunnery sergeant Valentine had also brought into the plan in its formative stages. Hanson had given the operation its name: Double Boxcars. The crap pit slang described Hanson's estimation of the scheme's chances of coming off as planned, rolling two sixes with two dice. Twice in a row.

"But even if it's a cluster fuck, we'll cause a hell of a lot of damage."

Styachowski had spent hours with Valentine writing on the Ping-Pong table that afternoon. She'd taken to wearing baggy cargo shorts because of her cast, and she'd loosened her shirt to give her more freedom of movement as she reached across the table to draw, fighting an occasional sniffle. Valentine coudn't help but admire her splendid body, though it seemed that her gymnast's legs and swimmer's shoulders had sucked all the vitality from the rest of her: she was still as pale and bloodless as ever, even on the hearty, well-balanced meals issued by Xray-Tango's commissary.

Her constant questions as she wrote out orders helped sort his own ideas. The men would have to get rid of their TMCC uniform tops; the rules of war, such as they were, allowed ruses in enemy uniform as long as the uniforms were changed before taking hostile action. The men would dispose of their tunics. Narcisse was already dyeing their undershirts black. To further distinguish friend from foe in the dark Ahn-Kha had suggested bandoliers of red demolition tape. There were rolls of it lying around, used to mark off areas known to contain mines, unexploded munitions or construction blasting.

Each quadrant of the table had a sketch of a critical zone in the plan: the wharf and supply warehouses, the train line running through New Columbia, the prison camp, and the Kurian Tower.

The last was the result of a cryptic comment from Mantilla as they'd loaded the beams onto the foredeck of his aged barge, after his faked grounding had been ended. "Good luck, Colonel. Be sure you hit the tower. Go down. Not up. The rat's in the cellar. Here's a little gift from the Redhead. You'll need it soon, I think." He'd given Valentine a bag with two bottles of bourbon. It had a false bottom. When Valentine found the hidden zipper he came up with his pair of Cat "fighting claws," and a little box with five flash-bangs inside. They were about the size of yo-yos, and each had a lacquered picture from a matchbook on it. Valentine recognized the matchbooks; they were bars and restaurants he and Duvalier had dined in while posing as husband and wife in New Orleans. A note from Duvalier rolled up in the box read:

G -The Good captain kept these for me, for you.
Luck - s

A second, rolling, blackboard stood against the wall, where Valentine had drawn the rail line running north from New Columbia, adding times for the trip up to Third Division's position.

If there were an unexpected visit from Xray-Tango, Styachowski's Ping-Pong table would be covered with plastic and a tablecloth, then heaped with food. Hopefully the visiting general wouldn't notice the detailed drawing of the Consular Residence along the way, and Valentine could look like he was giving a simple briefing about their shift north to join the TMCC's lines south of the Boston Mountains.

There were the usual questions. Dumb ones from officers who'd already had their role explained to them, and just wanted to hear it repeated again. Smart ones about what to do if there were a disaster at another component of the plan. Styachowski answered all questions, never once needing an assist from Valentine. She'd absorbed the details of Boxcars like a sponge taking in water, but had chafed at not having a more active roll in the operation.

"If the train's SNAFU, go to the barge," Styachowski said in answer to a question about failure in one part of the operation. "If the barge is underwater, go to the train. If they're both impossible, we'll get what we can across on the ferry."

Then there were the inevitable what-ifs. Valentine finally called a halt to it.

"Things are going to go wrong. Improvise. This plan boils down to getting to Objective Omega with everything you can haul. Supplies. Medicine. Prisoners. The tubes. But getting the men there comes first. I'd rather have you alive on the hill than dead trying to haul another mortar up there."

"But there's bound to be fighting," a sergeant said.

"At the docks and warehouses it'll be supply sergeants and clipboard-holders. Everything else, save the Kurian Tower, are sentries and police. Other than the guards at the prison camp, they're not used to carrying weapons every day. You'll outnumber and outgun them. The nearest real troops are watching the river and the roads from Pulaski Heights. If they move, their orders will probably be to go secure the Kurian Tower. They can't hurt us with anything but their mortars, and I don't think they'll fire into the town. If they do, they'll just help us do our job."

"As we said at the beginning," Post added, "we're like bank robbers. Scare everyone shitless, grab the money and haul ass before the cops arrive. And that's all." The men chortled at that. "How you scare 'em, how much you take and how soon the cops show up are variables we can't know until we're in the middle of the robbery. So you're going to have to do some thinking."

"What about the security guards?" Lieutenant Zhao asked, extending the metaphor.

Valentine tapped the corner of the map showing the

Kurian Tower. "You don't have to worry about that. It's my job. Even if we don't get him, we should be able to stop him from coming after you with the Hoods."

Styachowski's face went blank. She would assume command of the operation if something happened to Valentine's group. "Okay, our train up to the front is in two days. Those of you on the train detail, watch them send out the train north tomorrow morning. See where the guards are. They'll be expecting spectators; it's the first train to cross the bridge. Be sure to cheer your lungs out as it goes over."

The meeting dispersed, but one soldier waited outside with the patience of a plowhorse. Jefferson, the Texas teamster, smoked a cigarette wrapped up in the distinctive gray-green paper of a discarded New Universal Church *Guidance* propaganda sheet.

"You had something for me, sir?"

"Two things, Jefferson. First, these." Valentine handed him a half dozen of the boxes of cigars he'd acquired from Mantilla in a waterproof canvas pocket. Jefferson smelled the tobacco as though it were a bouquet of roses.

"Thank you, sir." The teamster couldn't keep his eyes from narrowing in suspicion, though.

"You're right, Jefferson, it's a last favor. You've gone above and beyond the past couple of months. You were just supposed to get the wagons safely to a Southern Command outpost, and ever since the ambush outside of Bern Woods you've been running with us. Time for you to go home. If you'd like to try, that is."

As Jefferson smiled, Valentine could see the spaces where the Quislings had knocked out teeth. "I sure would. But I want to be here for this fight."

"Sorry. I'm giving you my horse, a TMCC map and a courier warrant clearing you to Hot Springs. One favor, though. I've got some papers I'd like you to drop off with Colonel Meadows at Bullfrog's Station. Can you find it again?"

"Easy enough, if I've got the right ID." Valentine liked the cheery confidence in his voice.

"You can leave whenever you like, but the sooner, the better."

Jefferson took a long drag on the homemade cigarette, muscles at the corners of his mouth working.

"Out with it, Jefferson."

"You got some good men here, sir. I hate to leave them if a fight's in the cards. Feels too much like running."

"It's not Texas' fight."

"There's a lot who think that way. I'm not one of them."

Valentine offered his hand. "Jefferson, get to Meadows and you'll have done more for what's coming than a whole company of riflemen. And when you get back to Texas . . . there's no way I can make this official, but any pressure that could be brought to bear on Oklahoma or Dallas . . . it'll help us if they start screaming to have their troops returned."

"I'm a Ranger teamster, not a general."

"Jefferson, I'll write up a promotion for you to lieutenant in Southern Command. That'll make you an official emissary, if you think that'll help."

"It might at that." Jefferson tried a salute on for size. "Thank you, sir."

Valentine touched his eyebrow in return. "Take good care of that horse. He'll get you there."

With the paperwork done, Jefferson rode out after the midday meal. Afternoon gave way to a warm evening; spring was truly on the way. Valentine and Ahn-Kha sat on mats on the floor of his tent, playing mahjong with the pieces Carrasca had painted for him.

"It's a good plan, my David. Stop chewing on it and swallow."

"I feel like I'm making a mistake. I'm basing this on Solon's reaction. Suppose he just cordons us off and lets us sit?"

"Maybe we'll catch him in his hole."

"He's off to Pine Bluff, trying to hurry up the rail gangs

and get his precious airfield built. Don't know why, since there aren't any airplanes to bring in. Then it's down to Hot Springs to see how the relocation of TMCC headquarters is coming."

"He doesn't want to put too many eggs in any one state, I notice," Ahn-Kha said, removing a green dragon pair.

"I shoulda seen that coming," Valentine said.

"Colonel! Colonel!" someone shouted from outside.

Valentine stood in a smooth motion, as if he'd been pulled up by wires. He went to the tent flap.

"Yes, Yvaro?"

"There's been . . . Sergeant M'Daw, he's stabbed, on the edge of camp. I think he's dying."

The night turned cold and unfriendly. *What in God's name?* With Boxcars so close he'd been having M'Daw watched. Valentine still wondered if he wouldn't return to his old allegiance when the time was right.

"Ahn-Kha, tell Lieutenant Nail about this, and have him bring a stretcher. Let's treat him here. Okay, Yvaro, what happened?"

"He'd turned in for the night. I thought so, anyway. Then I hear a shout from the latrine. It was him, and I ran over and saw him. Someone stuck him in the back with one of those wooden spears the Smalls made."

"Your breath smells like coffee," Valentine said. "You got a cup to help you through the watch, I suppose."

"How—yes, sir, sorry sir."

"Just take me to M'Daw. We'll worry about it later."

Valentine ran to the NCO latrine and showers. The men still lived in tents, but Valentine saw to it they had huts for shower and privy. The corporal panted, trying to keep up with Valentine.

M'Daw was unconscious. He lay behind the showers. He'd pulled out the spear and lost a lot of blood. Soldiers were gathered around, and one had a bloody dressing held tight against M'Daw's lower back. Across the mounds of rubble, the lights of the other installations of New Columbia were alive. Valentine did a quick search from the top of a ruined wall, but whoever had stabbed him could easily get away without being seen among the smashed buildings.

Hank Smalls ran up one of the hills toward the camp, crying. Blood ran from his nose and drops covered the front of his shirt.

"Hank!" Valentine called.

"Captain!" Hank sobbed, sinking to his knees.

"Raintree," Valentine called over his shoulder to one of the medics. "Help me here. It's the boy."

Valentine went to his knees and hugged Hank. The boy was a sniveling mess.

"Sir, my folks are running. Decided to run and tell the others about y'all. I din't know about it. Mister M'Daw tried to stop him and Pa stuck him."

Good God. We're dead.

"Where's he gone?"

"They want to turn you in. Did I do right?"

Valentine couldn't tell a boy that turning in his parents was the right thing to do, no matter the circumstances. Even as his mind regained its equilibrium, he grew angry with himself for not just telling the Smalls the whole truth. They knew he was lying. They'd just misinterpreted his lies.

"If you thought it was right, it was right. This is important, Hank; do you know where they were headed?"

Hank rubbed his eyes and climbed a mound of concrete to get a better view. He held a reinforcing rod and pointed.

Please don't let it be the Kurian Tower, Valentine prayed.

"That building."

Valentine followed Hank's finger. He was pointing at Xray-Tango's headquarters.

"Raintree, get Hank and M'Daw to the first aid tent. Do what you can for both of them."

Valentine had learned to run and think in his years with the Wolves. He ran to his tent, grabbed his gunbelt, and stuck his fighting claws in the cargo pockets in his pants. He took up the flash-bangs and his bolo knife, putting the first in his pocket and the second on his belt. *What else, what else?* He grabbed a few pieces of wax-paper-wrapped gum from the little box of luxuries beside his bed.

As he pulled his tunic back on, Ahn-Kha, Post, Styachowski, Nail and assorted faces gathered outside his tent, all in various states of undress.

"What's going on, sir?" Post, a flare gun in his hand, asked as he emerged.

"We've set a new record for things going wrong in an operation. It's started to fail thirty-six hours before the jump-off hour. Our masquerade is over."

"Miracle it lasted as long as it did," Nail said.

"No miracle," Narcisse said, appearing from the darkness. "Magic of the right hand."

Valentine took the gun and a satchel of flares from Post. "We're going to start Boxcars in thirty minutes; you all are going to be occupied. First thing is to get everyone up and ready. Don't go yet. I've got to run down a renegade. I'm taking Ahn-Kha. If you see a red flare from Xray-Tango's headquarters, we're aborting; head west into the mountains and do your best. A green flare from the Kurian Tower means commence Boxcars. Just hit whatever you can as soon as you can. Nail, your team has farthest to go, get your team to Alpha and I'll catch up. I've got to go confuse the issue. Post, get the pikes and stabbing spears, and the spare guns; I hope we'll need them. Make sure Ahn-Kha's platoon gets to the ferry. Styachowski, set up operational HQ at Alpha. You're in charge. Remember, red, run; green, go."

"Make it a go, sir, I've been running for near a year now," Hanson said.

"You're the best hope of the Ozark Free Territory. Act like it." Valentine gave them all a salute. "Ahn-Kha, let's go. Good luck, everyone."

The Golden One slung Valentine's old PPD—Ahn-Kha had made a few hundred Mauser reloads for it by hand—and trotted into the darkness.

"By now Smalls has had time to tell his story," Valentine said as they ran together, Ahn-Kha moving at his Grog canter using both hands and feet. "Xray-Tango's been woken up. Will they come for me or call an alert?"

"They'll ask Smalls more questions."

"Hope I can get there before Xray-Tango makes any decisions."

Ahn-Kha slipped the red flare into the gun as they approached the old bank. "My David, let's just fire this. We can get away clean into the hills. Much better off than when we walked up to the Ruins. We'll still cause them trouble in the mountains."

"Old horse," Valentine said, sticking a piece of chewing gum in his mouth. "I want them mad as hornets. I want Solon so peeved that he won't rest until I'm hanging from a gallows. I don't want to just be a distraction; I want to be an obsession. Put a green flare in. I'll be out in a couple of minutes."

Valentine left Ahn-Kha well hidden with a view of the headquarters building. With the gum softened he pulled it out of his mouth, shaped it and stuck a piece in each ear. He trotted out to the street, and came up to the guards in front of the building.

"Did some civvies just run in here? Man and a woman?" he asked the corporal.

"Yes, Colonel Le Sain, they—"

"Thank God. They don't come out the door, and if you see them climb out the windows, you shoot."

"Uhhh—"

"Surround the headquarters with your men. Right now, Corporal. I don't want them getting away with this."

Valentine ran up the stairs and into the light of the headquarters. One of Xray-Tango's staff had a field phone to his ear. He tapped the lieutenant on the shoulder.

"Yes, a security detail. Something's—" the man began, and then turned, recognizing him. "Just a moment," he said to the phone.

"There's been a murder in my camp. A sergeant is dead. I need to find General Xray-Tango."

"Downstairs, Colonel. Ummm . . . a man and a woman

came in . . . it's rather confused, sir. You're to be taken for questioning."

"I've got some angry answers. Where are the Smalls?"

"Downstairs, with . . . Wait, sir, you can't go down there with your weapons."

Valentine took off his pistol belt and hung it on the chair in front of the lieutenant. "Easily done. Send the security detail downstairs, too, there's someone I want arrested."

He didn't wait for any more protests. He descended the stairs and listened for voices in the quiet of the basement offices. Even through gum-clogged ears he could hear questions and crying coming from a room down the hall, in a different direction from the one where he had his conversation with Mu-Kur-Ri's avatar. A military policeman stood outside the door.

"That was quick work," he said, looking behind Valentine expectantly.

Valentine advanced on him. "Sorry, Corporal, I beat the detail here. Where's that renegade, Smalls? I want you to put him under arrest for murder."

"He's being questioned now. Wait, sir, you can't—"

"You're under arrest," Valentine said. "Insubordination, for a start." The corporal shrank back as if Valentine had waved a hot poker at him.

The Smalls were already under what might be called intensive questioning. They sat in chairs, side by side, in a darkened room with a bright light shining on them from a desk set in the center of the room. Their questioners stood with backs to Valentine. He could see blood on Mrs. Smalls' hands and frock, the fear in Mr. Smalls' eyes at events spinning out of control.

An MP, three officers, Xray-Tango and the Smalls. Seven.

"Now it's not just Le Sain, it's the whole battalion? Seven hundred men?"

"Horseshit!" Valentine roared, unscrewing the bottom of his flash-bang. The trigger button popped out. *Armed.* "You left something behind, Smalls. Take a look, everyone."

"Le Sain, what—" Xray-Tango began, but Valentine

shouldered his way through the questioners, pushing the general up against a wall, and slammed the flash-bang down on the table—triggering the button on the bottom. *Three seconds.*

The top was hand-painted with a vintage nude. Marilyn Monroe knelt against a red satin background, her arms behind her head, back arched, milky breasts lifted, a go-for-broke smile on her face.

He swung toward Xray-Tango, turning his back on Marilyn. He shut his eyes and shoved his hands in his pockets. "General, I'd like—" he said, and clapped his hands over Xray-Tango's ears.

Crack!

It wasn't a concussive explosion—more like someone loosing both barrels of a twelve-gauge—though even outdoors it left unprotected ears ringing. In the confines of the underground room the noise hit like a hammer blow. Even worse was the flash. Through his screwed-shut eyes Valentine still saw orange. Valentine popped Xray-Tango between the eyes with a strong jab. As the general's head *thunked* against the wall like a tossed coconut he followed through with a body blow to the solar plexus. Xray-Tango let loose with an asthmatic gasp and folded. Valentine slipped on his fighting claws.

He waded into the stunned Quislings. They were staggering around in ululating confusion, a six-player game of blind-man's bluff held under the influence of bad LSD. The confusion turned to screaming when Valentine opened the first throat with his claws. The questioning officer had caught himself in a corner. Valentine dug his claws into each side of the man's neck and pulled. The blood of opened arteries went everywhere. He raked another across the kidneys. The man went spinning in shrieking pain into Smalls, knocking both to the floor. Mrs. Smalls could still see; she turned her face from her husband to see Valentine advancing on her.

"You—not—no," she cried, more or less able to see what was coming.

He caught her with an elbow in the temple, and she sagged. He stabbed her husband in the Adam's apple, driving the extra-long straight middle claw into his voice-box. Maybe the Reaper would be in a forgiving mood, and delay killing him until he could tell the story in a few weeks.

But he doubted it.

It was awful, and it took too long.

Valentine looked around the abattoir. The knocked-over desk lamp illuminated walls splattered with blood, a floor painted in black and red depending on the fall of the light. The man with the slashed kidneys still twitched, in too much pain to rise again.

"General," Valentine said, lifting Xray-Tango to his feet. "General!"

"Spots. Alls I seeze spots," he said, drunkenly.

Valentine shook him in frustration.

"Scottie! Scottie!" he barked.

"Huh? Le Sain, what the hell—" The general's face fell into limp horror as he picked out a few details of the room with his damaged retinas.

"Everything the Smalls said is true. I'm a soldier with Southern Command. It's a rising, all over the TM," Valentine said, exaggerating the last a little. "I want you to join us. Fight the Reapers, instead of feeding them."

"God, the blood—"

"What'll it be, General? Fight or feed?"

"Ouch, you're hurting me, dammit."

Valentine felt a Reaper coming. Coming in anger, coming in fury, coming in haste.

"No time, General."

"Good God, they're all dead."

Coming fast.

"With me, General. You back me up, or I'll kill you. Give me that!"

Valentine gripped the pistol being taken from the general's holster. It turned into a wrestling match—which he had no time for. He raked his claws across the generals forearm, opening skin. The pistol came free. Valentine kicked it away, slipping off his claws.

He retrieved the gun, a standard KZ officer's revolver, rugged and reliable. He pulled back the hammer; the click sounded muted to his recovering ears.

"Out the door. I want you in front of me if anyone's shooting."

He heard banging somewhere below. In the direction of the Reaper. *Locked in an underground chamber? "In case of emergency, wake the vampire"?*

Xray-Tango poked his head into the hallway. Neither bullet nor Reaper claw removed it.

"It's clear. Don't get nervous, that thing triggers easy."

"Hurry, there's a Reaper coming."

"Jesus."

"The stairs. The gun stays pointed up as long as you keep quiet."

Valentine took a good two-handed grip on the gun. He heard a door give way and shoved the general with his shoulder. "It's coming. Upstairs! Upstairs!"

He pushed the general to the stairs and through the crash door at the bottom. As he slammed it behind them, he saw a shadow fly across the hallway and into the interrogation room. Mr. Smalls squealed—for the last time. Valentine shut the pathetically tiny bolt on the door.

"A bodyguard went nuts! Fuckin' tore everyone apart," Valentine shouted upstairs, pushing the general up in front of him. "That Hood's berserk."

An MP and another Quisling soldier stood at the top of the stairs, both pointing guns down at them.

"General?" Valentine asked, putting Xray-Tango between him and the rifles, just in case.

"Put up those guns, damn it. Run, run for it, boys. Or we're all dead!" Xray-Tango shouted, which was probably true enough.

Thank God!

Valentine got the general to the top of the stairs as the MP ran. Valentine heard another door downstairs torn off its hinges. He heard the scream of some other unfortunate pulled from a hiding spot. Probably the MP. That was enough for the TMCC grunt at the stairs. He put up his rifle and ran for the door, with a convincing "Get out of here!"

His example was one to be followed. The other officers and men made for the exits. One threw a chair out the window, and was about to follow it when a bullet whizzed by. One of the sentries outside, hearing shouts and confusion within, had shot in panic.

"What the—?" the private said.

"Try the door," Valentine suggested, grabbing his pistol belt and heading for the second story. "C'mon, General, let's call for help," he said, waving the pistol to point upstairs. Valentine smashed a red case on the wall and extracted the fire ax from within.

Either he was moving fast or the general was slow; it seemed an eternity until they came through the door to the radio room on the second floor. The rest of the floor was a cavern of future construction. Two operators stood next to the radios, both armed and pointing their weapons at Valentine and Xray-Tango. A trio of message tubes stood up from the floor like unfinished plumbing fixtures.

"Fuck! FUCK! Hold it right there, mister," the radioman with sergeant's stripes said, eyes bulging at the sight of the blood on Valentine.

"Holy shit," the other added, shaking like he had a jackhammer in his hand instead of a revolver.

"Watch those weapons there, soldiers," Xray-Tango said.

"I'm the only one who made it out," Valentine said. "If I were you two, I'd get gone. It's a bodyguard. It's going nuts."

"Jesus, that happened to my cousin in Armarillo," the shaking one said. "Like it got ravies. It killed thirty people before they stopped it."

"If you've got a way out of here that doesn't involve the stairs, I'd use it," Valentine said. "We'll call for help."

"It's my responsibility," Xray-Tango said, his eye twitching madly and the words barely getting out. "Run along, boys."

The men heard a crash below and decided they knew a sensible order when they heard it. They scrambled out the window and dropped to the ground below.

Valentine offered Xray-Tango the ax handle. "You want the honors?"

"Sorry, Le Sain, or whoever you are. I was true to you, best as I could be. You weren't straight with me."

"Could I have been?"

"That's a 'what-if.' I don't like to waste time with 'what-ifs.' I'm no renegade. I can't let you smash the radio. The only other unit strong enough to send for help is at the quartermaster office at MacArthur Park, down by the warehouses, and if you smash that one too, no one will get here in time. Assuming you cut the field-phone lines north on the bridge, and south on the poles, that is."

Valentine shared a smile with his former superior.

There was a scream from downstairs.

"Sorry, General," Valentine said. He swung the ax handle, connecting solidly with Xray-Tango's temple. He reversed the grip and, with three precise blows, left the radio in pieces.

Valentine hid behind rolls of weatherproofing, ax across his lap, lowering his lifesign. He pulled inward, concentrating on a point six inches in front of his nose, taking it *down, down, down . . .*

He became a prowling cat, a hiding mouse, a buzzing fly. A pair of ragged claws scuttling across the floors of silent seas. The Reaper came up and took in the ruins of the radio room. It hissed and picked up the general like a distracted parent lifting a child's dropped doll.

"general! general! wake! wake and tell what has passed."

Xray-Tango gave a moan as the creature shook him.

Valentine couldn't let the Reaper go to the window, see the men streaming out of his camp. He couldn't risk a single footstep behind him. It would mean a leap. He gathered himself, and readied the ax.

Even with its attention on Xray-Tango, it felt him coming. It was full night, when a Reaper's senses and reflexes become unholy. Valentine still buried the blade of the ax in its side, missing the great nerve trunks running up its spine. It dropped Xray-Tango.

"Melted butter," Xray-Tango murmured. At least that's what it sounded like to Valentine.

"you!" the Reaper spat.

Valentine fired Xray-Tango's gun into it, but he might as well have been throwing spitballs. It sprang.

He ducked, so fast that the air whistled as he cut through it. The Reaper sailed head-first into the framework of a wall, crashing through two-by-fours into the next room. Valentine ran, throwing himself out the window like a swimmer off the block. He jackknifed in midair, landing lightly, but his bad leg betrayed him and he sprawled into the dirt.

It flew out the window after him, ax-pinioned cape flapping like some hideous bat as it descended in a long parabola to the ground. It landed between him and the Ruins.

They faced each other. Valentine drew his .45.

"C'mon, you bastard," Valentine said, sighting on its yellow eyes.

It turned, looking over its shoulder. Valentine saw a hint of movement among the ruins and flung himself sideways.

A blast from the PPD illuminated Ahn-Kha's gargoyle features; the gun's rattle was music to his ears. The bullets caught the Reaper as it spun, knocking it to the ground. It tried to rise, but Ahn-Kha flattened it with another burst as the Grog took a step forward. Valentine rose, hand on the hilt of General Hamm's knife. Ahn-Kha stood, ten feet away from the crawling monstrosity, drum-magazined gun to his shoulder. He loosed another long burst, emptying the weapon. He lowered it, smoke pouring from the barrel filling the air with the peppery smell of cordite.

But the Reaper still lived. Valentine came up with the knife, pressed its head to the ground with his foot, and

swung for all he was worth. The blade went in deep, sever-
ing its spine. The Reaper's limbs gave one jumping-frog
spasm and went limp. Valentine pulled the blade out before
the black tar clogging the wound could glue it in place like
the ax head in its side.

Valentine kicked over the body as Ahn-Kha put a new
drum on the gun. The Reaper's eyes were still alive with
malice.

"Mu-Kur-Ri," Valentine said into the still-functioning
eyes, for the Reaper's head still lived and could still pass on
what it sensed to the Master Kurian at the other end. "The
Dau'weem sent me to kill you. My name is David Valentine.
I come for you now."

The Reaper tried to say something but Valentine swung
again. The blade bit deep; the head separated. He picked it
up by the wispy hair and sent it flying off into the darkness.
He pitied the rat that might taste the flesh.

"Neither of us remembered to bring a spear," Valentine
said. "We're a pair of idiots."

Valentine's eyes picked up a Quisling soldier or two,
watching them from hiding spots. "The headquarters is
clear," Valentine shouted at one. "The general's hurt. Call
the medics. There might still be someone alive in the basement." He clapped his hands. "Hustle, hustle!"

The soldier scampered off.

"Let's go," he said to Ahn-Kha.

They trotted into the Ruins and circled around to the road
paralleling the communications lines. Valentine surveyed
the line of wires until he found the utility pole he wanted.

"Those are the field-phone lines south. Gimme that sling.
I'll cut these; you'll need to do the ones at the railroad
bridge. Flare gun, please."

"I can guess which one you want in it," Ahn-Kha said,
slipping the flare inside and handing it to him. "I agree. It
will be glorious, even if it fails."

Valentine attached the PPD strap to his waist after wrapping it around the pole. Using his claws, he shimmied up the
pole easily enough. There was a crossbar for him to sit on at

the top. There, four communications lines and one power line shared space on the pole. Careful to avoid the last, he took out General Hamm's light infantry machete and shoved the first phone line into the notch. He used the utility cross-beam as a leaver. *Twang*—it parted with a push. Valentine looked again at the knife, smiling wryly.

"Nice work, Hamm."

The other lines were easily severed. Ahn-Kha watched the road, ears twitching.

Valentine looked around at New Columbia from his pole-top perch. Here and there he picked out his companies, the red tape hung across their bodies muted in the dark but identifiable, moving silently toward their objectives. They'd been told to say their orders were to reinforce the guards at the vital spots: warehouses, dock, bridge, rail yard, prison camp. With all the confusion in the night, Valentine felt they would have a good chance of being believed. Searchlights were lit at the Kurian Tower, probing the darkness around the Tower as guards deployed to hardpoints and Mu-Kur-Ri braced for his coming. At the prison camp, a hand-cranked siren wailed as the guards turned out. He saw truck headlights descending the winding road from Pulaski Heights. The Kurian had already sent for help.

Valentine cocked the flare gun. He looked down at Ahn-Kha. The Grog knew enough human gestures to give him a thumbs-up. He fired the pistol; the flare shot into the air with a sound like a cat spitting. The parachute opened and the signal drifted, a bright green star slowly descending, pushed by a wind from the southwest.

It sparked and sputtered across the sky on March 21, 2071, at 23:28—Captain Moira Styachowski made a note of the flare's time in her order journal. Valentine's Rising had begun.

Chapter Nine

New Columbia, March of the forty-eighth year of the Kurian
Order: Risings. Widespread revolts in the Kurian Zone are
rare, successful ones are exponentially rarer. While a number of the Freeholds of 2071 can trace their origins to uprisings against the New Order in the first decade of Kurian
rule, since that turbulent period examples of large-scale re-
bellion hardly exist. The few exceptions succeeded only in
cases of geographical isolation i.e. the Juneau Insurrection
along the islands and coastline of southeastern Alaska and
the more recent Jamaican revolt, or small populations on
the fringes of the Freeholds who manage to hold out long
enough for help to arrive: Quebec City, the Laramie Mountains, Las Cruces. Stacked against those few successes are
the legendary slaughters at Charleston and the Carolina
Coast, the Dallas Corridor, Cleveland, and Point Defiance
between Mobile and Biloxi. Ten times that number as
bloody, but not as famous because of the lack of surviving
chronicles, could easily be named. Then there are hundreds,
if not thousands, of small actions, where individual groups
of desperate sufferers on a city block or two, at a collective
farm, or within a factory managed to wrestle the weapons
out of their keepers' hands and go down fighting. Sadly, we
know virtually none of these stories beyond a faded scribble
of names on a wall or a brief radio transmission like a cry
for help in a ghetto night.

   Whether it's two men with pistols or twenty thousand with
a city, the Kurians are masters of suppressing risings. Even
if one Kurian principality falls, the six surrounding immediately invade, with the twin goals of preventing the revolu-
tionary virus from spreading and claiming new feeding

*grounds for members of their own hierarchy. Quisling sol-
diers know there are brass rings and ten-year exemptions to
be won in putting down revolts; their vengeance is all the
more brutal when they see their comrades strung up or lying
in piles against execution walls. The Reapers return in an
orgy of feeding. The aftermath is shown through slide shows
at New Universal Church lectures and becomes the subject
of homilies about the futility and madness of violence.*

*But while the flame of revolt burns, it burns brightly, fed
by the liberated energy of the human spirit. Now it takes the
form of a green flare falling slowly toward the center of Little Rock.*

By the time Valentine got to the bottom of the pole the
flare had returned to earth. Its green glow pulsed from behind a pile of debris-flattened automobiles stacked like rusty
pancakes.

"This is it, old horse. I'll see you on the other side."

"My platoon has a good sergeant. Let me come with
you."

"I'll be able to do this a lot better if I know you're waiting at the station. Otherwise I'll spend the next two hours
worrying about what's happening on that hill. Get out of
here."

"Until we meet again, my David . . . in this world or the
next." They clasped each other's forearms in the Grog hand-
shake.

"*Arou ng'nan,*" Valentine said. Every language has a
form of "good luck," though the Grog form was a little more
prosaic, hoping that spirit-fathers would intercede on one's
side.

They trotted off in opposite directions. Valentine stayed
clear of the road, tracing the route out to the edge of the
Kurian Tower that he had walked while forming his plans.
The foundation of the tower and the construction grounds
around it were floodlit, and searchlights from strongpoints
atop the first story probed the night.

Nail and five of his six Bears were crouching in the cover

of a filled-in cellar. Valentine looked at the faces above the guns pointed at him. The Bears' Quisling uniforms lay in a pile that smelled of kerosene. The Bears didn't need black T-shirts or red sashes. They were in their battle gear, the savage-looking Bear mélange of Reaper cloth, leather, combat vests, fur and Kevlar. Rain cradled a combat shotgun in chain-mail-backed leather gloves. Another Bear Valentine knew vaguely as Hack wore a massive girdle with Reaper teeth fitted into the leather. He held a machine pistol in one hand and one of Ahn-Kha's Quickwood spears in the other, its end decorated with eagle feathers like a Comanche war lance. Red, whose freckled face narrowed and ended in a jaw so sharp it looked like it could split logs, had Reaper scalps—at least Valentine hoped they were Reaper scalps— at his shoulder blades and elbows. More strings of black hair hung from the belt-fed machine gun so tied to his combat harness that it looked like part of him. Lost&Found had a shining cross over his heart and Brass, almost as wide as he was high, had painted his face so it resembled a skull. A red-eyed plastic snake head had been slipped over the mouth of his grenade launcher, and he'd wrapped the butt and grips with snakeskin and painted "The Fire Dragon" on the side of the support weapon.

"Where's Groschen?"

"He's got the Grog gun, forward. We like to have a good sniper ready when we go in."

"Signal him to pull back. I'm aborting this."

Nail exchanged looks with another Bear. "But the green flare—"

"We're still throwing the dice for Boxcars. We aren't going to hit the tower. I got an opportunity to throw a scare into Mu-Kur-Ri. He's protecting his precious aura with everything he's got. Going in there with some kind of surprise is one thing. Breaking down that door into the teeth of six or seven Reapers, and troops besides—I won't do it. In five more minutes there'll be troops from Pulaski Heights here. We'd have as much trouble getting out as going in."

"You're the boss," Nail said. He looked up and out of the

basement and made a buzzing sound. "Damn, we're almost in spitting distance of that bas—Groschen's pulling back, he'll be here in two minutes."

"Very good, Lieutenant."

"Sir, you look like hell."

"I feel like it, Nail."

The men got to their feet, slinging their weapons. One gathered up the kerosene-soaked clothes.

"Why are you bringing those?" Valentine asked.

"A little ceremony," Nail said. "We'll save it for another day."

Groschen, now clean-shaven, returned to the basement, the long Grog gun over his shoulders. "The tower's off. Hope you aren't bleeding yet," Nail explained.

"No, suh."

"You may still get to do it tonight. They sounded the alarm over at the prison yard."

Valentine checked their line of retreat and led them out of the basement. When they were clear of the tower's sight-lines, Valentine gathered the Bears.

"Keep back about thirty feet. I like to be able to listen."

They cut through the Ruins, zigzagging around the grave-yard of a civilization. They struck another field-phone line, strung on four-foot posts, and cut it. As they neared the road to the prison camp Valentine heard a mass of men moving away from the prison yard. Had they stormed it bloodlessly?

Lieutenant Zhao led his men up the road, away from the camp, in files at each side of the road. The men looked spooked. Valentine thought it best to call out from cover.

"Lieutenant Zhao. It's Valentine."

Zhao waved his right hand like he was wiping a table. The men crouched from the front of the lines and rolling backward, like rows of dominoes tumbling.

"Valentine who?" Zhao said. His hair was unkempt, his face was pitted from acne and he wore filthy glasses, but the only thing lacking in him as an officer was experience. Valentine had learned he was smart, hardworking and organized, which had led him to give him a company. But he'd evidently lost his head.

"Captain Valentine. Careful with the guns, men," Valentine said, stepping out from the rubble.

"Sir, did the Kurian go down?"

"I called it off. What happened at the camp?"

"The guard-tower had a machine gun for covering the yard," Zhao explained. "They slung it around and started shooting. Maybe they have night vision gear. We didn't go any farther. There's no cover for a hundred yards around the wire. I didn't want to risk those kind of casualties."

"Lieutenant, there's five hundred men in there, maybe more. Five hundred of our men, POWs. I want them back."

"I . . . I . . . I was using my judgment," Zhao said.

"I won't question it. Let's go have another look."

"We're going back?" a private said.

"If you were behind that wire, what would you want us to do?" Valentine said, looking at the objector. "Let's turn around, men. Who's in charge of your rear guard, Zhao?"

"Sergeant, umm . . . Franks is in charge of the tail of the column."

"I didn't say tail of the column. I said 'rearguard.'"

Zhao looked at his feet, miserable.

"Let's turn it around, Lieutenant. I'll scout ahead with the Bears."

"Thank you, sir."

Valentine and the Bears doubled the column.

"Christ, I hate all these little generators," Nail said. The lights of the prison yard glowed beyond the tumble of shattered buildings.

"Do you?"

"Of course."

"Be glad for them. I think Groschen is going to get his chance with that gun."

Time enough? Time enough? Valentine wondered.

Valentine had seen Kurian concentration camps by the dozens. This had to be one of the shabbiest he'd ever seen.

The camp was wired into sections of thirds, one-third for women, the center third for guards and the most crowded part for the male prisoners. A single tower stood over the central common yard—judging from the road ruts, trucks came to pick up and drop off prisoners. The fence, just a series of stout poles to hold concertina wire was not even double layered, or electrified, or topped with razor wire. At each corner of the camp, outside the wire, was a sandbagged guard post. Prisoner and guard alike lived under prefabricated roofs; the walls were nothing more than pieces of tent and tarp, though the guards' tents in the center had openings that served as windows. Valentine's nose picked up the smell of corn flour baking in the only complete structure in the place—a Quonset hut set in the guards' section.

The guards' section was a frenzy of activity. The guards were piling up boxes and sandbags at either end of their Quonset; nervous men peered out from under their helmets, rifles ready. Zhao had thrown enough of a scare into them that they had abandoned the outer guard posts, but four men still remained in the tower. The machine gun that so frightened Zhao was positioned to cover the road.

"What do you think?" Valentine asked Nail, after having Zhao take his men and spread them out to the front of the camp. He watched another Bear, the quasi-giant Rain who'd bearded Martinez, heat the blade of his knife with an old liquid lighter, careful to keep well out of sight of the camp. Not that the men would have much night vision outside the brightly lit camp.

"Piss-poor layout, even for a temporary camp. Why do they still have all the lights on? It's like they want us to pick 'em off."

"Look at that," Rain said. "The poor bastards in there aren't waiting for us."

A trio of men were working at the concertina wire behind their tent in the tower's blind spot. Someone among the prisoners had been waiting for this moment; two men were working at widening the hole with pieces of wood as the first crawled through, cutting.

Valentine spoke: "Saves us the trouble. Nail, go back and tell Lieutenant Zhao to spread for skirmishing. Meet up with us there, at those concrete pilings that look like tree trunks. See them?"

"Sure, sir."

"Zhao should just demonstrate. It's not a real attack. I want them to shoot at the tower, once we start. If they kill them all the better. I just don't want that gun aimed at us. Oh, be sure to call out before you come up on them. They're nervous."

"Yes, sir," Nail said, disappearing into the darkness.

"Groschen, Rain, let's work our way around to the north side of the camp. Try and find something we can throw down on that wire."

By the time Nail caught up with them in a skeleton of reinforced concrete, the Bears had found an old metal fire door and pried it off its rusted hinges. It was a heavy, awkward burden, but Rain managed to get it up on his back.

"They're almost through the wire. What the hell are you doing?"

Nail looked up from the pile of TMCC uniforms he was lighting. "We're going Red, sir. It's a ritual. Haven't you ever seen Bears go into action before?"

"Not up close. The tower might see some of the light from that fire."

"Let 'em. Nothing makes the Quislings shit like Bearfire."

Valentine tried to keep his attention on the camp, but the little circle of Hunters going through their ritual distracted him. It was something out of another time and place, when men in animal skins nerved themselves for action through tribal custom.

They stared into the fire for a few minutes, sitting cross-legged and silently contemplating the blue-bottomed flames. First Nail began to sway; in a moment the others joined in, until they were moving in synch like seven metronomes, first right, then left, then right, all the while staring into the fire. When they were all moving in unison, exchanging grunts that meant nothing to Valentine, Nail rose onto his haunches and the others followed suit. Rain took out the knife he had sterilized, raised his Reaper-robe sleeve, and revealed a long line of little brown scars, hash marks running up to his triceps. He reached up with the blade and added another cut, parallel to all the others. He passed the blade to the next man, then sprinkled gunpowder out of a shell casing into the wound.

The knife traveled the circle, the men holding it out across to each other over the flames, until Valentine's own arm began to hurt in sympathy. The blade traveled from Rain, the one with the most scars, to Nail, and then to the others, each solemnly dusting the wound with the powder from their own shell casings. Valentine found himself wondering about hepatitis rates among the Bears.

When it was done Nail rose, a little drunkenly, and came up to Valentine.

"We're ready. They through the wire?" he said. Nail was enunciating a little thickly.

"Yes, men are starting to slip out. Someone's keeping them together at the edge of camp, though. Let's go meet them."

The Bears took up their assortment of weapons and the steel door. They ran, hunched over, up to the gathering point of the escapees.

"Someone's—" a tattered lookout said, before a Bear came from the shadows to clamp a hand over his mouth.

"Easy, men," Valentine said, holding out a hand as a couple of the prisoners took up rocks. "There's a Bear team here. Nice work on the wire. If you don't mind, we'd like to use it to get in. Who's in command, here?"

"I am. You've got a familiar voice, Bea—is that you, Valentine?" said Captain Beck, former commander of Foxtrot Company, and the officer who had Valentine drummed out of the Wolves.

* * *

"How's the arm, Captain?" was all Valentine could think to say. Beck had his right arm tucked into his shirt, Napoleon-style.

"Nerve damage. You back from Minnesota? What the hell's going on?"

"Long story, Captain. Gather the men here—"

"The women—"

"Please don't interrupt me, Captain. The team's going in for the women."

"Thank God for that. You wouldn't have a spare rifle or two, Lieutenant?"

Valentine didn't bother to correct him. "Nail?"

"We're light enough as is," Nail said. "Let us at those guards, we'll get you some guns, sir."

Beck nodded. "I like the sound of that. I'll take you into the men."

Valentine led the Bears through the wire, past an astonished line of men waiting their turn. "Keep it moving, men. There's going to be shooting, the more of you outside the wire the better."

"Gimme one o' them auto pistols an' I'll give—" one began.

"You'll get your chance soon enough, Corporal," Valentine said, looking at what was left of his uniform. "Move along, men."

They passed into a tent. The stench of the dark tent was palpable, a warm, cloying shroud enveloping them. The men didn't even have cots to lie on, there was just bedding on mats on the ground and some hammocks. "This and the barrack next to it are the only ones they can't see too well from the guards' hut." Beck said. "We were going to open some more holes in the wire from the outside so the others could get out."

The men gaped at the Bears.

"Do you have a signal system between the tents?"

"Yeah, we whistle," Beck said.

"Whistle them to keep their heads down, Captain, if you please."

"Johnson, do the 'watch out' tune. Alert for all barracks," Beck said. A rag-and-bone private let loose with three hacking coughs that could be heard a mile away and began a querulous whistling.

"Nail?" Valentine asked, looking through the tent flap. "What do you think?"

The guards were still piling sandbags around each end of the Quonset hut. Valentine could see a machine gun at the pile opposite the main gate, covering the back of the camp. *Too late, guys, we're already in.* The other Bears, at a signal from Nail, were opening window-sized gaps in the tenting.

"It's up to you, Lieutenant," Valentine said to Nail.

"They're worried about the prisoners storming the wire," Nail said. "We'll go in through the middle. Two grenades to each end of the hut. Hack, try and get yours behind the sandbags this time."

"Five seconds," Nail said, nodding to Valentine. The Bears pulled the pins on their grenades. He squatted, and motioned for Beck to get down. The men left in the tent fell to the floor. Two Bears threw, the others held the tent flaps open. Everyone covered their ears.

The cry of, "Grenade!" never came; the prison guards must have been some combination of inattentive and poorly trained. Just four explosions, less than a second apart.

"Blitz! Blitz! Blitz!" Nail shouted, tearing open the tent.

The Bears charged the wire. Rain went first. He threw himself at the wire like a breaching dolphin and crashed down on the concertina. He pivoted, holding the wire apart with gloved hand and boot as the other Bears stampeded over him. Valentine brought up the rear, pistol ready, but only smoke and pained cries came from behind the piled footlockers and sandbags. A severed arm had been flung into the wire—its fingers still moved. Groshen threw himself down in the space between the Quonset hut and the wire, his unwieldy Grog gun on a bipod and pointed at the tower. Hack covered the other end of the building. "Motherfucker!" Lost&Found shouted. He made a tight fist and drove his leather-gloved hand through the aluminum in the side of the hut. Brass stuck the Dragon's snake-head muzzle through as soon as Lost&Found pulled his bleeding hand out and the grenade launcher hissed as he swiveled the muzzle: *fssssssh fssssssh fssssssh.*

Groschen saw a shot and took it, but Valentine ignored the .50 caliber report and its effect.

The grenades roared within the hut, blowing ventilators off the arced roof. Rain got to his feet and grabbed the aluminum in his chain-mail gloves. He planted a foot against the wall. Muscles on his back strained and he peeled open the aluminum side of the hut.

Valentine heard scattered gunfire; Zhao's company was shooting at the tower. He upbraided himself for not giving strict orders to only shoot the tower. The soldiers might start firing at his Bears in the confusion.

Rain extracted himself from the wire and pulled his knife and hooked ax. He plunged into the smoke boiling out of his improvised door. The other Bears followed drawing blades, hatchets and, in Brass' case, a folding shovel.

Nail followed his men in, machine pistol held tight against his shoulder.

Groschen shot again. "That'll teach you to peek," he muttered as he chambered another round.

Valentine heard screams from within the Quonset hut. A Quisling, blood running from his eyes and ears, stumbled blindly out the back door. He hit the sandbags and went over head-down-feet-up like a teeter-totter changing balance. Hack put a single shot into his armpit.

"We surrender. Surrender," a voice from the tower yelled faintly across the yard.

A pained scream bounced off the corrugated walls of the hut. He noticed Captain Beck at his side. "Helluva Bear team you have, Valentine."

Valentine had no time for him. "Throw your guns outta there," he shouted at the tower, his voice dry and hoarse in the smoke and cold night air.

The machine gun and some rifles flew out of the tower. One discharged as it hit the ground.

"Stop shooting, we surrender," the invisible Quisling shouted.

"Idiots," Groschen said. He picked up his Grog gun, holding it with the aid of a sling. "Let's go get them."

Valentine looked to Beck. "Wait here, Captain," he said. He shuffled crabwise to the sandbags covering the front of the hut. He followed his gun muzzle over the side. Two bodies and a third guard, whimpering out his confusion, lay there. The man must have been in shock, otherwise he'd be screaming, judging from the absence of his foot.

The man's pain still triggered instincts not wholly lost.

"Groschen, help this man."

"Sure thing, sir." Groshen drew a palm-sized automatic from his vest and shot the man through the ear. It was carried out with the same smooth, careless motion that he might use to toss away a gum wrapper.

"That's not what I meant," Valentine sputtered.

"Sorry, sir, but it's just a Kurpee."

Who are you to judge? Valentine had killed helpless men in anger, in desperation, in fear. He'd machine-gunned helpless sailors and murdered men in their sleep—and been giddy and sickened by the act. Maybe Groschen was better than Valentine after all; he didn't look like he'd enjoyed it.

"Coming out, Gross," Brass said from the doowary.

"Come ahead."

Brass came out, splattered with blood. "Even dozen. Rain's taking the heads now."

"You two, get the prisoners out of the tower. I'm going to see about getting the women out."

Groschen and Brass walked toward the tower, Groschen keeping his gun pointed up, holding it from the hip like a Haitian erotic fetish Valentine had seen in the Caribbean. He took one more look at the executed Quisling—he'd seen the man's face before, standing watch over prisoner labor. Whatever thoughts, ideas, dreams, or regrets had lived within that bloody head were forever lost.

Bullets flew. Shots from outside the camp made Brass and Groschen throw themselves to the ground. Valentine vaulted over the sandbag wall and landed on one of the splayed bodies.

"What the hell?" Nail said from the doorway.

"It's Zhao's company," Valentine said. "They're shooting at us."

"Fuck!" Lost&Found swore. For a man with "Born Again to Kill" written on his helmet, he had a distinctly un-Christian way of expressing himself. Brass and Groschen both hollered "Cease fire" as best as they could with their faces planted in the common yard's dirt.

"Doesn't that hurt?" Valentine asked, looking at Lost&Found's swollen hand.

"It will tomorrow. Don't worry, sir. She'll heal up."

Valentine caught motion out of the corner of his eye; a figure ran out to the gate of the camp.

"What's that idiot doing?" Nail said.

Valentine peeped over the edge of the sandbags. Beck stood in the open, waving a white rag with his remaining active arm. "Hold your fire!"

"My former captain," Valentine said. "Never short of guts."

There was another shot from the darkness. Beck didn't even flinch. He kept shouting and signaling.

"Boy's wiring is definitely not grounded," Nail observed.

Fifteen minutes later some order had been restored to the camp, now darkened by the destruction of the generator. Zhao's men were in a screen around it, their guns pointed in a less dangerous direction while Valentine organized his prisoners. Some blocks away a building burned; Valentine guessed it to by Xray-Tango's headquarters.

A quick headcount gave him five hundred twenty-seven men and sixty women. All were in this particular camp because they had been captured in Southern Command uniforms. Beck explained the half-assembled nature of their accommodations in a few terse sentences.

"The expected us to just be here a couple days. Then they found work for us, the flood started—a few days turned into weeks. Men were scheduled to ship to Texas, women to Memphis, by rail or water, whichever opened up first."

"Solon owes his neighbors for the loan of troops," Valentine said.

"Yes. We're the only currency the Kurians accept. During our captivity, their investment accrued interest."

This last was with a jerk of the chin toward the women. About one in four were visibly pregnant. Fertility drugs in the feed, perhaps.

"Don't let the expectants fool you," a woman who introduced herself as Lieutenant Colonel Kessey said, when Valentine waked over to the crowd of women wrapping up their belongings in bundles. "Most have combat experience." Kessey had an eyepatch and some burn tissue across her scalp, but put up a hard-nosed front as she organized her rescued women. "The guards used us like their common harem. They used to laugh and say we should thank them— pregnancy keeps you off work detail, saves you from the Last Dance."

"Can't say that I blame them," Valentine said.

She lowered her voice. "All the women get the lecture in basic. Rape Survival Strategy, given by women who've been there and made it back. I used to joke about it. 'In case of capture, break his balls.' Not so easy when there are six of them."

"How many can walk as far as the river?" Valentine asked.

"All of them, sir," Kessey said. "We have litters, just in—"

A scream from the Quonset hut cut her off. It was followed by another.

"Excuse me, would you?" Valentine said, hurrying off to investigate. Shouts blended in with the screams.

It was what he dreaded. The two guards captured in the tower had been strung up by their heels inside the hut. One had blood pouring down his body. Amid the bustle of Beck's prisoners grabbing weapons and anything else remotely useful, some of the vengeful prisoners had taken matters into their own hands. Two women, thin and hollow-eyed, stood in a circle of hooting men. Both had knives; one held the wounded guard's severed genitals before the other's eyes. Some of the male prisoners were tying together the legs of another man with a bloody wound in his leg, ready to string him to the ceiling fixture when the castrated man died.

"Stop that!" Valentine shouted. "Lieutenant Nail!"

Nail sat on an overturned desk, smoking a captured cigarette as he watched the show. "You want to interfere with those hellcats, you go right ahead," Nail said.

"Nail, you're relieved. Sergeant Rain!"

"You'll just have to relieve me too, sir," Rain said.

Valentine went over to the woman with the bloody knife. She'd already opened the trousers of the next man, who was babbling for mercy. Valentine took one look at his red, contorted face and held out his hand to the woman. "You there, hand it over."

She tried to give him her bloody trophy, with a smile. Valentine felt sickened, the way some go faint at the sight of another person's blood but can calmly hold a bandage over a pulsing wound of their own. Not many months ago he'd been the one mutilating corpses. He lifted his hand to push the slimy object down, out of sight of the others—

She flinched at the gesture, flinched with the fear in her eyes of someone who had been hit before, many times. Valentine felt a hard hand on his arm.

"Mister Bear," the other woman said. She had wide-set round eyes set beneath short white hair and a hard line of a jaw. "Yolanda has to wear a diaper all the time now. These men gang-raped her. They said her ass was too tight. So they took a knife and cut it so it'd open wider. That man bleeding to death, he had the blade, and this other piece of shit helped hold her down."

"Wasn't me, sir," the inverted man said. "We surrendered proper n'all."

Valentine looked into the haunted eyes of the woman who had stayed his arm, and then to Yolanda's face. He stud-

ied the profile; her darkly beautiful features reminded him
of his mother's in another time and place.

"It's justice, sir," Nail said.

"No. It's not justice. It's vengeance." He looked down at
the flushed face of the guard. "You decided to live like a
savage, soldier. For that you get to die like one. Nail, I'm
going to go out and talk to Lieutenant Zhao. I'll be back in
fifteen minutes. I want this camp ready to move then."

As Valentine walked out, he heard Yolanda's friend ad-
dress the strung-up man. "Fifteen minutes. Boy, you're getting off easy."

They left the camp with one of Zhao's platoons in front
of, and one behind, the liberated prisoners. The third platoon
walked to either side of the files. Some of Zhao's men had
already managed to lose their red-tape sashes. Beyond the
column, in the darkness that matched Valentine's mood,
Nail and his Bears reconnoitered.

Valentine walked beside Zhao. The lieutenant had made
a hash of things, and Valentine's anger could easily give way
to what Zulu Company's Sergeant Patel used to call a "two-
boot stomp" dressing-down. It might let Valentine blow off
steam, but whether it would do the rattled Zhao any good
depended on the resilience of the man. Dawn was still hours
away, but already the Quislings were reorganizing. Here and
there in the dark, isolated snipers were taking potshots at the
column. So far all the shots were misses, but they were un-
settling—especially to the unarmed prisoners.

"Sir, the company hasn't had enough time together,"
Zhao explained. "It's not like all these men have combat ex-
perience. Some were militia called up during the invasion.
I've only got a handful in each platoon trained as infantry."

"Lieutenant, I know you feel like you've been asked for
miracles. That you even got everyone to the camp, in the
dark, along a route you weren't that familiar with is a credit
to you. You got all this going at a moment's notice. Don't
worry about the rest."

"That Captain Beck—"

"Beck's not in charge."

"What's going to happen at Omega, sir?"

"A lot of work."

"More fighting?"

"I expect. They'll be coming for us, though. We're going to play defense for a while."

"That's good, sir. I've had some experience with that."

"What was it like when you hit the camp? The first time, that is."

"I was scared. I saw their rifle barrels everywhere. I was scared more troops were going to come rolling down the road behind me while I was looking at the camp. When we started toward the wire and the machine gun opened up—I just lost it, sir."

Somewhere behind him Valentine saw the Abica brothers embracing. The younger playfully cuffed his older brother across the back of the head. *The green flare was the right decision. . . .*

"You acted according to your judgment. You were there and I wasn't. A machine gun can kill a lot of men in a few seconds. But remember what was in your head next time you see the enemy coming at you. I know it sounds like they're howling for your blood and nothing can stop them. Remember how you felt; sometimes the noise is just fear let loose. Now that you know their fear you can work it."

"How do you stop from being scared in the first place, sir?"

"Zhao, I asked my old captain in the Wolves that exact question. I'll tell you what he told me: Don't. It'll keep you sharp."

"Send a runner ahead to that post," Valentine said to Zhao, pointing into the darkness around the warehouses. "Make sure they're our men."

While Zhao organized that, Beck and Kessey rested their prisoners. Some of them had surreptitiously gorged themselves on food from the Quonset hut and were being quietly sick along the roadside.

"Once we're across the river, we'll be back in our own lines?" Beck asked.

"Captain, you're addressing a fellow captain, you know," Zhao put in, after his messenger moved off.

"Never mind that, Lieutenant. Captain Beck and I go back far enough that the niceties don't matter. In answer to your question, Captain, the only lines in the neighborhood are the ones we're about to draw. This is a deep penetration raid, you might say. My orders are to tie down as many troops as possible."

"Where do we fit in?" Colonel Kessey asked. "Don't worry about my rank, Mr. Valentine, as far as I'm concerned I'm under your orders. This is your op. I'll do as you say."

"Couldn't stand to see friends behind barbed wire, Colonel."

Beck shook his head. "Seems to me I once criticized you for rounding up strays, Va-Captain. Looks a little different to me now. Thanks for getting me out of the frying pan."

"We in the fire are glad to have you. What sort of mix do you have?"

"There's a few Wolves, incognito. They put on militia uniforms in case of capture. The rest are mostly guards. I have infantry, heavy weapons, signals, some engineers and mechanics. Backwash from the big bugout that didn't make it to the mountains."

"And you, sir?" Valentine asked Kessey.

"The usual mix. I've got a first-class gunsmith, you might find work for her. A couple of doctors and a nurse."

A runner interrupted their talk.

"We were hoping to link up with the prison party, sir," the private reported. "Captain Styachowski didn't know you'd be with them. She sent out a scouting party to observe the Kurian Tower, but they came back and said nothing had happened there. I'm to take you to her; she's down by the docks. She's made space for the prisoners on a barge."

"Good. Captain Beck, Lieutenant Colonel Kessey, if you could get them up again, please."

Valentine heard an explosion in the darkness. "What's that?"

"I think it's mortars from the Heights. They're dropping shells around the docks. It's blind fire, sir, they're not hitting anything but rubble."

"When the sun gets up that'll change. Zhao, get them moving. Best pace the prisoners can manage."

Styachowski was in the wheelhouse of the barge, using the radio there. The barge was to be used to get the men across in case of catastrophe at the railroad bridge. She held the microphone in one hand, a cane in the other, her face lit by instrument telltales. She visibly sagged in relief when Valentine appeared in the doorway.

"The train's almost empty now," Valentine heard Post crackle from the radio. "Still no action here. You want me to send it back? Over."

"Yes, send it back. Over and out.

"Thought something had happened to you, sir," Styachowski said.

"Some confusion at the prison yard." Valentine was relieved to see her alive and well.

A soldier ran up the side stairs and entered the cabin.

"Should the people from the work camp be put on board?"

Styachowski looked at Valentine. "You're in charge of the warehouses and docks," he said.

"Yes." The private backed out of the cabin and made a noisy exit down the stairs.

"What's the situation, Styachowski?"

Another mortar shell landed amongst the Ruins.

"The supply train to go north was just waiting there. I figured we could use what was on it as well as the opposition. Here's the juicy part. There were four 155mm guns loaded on flatcars and ready to go, along with a bunch of other goodies. Post had his men ride the rooftops, it was quite a sight."

"Have you heard from Ahn-Kha?"

"They took the bridge, no problem; just a couple of corporal's guards at either end. After securing it he went overland to Omega. Called us on Solon's own transmitter. There was a little shooting. Someone was wounded up there, but he took the Residence intact."

"So where are the Quislings?"

"Sitting tight, waiting to be told what to do. I don't think it's sunk in to anyone what's happening yet, except maybe your Kurian in his tower. The prisoners we took here said they sent everyone with a gun there to guard him."

"How many prisoners?"

"A few dozen. Night watchmen type MPs making sure nobody pilfers, at least without giving them a cut. They're sitting under guard in the canteen here. We hauled Xray-Tango back, he was conscious for a few minutes and cursing you up and down. Seeing his headquarters on fire could have had something to do with that. I've collapsed into a little pocket here. I wasn't sure if I should burn the headquarters; I didn't want to give the mortar guys another reference mark."

Valentine wondered if he could have handled it half as well. "Nice work, Styachowski. I'm—we're lucky to have you with us. Really lucky."

She flushed to the corners of her eyes and wavered a bit in her at-ease pose. "It's been a nail-biter every second."

"What's this about sending the train back? That wasn't part of the plan."

"It was loaded. We couldn't fit everyone without dragging boxcars around. There's still plenty of stuff in the warehouse we can use."

"Do you have the manpower to load it before dawn?"

"We can try."

"Use the men we took out of the camp. Medical supplies, food, ammunition—especially for those guns. In that priority. Forget the rest. After the train pulls out send every pickup you have after it. They can bump their way over the bridge easily enough. We'll need transport to get it all from the station up the hill to the Residence. At first light set everything else on fire."

"Can do, sir. Excuse me, I'd better start giving orders."

"I'll give you my standard speech," Valentine said to the thirty-odd men under guard in a corner of one of the warehouses. The warehouses were shells of better-built structures that had survived the blast. Their drafty, burned-out interiors smelled of rat feces and cat urine, but they were space out of the rain. New walls of corrugated aluminum were wired onto the reinforced concrete. Styachowski's soldiers and the liberated POWs were filling hand carts and shuttling goods out the door in a frenzy.

"Anyone who joins us gets a new life in the Free Territory. You'll come with us as civilians. You'll work harder than you did under the Hoods, but you'll be able to do it with a clear conscience. This isn't an 'or else'; we're going to leave you somewhere safe. You might want to think about what'll happen when they start investigating all this. Angry Hoods aren't particular about allocating blame where it belongs. Heads are going to roll for this one. You might think about the chances of it being yours.

"This is Corporal Lopez," Valentine said, bringing forward the noncom after he gave his words a moment to sink in. "Any of you who want to take us up on the offer of a fresh start, just speak to him. Again, we're not threatening you with anything if you don't stand up. We leave that to the Kurians. Maybe you've got family back in the KZ, I don't know. Choice is yours, but make up your minds fast—we're in a hurry."

Valentine walked over to the sliding doors to the main aisle of the warehouse. One of the advantages of higher rank was the ability to stand around where and when you chose, just observing. He looked at the carts going out to the pickups and vans, rattling out their machine-gun-fire exhaust through straight pipes. Sacks of rice, cases of ham, tins of butter, dehydrated fruit, cotton balls and motor-oil . . . His real intent was to get a read on the faces, especially Xray-

Tango, who had sat through his lecture in contemptuous silence. If anyone had his neck in a noose, it was he.

Xray-Tango remained seated, holding a washcloth to the side of his head.

Only three volunteers stood up to join Lopez. Valentine wondered if they knew something he didn't.

Two men, both POWs of Beck's, were wounded by long-range fire while the second train was being loaded. Valentine sent Nail and his Bears out to find the snipers, but they returned to report they'd shot and run.

There was only one company left, spaced out wide to cover the roads, rail platform, warehouses and dock. They knew they had to pull back and get across the river when Valentine's flare went up, or dawn, whichever came first. Valentine was watching the road leading to the Kurian Tower, where the remaining flames of Xray-Tango's headquarters gave him a good view of the road. The road wasn't concerning Valentine; what was approaching on it had him worried.

"Armored cars," Valentine said. "Snowplows, I think. Two of them. Pickups behind, double axles with light armor tacked on."

"Snowplows" was Southern Command shorthand for long, heavy armored cars with pointed prows for pushing through roadblocks. Armored cupolas with machine guns, or sometimes a 20mm gun nicknamed a "Bushwhacker" stood high and gave the gunner a towerlike view. They were built on the skeletons of garbage-truck-sized vehicles.

"They're in for a shock," Nail said.

"As long as our heavy-weapons guys know what they're doing."

"Two minutes," Valentine said. "I'll be right back."

Valentine gave his men, squatting next to their stovepipe-like recoilless rifles, a thumbs-up and ran back to the train platform.

"Styachowski! Roll, roll, have everything roll!"

She nodded and signaled to the man working the engine,

a Quisling officer's machine gun bumping at her hip. A soldier helped her into the back boxcar. "The rest of you, fall back to the barge. The barge! Follow the women!"

Styachowski had used the female POWs after all. They stood along the road holding emergency candles. The lights weren't bright enough to be seen by the distant snipers, let alone the mortars on Pulaski Heights, especially with the warehouses beginning to burn. The men began to pull out, some carrying a last load between them, guided to safety by the candle-holding women.

Valentine pulled the flare gun from his shoulder bag and broke it open. He fired it. Before its parachute opened, he was already running back to the Bears. He glanced up and the white glare traced an angry scrawl on his retinas.

"Here they come!" Nail called, the growl of motors growing louder. Valentine could see the turreted tops of the armored cars above the rubble, coming toward them like the dorsal fin of an attacking shark. The Bears had arranged rubble to cover their heads and shoulders.

Valentine joined one of the teams with the light artillery. A box of forearm-sized shells was laid out, ready for loading, and a soldier knelt next to the tube, looking down a crosshairs bracket as he adjusted the barrel with levers.

"Let them have it as soon as you can," he told the gunner.

"Yes, Colonel," the man said. "Err . . . Cap—"

"Don't worry about it. Just put a shell into them."

The first armored car rounded the corner, the pointed prow on it filling the street.

"Clear!" the gunner yelled, but the other two in the crew were already well away from the back of the weapon.

It fired with a *whoosh*, more like a rocket than a shell. The backblast kicked up a shroud of dust, blinding Valentine for a moment. He heard an explosion somewhere down the road. The loaders opened the crossbars at the back and slid in a brassy new shell.

Valentine heard the Bears shooting. The front snowplow had been stopped, and smoke poured from the front. It was firing back; tracers arced from the turret, their brightness leaving strange echoes on his retinas. He saw vague shapes of troops exiting the armored car behind it before the recoilless rifle fired again.

"That's it. Wreck the tube," Valentine said.

"One more shell, sir," the gunner said, as the others loaded.

"Shoot and fall back." He raised his voice. "Nail, get out of it!"

More tracer streaks lit up the street. The gunner fired again, blindly. Valentine waited to see Nail and his Bears run for the burning warehouses, and pulled the gunner out by his collar. The loaders put another shell in the tube, and placed the spares beneath its massive tripod.

Tracer fire began to seek the recoilless weapon like a probing finger. "Better get going, sir," the gunner said, throwing a bag over his shoulder. He pulled out a shining new grenade.

Valentine looked up the street and made his dash. He gestured to the gunners, trying to encourage them to hurry. The gunner nodded to the other two and tossed the grenade in with the shells under the tube. The three of them ran.

From the platform Valentine looked at the rail bridge. He saw the tailgate of a pickup, bumping as the tires negotiated the ties. Men walked single file on the pedestrian walkway, crossing over to the north side. Others were setting charges.

"Nail," Valentine said, as the Bears came up behind him with the recoilless gunners. "It'll have to be the boat. They're getting set to blow the bridge."

Nail nodded, and they turned for the riverbank. A few members of the rearguard were hurrying for the dock. Mortar shells were dropping around the train station.

Nail clapped Valentine on the back. "We really—"

An explosion boiled all around them. Valentine felt a warm hand give him a gentle nudge. He realized he was on the ground. Nail lay facing him, his leg on top of Valentine's, like two lovers in bed.

"You okay?"

"Sure," Nail gasped. He started to pick himself up. Neither of his legs moved.

Valentine tried to help him up. "Rain, anyone . . . help!" His voice sounded like a far-off whisper.

"Legs . . ." Nail said, looking up at Valentine. He'd never seen fear in the Bear's eyes before.

Valentine picked him up in a fireman's carry and trotted down toward the pier. The barge waited, huge and comforting.

"Cast off, cast off," the sergeant handling the loading called. Zhao was running between little groups, clapping them on the shoulder and pointing toward the barge. Valentine saw his old marines from the *Thunderbolt* leave the piled sandbags around the dock—sandbags were easily found around the riverbank—and run up the gangplank to the barge. There was a hint of light in the sky; by it Valentine saw the main deck of the barge piled high with sandbags. The cargo carrier in front was filled with people, mostly prisoners from the camp, and Zhao's company.

"Bandages!" the sergeant called, looking at Nail and Valentine. "Take him to the foredeck, sir. The wounded are there."

Valentine boarded, and went forward. Just below the pilot house a man in splints and one of the women lay under blankets next to Beck's two wounded. Field medics helped Valentine lay Nail out.

"Sorry about this, Nail." The inadequate words made him want to bite his tongue.

"Don't feel a thing, sir. Hardly hurts."

"Shrapnel," the medic said. "His back's kind of tore up. I've stopped the bleeding—most of it."

Valentine heard the muttering boat engines gun, and the barge moved away from the dock, heading upriver.

"Can I get you anything, Nail?"

"I want to see."

"You want to see?"

"The bridge go."

Valentine looked at the medic, who shrugged. "Let me

get this dressing finished. Then we'll see," he said. Valentine couldn't remember giving orders about having an aid station set up on the boat. One of Styachowski or Post's additions. He heard bullets plinking off the old scow. The side of the boat was an irresistible target for any Quisling with a rifle and a view.

They passed under the old pilings of the railroad span. Valentine heard the distinctive clatter of a Kalashnikov fired from the River Rats' town.

When the medic finished with Nail's dressing Valentine pulled a soldier and they carried his stretcher to the back of the tug. The screws were churning the muddy waters of the Arkansas. Behind them they could see the bridge framed against a pink sky. The warehouses were going up, a ground-level fireworks explosion.

"We fucked with them good," Nail said, his eyes bright and excited. "That sight's worth getting all tore up over." The sky was growing brighter by the second.

"C'mon, guys, don't wait and try and take a few with the bridge," Valentine said. "Just—"

Explosions ripped across the bridge, and wood and rails spun into the sky.

"What the hell?" Nail said.

The bridge still stood.

"Shit. Didn't they use enough C-big?" Nail said.

"It's not that," Valentine waited, hoping for the structural integrity to fail. The bridge still stood. "They used plenty. They just used it all at the bottom of the bridge, where it meets the pilings. Spread it out too much, too. They tore up the track good, that's all. On a truss bridge the load is all borne by the joints at the top. If they'd just blown out the tops of the span we passed under, it'd be in the river."

A mortar shell landed in the water astern of them.

"This boat trip's gonna get cut short," Nail predicted.

The barge edged toward Big Rock Mountain. Valentine felt it shudder. The soldiers went to the rail, concerned.

"We're aground!" someone shouted.

"Shit!" Nail said.

"Okay, just wade, swim, whatever," Valentine shouted. He ran forward, leaving Nail for the moment.

"Out of here. Over the side . . . just go!" he yelled. "Manfred, help the women. We need stretcher-bearers. Who wants to carry?"

Part evacuation, part shipwreck, they got the soldiers and some of the supplies overboard. Valentine stayed with the wounded until the stretchers were ashore. The water helped deaden the effect of the mortars; they did little more than create brief fountains of water as they exploded.

"There's still a lot of cargo on the barge," Zhao said, dripping from the armpits down.

"Forget it. We need to get up the hill."

It was easier said than done. The hillside rose two hundred feet at a 3:1 grade, where it wasn't a cliff. There was an old switchback road going up the side. Valentine sent up the stretcher-bearers in groups so they could replace each other. He stood among the trees at the base of the hill, watching the mortars drop shells into the barge. The Quislings seemed to be taking strange pleasure in wasting shells on the wreck, rather than dropping them on the hillside where they might do some damage.

He heard a heavy tread, and looked up to see a mountain of muscle.

"Good morning, Ahn-Kha," he said.

"I'm glad to see you, my David. It's been a long night."

"For both of us."

"Post and Styachowski arrive?"

"Styachowski is at the Residence now. Post is still unloading the second run."

"What's the TMCC doing about it?"

"At first light I heard some shooting, far to the north. My guess is two patrols ran into each other."

"So you don't think they've figured out where we are?"

"They'll know soon, my David."

"What do you think they'll do?"

"I leave outthinking them to you. I just try to outfight them."

"If you had to outfight me right now?" Valentine asked, looking across the river. He could just see the tip of the crane building the Kurian Tower, though he supposed the construction schedule had been set back.

"I'd try you soon, before you could organize. Today, tonight."

"Wouldn't hurt to pretend you're giving the orders across the river. Let's get up the hill."

It was full light by the time he approached Solon's Residence across the bulldozed hilltop. A bulldozer was at work, digging pits into the ground in front of the house beyond the turnaroud. Post stood in front of the entrance, giving orders. A truck pulled up and a team of men hurried to take the crates out and manhandle them inside. With the bed emptied, the pickup turned around and drove back down the road to the station.

Post looked up as Valentine approached.

"The hill is secure, sir. Ella, Daltry and Pollock have their companies north, east and southeast. We've got observers watching the river. Styachowski is holding the station until we get the rest up here, unless they come in force. This is a choice piece of ground. I can see why Solon picked it. Great view."

"Where are the wounded?"

Post pointed to one of the building shells. "Lower level of that one, sir. The doctors are getting set up in there. There was already a little dispensary for the construction workers, and they're expanding it. They could use some trained nurses. Dr. Brough's already bitching."

"I know of one. Get Narcisse in there as soon as you can."

"She's with the wounded at the station," Post said, shrugging his shoulders the way some men do at a heavy rain that can't be helped. "Nothing serious, but you know her. If someone's in pain—"

"I'm glad you had the sense not to stop her. Let's get the

prisoners organized, Colonel Kessey—she's got an eye-patch, easy to spot—said she had some doctors."

"I saw her come over the hill," Post said. "She's talking to the men placing the guns now."

"Every company has Quickwood spears, right?"

"Having them is one thing. Getting them to use them is another."

"We've got today, at least. They won't hit us with Reapers until dark. Carry on, Will. Lieutenant Nail's been badly wounded by shrapnel. Hit in the back."

"Damn. You know, I don't think anyone's been killed yet? On our side, anyway. Who ever heard of that?"

"Maybe our luck's finally turned," Valentine said.

To the extent that there were still MDs, Major Brough deserved her title. She was a field surgeon with ten years experience in the Guards, and had seen everything metal could do to the human body.

"I'm not hopeful, sir," Dr. Brough said, when Valentine asked her about Nail. "Tore open his back. One kidney's gone, the other's probably damaged enough so it might as well be gone, too. His back's broken, and there's massive nerve damage. I'm surprised he was even coherent when they brought him in."

"He's a Bear. They're tough."

"I'm a surgeon. Lifeweaver mysticism isn't my field."

Valentine absorbed the news. Dialysis machines had gone the way of the dodo, as far as he knew. Nail was dead, it was just a question of how long.

"So he's still conscious?"

"I gave him a shot. I expected him to drop right off, but the morphine just relaxed him. He's in some kind of wide-awake shock, low blood pressure, fast heart rate, eyes a little dilated. Lots of perspiration."

"Mind if I have a word?"

"Go ahead. Sir, I have a request."

"Shoot, Doc. Anything for Nail."

"No, it's not that. I understand there's some kind of housing up here. If they've got a cookhouse, could you look for a refrigerator or a freezer? Without somewhere to store blood and plasma, wounded turn to corpses a lot easier. Your men have been stockpiling food and bullets. If it's going to be a fight, I'm going to need to do the same with blood. Some kind of donation schedule would help."

"Any coolers we find go to you."

"Thank you."

"If you need anything else, ask myself, Post or Styachowski. You'll get priority. But I hope you're very bored down here."

"Save the cheerful hero stuff for the troops. Years of amputations have made me a cynic."

Valentine walked over to Nail, who was resting on a folding cot. Nail's gear had been placed beneath the cot. Valentine picked up a tube he couldn't identify. It looked a little like a metallic zither. A wastebucket with a blood-soaked dressing lay next to it, and the coppery odor brought back memories of the headquarters cellar. He didn't want to think about that for a while.

"They have you comfortable, Nail?"

"Yesss, sssir," Nail slurred. "Damn sorry I'm out of commission for a while."

Valentine lifted the canteen lying beside the bed.

"Water?"

"Yes, thank you, sir." He sipped. "I could use a meal. Been running around since the meeting."

"I'll see about it." Valentine wobbled the tube in his hand, like a baton.

"You like that, sir? You can have it. Brass came up with the idea."

"What's it do?"

"Gimme." Nail took it from him, aimed at the ceiling, and pushed a button. A dart flew out and buried itself there. Dr. Brough gave him a dirty look. Nail stifled a snicker like a schoolboy caught shooting spitballs.

"There's a real serious spring inside. The winder's on the top, and you turn it clockwise to ready it. There's a safety at the front you need to flick off . . . To fire it you just push the button. I've got some Quickwood darts for it in my bag. I won't be needing it for a while. I hate being fucked-up and useless!" He pounded an unoffending blanket.

Nail wasn't speaking like someone with a shot of morphine inside him. Valentine had heard that Bears were hard to settle down after a fight.

"Lieutenant, I need your help. We might have some Reapers in our laps tonight. Do you think it would be better to space your Bears out with the companies to steady them, or should I keep them back here, and commit them when I know where the attack's coming from?"

Nail thought it over. "They're used to working as a team, sir. Keep them back. Chances are the Reapers will just try to claw through your guys to get to the rear where they can do more serious damage. My team'll clobber 'em."

"Thanks, Nail."

"Just give me a few days, sir. A week, then I'll be back. Rain can run the team until then. If . . . if . . . I don't, give him my bars. He's earned 'em."

"Nail, now that you've got some downtime, you want to write some letters? You have family, a girl?"

"I'm a Bear sir. My only family's rooting through that supply dump out front looking for chow. If they find something to eat, have 'em remember me in here, laid out and hungry."

Bear appetites were notoriously hard to sate. Valentine had seen them chew bark from the trees on the march through the Ouachitas after leaving Martinez. "I'll see that you aren't forgotten. It's a promise."

Valentine, exchanging a look with Brough, wondered how *it's a promise* would look on Nail's tombstone.

Chapter Ten

Big Rock Mountain, March of the forty-eighth year of the Kurian Order: Viewed from above, the outline of Big Rock Mountain looks like a cameo of a Regency buck, or perhaps Elvis Presley done during his last Vegas days. The Arkansas River flows west into the King's forehead, complete with lock of hair hanging down, where it's stopped by the cliff face of a quarry and turns south. After the small bulge of the nose the river passes a protruding jaw. The hill curves off east, gradually leaving the river, into an oversized collar tucked into the hair flowing down to North Little Rock. What was Interstate 40 runs up the base of the north side of the hill.

It's a picturesque prominence, named "La Grande Roche" by Bernard de La Harpe in 1722 as he traveled among the Quapaw Indians. The climb up the 580-foot hill is worth it, for the view west and east along the two gentle bends the Arkansas makes as it flows into Little Rock. Or so it must have seemed to the man who built a luxury hotel upon it for the swells of the Gilded Age. But hotels are a chancy business; the hilltop property became Fort Logan H. Roots, when men trained for the Great War in the swampy ground of Burns Park north of the hill.

Following a progression so logical that it verges on the sublime, the fort became a Veterans Administration Hospital for those shattered in the staccato series of twentieth-century wars. It became a warren of buildings, from elegant Grecian structures complete with solemn columns to the smallest maintenance shack and pump house, surrounded by parks full of oaks and a hilltop lake, memorials and greenways.

That was before the Blast. The twenty-megaton airburst, part of the nuclear fireworks that helped end the reign of man in the chaos of 2022, went off at ten thousand feet somewhere in the air between the Broadway Street and Main Street bridges over the Arkansas. It left nothing but foundations ten miles from the epicenter, barring reinforced concrete construction.

And a limb-shorn oak that had seen it all, like one of the shattered veterans of the former VA hospital.

The men were gathered beneath the grandfather oak. The tree, perhaps because it was partly sheltered by one of the great buildings, had survived the blast and the fires that came with it. It had the tortured look of a lightning-struck tree, scored on the southeast side and shorn of older branches from two o'clock to four, and from seven to ten, though knobby amputations showed where the once-leafy limbs had been.

Valentine looked at the expectant faces in the afternoon sun. They were haggard, unshaven, tired. Post and Styachowski had pushed them to the extreme of what could be expected of soldiers, and then beyond. The former POWs were mixed in with the men he'd brought away from Martinez—though they looked better, strangely enough, than when they first arrived.

Almost anything is perferable to being inside barbed wire.

Post has assembled a list of operational specialties from the prisoners. The hilltop redoubt was well supplied with ration processors—women and men who were experienced canners, food dehydrators, pickling and drying specialists. There were no herds to slaughter or bushels of fruit and vegetables to puree and seal. "If they come up the hill, we'll just can the AOT troops like sardines," Post said with a fatalistic shrug. Valentine had almost a whole motor pool from Pine Bluff; invaluable to Southern Command with their wrenches and hoists, but they would have to put rifles in their hands and cartridge cases around their waists.

In this he was blessed, as Southern Command had a tradition of rotating men between front line and support duties, allowing the freehold to rapidly convert support units to combat operations. All of them had heard bullets fly and shells land in dreadful earnest. He wished he had more time to get to know them. Post and Beck would have to rely on volunteers to put together an NCO grid.

The four big guns were spaced out like the bases on an oversized baseball diamond in the open ground in front of Solon's Residence, each in its own pit, dug by the bulldozer, and ringed with sandbags. The backhoe was still making trenches to the ammunition dump, buried deep beneath a layer of sandbags, dirt, railroad ties and rail beams. This last came from the dismantled rail line the now-destroyed train had run on to the station near the old interstate.

Apart from the occasional shell from Pulaski Heights, the only military action to take place in the last forty-eight hours was a skirmish already going into the Free Territory folklore as the Great Howling Grog Chicken Raid. Ahn-Kha had led two platoons into the outskirts of North Arkansas and snatched up every chicken, goose, goat, piglet, calf, sheep and domestic rabbit they could run down and stuff in a sack—at the cost of the commanding officer getting a buttock full of birdshot from a twenty-gauge—while a third platoon blasted away at the men guarding the partially blown bridge from a thousand yards. Ahn-Kha had been running from a henhouse with a pair of chickens in each hand when the birdkeeper peppered him with shot that had to be dug out by a medic named Hiekeda with sterilized tweezers. In tall-tale fashion, the circumstances of Ahn-Kha's wounding and subsequent extraction of the pellets were exaggerated until, in one version already being told over the radio, Ahn-Kha was sneaking past a window with a sow under each arm and six chickens in each hand when an eighty-year-old woman stuck a gun out the window and gave him both barrels as he bent to tie his shoe. The shot, in that particular version, had to be dug out by a Chinese tailor working with knitting needles used as chopsticks. But the raid was the Big Rock Mountain garrison's first offensive success of the campaign. As a bonus, a baker's dozen of forgotten milkers were rustled from their riverside pasture and driven up the two hairpins of the switchback road on the south side of the Big Rock Mountain.

"Men," Valentine said. "You've been following orders that haven't made much sense for three days straight. You've done your duty without questions, or answers that made any sense. I'm going to try to straighten you out now. Please pass on what I say to everyone who is on watch at the skyline."

The "skyline" was the men's name for the edge of the hillside, where a series of foxholes and felled trees traced the military crest: the point where the slope could be covered by gunfire. They didn't have a quarter of the trained men they needed to man the extended line; by using three companies he could place a soldier about every fifteen yards along the line, if he didn't cover the cliffs above the quarry with more than sentries.

"We were the first move in an effort to take back the Ozarks from Kur."

He couldn't get any farther; the men broke into cheers and the corkscrew yip of the Southern Command Guards. Valentine let the cheers stop. He said a silent prayer of gratitude for the high spirits of the men, tired as they were.

"We're about as far behind the lines as we can be. There are divisions of Quislings between us and the forces north and south, which will soon be driving for us."

Valentine knew he'd be roundly damned for what he was telling them; by the men if they found out he was lying, by his conscience if it was successfully kept from them. It was a guess at best. For all he knew, Southern Command was going to move toward Fort Scott or Pine Bluff. Since the men holding the Boston Mountains were a charade of an army, there wasn't a snowflake's chance in hell of being relieved from the north, and as for the south . . .

"We're in radio contact with Southern Command. They know about the blow we struck the night before last. We threw a wrench into the gears of the TMCC. You know it, I know it and the Quislings will know it when they start going hungry and running out of bullets to shoot at your comrades."

All that was true enough. With only Post in the basement radio room, he'd made a report to Southern Command, and after an hour's pause they contacted him only to say that he'd been promoted to major and was now part of "Operations Group Center" under the titular command of General Martinez. They told him that he was to tie down as many troops as possible and be prepared to operate without the direct support of Southern Command for an "indeterminate time frame." Valentine didn't think that clumsy phrase, or the mention of Martinez, would bring cheers.

"From this hill, with the guns and mortars taken in our raid, we command a vital rail, road and river crossing. Consul Solon had to give up his old headquarters at Fort Scott to the Kurians of Oklahoma. He was in the process of transferring it here. Now we've taken his new one, right down to his personal foam-cushioned toilet seat, which I placed under new management this morning." The men laughed.

"We're in a strong position with plenty to eat and shoot. I hope you like the view; you're going to be enjoying it for a long time. But the work has just begun. I'm going to put every man in this command under the temporary command of Captain Beck, the officer commanding the prisoners we brought out of Little Rock. I served, and chopped, and dug, under him. He's been in two corners as tight as this one, outside Hazlett and commanding me at Little Timber Hill, and I'm still breathing because he knows how to fortify. He's going to work you until you drop. Then he'll wake you up and work you some more, but you'll be alive at the end of this because of it."

Liar.

Beck pulled Valentine aside as Lieutenant Colonel Kessey took over the assembly.

"Major Valentine needed a trained artillery officer," she

said, "and I, for my sins, happen to be one. I need more crews. The one I put together to set up the guns won't help me much to shoot the other three. Anyone who's got experience as a gun-bunny, cannon-cocker, or ammo-humper, please raise your hand. Not enough. Anyone who knows what those words mean, raise your hands . . . anyone who thinks they might know. Finally. Good news, you're all in the artillery now."

"What are the latest regs on friendly fire casualties?" Beck asked sotto voce.

"Be thankful they don't have to counterbattery the mortars on Pulsaki Heights just yet."

"We won't hear from them for a while. They shot their ready reserve and we've got the rest. That, or they're saving it for a charge up our hill."

"What do you need, Captain?" Valentine asked.

"Valentine, what happened after Little Timber . . . I'm sorry. This arm meant no more duty in the Wolves."

"It meant no more duty in the Wolves for me, too, Captain."

"That's my fault."

"Doesn't matter now. You're a helluva fortification engineer. The best officer I ever served with was Le Havre in Zulu Company, but if I had my choice of him or anyone else in Southern Command for this job, I'd want you."

Beck swallowed. "Thank you . . . sir."

"It won't be easy. We don't have anything like the men we should have to defend this position. You've got to make it look like we do. Sooner or later they're going to get around to trying us."

"The firepower we have is better than what we had in the Wolves. Supports, heavy weapons, mines. That counts for a lot."

"When the construction equipment is done with the artillery, it's all yours."

Beck nodded. Valentine saw his jaws tighten. Back in his days as senior in Foxtrot Company he'd known that meant Beck was thinking. Valentine reminded himself to give Beck

Consul Solon's humidor of cigars. Beck enjoyed a good smoke while working.

"Rough out what you want and run it by Styachowski. She's sharp. I've told her and Mr. Post that you're in charge of getting us ready. They'll follow your orders. If there's anything I can do, let me know."

"You've done more than enough. How long are we going to have to be here?"

"How long were you going to hold that road to Hazlett?"

Beck thought it over. "It's like that, sir?"

"We've got to keep as many troops occupied as possible for as long as we can. We're right at the nexus of river and rail traffic in the Ozarks. We need to make sure they can't use it. At least not easily. We've got to protect the artillery covering the river and rail lines."

"Then I'll build a redoubt around these buildings and foundations. We have to figure on them getting on the plateau. More railroad rails and ties would be nice."

"There's the line running to the quarry. The Pulaski Heights boys might have something to say about us working right across the river from them."

"Maybe the 155s can say something back to them if they do."

Nail was a little pale, but he was eating and sleeping well.

"Better than I'd've expected," Dr. Kirschbaum said. Valentine didn't think she looked old enough to be a doctor, but wasn't about to ask her for a diploma. "Could be that kidney's in better shape than the triage report says. You should see this."

The doctor led him over to Nail. The Bear lay on a bed now; they'd taken mattresses from the construction huts and moved them into the hospital—along with the generator and a refrigerator that had been holding beer.

"Lieutenant, you've got another visitor," Kirschbaum said.

Nail managed a tired smile. "I'm about visited out, Doc. Unless he's got more of Narcisse's gumbo."

"You need a second nurse to handle your dishes and bed-pans as is, soldier."

Nail drained his canteen and handed it to the doctor. "More."

"Do your trick first, Lieutenant."

"What trick is this, Nail?" Valentine asked.

"Check out my toes, sir."

They were wiggling.

"You don't have a battery under here, do you?" Kirschbaum said, pretending to check under Nail's bed.

"Ever treated a Bear before, Doc?" Nail asked.

"I've seen some DOAs. You boys take a lot of killing, judging from the holes. I'll leave you with the lieutenant, Major. Or are you going to ask him for a quickie, too?"

Nail winked.

Valentine swung around the chair next to Nail's bed. "I'm glad you're feeling better. What's in that gumbo?"

"Part of being a Bear."

"This isn't healing, Nail. This is more like regeneration."

"You know Lost&Found, sir? You know why he's called that? He's got me beat. He was dead, like body-getting-cold dead, and he came back. He was in the fraggin' body bag, sir. Zipped up and in a pile. He came to when the gravediggers picked him up. It's like a legend, this story. Sat up and asked his mom for griddle cakes. Three men there had simultaneous heart attacks. He kept the twist tie on the tag they stuck through his ear. We try to keep it quiet. In case we ever get captured, we don't want some Quisling cutting a notch in our arm just to see how quickly it heals."

Valentine found Narcisse in the basement of the hospital, pouring honey down the center of loaves of bread, risen and ready to go into the oven. She was organizing the kitchen with the help of one of the pregnant POWs and a former Quisling soldier, one of the three from the captured bunch at the warehouse, who looked about fifteen.

"Where's Hank?" Valentine asked. "I thought he was helping you out."

"He volunteered for the artillery. That woman Kessey came through earlier today, she adopted the boy."

"How's he doing?" Valentine had avoided Hank since the night they broke out of New Columbia.

"He told me he hated his parents. He hopes they're dead."

"No, he doesn't. Would it help if I talked to him?"

"Daveed, I don't know what you did when you went off that night. I don't want to know. I think it'd be best if Hank, he never know either. You tell him his parents, they run away."

"What makes you think they didn't?"

"Your eyes. They are your grief. They say, when you leave that place, you were dipped in blood."

"Enough with the juju stuff, Sissy. What have you been putting in Nail's soup?"

"Sausage, rice, celery, no chilis or nothing; the doctor, she say keep it mild—"

"That's not what I mean. He had nerve damage. It's healing. I'd heard Bears recovered from stabs and bullet wounds fast, but I've never known of a higher animal doing this."

"'More t'ings in heaven and earth,' Daveed. If I knew how to make a gumbo that make cane-man walk again, I use him on myself and get new legs."

"Colo—Major, passing the word for Major Valentine," a soldier called in the hospital.

"Down here," Valentine yelled back.

A private from the command company made a noisy descent to the kitchen, a signals patch on his shoulder. "Major! Sergeant Jimenez needs you in the radio room. Priority broadcast from Southern Command. For all troops."

"Did you say broadcast?"

"Yes, sir, not direct communication. The Sarge said you needed to hear it."

"Thank you, Private. I'm coming."

Valentine stole a fresh heel of bread and dipped it in honey.

"You too bad, Daveed," Narcisse said. "This galley supposed to be for hospital."

"Impossible to resist your cooking, Sissy," Valentine said, moving for the stairs.

Word had passed among the men that something was up. There were a couple of dozen sandbag-fillers trying to look busy in front of the Federal-style command building. A new long-range radio mast had gone up atop its molding-edged roof since the previous day. The signals private held the door for Valentine.

"Does Jimenez have the klaxon rigged yet?"

"I helped him, sir. Klaxon, PA, he can even kill electricity."

"Quick work."

"To tell you the truth, sir, it was mostly rigged already. We just added the kill switch for the juice."

The radio room was a subbasement below the conference room where Solon had laid out his scheme for finishing off Southern Command. Solon had a sophisticated radio center. A powerful transmitter, capable of being used by three separate operators, was surrounded by the inky flimsy-spitters capable of producing text or images from the right kind of radio or telephone signal. Sergeant Jimenez had a pair of earphones on, listening intently.

"What's the news, Jimenez?"

"Oh, sorry, sir. Lots of chatter. Something big is going on down south. I'm scanning Southern Command and TMCC. Chatter north and south, but it sounds like there's action somewhere on the banks of the Ouachita."

"What about west? Anything from Martinez?"

"Not a word, sir. Like we don't exist."

"What did you call me here for, then?"

"There's going to be a broadcast from the governor. Thought you might like to hear what he had to say."

"I'm not the only one, Jimenez. Can you put this on the PA?"

"Uhh . . . wait, I can. Just give me a sec."

The radio tech rooted through a box of tangled cords in

the corner, pulling up wires and examining the ends. He pulled out a snarl of electronics cable and unwound what he was looking for. Valentine put an ear to the headphones, but just picked up a word or two amongst the static. His eyes wandered over the Christmas-like assortment of red and green telltales, signal strength meters and digital dials. The apparatus was a Frankensteinish creation of three mismatched electronic boxes, placed vertically in a frame and patched together. The electromagnetic weapons that darkened so much of the world in 2022 took their toll on everything with a chip; the more sophisticated, the more likely to be rendered useless by an EMW pulse. Sets like this were an exception—restored military com sets with hardened chips. The Kurians frowned on any kind of technology that allowed mass communication; radios were hunted down and destroyed as though they were cancers. An illegal transmitter was a dangerous and practically impossible thing to have in the Kurian Zone. Only the most trusted of the Quisling commanders had them for personal use. Southern Command made transmitter/receivers by the hundreds, and receivers in even greater quantity, in little garage shops for smuggling into the Kurian Zone, and of course had encouraged the citizens of the Free Territory to own them as well, even if they were on the telephone network. Caches of radios had probably been hidden along with weapons when Solon's forces overran the Free Territory. If Governor Pawls was about to make a statement, chances were he had in mind speaking to those of his former citizens who still possessed theirs, and if they still had radios they probably had weapons. Valentine hoped for a call to rise. The Ozarks, especially near the borders, were full of self-reliant men and women who knew how to organize and fight in small groups. With his guns at the center of the Quisling transport network, the Kurians would have difficulty stamping out fires.

"We're live, sir. Just let me know when you want to pipe it through," Jimenez said. Valentine heard a voice through the padding on the earphones. He picked up another pair.

"When's the broadcast?"

"Soon, sir."

"I'm just getting static."

"I'll fix that," the technician said. He sat and worked the tuner. "Code messages again. Something's happening."

"Why aren't they doing it in the dead of night?"

"They usually do; reception is better. Maybe they want to get it rolling today, before the Kurians can react."

"Or tonight."

"Could be, sir. Oh, just a sec. Five minutes."

"Give me the microphone." When Jimenez handed it over, Valentine tested the talk switch. He heard an audible click outside. "Lend an ear, men. Lend an ear. We've got a broadcast coming in from the governor. I'm not sure what it's about, just that it's a general broadcast to what used to be the Ozark Free Territory. I figured you'd want to hear it. We'll pipe it over as soon as it comes on."

"They've got cassettes, so I can tape it," Jimenez whispered.

"For those on watch, we'll tape it and play it back tonight. That is all."

To pass the time Jimenez took Valentine through the shortwave spectrum. There were notes on a clipboard about where to find the bands for the Green Mountain men, the Northwest Command, even overseas stations like the Free Baltic League.

"We'll have to set up a canteen where you can play the news," Valentine said. "Solon has enough office space down here; we can knock down some of these walls—"

"Just a sec, sir. He's coming on." Jimenez nodded to himself, then flicked a switch. Faintly, Valentine heard Governor Pawl's voice from the loudspeakers outside. Jimenez unplugged the earphones and the sound went over to the old set of speakers bracketed to the wall. Valentine had heard the old Kansan's rather scratchy voice on occasions past, explaining a new emergency measure or rescinding an old one, eulogizing some lost lieutenant or passing along news of a victory against the Kurians overseas.

"—and all our friends and allies who may be listening.

Late last night, after speaking to Lieutenant General Griffith, my interim lieutenant governor, Hal Steiner, and what members of the Ozark Congress are with me at Comfort Point, I gave the order for the counterattack you've all been wating for in this, the darkest year of the Free Territory. A combination of weather, enemy movements and a fortuitous raid on the Quislings at the old Little Rock Ruins—"

"Hey, that's us," Jimenez said, smiling. Valentine nodded, listening.

"—I took as portents that it is time for the storms and shadows to disperse. Therefore I gave the order for 'Archangel' to begin."

"Archangel" must have meant something to the men outside; Valentine heard cheering.

"The first shot was fired before dawn this morning. As I speak, in the south we have seized Camden and are on the march for Arkadelphia; in the north we descend from the mountains and onto the plateau. So now I ask the men and women of the militia, when they hear the sound of our guns, to gather and smash our enemy, hip and thigh. Smash them! Smash them to pieces, then smash the pieces into dust. For the outrages inflicted on us, smash them! For the future of your sons and daughters, smash them! As you are true to your heritage of liberty, smash them! For the honored dead of our Cause, smash them! Now is our time. With courage in your heart, you will know what to do. With steel in your arm, you will have the means to do it. With belief in your spirit, you will not falter but shall see it through. We have lived through the night. Now let us make a dawn, together."

The broadcast switched over to a marching song of Southern Command, based on an old marching ditty. Valentine left the radio room and went out to see the men, the song ringing in his ears:

We are a band of peoples, granted through our creed
The Right to Life and Liberty: our Founding Fathers' deed.
But when those rights were taken, our duty then as one:
Cry "Never!" to the Kurian Kings, and take up arms again.

Never! Never! Our sacred trust . . . Never!
"Never!" to the Kurian Kings, we'll take up arms again . . .

Outside, Valentine heard the men join in the song. It spread across the hill, even to the pickets on the crestline. Though most of them couldn't carry a tune with the help of a wheelbarrow, they did slap their rifle butts, or shovel blades, in time to the "Never!" It was a rythmic, savage sound. He hoped the Quislings across the river were listening.

Valentine found Hank Smalls learning his duties as a "runner." The boy's job was to pass oral messages between the guns and the main magazine, headquarters, or the forward posts in the event of a hard-line breakdown with the field phones. He and a handful of other young teenagers were being escorted around the hilltop and taught the different stations still being put together by Beck and his construction crews.

"Can I borrow Hank a moment?" Valentine asked the corporal walking the teens around.

"Of course," the corporal answered. She had the near-sighted look of a studious schoolgirl entering her senior year, despite the "camp hair" cropped close to her scalp. Valentine stopped the children as they lined up, as though for inspection.

"Excuse me, Corporal." He drew Hank aside. "How are you getting on, Hank?" Valentine asked the boy. Hank wore a man's fatigue shirt, belted about the waist so it was more of a peasant smock. Mud plastered Hank's sandal-like TMCC training shoes, but the old tire treads were easy to run in and then clean afterwards.

"Busy. Lots to remember about fuses, sir."

"Are you getting enough to eat?"

Hank looked insulted. "Of course. Two hot and one cold a day."

Valentine had a hard time getting the next out: "Worried about your parents?"

"No." But the boy's eyes left his this time. Valentine went down to one knee so he was at the boy's level, but Hank's face had gone vacant. The boy was off in a mental basement, a basement Valentine suspected was similar to his own.

"Keep busy," Valentine said, summing long experience into words. The boy looked like he needed more.

"Hank, I'm going to tell you something a Roman Catholic priest told me when I lost my parents. He said it was up to him to turn me into a man since my father wasn't around to do it. He'd never had kids, being a priest, so he had to use the wisdom of others. He used to read a lot of Latin. Roman history, you know?" For some reason Valentine thought of Xray-Tango and his *groma*.

"They had gladiators," Hank said.

"Right. A Roman statesman named Cicero used to say that 'no Roman in any circumstance could regard himself as vanquished.' You know what vanquished means?"

"Uhhh," Hank said.

"What Cicero meant was that even if you were beat, you should never admit that you were. Especially not to the people who'd beaten you."

"Like Southern Command keeping together even after all this," Hank said. The boy's eyes had a sparkle of interest, so Valentine went on.

"Cicero said a man had to have three virtues. *Virtus*, which meant courage in battle. Not minding pain and so on. You also have to have *gravitas*, which means being sober, aware of your responsibilities, and controlling your emotions. Even if someone has you madder than a stomped rattlesnake, you don't let them know they've got you by the nose, or they'll just give you another twist. Understand?"

"Virte—*virtus* and *gravitas*," Hank said. "I see. But you said there was another."

"This is the most important one for you now. *Simplicitas*. That means keeping your mind on your duties, doing what most needs to be done at the moment. In fact, I'd better let you get back to yours. I don't want to keep the corporal and the rest waiting."

"Yes, sir," Hank said, saluting. The vacant look was gone.

Valentine wanted to hug the boy, but settled for a salute. *Gravitas* required it.

All through the following day the sound of distant trucks and trains could be heard.

That night, though the men were exhausted from laboring on what was now known as the "Beck Line," they danced and cheered at the news that Arkadelphia was liberated, and the Quislings were falling back in disarray. Southern Command would soon be knocking on the hilly gates of Hot Springs, barely fifty miles from New Columbia.

They'd had their own successes. The mortar crews had prevented repair gangs from working on the rail lines during the day, and the occasional illumination shell followed by 4.2-inch mortar airbursts slowed the work to a crawl at night.

But strongpoints with machine guns were now all around the base of the hill, and the mortars on Pulaski Heights had begun to fire again, scattering their shells among the buildings of Solon's Residence. Two men laying wire for field phones were killed when a shell landed between them.

Big Rock Mountain added a life when one of the women gave birth. The eight-and-a-half-pound boy was named Perry after one of the dead signals men.

"That's pretty damn arrogant of them," Valentine said, taking his eye from the spotting scope the next day. It was late afternoon, and the shadows of the hills were already stretching across New Columbia. "Bringing a barge up the river in daylight."

"I'd say the river's too tricky to do it at night," Post said.

"Then we'll make it too tricky for them to do during the day."

They stood at an observation post above the switchback road running up the southeastern side of the hill, looking through a viewing slit with the protection of headlogs. There were snipers at the base of the hill good enough to get them, even with an uphill shot. There had been minor wounds among the work parties until three-man teams of counter-snipers had been sent down the hill to hunt out the marksmen. Valentine knew there was a gritty war of precision and patience being waged through scoped rifles two hundred feet below, but he had to keep his mind on the river, or rather denying its use to the enemy.

"They're trying to time it so they can unload at night," Post said. The barge was still far from the docks, behind the old brush-covered roadway of the interstate loop.

"I'd like to see if Kessey's guns can make a difference. Durning, you're forward observer for this side, I believe?"

The corporal in the post looked up. "Yes, sir."

"I want that barge sunk. Can you do it?"

"A crawling target like that? Yes, sir!"

Valentine listened to him talk into the field phone to Kessey, acting as fire direction controller, and the far-off squawk of the alarm at the gun pits. Kessey had decided that, because of the lack of experienced crews, she could only put two guns into effective action at once. The other two would be used once some of the raw hands gained experience. Within three minutes the first ranging shot was fired as the barge negotiated the wide channel around the swampy turd shape of Gates Island.

"Thirty meters short," the observer called, looking through the antennae-like ranging binoculars. Kessey tried again. Valentine heard her faint "splash" through his headset, letting him know another shell was on the way. Through his own spotting scope, Valentine saw the white bloom of the shell-fall well behind the barge. He took a closer look at the tug. Thankfully, it didn't belong to Mantilla. The observer passed the bad news about the miss.

"Sir, it's the damn Quisling ordinance. Their quality control sucks sewage."

"The target's worth it. Keep trying."

The Quislings on Pulaski Heights tried to inhibit the crews by raining shells down on the battery. Valentine heard the crack of shells bursting in the air.

The observer was happy with the next shell, and he called, "Howizer battery, fire for effect."

The shells traveling overhead whirred as they tore through the air. Valentine stepped aside so Post could watch.

"Keep your heads down, boys. Nothing to watch worth a bullet in the head," he called to a pair of men resting concealed behind rocks and earth along the crestline to his left.

"I think there were two hits to the cargo, sir."

"Secondary explosion?"

"No, sir."

"Probably just a cargo of rice then. Worth sinking anyway. Corporal, keep it coming."

The sun was already down beneath the trees behind them. Three more times the guns fired, with the forward observer relaying results.

"Another hit!" Post said.

"Sir, the barge is turning," the observer said.

"They cut loose from the cargo," Post said. "There's a fire on board. Black smoke; could be gasoline."

Even Valentine could see the smear of smoke, obscuring the white tug beyond. "Forget the cargo, sink that tub."

It was getting darker. Tiny flecks of fire on the sinking barge could be made out, spreading onto the surface of the water. There had been some gasoline on board.

The observer cursed as shells continued to go wide. Valentine could not make out anything other than the guttering fire.

"Illuminate!" the observer called.

A minute later a star shell burst over the river.

"Hell, yes," Post chirped.

Under the harsh white glare, Valentine squinted and saw the tug frozen on the swampland shallows of the northern side of Gates Island. The pilot had misjudged the turn in the darkness.

"Fuze delay, fuze delay . . ." the observer called into his mike.

Shells rained down on the barge. Its bulkheads could keep out small arms fire, but not shells. The star shell plunged into the river, but an explosion from the tug lit up the river. Another illumination shell showed the hull torn in two.

"We got her," the forward observer shouted. "Cease fire. Cease fire."

"Pass me that headset, Corporal."

Valentine put on the headset. "Nice work, Kessey."

"This isn't Colonel Kessey, sir," the voice at the other end said. "It's Sergeant Hanson, sir. She was wounded by the mortar fire. Permission to redirect and counterbattery."

The mortars on Pulaski Heights were scattered and in defilade; the number of shells required to silence even one or two was prohibitive. "Negative, Sergeant. Get your men to their shelters. I'm promoting you to lieutenant; you'll take over the battery. What's the situation with Colonel Kessey?"

"Blown out of her shoes, sir, but she landed intact. I'm hoping it's just concussion and shock. She's already on her way to the hospital, sir."

Valentine kept his voice neutral. "Thank you, Lieutenant. Over and out."

Later that night Valentine went through the solemn, and rather infuriating, ritual of composing his daily report to General Martinez. He labored over the wording at the end of the report.

> At approximately 18:20 we sighted a barge moving up the Arkansas River. Our howitzer battery took it under fire. After ten minutes sustained shelling the tug cast off from the sinking cargo. The battery shifted targets to the tug, which ran aground and was subsequently destroyed by howitzer fire.
>
> Counterbattery fire from the Pulaski Heights mortars caused two casualties. A loader was wounded in the foot and the battery Fire Direction Officer, Lt. Col. Kessey, suffered head trauma resulting in a concussion when a shell exploded near her. I hope to report that she will return to duty shortly, as she was still training and organizing her crews. The battery is now under the command of

a first sergeant I promoted to lieutenant. Lt. Hanson completed the battery action.

Enemy troops continue to concentrate in front of us. Eventually larger weapons will be moved to Pulaski Heights, making our current position untenable and offensive action impossible. The mortar tubes are dispersed and guarded from the river side, but I believe the New Columbia area to be open to attack from the hills in the west. I respectfully suggest that a movement by your command in our direction will allow us to control central Arkansas and pressure Hot Springs from the north as other commands push up to join us.

My staff has a detailed plan worked out. Establishing closer contact would go far toward coordinating the actions of our commands to the benefit of Southern Command in general and the detriment of Consul Solon and the TMCC in particular.

Writing Martinez was an exercise in futility, but it had to be done, no matter what taste the task left in his mouth.

Valentine put a code card in the envelope and sent it to the radio room. He looked around the basement room that served as his office and sleeping area. If a man's life could be measured by his possessions, his life didn't amount to much. A little leather pouch of Quickwood seeds. A toothbrush that looked like an oversized pipe cleaner. Field gear and weapons. A report from Styachowski on her progress in organizing the POWs from the camp into battle-ready infantry. Pages of notes. A terrain sketch on the wall. He was a man of lists. Lists of officer rotations. Lists of Quisling brigades and regiments identified in the area—it had doubled in length in the past week. A list of needs for the hospital—God knew where he'd find an X-ray machine, why did they even ask? Xray-Tango. A man who wanted and needed to switch sides thanks to intelligence and conscience, but who couldn't bring himself to do it.

He collapsed into his bunk, palms behind his head. His scalp was getting past the prickly stage, and the returning black hairs on his head made him look rather like someone on a long walk home from prison; the visible skin of his scalp made even more odd-looking thanks to their presence. He let his hearing play around the headquarters building. Fresh construction made the most noise: hammers and electric saws turning Solon's future meeting rooms and art galleries into living space, with fainter splats from the ground floor above as windows were bricked up into firing slits. Typewriters clattered as clerks catalogued and allocated the stores from the warehouse raid. He could hear Post and Styachowski talking with the top sergeants and a smattering of lieutenants as they worked out the organization of the hilltop's men; many of the prisoners were getting their strength back after a few days of balanced rations and could now be blended into other units. From the communications center he heard field phones buzzing or jangling—they'd come away with two kinds, the ones that buzzed doubled as short-range radios, the jangling ones had been used by Solon's construction staff—now shakily melded together in a single network rather like Valentine's *ad hoc* command.

The Consul hadn't reacted to his seizure of the Residence as quickly, or as violently, as he'd expected. The Quislings under Xray-Tango had just concentrated on keeping him where he was rather than prying him off the hill. The forces they'd assembled could overrun him, at no small cost, but so far they hadn't moved beyond the engagement of dueling sniper rifles. Perhaps they couldn't afford a Pyhrric victory with Southern Command still on the move in the south.

Did they want to starve him out? He had just under sixteen hundred soldiers and captured Quislings—the latter were digging and hammering together log-and-soil fortifications under Beck's direction—that he could feed for months, if necessary, at full, balanced rations. After the canned meat and vegetables ran out he could still manage beans and rice for another ten or twelve weeks. They must have known the contents of the divisional supply train he'd made off with. Of course, the food would run out eventually, but not before Solon had to send most of his boys back to where he'd borrowed them, or Archangel had been decided one way or the other. A few shady Quislings had made contact with the forward posts, offering to trade guns and small valuables for food. Valentine's hilltop forces were, temporarily at least, better off than the besiegers. He could just wait for Southern Command to move up after taking Hot Springs, or the less likely relief from Martinez. If he were Solon, he'd destroy the the forces in his rear as quickly as possible, before turning his attention to the new threat from the south.

But you're not Solon. You don't know the cards he's holding; he knows exactly how many aces you've got. Except for the Quickwood. Valentine hoped a few dozen Reapers had already been turned to wooden mummies by the beams he'd passed to Mantilla.

A whistle sounded from outside. Barrage?

Valentine took up his tunic and ran through the officers' conference room, with Beck's proposed layout still on the blackboard. He entered the radio lounge, where off-duty men gathered to hear news and music piped in by Jimenez and the other operator.

"What's the whistle?" he asked Styachowski, who was sitting below one of the speakers, fiddling with Solon's old bow and quiver. She'd had an idea to use Quickwood chips for arrowheads. The cane she relied upon was conspicuous by its absence.

"Thought I heard someone yell 'star shell.' I haven't heard it followed up with anything. Maybe it's a psych job."

"Get to the field phones, please. I want you in the coms center in case it isn't."

Valentine hurried out to the front of the headquarters building. Sure enough, a star shell was falling to earth. A second burst far above the hill as the first descended. Valentine saw the men atop the building pointing and chatting. A few figures hurried to shelters, assuming real shellfire was on the way.

"Sir, you don't want to be standing there if a beehive bursts," a private behind the sandbag wall filling one of the arched windows called to him, referring to the flechette-filled antipersonnel rounds fired by larger guns.

The Cat stood, anxious and upset, listening to the night. There was a droning in the sky, faint but growing. Suddenly he knew why he was anxious. *The chills . . .*

"Reapers!" Valentine shouted to the men on the rooftop. "Reaper alarm!"

The sentry froze for a moment, as if Valentine were shouting up to him in a foreign tongue, then went to the cylinder of steel hanging from a hook on the loudspeaker pole atop the building. He inserted a metal rod and rang the gong for all it was worth. Valentine picked up the field phone just inside the headquarters entrance and pushed the button to buzz the com center.

"Operator," the center answered. Another star shell lit up the hilltop, creating crossing shadows with the still-burning earlier one.

"This is Major Valentine. Reaper alarm." He heard the woman gasp, then she repeated the message with her hand over the mouthpiece.

"Captain Styachowski acknowledges, thank you," came the flat response.

Ahn-Kha appeared in the doorway behind him, a golden-haired djinn summoned by the clanging alarm. He had a Grog gun in his arm and a Quickwood stabbing spear between his teeth. A second spear was tucked under his arm.

"This is going—" Valentine began, then shut up as he saw what was coming from the east. In the glare of the star shell, he saw a little two-engined turboprop, the kind used by pre-2022 airlines to hop a few passengers between small cities, roar into the light at a hundred feet. The rear door was open.

"What the fuck?" one of the soldiers on the roof said, watching. A figure plunged from the plane, trailing a cathedral train of material that whipped and flapped in the air as it fell. A parachute that failed to open? A second one followed it, and a third, all with the same flagellate fabric acting as a drogue for the plunging man-figures. Valentine saw another plane behind, a different make, this one coming for him like a missile aimed at his position, its daring pilot almost touching the treetops.

"Your shoulder, my David," Ahn-Kha said, as Valentine felt the barrel of the Grog gun fall against his shoulder. Valentine froze, a human bipod.

"*Nu,*" Ahn-Kha said, and the gun jumped on Valentine's shoulder as the Grog fired.

The boom of the .50 echoed in the hallway. The plane reacted, tipping its wings to the side. At that height there was no room for error; the plane veered into the treetops. It roared through them to the music of snapping wood, then struck a thicker bole and pancaked. Exploding aviation fuel flamed yellow-orange in the night.

"Good shot," Valentine said, hardly believing his eyes.

"Good luck," Ahn-Kha returned. "I guessed to which side the driver sat."

The star shells lit up the first figure's landing in white light and black shadow. It hit the ground running, shrugging off the drapes of fabric attached to it. Only a Reaper could survive such a landing with bones intact . . . as did the next, and the next, striking earth to the sound of clanging alarm gongs.

Valentine watched, transfixed, and his "Valentingle" told him where the others were. To the west. Climbing the sheer face of the quarry, the one part of the hill almost unclimbable and therefore almost unguarded. He took one of Ahn-Kha's spears.

God, two were headed for the hospital.

"Ahn-Kha, get the Bears!" he shouted, hurrying toward the hospital building. He ran past the old stable building that now housed the dairy herd. He paused in his race and threw open one of the barn doors. If these were the "unguided" sapper Reapers, they might be drawn to the heat and blood of a cow more than a lighter human.

A Reaper ran across the hillside, leaping from fallen tree to earthen mound like a child hopping puddles, making for the hospital.

"You! You!" Valentine shouted, waving his arms.

It turned, hissing, face full of malice, eyes cold and fixed as a stuffed snake's. It squatted, and Valentine braced himself for the leap.

Tracer cut across his vision like fireflies on Benzedrine. Men in a hidden machine-gun nest, covering the open ground between the buildings and the artillery pits, caught the Reaper across the side. It tumbled, closing its legs like a falling spider, and rose dragging a leg.

Valentine was there in two Cat leaps, but he must have looked too much like a jumping Reaper to the machine-gun crew. Bullets zipped around him. Valentine dropped to the ground.

The Reaper staggered toward him, one side of its body recalcitrant, like that of a stroke victim learning to use his worse-off half again. Valentine heard screams from the machine gunners: a Reaper was among them.

He rose, spear ready, and realized that once he used Ahn-Kha's point, he'd be unarmed. The nearest weapon was with the machine-gun crew, now dying under the claws of a sapper. Valentine ran for their gun pit, pursued by the half-leaping, half-staggering stride of the shot-up one.

The Reaper in the gun pit was feeding, back to him. Valentine jumped from ten feet away, landed atop its back and buried the Quickwood in its collarbone. The beast never knew what hit it; the Quickwood sank into the muscle at the base of its neck before the handle snapped off. Valentine's body blow knocked it flat. It stiffened, legs kicking and hands pulling up fistfuls of earth in black-nailed claws.

Valentine ignored the bloody ruin of the soldiers in the machine-gun nest, noting only that one was a promising soldier named Ralston, who'd qualified at the bottom in marksmanship with his rifle, but when given a tripod and the sliding sights on a Squad Support Gun, came to the head of the class with his accurate grouping. He tore the machine gun from Ralston's limp fingers and fired it in time to see the flash reflected in the eyes of the oncoming Reaper, lit up in the gun's strobe light of muzzle flash as it came toward him. The 7.62mm bullets tore through even the Reaper cloth, blasting back the staggering nightmare into a jigsaw cutout of tarry flesh and broken bone. What was left of the thing rolled around aimlessly, clawing at and opening its wounds in search of the burning pain within, a scorpion stinging itself to death.

He opened the gun, put a new ammunition box on the side, let loose the tripod catch, and ran for the hospital.

The next fifteen minutes were a blur, and would remain so for the rest of his life. Not that he wanted to remember any of it. The fight lived on in his mind as little snapshots of horror. The hospital, looking as though a scythe-wielding tornado had passed through it, leaving Dr. Kirschbaum and Lieutenant Colonel Kessey in mingled pieces. Nail standing, eyes bulging, holding down the Reaper as it stiffened with his spring knife in its eye, feeling its clawed hand digging bloodily into the muscle of his thigh, searching for the femoral artery as it died. The wave of Reapers, a dozen or more, coming across the hillside, throwing aside men like a line of hunters knocking over cornstalks for fun. One Reaper descending into the ready magazine for the 155s and a resultant explosion, lighting up the night and sending a railroad tie skyward like a moon shot. The Bears and Ahn-Kha meeting them, backed up by the *Thunderbolt*'s old marines, clustered in a protective ring around Valentine, pikes and guns working together to knock over the death-machines and then pin them until they stiffened. Styachowski, fear-whitened face like ice in the moonlight, carrying Solon's bow and sending an arrow into a leaping Reaper just before it landed on Post's back. When another Reaper broke the antique as she used it to ward off a blow that threatened to remove her head, she thrust up with another arrow held near the tip, putting the Quickwood into its yellow eye. Max the German shepherd, a pet of one of the construction engineers, licking the face of his dead owner, stopping only to snarl and stare at anyone who approached the body. The screams of panic from the maternity ward, where the pregnant women had drawn one of the sappers, a dozen men dying as they tried to pull it down as they protected the mothers to be with nothing but their knives and scissors. Hurlmer finally sticking a pike into it, his head torn off for the act. The fearful, confused eyes of the last Reaper to die, a wounded beast trying to escape by crawling amongst the cows, harried by bullet and pike until it died beneath a feed trough, corn-meal dust sticking to the blood coating its face.

All the while there was rattling fire from the crestline, as Quisling troops probed the hill.

At dawn there were fifty-three corpses lined up. Thanks to the backhoe and a lot of sweat from soldiers with shovels, each would have an individual grave. Woodworkers were hammering together the arrowhead tepee-cum-cross design of a Southern Command grave post and passing them on to painters. The men were gray and haggard after last night's bitter fighting and the probe up the hillside. Valentine pulled as many men out of the line as he could and gathered them by the graves. They had to follow a circuitous path to get there to avoid observation from the spotters on Pulaski Heights; any gathering of men in the open drew mortar fire.

Ceremonies weren't for the dead; they were for the living. There was a lay preacher to say the right words over the bodies. When they were rested in their graves, Valentine walked down the line of bodies in their shrouds, searching for words to add meaning to what had been random slaughter.

"We're in a siege, men. This hill is like a medieval castle, and the enemy is at our gates. That enemy, the TMCC, is in the first phase of taking a position by siege. It's called the 'Investment.' He's already put an effort into destroying us. Last night we killed eighteen Reapers, thanks to the Quickwood. Eighteen Reapers." Nothing else could explain the malevolent choice of targets: the magazine, the infirmary, the maternity ward. "That means there's more than one Kurian Lord in the area, perhaps four or five . . . even six. Not many Kurians can work more than two or three Reapers at once. Thanks to the rising that we began across the river, I suspect some governors have already been kicked out of their holes."

He picked up a handful of dirt, and tossed it on the row of corpses.

"Last night they tried to get our lives cheap. We kept the price up, thanks to the Quickwood, your courage and especially the sacrifice of those killed last night. Solon's investment isn't paying any returns yet.

"The fifty-three soldiers we're putting in the ground pinned down thousands of troops with their lives. Those mortars, and the guns that will probably soon support them, could be used outside Hot Springs, or against the Boston Mountains. The forces around the hill, from the snipers to the machine-gun crews, are looking up the hill at us instead of at Southern Command's Archangel operation. They're here because our guns are covering the rail and water nexus for Solon's territory. There's no fast and easy way around us; it means moving on broken-down roads, crossing bridgeless rivers. Nothing moves by water or rail, east-west or north-south, without our stopping it. They're not able to shift troops fast enough, and Southern Command's eating up what they can move piecemeal."

They liked the sound of that. Bared heads of all skin tones and hair colors, sharing a common layer of sweat and dirt, lifted, nodded, turned to each other reassuringly.

"Every town Southern Command takes is liberated partly by us . . . though at the moment we're doing nothing here but having the occasional mortar shell dropped in our laps.

"Unless we're lucky, the fifty-three here are going to have more company as the days and weeks go by. It could be that we'll all end up on this hill with them. If that's our fate, I hope we cost the TMCC as much as they did. If any of you want to say anything, now's the time."

"I've something to say," Yolanda, the woman who had mutilated the captured guards back at the prison camp, began. "It is not right for such men to go into the ground without a flag to be under. They are soldiers. Soldiers are their flag."

Free Territory flags weren't stocked in the warehouses we raided, the overtired part of him said.

"So I made them one. The men who came in to get us, I thought of them as I made this. Styachowski helped me with the wording, and Amy-Jo on the mortar team drew the animal."

She held it up. It was not a big flag. The base of it was red, rimmed with blue and gold roping . . . probably from a curtain somewhere in Solon's imperial Residence. In the center was a silhouette of a tusked Arkansas razorback in black, pawing the ground angrily and lowering its head to charge. Blue letters stood out against the red as if luminescent. DON'T FEED ON ME read the block-letter slogan.

The men laughed, not at the amateurish nature of the flag but at the pithy sentiment it expressed. They liked it. Valentine felt a little electricity run through the men as she turned it so everyone could see. It was a fighting flag: black and blue set against red, the colors of a brawl. A team could rally round the image of an animal—that was part of the Lifeweaver Hunter Caste appeal—and a savage boar was as good as any. Wily, tough, stubborn, a brute that would gore any animal that dared hunt it—and ugly as its mood when challenged—it suited the dirty funeral attendees.

Valentine went to Yolanda's side, and Styachowski came forward to admire the flag in the sun. Three parallel wounds, probably Reaper claw marks, stood out on her forehead.

"Let's have it up," Valentine said. "Ahn-Kha, where's the pike Hurlmer got that one with?" Ahn-Kha walked along the graves until he found the aluminum conduit pipe.

It took a few minutes to rig wire through the grommets and fix it to the pole. Valentine recognized Yolanda from the prison yard, but he only knew Amy-Jo as one of the heroes from the hospital fight. She'd snatched up the infant Perry and barricaded the babe and his mother in a bathroom, holding the door shut as the Reaper pried it off its hinges before it was swamped by pursuing men.

"Where do you want it, sir?" Yolanda asked.

"Here at the graves," Valentine said. "You said they deserved a flag above them. Can you think of a better place?"

"Make some more," Ahn-Kha said. "Or at least another, for the headquarters. This battalion needs an emblem."

"Hell, with the prisoners, we're a regiment," Styachowski said.

"Valentine's Razors," Post suggested.

The phrase passed up and down the ranks and more cheers broke out.

Valentine looked at his feet, embarrassed for the tears in his eyes.

Styachowski dug the pole into the ground and Amy-Jo and Yolanda found rocks to pile about its base. It wasn't a big flag, nor was it high off the ground, but every eye was on it as it flapped in the fresh spring breeze.

"What kind of shape is the battery in, Hanson?" Valentine asked, after the memorial service dispersed.

"Is 'piss-poor' an appropriate military description?" the new lieutenant asked.

"Can you quantify it a little more?"

Hanson scratched the growth on his chin. "Those Reapers that came up the cliff, half of them made straight for the guns. That suicide mission into the ready magazine—I lost men there. Ives, Lincoln and Lopez bought it in their gun pit. We found Streetiner in a tree. Smalls is missing, Josephs—"

"Smalls? Hank Smalls?"

"Yes. He was a designated as a messenger. When I heard the firing at the base of the hill, I sent him to tell the mortar pits to start preregistered fire missions. He never came back. There's still some woodland that we haven't searched yet. Maybe he ran and hid, and has been too scared to come out yet. Can't say as I blame him."

Valentine tore his mind away from Hank. He feared for the boy, but had to keep the rest of his command in mind. "How many guns can you have in action?"

"I'm jimmying the lists so I can keep three firing, sir. It

won't be quick fire, and I'd like another twenty men to start training."

"We're thin as it is. But ask Lieutenant Post about it."

"Thanks, sir."

"Feel free to practice on the Kurian Tower. No shell fired at that is wasted, as far as I'm concerned."

"In all honesty, sir, I'm not sure I'm up to being battery officer. Could you give me a new commander? Like Styachowski? She knows the theory, and she's good at putting theory into practice."

It took guts for Hanson to tell Valentine that he didn't feel up to the job.

"I'll talk it over with her."

"Thanks, sir. We'll get 'em firing again."

"I'll talk to Beck about getting your ready magazine rebuilt."

"Yeah, it's probably landing in Berlin right about now."

Valentine finished his walk of the perimeter. The men were in better spirits than he would have expected; killing the Reapers and resisting the probe had made them confident.

What success they enjoyed should be shared with Beck's defenses. There were clearings along the easier paths up the hill for open fields of fire, and a series of foxholes and trenches, many lined with logs, for the men to do their shooting. They were still digging dugouts for the men to wait out shellfire, adding interconnecting trenches and access to the flatter hilltop so the men could bring food and water forward safely, and laying mines and wire along likely alleys of approach. Valentine saw one of Kessey's—now Hanson's—forward observers teaching the other soldiers the defensive fire mission zones. With the use of a simple code word, they could call in mortar fire on their attackers.

He returned to the headquarters building, and asked around for Styachowski. She was in her usual spot, beneath the speaker in the radio lounge, eating a bowlful of rice and milk. Her skin had that translucent look to it again; she'd been pushing herself too hard.

"What is that?" Valentine asked.

"Rice pudding. Narcisse made it."

"Don't you ever sleep? You were up all last night."

"Listening to the radio is like sleep. I can zone. What I really need is food."

"I'd still rather see you flat on your back."

"Major, under the Uniform Code, I believe you've just made a sexual suggestion."

Valentine snorted. "That's not what I meant and you know it."

"I was trying to make a joke. You look like you need one."

"Hank Smalls is missing. Since last night. Hanson sent him with a message . . . He never came back."

"A Reaper?"

"Could be. We never knew how many they sent in, just how many we killed. Poor kid."

"And naturally you're blaming yourself."

Valentine left that alone. "I did dig you up for a reason," he said. "I need your help. How would you like a change of duty?"

She brightened visibly. "The Bears? I know Lieutenant Nail's hurt again—"

"Sorry. Hanson isn't confident in his ability to run the battery. I want to put you in charge of it."

Styachowski pursed her lips. "I only know mortars."

"But you know the theory, right?"

"Of course."

"You've done everything I've asked you. You can do this, too. Those guns have to be kept good and lethal. They're the reason the Quislings are all corked up."

"Major Valentine, I've got a question for you, if you don't mind."

"Shoot."

"Last night, you sent me down into the communications bunker. That's the safest place on this hill. Even a Reaper would have trouble clawing through that door Solon had put in. Why did you want me there of all places?"

"I notice you didn't stay. You're my second in command. I couldn't risk us both being killed."

"I'll take over the battery if you take my place in the headquarters. I heard what you did last night, running around in the dark with Reapers everywhere. I've been scared all day thinking about it."

"Are you afraid of having to take command?"

"Not that. I—"

"Courier, Major Valentine," a staff soldier called. "A courier's come in. She's asking for you, and she said for you to hurry."

"She?"

"Yes, popped up on the west side. Pretty gal, red hair, says she's your mama but she's too young for that. I think she climbed the cliff, just like the Reapers."

"Where is she?"

"Eating in the main galley."

"Thanks." Valentine turned to Styachowski. "Sounds like we're getting intelligence. Want to come?"

"For news? Naturally."

They found Alessa Duvalier shoveling rehydrated scrambled eggs into her mouth. She had changed into an outfit Valentine knew as her "traveling clothes." She wore a long, deep-pocketed riding coat, wide-brimmed hat, hiking boots and a backpack blanket-roll combination.

"Hello, Ali. Tired of the showgirl routine?" He and Styachowski sat down opposite her. The cook brought a plate of fried potatoes and Duvalier loaded them with salt before digging in.

"They've got you boxed in tight here, Val. I had to wade across a swamp to even get to that damn cliff. This sort of reminds me of the day we met."

She still had her fast, deft hands, now working knife and fork instead of tying dressings. Both of them had added a few pounds since then. They shared a smile at the memory.

"Then it must be important."

"First, Hamm's back in town with his whole division. Another is moving for Pine Bluff. They won't be there for a couple days maybe; bad roads, guerillas, mines and no rail. Hamm's going to be going across the river in small boats to get south."

"You're not going along?" Valentine asked.

"He's always been unpleasant. Last night he was a bastard. Mean as a stuck pig. The Trans-Mississippi is crashing down around his ears, he's angry at everyone. Executed a junior officer himself."

"Anything from us?"

"Yes. Two days ago a Cat came in from Mantilla. He got your answer, and it's in this letter." She reached into her coat. "What good can come of it beats me. We had to run risks to get this to you. Hope it was worth it."

Valentine opened the envelope and looked at the page. A few bare paragraphs, handwritten, told him what he suspected.

"Where are you off to, Duvalier?"

"South. Every Cat's on the hunt for Solon. He was supposed to be assassinated at the outset of all this, but the Cat shadowing him missed. He disappeared and the Cat's dead."

"Damn. Hamm's division is moving on too?"

"He was supposed to dust you off this hill cheap. They were supposed to take you out while the Reapers were up here causing trouble, but there was some screw-up at headquarters. Only half his division got here in time. The Ks lost a lot of Reapers. I think they're gonna blame him."

"What happened that made you choose last night to leave?"

Duvalier's eyes shifted to her eggs. She added more salt. "He said something about wanting to climb this hill and piss on your body. Accused me of sneaking with you. I think I was going to be arrested. When he went to the CP, I took off; around morning I came up on some pickets along the old interstate north of you. They were talking about how you were still up there. Thought I might as well deliver the message before moving on."

"And check to see if I was still breathing?"

"I brought you along as a Cat. Call it a family interest. Hope the packet helps."

"Your soaking was worthwhile. What's your opinion on Xray-Tango?"

She shrugged. "Typical high-ranking goon. I did hear a rumor from Hamm. The Reapers took his wife away some years back. They thought she was a Cat."

"Remember our Invocation? The blood in our palms?"

Duvalier scrunched up her eyebrows. "Yes. Of course."

"Wonder if that's what passed on our abilities. Something in the bloodstream. Maybe she somehow passed on some abilities to him."

"I don't know Lifeweaver technomagic. Hope it's not something that would show up on some kind of blood test. Might make it easier for them to find us."

"Perish the thought," he said.

She finished her meal and drummed her fingers on the table, so fast each tap combined into a single dull noise. "Sorry I can't be more helpful. Don't try to figure Quislings, especially high-ranking ones. Might as well try to win over a scorpion."

Valentine took his eyes away from her hands. "Feel free to load up with whatever you need. I'd like to ask one more favor of you, though."

"What would that be?"

"The sound of your voice."

It felt a little like a producer doing radio theater that night. Valentine, Styachowski, Jimenez and Duvalier were crammed into the little room, each holding a page of notes. Jimenez twiddled the dials.

"We're on TMCC New Columbia band now," Jimenez said.

"Contact GHQ New Columbia, do you read? Over," Jimenez said. There was a pause of just a moment.

"GHQ here, reading five-five," the speaker crackled back.

"I have priority com from Colonel Le Sain on Big Rock Mountain to General Hamm. He requests that the general come to the mike, wishes to discuss terms of surrender, over."

"Nulton, cut the crap," the voice said.

"Check your RDF and signal strength," Jimenez said. "I'm just up the hill from you, over."

Valentine pressed the transmit trigger. "This is Colonel Le Sain, boy. Get the general to the radio rikki-tik, would you? Standing by."

"Ack—acknowledge," the voice responded.

Jimenez cut the static as they waited.

"You really think turning this into a soap opera will work?" Duvalier said.

"Life's been hard on him lately. I want to make it all my fault," Valentine said.

The minutes passed. "This is Stanislaw, GHQ New Columbia, with General Hamm online. Do you read, over?"

"Zippety do-dah," Duvalier said. "He went for it."

"Colonel Le Sain here. Put the general on the phone."

"I'm here, you turncoat," Hamm's voice cut in. "They said you wanted to do a deal."

"Yes. I'm in charge of guerrilla activity north of the river. I'm in a position to accept your surrender."

"Drop dead, dunk. Signing off."

"Any unarmed man who comes up the switchback road will be taken prisoner, no reprisals."

"Le Sain, if you called me here to joke around—let me tell you my terms."

"Hey, Hambone," Duvalier cut in. "Guess who this is?"

There was static at the other end.

"Yes, sir, I'm up here, too. You were right about one thing, Knox and I had a little fling. He's a man with a future, treats me good, and you know what they say about Indian guys—"

"Get stuffed."

Duvalier checked her notes. "I told him all about you, Hambone. To all those out in radio land, tune in at oh-one-hundred for a detailed description of just how pathetic General Hamm is in bed, complete with what he begged me to do to him. Sorry, General, Knox said this was just too good to keep from the world. We had quite a laugh."

There was no response. Styachowski took over the microphone, and Jimenez switched it to a different frequency.

"This is Ozark Central Command. Ozark Central Command to all stations. Latest intelligence has Third Division moving south of the river. Activate Zones Nuthatch and Finch, alert Jay and Crane. Authentication Z-4, repeat Z-4, P-9, repeat P-9. Signing off."

Jimenez killed the transmitter as she finished the farrago of nonsense.

"That'll give him something to chew on," Styachowski said, looking over at Duvalier.

"I hope he chokes on it," she said.

Valentine put Duvalier in his room, ordering her to get some sleep before her after-midnight broadcast. "Makes me feel like a whore, but if you think it'll help," she said, as Valentine transcribed a few bedroom details about General Hamm. Valentine wrote it so there were five minutes of gossip, then a teaser for the next night's performance, describing what Hamm liked to do to elicit an erection.

Then he had the observers fire a star shell above the river while the moon was down. There was no sign of boat activity; the Third Division showed a lot of activity in its posts.

He gathered Styachowski, Post and Beck for a late-night briefing.

"I want us to be extra alert this morning. Anyone else noticed an increase in activity?" Valentine asked.

"Yes, spotters saw a ferry shuttling back and forth upriver in the last four days," Styachowski said.

"I'd rather have that division busy with us than moving down to Hot Springs," Valentine said. "Earlier this evening we stuck a couple of banderillas in Hamm. Tonight Smoke is going to wave the red cape. He might charge at dawn."

"With the division?" Beck said.

"That's my guess. He'll try to overwhelm us. Captain Post, get every man you can into your line, but quietly. Captain Beck, I want you in the western command post. Send out pickets to listen—again, quietly."

"Yes, sir," Beck and Post said.

"Styachowski, have all your gun crews ready. Good people on the mortars; we'll be dropping shells close to our lines."

"I'll have everyone on station at 3 A.M."

"Major Valentine, report to the radio room, please," the PA blatted.

"Excuse me, please," Valentine said.

He made his way down the hall and to the stairs. There were crowds of men in the radio lounge, grinning and joking.

"Sir, we're going to be on the news," a private said.

"Really? Well, by God, we should be. You're causing Kur a lot of grief, for only fourteen hundred men. We're tying down something like ten thousand, you know."

"Go tell the Spartans," a better-read soldier commented quietly to a friend, but Valentine's ears picked it up anyway.

Valentine went down to the radio room, where Jimenez's relief was at the headset.

"I've got Baltic League on shortwave, sir. They're doing the news. In the news summary they mentioned us, and we're about to catch the repeat broadcast."

"Pipe it up, good and loud. Hell, put it on the loudspeakers."

". . . in the Caucasus continues," the vaguely English-accented voice announced. "Another Kurian Lord in the Rhone Valley went the way of his cousin last month when humanist guerillas seized his chateau, proving that the flames of resistance still burn in Western Europe. This is Radio Baltic League, broadcasting in the first language of freedom to humanity's patriots around the Baltic and around the globe, finishing the European part of the broadcast. Turning to America, an update on the news flash earlier. We have more details from Southern Command in the Ozark Mountains, lately the scene of heavy fighting. General Martinez reports that forces in his organization infiltrated, seized, and destroyed a major supply base on the Arkansas River, formerly the city of Little Rock. For those of you mapping at home, that's a major red-white-and-blue flag for our Cause. General Martinez's command has guns on a nearby hill commanding the entire town, and recently sank river traffic moving to resupply the forces engaged with Southern Command on the South Arkansas Front. He reports that the senior officer on the scene in command of the guns, Lieutenant Colonel Kessey, was wounded in the action, but has hopes for her speedy recovery. Congratulations to the daring and resourceful general, this morning's broadcast is in tribute to you and your men fighting on the Arkansas. Turning to other news from America, with spring coming to the Green Mountains and the Saint Lawrence Seaway—"

Valentine forced a smile across his face and went up into the radio lounge. The men gathered there looked like they'd been slapped.

"What the hell was that, sir?"

"Yeah, Major, that ain't right."

Valentine looked around. "What part isn't right? Did they get the location wrong?"

"No . . . no . . ."

"The lieutenant colonel is dead, but you can't expect them to know that detail. I've only just reported it."

"It's not that sir," Sergeant Hanson said. "They didn't mention you. Valentine's Razors. We're the ones that done it. Martinez, he's—"

"He's in charge of the central part of Arkansas. I send my reports to him, and he communicates them to Southern Command. They don't know everything that happened in his camp yet."

"But it's not right for him—" Hanson persisted.

"Sergeant, let's try to stay alive until this is over. They'll get the story right. It just takes some time. Get some food and rest, men. We might be busy tomorrow morning."

The next morning, they came in fire and thunder.

Duvalier's short broadcast gave the men a chuckle before

they crept into Beck's fortifications. Soldiers always enjoyed a general getting his ego pricked.

The harassing fire started at three A.M., the mortars on Pulaski Heights peppering the whole hilltop with shells. Most of the men were in their trenches and posts, and those who weren't underground ran to safety in a hurry.

Valentine participated in the battle from the basement of one of the smaller buildings on the hilltop, between the gun pits and the western command post. All he saw of it was shellfire, all he heard of it was over scratchy field phone lines.

The men on Pulaski Heights came first. They'd obviously been given orders to pressure them with a river crossing, to look as if the attack were going to come by water. Styachowski dropped a few flechette shells among their boats, and the Quislings thought again about sacrificing their lives just to draw the attention of the artillery.

The listeners returned to their lines before light, with reports of men coughing, swearing and giving quiet orders. Beck ordered his handful of claymores—mines that swept the ground before a position with bursts of dartlike fragments like an enormous shotgun shell—placed above where they were concentrating.

When dawn came the artillery started. The divisional artillery was on the other side of Park Hill; Valentine wished he had a few trained men and a radio somewhere with a view. If Southern Command saw fit to send him a company or two of Wolves and a Bear team—

Their shooting was poor, compared to the mortars across the river. Shells landed all over the hill, damaging little but the turf.

The besiegers were at the bottom of the hill in the predawn gloom. Valentine listened in to the field-phone chatter. Kessey had her guns set up so the observers and officers on the line called the mortar pits directly without going through her, trusting the individual mortar crews to prioritize the use of their shells. Styachowski had been relentlessly training the men on the system ever since. The mortars went into action first, dropping their shells all around the base of the hill.

The assault came. Hamm struck from two directions, the north and the east, both driving to cut off the men at the tip of the finger of the hill extending eastward, to get control of the road going up the hill Valentine had used on his first trip to Solon's Residence. Styachowski used her guns to form a curtain of steel along the north face of the hill. Valentine paced and waited, watching the trees along the top of the eastern finger for signs of the Quisling troops. He forced himself not to call every time the firing quieted, and the company commanders had enough on their hands without him calling for status reports in the middle of action.

"Danger close! Danger close!" the voice of one of the forward observers crackled over the phone. He was calling in fire just in front of his own position—that the Quislings were partway up the hill this soon was troubling.

"Post, take over here. I'm going forward," Valentine said.

"There's no trench, Maj—" Post objected as he left.

Valentine had a soldier's eye for ground. His route to Beck's command post was determined by cover rather than directness. He scrambled through the fallen scrub oaks, along foundations of old buildings and then up a little wash to Beck's position on the north face of the hill.

Beck was at a viewing slit in his wood-and-earth bunker, looking west down the ridge pointing toward the train station. He had a band of dirt across his face the same size as the slit, giving him a raccoonlike expression.

"They're not having any luck from the east," Beck said. "Too much fire from the notched hill by the war memorial. They're coming up hard on the north side. Jesus, there it goes again . . . They're using flamethrowers. Sergeant, call in more mortar fire where that flame's coming from."

Valentine looked at the little gouts of flame as the sergeant spoke into his field phone, binoculars in his other hand. Beck passed his own glasses to Valentine. Valentine surveyed what he could of the north side of the hill; there were mottled TMCC uniforms all along it, all lying in the same direction like freshly cut hay.

Some gutsy company officer fired a signal flare, and the aligned figures stood and began to run up the hill. Beck tore the glasses from his face and flicked a switch on a fuse box. Explosions blossomed across the hill as the signal traveled the wire, little poofs of smoke shooting down the hill like colored sugar blown through a straw.

"The claymores," Valentine said. He saw the Abica brothers moving forward, great belts of ammunition about their necks like brass stoles.

"They're turning around."

"Lieutenant Zhao is back in the machine-gun post," a soldier reported. "He says they're heading back down the hill."

They tried again. According to Beck the second attack showed nothing like the patience and skill of the first. Hamm concentrated all his gunfire on the easternmost tip of the hill, until a permanent cloud of thrown-up smoke and dirt hung at the end of the hill, constantly renewed by further shellfire. But the men there held; the machine guns weren't silenced. As fast as they came up, they turned around and went down.

"We broke the second wave!" Beck's forward observer shouted. "They're running!"

"And the Third Division's bad luck continues," Valentine said. "Cease fire. Cease fire."

"Why?" Beck asked.

"Let 'em run. I want the others to get the idea. So next time they come, they have to start from scratch, not from halfway up."

"Hurrah for the Razors!" a soldier shouted as Valentine surveyed the devastated ridge. Stretcher-bearers braved sniper fire to bring in the wounded, and Valentine had come forward to see to those wounded. Pickups converted to ambulances were bumping across the shell-holed road to take them back to the hospital building.

God, and there's only one doctor.

"Valentine, time for me to be moving on," he heard, as he knelt beside a wounded man.

Valentine glanced up at Duvalier. "Interested in lugging a radio up Park Hill tonight?"

"No, sorry. Suicide isn't my style. I've got another assignment. They think Solon's outside Hot Springs. The Cats are concentrating. Someone'll get him."

"Is he so important?"

"Wherever he goes the Quislings do better, for some reason. He's like a lucky charm."

Valentine went back to cleaning the soldier's face. The man's elbow was torn up, and the skin on his forearm and hand already had a gray look to it. He'd never use his right hand again. "They won't try that again, will they, sir?" the private said, smiling.

"They're dumb, but they're not that dumb," Valentine said. "You taught them about touching hot stoves."

"It was them Bears, sir. They backed up our platoon. When the flamethrower burned out the machine-gun crew, they went down and got 'em, then held the machine-gun post, flames and all. We took the line back after that."

"Good teamwork, hero." He looked up at Duvalier. She stared at him, strangely intent. "Take off. It's getting dark. If you pass a TMCC mail pouch while you're sneaking through the lines, drop a note in for Xray-Tango; tell him I want to have a word."

Duvalier's lip trembled. "Val, if you guys get pushed off here . . . make for the south bank. There's good cover in the hills."

"We're here to stay, Ali. In the ground or above it."

She hugged him from behind; he felt her lips brush the back of his neck. Then she was gone.

There was a week-long respite from all save harassing fire. The Quislings were being careful with their shells, so only one or two an hour landed on the hill. Sometimes they would ratchet up the fire into a bombardment, so every time a shell landed Valentine tensed, waiting to see if others would follow. It was exhausting.

The only thing Valentine remembered about the period between the Third Division attack and the arrival of the Crocodile was Nail's recovery. Dr. Brough reported that one day the wounded Bear simply sat up and swung his legs off the bed, then walked downstairs for breakfast. He returned to command of the Bears and reorganized his tiny but ferocious group. With wounds from the Reaper fight healed, his teams were back at full strength.

Which was something that couldn't be said for the rest of the command. The bonfire they'd held to celebrate the victory was lit with the flames of Pyrrhus. The hospital overflowed with the bloody debris of his victory over his old general. Beck's line was a series of points; if the enemy came again as they had the first day of the attack, they would go through it like floodwaters through a screen door.

Then the first "railcar" struck.

The men called them that because it was what they sounded like as they roared overhead, looking like red comets of sparks. They may have sounded like railcars, but they struck like meteorites, causing the ground to writhe and shake in an explosive earthquake.

The shells landed all through the long night, every hour at the hour, precisely. The timing made the shelling even worse. Each man, Valentine included, dreaded the rise of the minute hand toward the top of the clock. One overshot the hill and splashed into the Arkansas River, while others killed men just from the concussion. Valentine saw one man with either a part of a lung or a stomach sticking out of his mouth. Others died without so much as a tooth being found.

The explosions drove man and animal mad. Max the German shepherd had to be put down after he attacked anyone who came near. The wounded in the hospital had to be tied into their bunks to keep from crawling under them, tearing out IV lines.

"It's the Crocodile, sir," a rummy-eyed old Guard said to Valentine in the blackboard-walled briefing room. Post stood next to him. "That's what we called it, anyway. They tell me from a distance it's all bumpy and green, and the tug tower sticks up like an eye."

"I've never heard of it."

"It's a Grog thing, out of St. Louis. She shelled us from twenty miles away on the Missouri, when we were dug in during the siege on the Bourbeuse in '61. She's naval artillery. She goes on the water and they move her around in an armored barge, like a battleship. I think they put the gun together on the banks, but nobody knows for sure."

"Solon's called in the Grogs? He must be desperate." Valentine wondered what kind of deal Solon had made to get the Grogs to aid him.

"You may get a chance to find out," Post said. "A messenger came forward at oh-nine-hundred, on the dot, under a flag of truce. He had a letter from Xray-Tango. I guess Hamm's been 'relieved' because it's signed General Xray-Tango, CINC New Columbia State, Trans-Mississippi. No demands, just a parley."

"Colonel Le Sain," Xray-Tango said, when Valentine emerged from the lines. Nail and Ahn-Kha stood alongside, Nail carrying the white flag. They met on an old residential road at the base of the hill. The growth had been blasted and burned by shellfire.

"General Xray-Tango," Valentine said. The general's spasm-afflicted eye sent out mental distress signals like Morse code.

"Both still alive, I see," Xray-Tango said.

"I should have shot Solon and you when I had the chance on that hill back in March. Would've been a nice change; the commanders kill each other and the privates live."

"What are you suggesting, a duel? We both take our pistols, walk ten paces and shoot? The winner gets the hill?"

"Save a lot of blood, General."

"You know it's ridiculous. Change of subject."

"You sent the message, General. What are we to discuss?"

"Your surrender. Prevent the 'further effusion of blood.' I believe that's the traditional wording."

"You're working for the experts in the effusion of blood, General."

"Forget it, Le Sain. I'll go back and blow you off that hill."

"General, suppose we step over under that tree and talk," Valentine said.

"That's better. A smart man knows when his bluff's called."

They walked along the old road at the base of the hill, leaving Nail, Ahn-Kha and Xray-Tango's aides looking across the road at each other. A red oak sprouted from a crack in the pavement, now big enough to offer them some shade in the late-morning sun. A dead apartment complex watched them with empty eyes.

"Just out of curiousity, General, what happened to Hamm?"

Xray-Tango's eye twitched. "He was"—*blink-blink-bliiink*—"relieved."

"Permanently, I take it."

The general said nothing.

"What are the terms, General?"

"Very generous, Le Sain. Very generous, indeed. These come from Solon and all the governors. Each has allowed their seal on the deal."

"I can just hear my last words as the Reaper picks me up: 'The seals are in order.'"

"It's got my name on it, too, if that means anything to you. It says you and your men can walk away. You can travel wherever you want, with your small arms. Join Southern Command's lines for all we care. Just get out of New Columbia."

"That simple, huh?"

"We kept it simple so you could understand it."

"I need to contact my higher ups."

"Oh, Colonel," Xray-Tango said. "I almost forgot. One more gesture of good faith for you. Bring him forward."

One of Xray-Tango's aides waved, and two soldiers stood up from the bushes, a slight figure between them. It was Hank. Valentine held his breath as they brought the boy forward, fearing some sort of sadistic display.

The boy had his right hand swathed in bandages. He was thin and haggard.

"What did you do to him?"

"That's a story, Colonel. He was being questioned, you see. By General Hamm himself."

Hank looked up at Valentine. He read pride, and something like defiance in the boy's eyes.

"I didn't tell them anything, sir," Hank said.

"No, he didn't," Xray-Tango continued. "Hamm took the boy to a charcoal grill. He threatened to cook the boy's hand there on the grate, smash it down like a hamburger with a spatula. Wanted to know who the spy at his headquarters was, like some kid would know. Your boy here stuck his own hand into the coals. Stared right at Hamm until he passed out. One of the men there puked from the smell."

"Hank—"

"Take him back with you. Your whole command, in the person of a prepubescent boy. What'll it be, Le Sain? Do they live or die? Does this brave kid live or die? Up to you."

Valentine pulled the boy over to his side of the road. "I'll see you later."

"You have until sunset. After then, anyone coming off the hill is dead. You've already had some deserters. This is your last chance."

"No, General, it's yours."

Xray-Tango stared with his owl eyes. "Pretty pathetic threat."

"You're fighting two wars, General, one with me and one with your conscience. The things you've seen, the people you've helped. You've been on the wrong side your whole life. You should have talked to your wife more."

"Huh?"

"She was a Cat. Same as me. The Lifeweavers train us to assassinate Kurians, Quisling generals, what have you.

Maybe she was on an assignment, to kill you maybe, but she saw some hope in you, Scottie."

Xray-Tango's eye twitched. This time it didn't stop after three.

"That is . . . horseshit."

"Do you suppose they killed her quick, or slow?"

"Shut up. Shut up! I've made my offer. You have until sundown."

"They probably killed her. Maybe she was hung. In New Orleans I used to hear the guys in the wagons talk about a last ride for the women they—"

"Shut your fuckin' mouth!"

Valentine raised his voice in return. "What kind of sword is hanging over your head, General? How thick's the thread? You don't get us off this hill in hip-hop time and they'll haul you off, I bet. Brass ring or no. I saw one taken once. They jerked the ring right off, along with the owner's finger—"

Xray-Tango's eyes widened as he thought through the implications. "Balls," he howled. Xray-Tango's left fist exploded toward Valentine's jaw.

Valentine slipped under it, and just dodged a right cross that he only saw coming at the last split second. Xray-Tango moved fast for a big man. A jab by Valentine bounced off a beefy triceps. Xray-Tango paid it no more attention than a plowhorse did a fly.

Xray-Tango squared on him and the Cat's vision exploded into dueling rainbows; all the colors of the spectrum and a few Valentine didn't know existed danced to the ringing in his ears. He brought his forearms up to cover his face and saw a fuzzy apparition between his parallel radii.

Xray-Tango took the opportunity to work Valentine's stomach, the blows like the kicks of an entire team of mules. Valentine lashed out, but it only left him open for a combination that left him looking at the grass.

He fought for breath, took one and the mists cleared. He heard men shouting as he rolled to his feet.

Xray-Tango advanced, his fists turning tight circles in

front of his massive shoulders. "Should have taken your dose and gone down, Valentine."

Valentine saw men from both sides gathering, emerging from their holes and trenches and piled-rubble redoubts to watch the fight. Even those who stayed behind with their weapons stood atop headlogs and sandbags to see the action.

Valentine tried a combination, but the big arms came up and he just missed losing part of his jaw to Xray-Tango's riposte.

"Who do you really wanna hit, General?" Valentine said.

Xray-Tango stepped in with lethal speed and tried the uppercut that had started the music still echoing in Valentine's ears, but the Cat stepped out of the way. The blows came like an artillery barrage, but every time the general's fist cut nothing but empty air. Valentine sidestepped, backstepped, but there were no ropes to pin him, just an evershifting circle of soldiers.

"Shadowboxing, General. You're shadowboxing," Valentine gasped between breaths. "Quit fighting me and fight them!"

"They're fighting for the hill," someone in the crowd shouted as others came up. "A duel. General Extasy's winning against the Red Renegade!" An excited murmer went up from the crowd; every soldier's fantasy seemed to be coming true—the two big bugs fighting, instead of all the little worker ants.

Xray-Tango began to pant. "How are you going to win if you never hit back?"

Valentine bent under another combination, slipped under Xray-Tango's reach and came up behind the general, and tapped him on the shoulder.

"Did she ever ask you to desert, Scottie?"

"Narrr!" Xray-Tango bellowed, swinging laced fingers as though he held a sword to take Valentine's head off. Valentine ducked under it and the momentum of his blow carried Xray-Tango off balance. Valentine helped him to the ground with a cross.

The audience roared with excitement. "Southern Command is winning!"

"Extasy's a champ, you dunks," a seargeant from the other side shouted.

Xray-Tango rolled to his feet with the same grace that seemed so out of place in his big frame. Suddenly his feet were against Valentine's chest as he launched himself at Valentine with a two-heel kick, and Valentine felt something snap as both opponents fell backward to the ground.

The general rolled, got a hold of Valentine's leg and it was a ground fight. Against most other men Xray-Tango's weight would have ended the contest, but Valentine was a veteran of dozens of Zulu Company wrestling matches, often ending with Valentine facing the old top sergeant, Patel, before Patel won and went on to regimental competition. Valentine got ahold of an elbow and kept Xray-Tango's face in the dirt so he couldn't breathe. He forced the arm up, up—

Clack!

The arm suddenly gave way with horrid ease. Valentine sprang to his feet, let the general up.

"You're done," Valentine said.

"So are you," Xray-Tango answered. "We're going to roll up your men like—"

Valentine raised his voice toward the assembled Quisling soldiery. "The general lost. You're to retreat west, home to Texas or Oklahoma."

Dozens of faces suddenly brightened. An end.

"No!" Xray-Tango roared. "That wasn't what this was about."

"He's trying to back out of it," Valentine shouted over his shoulder to his soldiers. It was all lies; his men deserved more than lies, but if he could take the heart out of the Quislings, make them feel that their lives were being sacrificed after the general's loss of a duel—

"Back to your posts. Back to your posts. Open fire on this rabble," Xray-Tango shouted.

"Welshing Quisling!" a Razor shouted. Boos broke out on both sides.

"Back up the hill, men," Valentine said. "He lost and he's not squaring up!"

The two groups of men parted like magnets pressed positive to positive. Two floods of dirty soldiery retreated in opposite directions.

Valentine carried Hank up the hill himself.

Responsibility. Valentine had dreamed, on his long trip back across Texas, of being able to give up the burden, turn his command over to higher ranks. Let someone else make the decisions for a while, and lie awake nights because of the consequences. This was a decision he couldn't make.

He tried to consult higher authority. He had raised Southern Command on the radio, and got a colonel in Intelligence Operations who told him that "as the officer commanding locally, you're better able to evaluate the situation and reconcile your orders to keep as many as you can of the enemy tied down as long as possible, denying traffic across the enemy's road, river and rail network, rather than someone who had to be apprised of the situation over the radio."

"Thanks for nothing," he replied, fighting the urge to curse. He didn't want the techs in the radio room telling the others at breakfast that he'd lost it.

The anger at his superior officer was surpassed only by that with himself. He slammed the microphone down and retreated to his room. All over the camp, the story was spreading that Valentine and Xray-Tango had fought for New Columbia. Valentine had won, but the Quislings wouldn't leave. It made the men fighting mad, all the more determined to stay and win.

But Valentine lay in his bunk, feeling like a fraud.

The day's respite gave him a chance to gather the men in the open, in the afternoon sunshine. He gathered them at the grave site, where the fifty-three, now swollen to triple the original number, rested under their tiny hand-sewn flag. Valentine took in the faces. They reclined, his handful of Jamaican *Thunderbolt* marines, prisoners, Southern Command Guards, Bears, officers, NCOs and men, not a mass of uniforms, but a collage of faces. Faces he knew and trusted, under their dirt and bug bites. Only one or two had regrown the beards and mustaches they'd lost in the woods outside Bullfrog's phony station. Most had kept themselves as shorn as new recruits or in short, spiky hair—with showers a rarity, fleas, ticks and lice had multiplied.

He met the gaze of Tamsey, a corporal who'd shown him pictures of sixteen sisters. The boy had seen his mother die giving birth to his sixth sister, then his father remarried a woman with daughters of her own and jointly they produced more, and he knew every detail of each of their marriages. Next to him was a private named Gos, so nearsighted that he was almost blind, but an expert at feeding belts into a machine gun overlooking the switchback road on the southeast side of the hill. Gos could whistle any popular tune you could care to name, pitch-perfect. Amy-Jo Santoro, the heroine of the Reaper fight in the hospital, turned out to be an insomniac who sewed at night. She'd fix anyone's uniform, provided they gave it to her clean of dirt and critters; she had a horror of lice. There was Tish Isroelit, reputedly the Razors' best sniper, who'd stalked and then managed to bring down a Quisling colonel at dusk by the glow of his after-dinner cigar, shooting him through a closed window. She kept score by adding beads—Valentine had forgotten the exact ranking system, but it was color-coded—to braids in her chestnut hair. Sitting crossed-legged behind her was Denton Tope, a combat engineer whom everyone called "the Snake." Though a big man when he stood, he could press himself so flat to the ground one would swear his bones were made of rubber, useful for his trips out in the dark and wet to replace mines and booby traps at the base of the hill. He was always borrowing powerful binoculars at night to try to spot satellites among the stars. Dozens of other ministories, sagas that had briefly joined with his own and were likely to end on the churned-up hill, waited for him to speak.

"This is the deal," Valentine began. "There wasn't a duel for the hill, that was a private fight. Here's the truth: General

Xray-Tango has given us until sundown to walk off this pile on our own. He'll escort us, with our rifles, anywhere we want. Hot Springs. Up north to Branson, maybe; see a show.

"Or we can stay here. Let them waste their time and bullets killing all of us, instead of Southern Command soldiers liberating towns and villages full of your relatives. Make sure there are a few less of them at the end of it all. At the end of us."

"So it's a life-or-death decision. How many of you know what the phrase 'Remember the Alamo' means?"

Hands went up all across the command. His command.

"I see a few who aren't familiar with it. It refers to a battle fought two hundred and fifty years ago, or thereabouts. Some Texicans under a colonel named Travis were holding out against a general named Santa Anna at a little abandoned mission station on the Rio Grande. They were outnumbered, surrounded, but they fought anyway, gave a man named Sam Houston time to organize his own counterattack. It became a battle cry for an entire war.

"How many of you remember Goliad?" No hands this time. "I'm not surprised. They were also a group of men in that same revolt against Santa Anna. They didn't fight like the men at the Alamo. They surrendered. Santa Anna executed every one of them.

"I'm not saying we'll be remembered, I'm not saying we'll be forgotten. What we do up here may have an effect on the future. Whether that future remembers us or not . . . it's not for me to say. I'll tell you another thing about the Alamo. Each of those men made a personal decision to be there. Some say they stepped across a line in the sand.

"I'm not doing anything that dramatic. Any of you who want to leave can get up and walk down that hill. I'm staying, and Ahn-Kha's staying. Each of the rest of you have a decision to make. You have until sundown to get out of town, according to Xray-Tango. He's going to kill the rest of us. Well, he's going to try.

"I'm going down to the radio lounge. The smart thing to do is run. It may not be the right thing to do, but it's the smart thing. The dummies can join me for a drink. We need to be back in the line at sundown. I expect the Crocodile will start firing again."

Valentine used his knife to cut open a carton marked "snakebite serum," from the medical quarters. Mantilla had given him the case that night he'd passed most of the Quickwood on to Southern Command. He extracted a bottle of bourbon and broke the seal on the paper screwtop. He sniffed the amber contents. He flipped up two shot glasses on the bar.

"One drink for you, Colonel Travis, and one for me."

Travis didn't seem to want his, but Valentine left it there for him anyway. Ahn-Kha stood in the door.

"Good news," Ahn-Kha said. Nothing more. The Grog turned and went upstairs.

Valentine walked out the oversized doors, still on their hinges despite the shellfire. The soldiers stood in ranks, not neat, lines not dressed, and nothing but a proud expression was uniform, Post, Styachowski and Beck to the front.

"Thank you, men," he said, blinking back tears. "How many smart ones were there?"

"Nineteen," Styachowski reported. "Two were wounded. None of them women; they all wanted to stay."

Valentine saw a bright bandanna in the back.

"Couldn't get anyone to carry you out, Narcisse?"

"Didn't want to run again," she called. "Haven't had much luck with that; only have one arm left, sir."

Dr. Brough appeared with the case of bourbon. "Company commanders, to me. We've got some bottles to distribute."

"Okay, you dummies," Post said. "Back to business. Let's disperse, no point in getting killed all at once."

Valentine pulled the youngest member of his command aside as they dispersed.

"Hank, you sure you're fit to rejoin your outfit?" Valentine asked.

"Yes, sir."

Valentine disagreed. Hank looked sick.

"How's the hand?" Valentine said through gritted teeth. His nose picked up a faint, sweet smell from Hank's bandaged hand.

"Not so bad."

"Report to the doctor. If she says you're okay, you can get back to Captain Styachowski. She needs quick feet at the battery."

Hank turned away, dejected. Valentine whistled, and the boy turned.

"Hank, of all the men who stayed up here tonight, I'm proudest to have you with me."

The Crocodile opened up on them again as soon as the sun disappeared. The Grogs upped their rate of fire to three shells an hour, every hour. Their firing was wild at night, though the air-cutting shrieks and earth-churning impacts made sleep impossible. When dawn returned they began reducing Solon's Residence to rubble.

The men began to go as mad as Max the German shepherd.

One snuck out of his dugout at dawn and was spotted by an observer standing atop a heap of rubble, arms outstretched as though welcoming a lover's embrace as the sun came up in thunder.

Later they found a boot, Post reported, his incipient beard now going gray as well.

Sergeants had to put down furious brawls over nothing. The precise timing of the shells tightened everyone's nerves into violin strings as they waited for the next howl and explosion, leaving flung dirt floating like a cloud atop Big Rock Hill.

Valentine was coming up the stairs from the generator floor, where he'd been checking fuel feeds damaged by the shelling, and passed Styachowski in the stairwell when the 15:20 struck, burying its nose in the ground deep—and near—enough to cause a collapse at the floor above. Valentine threw himself at Styachowski, pushing them both into a notch under the stairs—unnecessarily as it turned out—and the lights flickered and died just as he smelled her hair and the feminine musk coming up from her collar.

They scooted up against an intact wall, Valentine covering his head as well as he could, and he felt a wave of dust hit him in the dark.

"You okay?" he asked, hearing rubble fall somewhere up the stairs. It sounded strangely far-off and muffled.

They sat there as the air settled. Valentine thought he heard a shout from above, but there wasn't a hint of light.

"I'll be dead soon, I think. It works on the mind. I'm smelling food, growing plants, coffee being warmed up. Listening to everyone."

"There's still hope," he said.

"You tell yourself that? Or just the rest of us?"

"They haven't whipped us. They aren't even close."

"That's not an answer."

He didn't supply one.

She pressed his shoulder with hers in the darkness. "You're an odd duck, sir. You look so . . ."

"So what?"

"Never mind."

"I'd like to know what you think. Might as well talk about something."

"How about that bacon we had yesterday? Talk about the bottom of the lot," she said.

"You've got me curious. I look so what?"

"Well, you look so soft, I was going to say. You've got really gentle eyes. They're scared, too. Sometimes. Like that night they dropped the sappers."

"I was scared. Till I saw you with that bow. You looked like you were at target practice."

She didn't say anything. He broke the silence. "Speaking of setting an example—I should go up those stairs and see—"

"No. Give it another minute. We're here, it's dark, and you smell . . . comforting."

"Is that a soft smell?"

"See, you are hurt."

"No. Interesting to see yourself through another's eyes. What another person thinks."

"I want it to be over. I'm down here in the dark pretending there's no fighting, no Crocodile. No memories of Martinez and his gang. You can't imagine how good it feels, to have all that gone."

Actually he could. Valentine had sought oblivion in lust in the past . . .

They sat in the dark, feeding off each other's warmth, conducted through her hard-muscled shoulder.

"Sir, why are you what you are?" Styachowski asked.

"You mean a Cat? And it's 'David' or 'Val' when I'm off my feet."

"Okay, Val. Why?"

"Why don't you go first?"

"I took up soldiering because I knew I could fight. When I was little, about six, I got into a scrap with a boy two years older than me. I beat him. When I say 'beat him' I really mean 'beat'—he ended up in the hospital. After that my mom told me about my dad. He'd been a Bear, in a column marching back from some fight in Oklahoma. Caught Mom's eye somehow, and they had a night before he moved on. She said she wasn't thinking—just doing patriotic duty she called it; I showed up nine months later. She said the hunting-men were like wild animals and I had to control myself and never lose my temper. The doc said that was superstition, but I dunno."

"Your mom may have been right. My father was a Bear, too."

"So you joined to be like him?"

"Something like that. I think it was my way of knowing him. He was dead by that time."

She sniffed. "Oh, I'm sorry."

"So the Bears didn't want you?"

"No. But I still want to be one. It's like this monster inside that wants to get out, wants to fight. I'm afraid that if the monster doesn't get to take it out on the enemy, it'll get out another way."

Valentine had never met someone with the same dilemma before. After a moment, he said: "You worried that you're a threat to others?"

"I meant myself."

Valentine brushed dirt off his kneecaps. "I wondered what my father's life was like fighting for the Cause, what made him give up and go live in the Northwoods. Now the only thing I wonder is how he lasted so long. There were other reasons. I believe in the Cause. I've got no time for the 'it's over, we've lost, let's just weather the storm, fighting makes everything worse' crowd. The Cause is no less just for being lost. Then again, being special appealed to me—meeting with the Lifeweavers, learning about other worlds."

He wanted to go on, to tell her that he worried that the Lifeweavers had also unlocked the cage of a demon somewhere inside him, to use her metaphor—even more, fed and prodded the demon so it was good and roused when it came time to fight their joined war. The demon, not under his bed but sharing his pillow, was a conscienceless killer who exulted in the death of his enemies at night and then reverted to a bookish, quiet young man when the fighting was over. He worried that the David Valentine who agonized his way through the emotional hangovers afterward, who sometimes stopped the killing, was vanishing. He could look at corpses now, even corpses he'd created—felling men like stands of timber—with no more emotion than when he saw cordwood stacked on a back porch. It made him feel hollow, or dead, or bestial. Or all three at once.

A voice from above: "Clear from here on . . ."

Valentine saw the flicker of a flashlight beam and got to his feet, reaching up into the dark to feel for the stairs above.

"Hellooo—" he shoulted as he helped Styachowski up.

"Stay put. On the way," a male voice called back from above.

Soldiers with flashlights, one carrying a bag with a big red cross on it, came down the stairs.

"Hey, it's Re—Major Valentine," one called to the other.

"That was fast digging," Styachowski said.

"There's not much of a blockage," the one with the medical kit said. "Just a wall collapse and some dirt to climb over. Ol' Solon built his foundations well."

Styachowski straightened her dust-covered uniform. "We're fine," she said, reverting to her usual brisk tone. "Let's get those lights in the generator room and see where the trouble is."

The last of her warmth left his skin as Valentine nodded. She turned, and he followed her and the soldiers into the generator room.

They had electricity within the hour, but Valentine wasn't sure how much longer he could transmit, so he composed a final report to Southern Command of two bare lines. He walked it down to the radio room himself.

Jimenez had the headset on. Jimenez took it off and threw it on the desk, upending a coffee cup. He didn't bother to wipe up the spill.

"They left Hot Springs yesterday. The official bulletin just went out."

"Then what's wrong? They're only fifty miles away. There's nothing between us and them."

"They're turning northwest. Heading for Fort Smith."

Valentine patted him on the shoulder. "There's a lot of Kurians in Fort Smith. Let's hope they get them."

"Right. Across mountains."

He placed his final transmission to Southern Command on the coffee-covered desk.

WE STAYED. WE DIED.

The shelling from the Crocodile went on for four more days. It was the closest thing to insanity Valentine had ever known. Nothing had any meaning except where the next shell would land. Styachowski's guns couldn't reach the Crocodile. One by one they were put out of action.

The radio room was buried by a direct hit, and Jimenez with it. The hospital had to go underground when a near miss blew down its southern wall. Beck died on the third day, torn to shreds as he turned the knocked-down remnants of Solon's Residence into a final series of trenches and fire lanes. Styachowski took over for him, pulling back what was left of her mortars and placing them in a tight ring of dug-out basements, along with a few shells they were harboring for the final assault.

They knew it was coming when the Crocodile's fire stopped. Thirty minutes went by, and the men gathered at their firing posts. An hour went by, and they began to transfer wounded.

The single remaining pack radio, kept operating by Post, crackled to life. For the past two days it had been rigged to the generator recovered from the kitchens. Post whistled and shouted for Valentine across the ruins. He hopped over a fallen Doric column, a piece of décor Solon fancied, and climbed down the wooden ladder to Post's dugout. A shell or two pursued him. Just because the Crocodile was silent didn't mean the mortars on Pulaski Heights quit firing.

"Urgent call for you, sir," Post said. "Scanner picked it up."

"Le Sain? Are you there, Le Sain?" the radio crackled, on Southern Command's frequency.

"Go ahead; not reading you very well."

"It's a field radio." Valentine heard distant gunfire over the speaker. "It's me, Colonel. The Shadowboxer."

"Go ahead, General. Another surrender demand?"

"It's Scottie to you, Knox. Or whatever. I'm the one that surrendered, using your metaphor. I took a few members of my staff on board the Crocodile. We wanted to see the gun in action, you see. For some reason the Grogs didn't think it was odd that I had a submachine gun with me. I shot the crew and pulled out a hand grenade. Grogs sure can run when they use all their limbs." He laughed, and it occurred to Valentine that he'd never heard Xray-Tango's laugh before. "Now I'm sitting between the magazine door and a shell. There's a dead Grog loader propping it open. This shell's a monster: it's got to be a fourteen-inch cannon. My driver and a couple of members of my staff are making their way around the other side of the gun through the woods. The

Grogs are running for dear life. Regular Cat trick, isn't it? Infiltrate, assassinate. All that's left is the sabotage. I've got a grenade bundle in my lap right now."

"Scottie, I—" Valentine began. Post had an earpiece in his ear and a confused look on his face.

"Going to have to cut this short, Colonel." Valentine heard automatic fire. "My driver almost has an angle on me. Apologies to St. Louis, looks like they aren't getting their gun back. You know what the best part is, Le Sain?"

"What's that?"

"Since I started dreaming up this plan night before last, my face hasn't twitched once. God, what a relief, it's wonderful. Over and out."

Something lit up the sky to the east and Valentine felt the ground shudder. He counted twenty-two seconds. Then it came, a long, dull boom. Valentine went back up the ladder, and saw the top of a mushroom cloud climbing to the clouds, white flecked with gray at the edges. He watched it rise and spread.

Until the tears came.

The shells stopped, but not the attack. On the thirty-fifth day of the siege they came up the north face, like the wind behind a rain of mortar shells. They came up the east ridge; they came up the switchback. They came up everywhere but the quarry cliff.

The Beck Line collapsed.

Valentine's men tumbled backward toward the Residence. What was left of the gun crews dragged the one remaing gun back to Solon's prospective swimming pool and set it up there.

Even the headquarters staff turned out to stanch the attack. Valentine watched it all from a tangle of reinforced concrete, a conical mound of debris looking out over the hilltop beside what was left of Solon's Residence.

"Officer by the switchback road," Valentine said, looking through some field glasses. He and Ahn-Kha occupied one of the higher heaps of rubble. Ahn-Kha swiveled his Grog gun. His ears leveled and he fired, kicking up concrete dust.

"They'll zero that," Valentine said. "Let's move."

They slid off the mound and into the interbuilding trenches. Rats, the only animals that didn't mind shellfire, disappeared into hidey-holes as they picked their way to the headquarters basement.

It still had a roof of sorts on it, three stories of collapsed structural skeleton. Among the cases of food and ammunition, Brough patched up wounds and extracted shrapnel with the help of her remaining medics. Bugs crawled in cut-off clothing, stiff with weeks' worth of sweat and dirt.

Brough didn't even look at the worst cases. After triage, performed by Narcisse, the worst cases were sent to the next basement over, which was only partially covered. There a few of the stronger-stomached women replaced bandages and murmured lies about recovery. That the men called the passageway to the next basement the "death hole" showed the general opinion of a sufferer's chances within.

Styachowski and Post bodily shoved the men into positions in the final series of trenches as the stream from the crestline turned into a trickle. They moved dully, like sleepwalkers, and collapsed on top of their rifles and slept as soon as they were told to stop moving. Soon, what was left of his command had to keep their heads down not just from mortar fire, but from machine-gun fire that swept the heaps of ruins.

Valentine looked around the last redoubt. In a year it would be a weed bed; in five these mounds would be covered by brush and saplings. He wondered if future generations would wander the little hummocks and try to pick out the final line, where the Razorbacks were exterminated in their little, interconnected holes like an infestation of vermin.

Hank was in the death hole. His burns had turned septic despite being dusted with sulfa powder, and Brough was out of antibiotics. The boy lay on the blankets someone else had died in, waiting his turn, keeping the tears out of his eyes.

"We sure stuck a wrench in their gears, didn't we?" Hank asked, when Valentine sat for a visit.

"With your help," Valentine said. "Wherever your parents are, they're proud of you."

"You can be honest with me, Major. They're dead; they have been since that night. You can tell me the truth, can't you? I'm tough enough to take it."

"You're tough enough."

Hank waited.

"They're dead, Hank. I went after them, and I killed them with the rest of the Quislings. They were telling about the Quickwood. About the ruse."

"My fault, sir," Hank said.

Valentine had to harden his ears to make out the tiny voice. "No."

"It is," Hank insisted. "I heard them talking after the baby—after you told us she was dead. 'We won't be sacrificed,' Pa said, and they started speaking with their heads together. I should have told you or Ahn-Kha or Mr. Post—but I didn't. Just Mister M'Daw and then it was too . . ." The boy faded back into sleep, like a child who has fought to stay awake until the end of an oft-repeated story but lost.

Valentine knew from fifteen years of regret what sort of abyss yawned before the boy. Agony rose and washed through him along with a gorge he fought to keep down, all the pent-up emotional muck of his losses breaking in his roaring ears and wet eyes. Maybe if he'd been tending to his ax and the kindling as was his duty that day, instead of corn collecting, he would have warned Mom of the trucks coming up the road to the house; she would have grabbed his sister and baby brother and gotten his father from the lakeshore—

Regret might haunt Hank, grind the child down, or drive him to God-knows-which bitter lengths to compensate for an imagined fault. Valentine couldn't allow that to happen to the boy—or man, rather. If anyone on the hill exhibited the manly virtues Valentine had listed when he sent Hank off to the guns, it was the septic boy in the cot.

Being able to forgive himself was a cause as lost as the Razors'.

There was still plenty of hot cocoa; it came in tins with little cups inside so all that was needed was a glass and hot water. He, Ahn-Kha, Post, Styachowski, Nail, Brough and Hanson met one final time. Their conference room was filled with wounded, so they gathered in the last artillery magazine. A few dozen mortar rounds stood, interspersed with sandbags, where once there had been hundreds stacked to the ceiling.

"You know what's always pissed me off about this operation?" Valentine asked.

"Your haircut?" Post asked. The officers had enough energy left to laugh.

"That railroad bridge. We never were able to bring it down."

"Isn't that in the 'too late to worry' file?" Nail asked.

"Not necessarily. If we get the men up and moving, we could punch through. Some of us would make it to the bridge. I doubt they've got reserves massed everywhere in case of a counterattack. Once we got off the hill it's only a mile."

"I'll go with you, my David," Ahn-Kha said. "I don't want to die like my father, in a burned-out hole."

"What happened to tying down as many troops as possible as long as possible?"

"Aren't you all sick of this?" Valentine said. "The dirt, the death? Sitting here and taking it?"

Styachowski and Nail exchanged looks. "If we do it, I imagine you'll need Lieutenant Nail."

"Of course I'd need him."

"Then I can't try my plan to save Hank," Dr. Brough said.

"What's that?"

"The boy, the one with the gangrenous arm. I've been curious about the resiliency of the Bears. I put some of Lieutenant Nail's blood in a dish with a bacterial culture. It killed it, like his blood was full of chlorine. I thought I'd try a transfusion; he and the boy have the same blood type. But it would take time for him to recover."

"You may not have that, Doctor. They'll attack again. I don't believe we're in any kind of shape to hold them off."

"Hank can't hold off the gangrene. It's system-wide."

Valentine finished his cocoa. "Nail, would you turn over your command to Styachowski? She's always wanted to be a Bear."

Nail tried walking on his wounded, mangled leg. He was still limping.

"I hate to miss out on a fight if my Bears are involved."

"I'll bring them back to you, if I can," Styachowski said.

The transfusion took place within the hour. It was done under fire; the Quislings launched a probing attack to see what sort of defenses the defenders still had. It left Nail drained, and after a tiny meal—by Bear standards—he drifted off to sleep.

As it turned out, they weren't able to try Valentine's plan that night anyway. The day's clouds dissolved and it was a clear night for the half moon. They'd be spotted on the river too easily. Valentine looked down at the bridge, and saw the white Kurian Tower beyond, shining under its spotlights like a slice of the moon fallen to earth.

The Quislings cleared the roads and brought armored cars up the hill. They prowled the edges of the ruins like hungry cats at rat holes, shooting at anything that moved. Styachowski and the Bears went out and buried what was left of the mortar shells where they had driven before. The next day they managed to blow the wheels off of one. It sat there, looking like a broken toy in a rubble-filled sandbox.

Then came the quiet dawn. The harassing fire slacked off, and the men were able to dash from hiding hole to hiding hole without anything more than a sniper bullet or two zinging past. Valentine was watching Hank sleep. He felt strangely relaxed. Perhaps it was because of the color in Hank's cheeks and his deep, easy breaths. The boy was on the mend. He worked out a final plan. His last throw of the dice, in the strange table run that had begun with Boxcars.

He talked it over with Ahn-Kha, Nail and Styachowski at the nightly meal. Post had been briefed early and would assume command of what was left of the Razors—mostly a noisome aggregation of wounded sheltering in dugouts and the basements of Solon's headquarters.

"It's worth a try," Nail said, looking at the weird, question-mark-shaped assault path Valentine had mapped out. He had a little of his energy back. "They won't be expecting it, after all this time, with them so close."

"It could take the heart out of them. Even more than the loss of Xray-Tango," Ahn-Kha said. The Golden One's ears drooped unhappily. He'd been tasked with his supporting role.

"The only heart I'm after is in that tower," Valentine said.

Nail joined them despite his weak state. Valentine wanted to leave him and Styachowski both back at the camp, but they presented a strangely united front, and he couldn't argue with both.

Their chosen path to the river was down the cliff face above the quarry. Valentine had only rappelled once, long ago, in an exercise as a trainee. Valentine, Ahn-Kha and the Bears crept out of the trenches and moved west, where they fixed ropes to tree stumps.

"I would like to come on this, my David," Ahn-Kha said.

"Sorry. I need your muscles to haul us back up this rock," Valentine said. "Don't stay here and die. If you get overrun, try for the swampy ground to the north. Go back to your people."

Ahn-Kha looked over his shoulder at the shattered walls and missing roofs. "My only people are here, now. I will wait. Unless a bullet finds me, I will wait here, yes, even through another winter and another like that."

Valentine gripped arms with his old ally. "I'll be back sooner than that." He looped a line through a ring on a harness improvised from an AOT backpack, and dropped over the edge.

Naturally, he burned his hands.

The Bears loaded their gear onto an inflatable raft as Valentine applied antiseptic and dressings to his hands. The raft was a green thing that rose at each end like a sliced quarter of melon. A box containing four of them had been on the first train brought to Big Rock Hill. With a little luck and a little more dark, they might be able carry the Bears to the other side without being observed.

They waited by the riverbank as they half inflated the boat. It only needed to carry their gear, and the lower its profile the better. A warm breeze blew down the river for a change. Summer was coming on, and the frogs were welcoming it with creaky voices. Bats emerged from their riverside lairs in the quarry and hunted mosquitoes with meeping calls Valentine's hard ears could just pick out.

Valentine and the men were nervous. Even Rain, who had started a second set of slanted brownish scars on his left arm, shifted position and mumbled to himself constantly.

The Bears huddled together as they worked the little bellows that inflated the raft, keeping watch for patrols at the riverbank. The AOT had lost men on this side of the hill to snipers and had given up trying to occupy the narrow strip of ground between the cliff face and the river, but they could never be sure there weren't dogs loosed at night.

"What's going red like?" Valentine asked. He'd heard various stories, including one from ex-Bear Tank Bourne, but he was curious if different men felt it differently.

"You can't control it too well," Red said, patting the belt-fed gun on his lap. "All that has to happen is a gunshot and over I go. You get all hot and excited, like you've just won a race or something. Everything seems kind of distant and separated from you, but you have perspective and everything, so when you chuck a grenade it lands where you want it, not a mile away. Pain just makes you hotter and ready to fight more. It wears off after everything's all over, but once in a while Bears drop over afterward and don't wake up. Their hearts burst."

"You feel like you can run, or jump, or climb forever,"

Hack put in. "Sometimes you have to scream just to give it all somewhere to go. Here's something they don't talk about at the bar, though. Most Bears piss themselves over the course of it. Every single red nick I've got on my arm means I've come back with a pantload of shit."

Nail nodded. "I always go into action with an extra diaper under my pants. The guys in Force Apache wear kilts— actually, more like flaps—that's another solution."

"Glad I'm a Cat," Valentine said. "What about you, Styachowski, what do you want for a handle?"

Styachowski looked up from where she sat, knees hugged to her chest, one hand wrapped with a leather wrist guard for her archery. "I'd like to be named by my team."

"How about 'Guns'?" Nail asked. "From the cannon. Plus, she's got the arms for it."

Styachowski looked down, flexed her muscles. "Let's wait until after tonight."

The chill of the Arkansas River's current was enough to geld the seven men. The river flowed differently every few yards, it seemed; for a few minutes they had to kick hard to keep from being pushed downriver too far, then they'd hit a pool of slack water in the lee of some sandbar. They swam like pallbearers with a floating casket, four to each side. They made for a spot halfway between the Pulaski Heights and the bridge, near the place where Styachowski had been buried by the fallen sandbags the day the river ran mad.

When their feet struck muddy bottom again, they halted, and Valentine went up the bank for a scout. He saw that the rail bridge was lined with sandbags, thick with men and weapons points. Cable was strung about ten yards upstream, festooned with razor wire and looking as though there were more lines underwater, barring access to the bridge pilings. The boats would never make it through without a good deal of work with bolt cutters and acetylene torches.

But his Bears were on the enemy side of the river. In the distance, the concrete tower of the Kurians stood like a white tomb in the rubble-strewn grave of Little Rock.

Each pair of Bear eyes fixed on it like lampreys. Any chance at a Kurian was enough to heat their blood. He took the team up for a look.

He wished his blood could run hot like the Bears'; the spring night was no longer as warm as it had been when they were dry on the other side of the river. The water beaded on his oiled skin. The greasy coating served two purposes; it helped him resist the water and darkened his face and torso. His legs protruded out of camp shorts. He slipped some old black training shoes, preserved dry in the rubber boat, over his feet and put on a combat vest and his gunbelt, then picked up a cut-down Kalashnikov and an ammunition harness. He would have preferred the comforting bluntness of his PPD, but it was out of 9mm Mauser and the gunsmith didn't have the right molds for reloads. Finally he put his snakeskin bandolier of Quickwood stabbers over his arm and checked his bag for the presence of a battered old dinner bell that had, until a day ago, served as a Reaper alarm in one of the trenches.

He felt the mental echo of a Reaper in the direction of the bridge. It was in motion, crossing to the north bank. Wiggling up the bank and into cover, he checked the bank. In the darkness in the direction of Pulaski Heights he saw the twin red eyes of a pair of sentries smoking cigarettes. They weren't near enough for him to smell the tobacco, even though he was downwind. The sentries wouldn't hear or see his Bears, if they were careful.

Valentine inspected the remains of the buildings along the riverbank. He found an old outlet for the storm sewer system and waved the Bears over. The concrete mouth was wide enough to store the rubber raft. No words were necessary; the Bears took up their weapons silently. Styachowski had armed herself with a silenced .223 Mini-14 along with her bow. Valentine issued each Bear a Quickwood stabbing spear, almost the last of the precious supply. Ahn-Kha and the squad of Jamaicans, who proudly bore the informal label "Hoodhunters," had the few others.

They cut through the Ruins, skirting their old TMCC

campsite. Their weeks at the camp—now occupied by a field hospital for those wounded in the siege—gave them a knowledge of the buildings that let them pick a route to cross the fallen city discreetly. They went to ground twice, once for a dog-led patrol that passed a block away, and a second time when Valentine felt a Reaper on his way to the hospital. Had the Kurians been reduced to feeding on their own badly wounded? Or did Mu-Kur-Ri fear to send his avatars far afield in search of auras?

They could see the Kurian Tower clearly now, no longer just a white blur in the distance. Valentine, then Nail, examined it through night binoculars from the vicinity of Xray-Tango's burned-out headquarters. The old bank had no flag before it as when Xray-Tango had made it his headquarters, though a few lights glimmered inside and a sentry paced back and forth behind it.

"Wonder how many are in there?" Nail asked. "Southern Command has to have driven a few out of their holes down south."

"I was hoping Solon had moved in," Valentine said. "I'd like to catch him in the temple of his gods." He swept the building with hard eyes, using the glasses and naked eyes alternately, naked eyes to spot motion, glasses to identify the source. "There'd be more guards if he had. Looks like the Quislings think the place is bad news."

"There's bars over the windows. And bunkers at the corners. How are you going to get through?"

"Don't worry about that. Just make sure you handle Xray-Tango's old building."

Nail smiled. "If there's anything they hate worse than Quisling soldiers, it's officers. They won't need a fire to look into to go Red."

"This is it then. When the shellfire starts, give me a few minutes. Then hit them. Look out for men on the roof."

"I didn't get the Bear bar on my collar by not knowing how to hit a building quiet. Take Rain at least, sir; he's worth a whole team of Bears."

"You're the hunter at the rabbit hole. I'm the ferret going in. I want to flush them, not fight."

"What if they hole up in a bunker and just work their Hoods?"

"Not your problem. Just get into that basement where I told you."

"Let me go with you, sir," Styachowski volunteered.

Valentine hesitated to say "no" and she filled the gap. "Lieutenant Nail and his Bears are a team; I haven't trained with them. . . ."

"Okay, two ferrets, Nail. See you below."

"One way or another, sir," Nail said, smiling as he gave a little salute.

Like a pair of rats, alternately hunting and being hunted as they went over—and under—the debris of old Little Rock, Valentine and Styachowski threaded their way toward the Kurian Tower. Construction hadn't stopped; they'd finished the second level and were starting on the third, even with the fighting across the river. It looked like an unevenly baked wedding cake with the layers stacked off center, or maybe a soft-serve ice-cream cone, Valentine couldn't decide which.

They found a rubble-filled basement loading dock just outside the glare of the tower's lights. The spiderwebs told them that the Quisling patrols didn't visit it, and they made themselves comfortable. They sat next to each other and looked up at the night sky through a gap above.

Valentine passed his time looking at the TMCC officer's handbook, a list of field regulations and procedures condensed to pamphlet size. He opened it to a page he had turned down and reread the passage he'd penned a tick next to. Even in their almost lightless refuge, the script stood out against the paper to his Cat-eyes as if it was on an illuminated screen. He finished and put the book back, trying to relax against the cold concrete. Rodents scurried somewhere farther inside the building.

*   *   *

The whistle-crash of the first shell ended the respite. The 155s came down with a terrifying noise—not as bad as the monster shells of the Crocodile, but unnerving all the same. He let five land to give the Quislings time to take cover, then nodded to Styachowski. They left their hideout.

They wriggled their way to a good view of the Kurian Tower, its white sides already smudged by the explosions. Valentine counted each shell burst; they arrived almost on the minute. After twenty had been fired, he grabbed Styachowski by the shoulder and they ran toward the tower, dodging their way through construction equipment and supplies. He heard one distant alarm whistle but ignored it. They made for the concrete bunker flanking the construction entrance to the tower. A scaffold with an electric elevator stood next to the entrance, on the other side of the bunker. Styachowski tore the colored tabs off a thick cylinder of a grenade, squatted listening to the fuse hiss—and threw it in the firing slit of the bunker.

"Hey!" someone inside shouted.

It would have been ideal if the next shell had landed at the same time as the grenade exploded, but they were seconds apart. The grenade went off first, followed by the louder, but farther off, explosion of the artillery shell.

Valentine had his own grenade to deal with. It was a green smoker. He pulled the pin and rolled it under a sluice on the steel curtain door of the construction entrance. It went off like two cats spitting at each other, and green smoke began to billow out from around the edges of the door. Valentine threw two more green smokers around the edges of the buildings. When the grenades were spewing he pulled the dinner bell from his bag and pulled out the sock he'd used to silence it. He rang it, loud and long.

"Gas! Gas! Gas!" he shouted. He rang the bell again.

"Gas! Gas! Gas!" Styachowski added, deepening her voice. She pulled out a pair of crowbars.

Valentine clanged the dinner bell for all he was worth, then tried the electric lift. No juice.

"We climb," he said.

Valentine went up first while Styachowski covered him, shrouded with green smoke. The gas warning had been taken up by men inside the building. Valentine heard a klaxon go off, three angry buzzes, followed by the triple "gas" call over the PA system within. He took the crowbars from Styachoski and pulled her up.

Valentine went up the scaffold to the platform on the first level. Styachowski joined him and they put their crowbars to work, pulling at a metal screen blocking a window. It was more of an iron grate than true bars, designed to explode an RPG aimed at the window. Nothing but cardboard stuck in a fitting for thick glass closed the window beyond, but the bars blocked them out.

Styachowski roared in frustration.

Valentine tucked his crowbar nearer hers. Together they pulled, shoulder to shoulder. Styachowski's muscles felt like machine-tool steel against his.

"Graaaaaa!" Styachowski heaved. She set her leg against the tower face. They pulled again—

The grate gave way, pulling the masonry at the top and bottom of the narrow window with it. Styachowski pulled an opening big enough for them to climb through.

Eyes wild and burning, Styachowski swung through, knocking the cardboard away. Wisps of green smoke could be seen within, and the gas alarm was still bleating its triple call every ten seconds. The tower's interior was still being worked on; the walls were nothing but cinder block coated with primer paint.

Valentine felt something crackling inside his mind, like a man running a sparkler firework across the field of an empty stadium. Or maybe two or three, waving and parting and separating like schooling fish. With them were the colder, darker impressions of Reapers.

"Downstairs! They're down, in the basement, heading north."

"How can you tell? I don't hear anything but that friggin' alarm," Styachowski asked from the other side of the room, covering the hall with her gun.

"I just do. Find the stairs."

The tower appealed to some kind of Kurian sensibility for architecture; the "stairs" were a tight ramp-spiral in a corner under the tallest part of the tower. Valentine could hear footsteps climbing the stairs above in between the klaxon bursts; the Quislings or construction workers or whoever were sensibly getting as high as they could above what they thought to be lethal fumes.

There was a change in the air as soon as they got underground. They came to a corridor; the lighting fixtures and flooring told Valentine it was pre-2022 construction. A man in a uniform with a gas mask over his face was leading another toward the stairs, the one behind had his hand on his leader. Neither could see much through the eyeholes in the dusty old masks, and they were going down the corridor like they were playing blind man's bluff. One had a radio bumping against his chest.

The Kurians were still below and moving away somewhere. Where was that rathole to Xray-Tango's old headquarters?

Valentine and the Bear hurried down the corridor, catching up to the men. Valentine heard the radio crackle.

"Townshend, Townshend, what's the situation? Is there gas in the tower?"

As Valentine passed him he lashed out with his fist, landing a solid jab in the radio-wearer's breadbasket. The man went to his knees, gasping. Valentine caught the other under the jaw with the butt of his machine pistol.

"Help——haaaaaaaaaaa——help," the radio man on his knees gasped into the mike. His battle for air sounded authentic enough. Valentine kicked out sideways, catching him in the back of the head. The Quisling's head made a sound like a spiked volleyball as it bounced off the wall, and he went face-first on top of the radio, unconscious or dead.

"Val, here," Styachowski said, checking a room at the end of the corridor.

It was a utility room. Snakes of cable conduit ran up from the floor and across the ceiling; boxes and circuit breakers lined the wall. Another stairway descended from a room beyond. The steel door had been torn off its hinges. Valentine recognized the nail marks of a Reaper. He picked up the mental signature of the fleeing Kurians again, this time clearer.

"You ready for this?" he asked Styachowski.

She nodded, giving him the thumbs-up.

He handed her two of his four Quickwood stakes. "Remember, they can make themselves look like a dog, anything. Just kill whatever you see. Unless it's another Bear, or me. No, strike that. If you see another me, kill him, too. I'll just hope you pick the right one."

"Yes, sir."

"Let's do it."

They went down to a boiler room, connected by another missing door—this one long since removed—to an arch-topped tunnel. Two Quislings, in gas-mask chemical weapon hoods, stood at the portal.

Styachowski's Mini-14 came up. She shot twice, the action on the gun louder than the bullet through the silenced weapon, and both men crumpled. As Valentine looked down the corridor she shot each Quisling again for insurance.

It wasn't much of a tunnel, only a little wider than the passageways on the old *Thunderbolt*. Old conduit pipes and newer wires ran along the walls and ceiling, lit here and there by bulbs encased in thick plastic housings like preserve jars. It smelled like damp underwear and bad plumbing.

Valentine went in first—trailing the psychic scent like a bloodhound—in the bent-over, lolloping run he'd picked up going through the underbrush in his days with the Wolves. He heard Styachowski behind; an occasional splashing footfall sounded as she hit a puddle in the damp tunnel.

He heard firing at the other end of the arrow-thin passageway.

The sparking mental impressions grew clearer. They were coming. With their Reapers.

Valentine pulled up. "They turned around."

"Shit! How many Reapers?"

"I don't know. Several." The corridor went dark. Styachowski pulled a flare out and lit it in a flash, then threw it down the corridor toward the coming Reapers. She reached for a fist-sized metal sphere on her vest.

She pulled the pin on the grenade. "Want to keep it?"

"No, throw it. When I tell you. If there's anything beyond Red . . . like Violet maybe, you might want to give it a try."

Styachowski pulled her bolo blade. It was a nice length for the tunnel. Valentine wished he had his old straightedged sword. He felt oddly light and fearless. Just a mouth like dry-rotted wood and hands greasy with sweat and aching from rope burn. He shifted his grip on Ahn-Kha's stabbing spear.

The Reapers came in a wall of death, three of them, jaws agape like Cerberus.

"Now," Valentine said. Styachowski threw the grenade and readied her Quickwood stabber.

The Reapers ignored the bouncing explosive. It went off behind them, throwing them into the Cat and the Bear in a wave of heat and sound. Valentine's mind felt pain and confusion—his own, and that of the Kurians.

Styachowski went into the first Reaper like it was a badly stuffed scarecrow. Valentine could see the fight as clearly in the faint red glow of the flare as if it were daylight. She chopped off an arm, then buried her Quickwood into its neck. Another jumped on her back like lightning leaping sideways to hit a rod. It got its hands around her, claws reaching to rip open her rib cage, but Valentine plunged his stabbing spear into its shoulder, trying to hit the nerve trunks descending from the armored skull. The spear went through its robes and bit deep, eliciting an angry shriek, the loudest noise Valentine had ever heard a Reaper make.

Suddenly he was flying through the air. He crashed against the tunnel wall, held by the piece of steel that was the third Reaper's arm. Its eyes burned into his. Valentine slammed the side of his arm down in a chop against the Reaper's elbow, hoping to fold its arm like a jackknife, but he stayed pinned. The Reaper grabbed his other arm, forcing it to the wall so he hung in the crucifixion pose. Its narrow face drew nearer, jaws opening for the sweet spot at the base of his throat. The stabbing tongue stirred within its mouth like a serpent coiling for a strike.

Valentine brought up his knees, putting his feet on the demon's chest. It bore in, an irresistible force, folding him until his spine would snap—Valentine screamed in agonized frustration.

Styachowski's face appeared above the Reaper's. She was atop its back, her hands black with Reaper juice, her own blood pouring in a river from her nose. She brought her blade across its throat, grabbed it by the handle and tip, and pulled toward herself. The improvised guillotine cut through its windpipe and circulatory system, but the thing dropped Valentine and reached its queerly jointed arms around behind itself for Styachowski.

Valentine, his vision a red mist, brought both of his hands up, uncoiling with his body and helping the blade travel the last few inches. The Reaper's head went up and off in a gristly *pop-snap*.

The Reaper's body staggered off sideways, clawing at the air. The ambulatory corpse did a U-turn, crashed into the wall, and flopped over. There was shooting coming from the far end of the tunnel.

"Your hands!" Valentine barked, as Styachowski was about to wipe her sweating face. She froze.

"Oh, yeah," she said. Reaper blood was poisonous, whether swallowed or taken in through a mucous membrane. Even the best Hunters sometimes forgot in the midst of a fight. The tunnel was filling with smoke from the grenade, and the fight elsewhere.

Footsteps. Another Reaper charged out of the smoke, robes torn, one arm gone, its body riddled with bullet wounds. Valentine and Styachowski threw themselves against the passageway and it passed without noticing them.

"Fucker!" Valentine heard Lost&Found shout, spraying bullets up the corridor after it.

"Cease fire, Bear! You're shooting at us," Valentine shouted.

The bullets stopped.

"Sir! Sir! We got two of 'em. Two blue bat-winged bastards!"

Valentine could hardly see them through the smoke. He made his way toward the sound of the voices with Styachowski in tow.

"Reapers?" Valentine asked.

"We got two down. One got away from us."

"He got away from us, too. But I think he was running wild," Styachowski said, meaning its Kurian had been killed.

Valentine could better make out the haggard four now. They'd almost passed through the smoke. The Bears were missing Brass and Groschen.

"Where are the other two?" Valentine asked. He felt nervous somehow.

Nail jerked his chin up the tunnel the way the Bears had come. "A Reaper popped Brass's head off. Sorry, sir, couldn't be helped. Groschen is keeping an eye on the other end of the tunnel. The old headquarters had been converted to some kind of communications center. Lots of field phones and printing machines. We took it out."

Valentine didn't listen. There was a problem with the smoke. It didn't smell like anything. Smoke also didn't make noise as it crawled along the ceiling.

"One got away," Valentine hissed. "A Kurian. It's heading back down the tunnel."

Without further explanation he threw himself down the tunnel. In the distance he saw a faint figure, running for its immortal life. The Kurian could move. Not as fast as a Reaper. Nothing that wasn't engine-powered moved as fast as a Reaper.

It dashed through the door of the utility subbasement, Valentine almost on its heels. Its skin was the color of blue ice and it gave off a sickly sweet odor like marigolds. So intent on the chase was he that he bounced off the chest of the

Reaper, which stepped out from behind the steaming boiler like a sliding steel door. The Kurian was safely behind it. The Kurian turned, looked at Valentine with red-black eyes, and then disappeared upstairs.

Valentine rolled backward and came to his feet.

The one-armed Reaper's eyes wandered. It extended its remaining clawed hand and pulled one of the boiler pipes free of its mount. Valentine heard the Reaper's skin sizzle against the hot metal, but the thing didn't even wince. It yanked the pipe out, so a firehose of steam flooded the passageway and the stairway behind it.

Then it advanced on Valentine.

"i know you," it hissed. *"our false friend from louisiana."*

"Valentine!" Nail shouted from behind him.

Valentine dropped to the ground. A hail of bullets filled the tunnel. The Reaper's face vanished in the tight pattern of a buckshot blast. It roared, and charged down the tunnel toward the sound of gunfire. With its eyes gone, it didn't see Valentine wriggling forward after Mu-Kur-Ri.

He heard fighting behind. Styachowski and Nail should be able to handle a one-armed, blind Reaper without him. He wanted Mu-Kur-Ri.

But the hissing steam blocked his way. There was nothing to do but . . . do it.

Valentine lifted his combat vest and got his head and arms tucked into as much of the material as he could, and held it closed over his face.

"This is for you, Hank," he muttered to himself. He took a deep breath; it wouldn't be pleasant to breathe in hot steam.

Later, when he'd forgotten the pain, he examined the burn marks in detail using a pair of mirrors. His lower back took the worst of it, from beneath his rib cage—where the combat vest ended—to the line of his camp shorts. That part must have been hit by steam shooting from the hose, and it turned into a girdle of scar tissue. The back of his legs got it badly enough that the hair only regrew irregularly, but there

was less scarring there than above the line of his shorts. The
thick cotton of the shorts and combat vest kept the rest of the
damage to first- and second-degree burns. Painful enough,
but they healed.

The pain drove him on instinct through the steam and up
the stairs. He caught up to the Kurian and fell on it like a
rabid dog. It squealed rabbitlike as he tore into the slippery
mass with fists and teeth. Cartilage crunched under his
knees, a pulpy mass of digestive organs slipped wetly
through his fingers, then its rubbery skull finally gave out as
he slammed it again and again and again into the concrete
landing, still shrouded in green smoke. Then he collapsed
atop the spongy corpse of Mu-Kur-Ri.

As he passed out he thought of Caroline Smalls.

The next thing he saw was Styachowski's face, gently
rocking as it floated above him. A pleasant warmth gave
way to pain, agonizing pain, pain like he'd never felt and
would shoot himself to keep from feeling again. It was so
bad he couldn't summon the energy to do more than whim-
per, his body paralyzed, living only in the endless moment
of the burn's agony.

*Think of something, anything, anything to drive the pain
away!*

"They think of a name for you?" Valentine croaked.

"Not yet," Styachowski said. She'd shoved expended
cartridge cases into her nostrils to stop the flow of blood.

Nail patted her shoulder. "You did just fine, you're a Bear
to be proud of. How about Ursa? Like the stars?"

"Wildcat?" Valentine said. "No. A woman who can be
anything. A Wildcard."

"I like Wildcard," Styachowski said.

"No, if you like it, we can't use it. Unwritten law," Rain
said.

Valentine turned painfully to Nail. "Make it an order,
Lieutenant."

The Bear shrugged. "After all this," Nail said, "it seems
we should call you whatever you like, Styachowski. Wild-

card it is. The drawn card that turned out to be an ace just
when we needed it."

"Wildcard, is he alive?" a voice that might have been
Nail's said.

"He's alive."

It was torture to his skin to be lifted and carried. Sensibly, his consciousness fled.

He later heard about the scattering of troops from the
Kurian Tower as Reapers ran amok, and the confusion that
allowed Lieutenant Nail to carry him and lead the Bears
back to the river, and how Lost&Found swam across with
Valentine tied to an empty five-gallon jerrican to keep him
afloat. As he heard the tale Valentine felt as though he'd
lived it, but couldn't remember much except for vague impressions of floating. He rememberd shelling but no further
large-scale attacks, just endless probes. He remembered
Post's daily reports of units observed moving east through
New Columbia, and the gun resting in the swimming pool
running out of ammunition so that all the hilltop forces
could do was watch. He remembered walking again, and
giving up his bed to another wounded man and sleeping on
a blanket on the concrete floor near where Narcisse worked
the hospital kitchen and rubbed him with oily-smelling
lotion.

Then came sounds of more trains in the distance and ve-
hicular traffic around the base of the hill, and he managed to
go outside. He'd meet the inevitable standing, even if he
stood in bandages.

"Sir, you're needed on the west side." One of the pregnant women, in a man's service poncho which gave her
belly growing room, reported from her station at the field
phone.

Valentine made a stiff-legged journey. His bad leg ached
all the time now, throbbing in sympathy with the healing
burns. Ahn-Kha helped him up a set of stairs and they
reached the observation point, what was left of Solon's
grand balcony. Three soldiers knelt, sharing a set of binocu-

lars, staring up the Arkansas River, a blue ribbon between the green Ozark hills.

"What in God's name is that?" Valentine asked.

The river was three deep in beetles. A flotilla of craft, none larger than thirty feet. Many towed everything from rowboats to braces of canoes.

"Reinforcements?"

"Depends on your point of view. Look—the mortars are shooting at them."

The tubes of Pulaski Heights were dropping shells into the mass of speeding boats, with little effect but wetting those inside.

Styachowski ran along the rubble-strewn base of Solon's Residence beneath them, tripped over a log and sprawled flat. She picked herself up, but didn't bother to wipe the mud from her chin.

"They're pulling back, sir," she called up, her voice squealing like a schoolgirl's in excitement. "Not the boats, the Quislings. They're coming off the hill."

"To oppose the landing?"

"They're just running," Styachowski said. "Running like hell for the bridge. A train just pulled out east, packed with men."

Valentine looked down the river, caught a familiar pattern. He snatched the binoculars out of the hand of the man next to him without apology, and focused on the boat trailing the leadmost pilot vessel. There was a flagstaff above the outboard motors. The State Flag of Texas flapped in the breeze.

The boats were a surprise to the Quislings as well. They abandoned the weapons on the Pulaski Heights and fled with the rest toward Pine Bluff. When Valentine was sure the hilltop was clear he brought up the wounded from their dreadful holes into the fresh air and sunshine. There were the dead to be sorted from the living, and sent on to the swollen, shell-tossed graveyard.

The Texans found him among the corpses, burying his dead.

"That's him. I met him in Texas," he heard a voice say. Valentine looked up and saw a Ranger he recognized, Colorado. The youth's shoulders had broadened, and what Valentine's nose told him was that motor oil stained the Ranger's uniform.

Colorado brought forward a bearded man. Valentine suspected that when the campaign started the colonel of the Texas Rangers was clean shaven.

"Nice to finally meet the famous Ghost," the colonel, whose nametag read "Samoza," said.

The idea of a famous Cat struck Valentine as a bit absurd, and he fought down a laugh. If his nerves gave way now he'd fall on the man, laughing or crying or confessing, and none were appropriate to the moment.

"We've come all the way from Fort Scott for you," Samoza continued.

The words took their time in coming. Valentine's shocked brain had to inspect each one as it came out.

"Thank you. Southern Command couldn't even make it fifty miles," Valentine managed, looking out over the graves.

"Southern Command opened the door for us. Archangel was a joint operation from the start. The Kurians sent troops up from Texas to take you boys down. We figured if they didn't want it, we'd like it back. We got more besides."

It all hit Valentine like a warm wave. Intellect gave way to pent-up emotion like the dike that had swallowed Styachowski, and he found himself shaking, with tears in his eyes. He hoped his brain remembered it all and would be able to sort it out later. "What's that, sir?" he finally said.

"We linked up with Southern Command just outside Hope. Ironic, wouldn't you say? Then it was north into Oklahoma, and down the river to you."

"What made you come all this way?"

"A Ranger teamster named Jefferson made a lot of noise in East Texas. Claimed we had to go help the man who started it all. He fought alongside us all the way to Fort Scott and lost a leg there to shellfire. Haven't taken it yet but figured it could wait. You couldn't."

Valentine held out his hand to the colonel.

"You came all this way for a few companies of men?"

"We're from Texas, friend. We remember the Alamo."

Chapter Eleven

The Saint Francis River, August of the forty-eighth year of the Kurian Order: The land was healing with the people. In the weeks following the relief of the Razors at New Columbia, even Fort Scott changed hands yet again, to the combined forces of the Ozark Free Territory and the Texas Republic. Solon and his Kurian Council collapsed like a house of cards, fleeing in all directions. There were losses, irreplaceable losses, everywhere across the fought-over land. In the chaos in the Missouri Valley Grogs pushed south and the Kur in Kansas took a piece of the Ozarks around the lakes, and sent their Reapers into the Mark Twain Forest.

But the leaders of the newly wedded Texas and Ozark Free Territories would have something to say about that, in time. They controlled an area larger than any of the former states of the union.

David Valentine crossed the Free Territory with his pouch of Quickwood seeds. He planted one on a windswept hillside where a sergeant named Gator was buried. He placed another one outside a stoutly built barn near the Lousiana border—a crippled ex-Wolf named Gonzalez helped him relocate it, where a little patch of earth marked the location of the first man to die under Valentine's command. A few frontier farmers turned up for the ceremony. In time, the locals called it Selby's tree, and a Selby Meadows grew up around that barn. He placed a ring of Quickwood trees at the ambush site outside Post 46, just northeast of the Red River, another on a devastated riverbank that looked like a piece of the moon, where the Crocodile had moored, and the rest shaded a cemetery on Big Rock Hill.

The rest save one. He took it to the empty little village of Weening on the Saint Francis. The inhabitants were scattered,

*the Carlsons had vanished and Tank Bourne was laid out,
months dead, in his cellar. Valentine buried him in the shade of a
willow tree by the river, and up near the riverside gate he placed
his last seed in the rich Arkansas soil, soil that had once soaked
up Gabreilla Cho's blood, and—though he did not know it—
Molly Carlson's tears.*

There was already a pamphlet printed about the fight at Big
Rock Hill. It was rolled up in Valentine's bag next to his order
book. He'd read a few pages—the author had relied on the col-
lected radio reports from the hill for a day-by-day record of
events, as interpreted for him by a decorated veteran of the Central Operational area named Captain Randolph—and given up
after it described Lieutenant Colonel Kessey's brilliant rising in
the prison yards of New Columbia, when a Quisling division was
put to flight by men keen on avenging their outraged women.
He'd heard they were renaming the battlefield Kessey Heights,
which was fine with him. Her body lay on it.

Folded into the pamphlet, for protection rather than as a book-
mark, was a radiogram from Jamaica.

TO: DAVID VALENTINE, SOUTHERN COMMAND
FROM: COMMODORE HOUSE, JAMAICA
CHILD AMALEE BORN 7LBS6 JUNE 19 BOTH
HEALTHY MOTHER SENDS LOVE CONGRATULATIONS
JENSEN

The Quickwood tree would have a nice life ouside Weening.
He found a boy from the Peterson family—they'd been the first
to see the empty homes of Weening for the opportunity they presented and move the extended family there. The boy was eleven
and watched him through wary but intelligent eyes. He seemed
old enough for the responsibility of watching over the tree.
Valentine didn't want some clown clearing brush to cut down the
Quickwood sapling.

Valentine tried to explain the importance of Quickwood to
Mr. Peterson, but to the literal-minded man it came down to a tree
that could grow a magic wooden stake that killed vampires.
Valentine left it at that. There were things to do, so many things

to do. Solon's dream of owning the Mississippi and its tributaries vanished with the consul, but far-sighted men from Texas to the Ozarks might be able to bring the evil man's idea to fruition—under new management, of course. Already there was talk of taking back New Orleans. Then the great gateway to the Caribbean would be open, a navy could be floated, and Southern Command would be able to put troops anywhere a keel could go.

And he could see his daughter.

Someday the Quickwood could be used properly. He'd returned to the Free Territory thinking the Haitian discovery would be a wedge he could drive into the heart of the Kurian Order, piercing it and breaking it up the way he did logs. But a wedge was only as good as the force driving it. All along, it had been cooperation between people, himself and Ahn-Kha, Styachowski and Post, Narcisse and Hank, Samoza and Jefferson, each doing their part in a whole that was even now being born.

How had the governor phrased it, after the formal military union of Texas and the Free Territory? "A new stake of freedom wedged between the Mississippi and the Gulag"? Something like that. Valentine liked to think of it as seed. A fast-growing seed, he hoped, and as deadly to the Kurian Order as the Quickwood he'd scattered over hundreds of square miles.

"Here you go, Gabby," Valentine said, covering the seed with moist earth fresh from the river. He knelt at the nongrave. "Keep it safe for me. Something happened this summer. A miracle. We took the worst they could throw at us—ended up the stronger for it. The Texans have the Dallas Triangle ringed in now, and we're sending captured artillery to finish the job. It's only a matter of time. I've got a daughter, if you can believe it. And here I've planted my last seed. It's a good day for me. It's a new beginning for us."

The future beckoned. The past, his regrets, his mistakes, all lay buried with the seed. No more looking back.

David Valentine glanced up at the hot noonday sun and wiped the sweat from his forehead, now beneath chin-length black hair, and wondered at the strange fate that saw him in the right place at the right time. Dreadful and deadly work still needed to be done, but it was work born of Hope.

Dallas, March, the forty-ninth year of the Kurian Order: Four square miles of concrete and structural steel smoke and pop and sputter as the city dies from the stranglehold of a siege.

Street fighting isn't so much seen as it is heard from a dozen different locations. Save for the sounds, a city at war seems strangely empty, save for scavenging black crows and wary, tail-tucking dogs. Vague rumbles like a distant storm mutter in the distance, or sudden eruptions of machine-gun fire from a few blocks away might be jackhammers breaking holes in a sidewalk in a more peaceful time. When men move, they move in a rush, pouring from doorways and crossing streets in a quick wave before the whine of shellfire can catch them in the open.

Valentine's Razors' regimental flag, a black-and-blue silhouette of an Arkansas razorback set under the joined Texas/Ozark flags, reads "Don't Feed On Me," though even a sharp-eyed youngster standing at the base of the Love Field control tower wouldn't be able to read the letters even in the bright morning sun.

The Razors shouldn't have worked. Soldiers thrown together under the most dire of circumstances, with unfamiliar corporals, sergeants, and officers putting together rifle platoons who had never trained together, couldn't be expected to stand up to a determined assault, let alone hold a precarious position alone in the heart of enemy country. That their famous stand on the banks of the Arkansas River succeeded might be considered a measure of their enemy's malice as much as of their own mettle—as well as of the improvisational skills of the officers who organized the Little Rock Rising.

One of those men crosses the outskirts of the airstrip as the sun rises. His mottled dark green-and-grey uniform is thick with "Dallas Dust," an oatmeal-colored mixture of pulverized concrete, ash, and mundane winter dirt. Black hair tied in a pigtail hugs his scalp, and a thin white scar on the right side of his face only serves to show off an early bronze tan indicative of ample melanin in his genes. A shortened version of his Razors battle rifle, with folding stock and cut-down barrel, bumps from its tight sling against leather battle webbing. The assault harness is festooned with everything from a wide-bladed utility parang to a gas mask hood, flares for a wide-mouthed gun at his hip, and a "camel" water bladder over his shoulder. Looking at him, a veteran of the Razors would point out the distinctly nonregulation moccasins on his feet and infer that the Razors' operations officer, Major Valentine, was back from another of his scouts.

David Valentine breathed in a last snootful of clean air and descended into the muskrat-den reek. He stepped down carefully, holding an uprooted young dandelion in his gun-free hand. The stairway to the old control tower basement was mostly gone. The entryway had been enlarged, replaced by churned-over earth paved with plywood strips dropping eight feet to the hole in the cinderblock side of the foundation where the basement door had been.

The entrance to the Razorbacks' headquarters resembled an oversized anthole, if anything. It fooled the eyes that sometimes drifted high above the besiegers' positions.

He rested his gun in a cleaning becket and stood on a carpet remnant in the entryway while he let his eyes adjust to the dim light within. Deaf old Pooter, one of the regiment's guinea pigs, rolled up onto his hind legs and whistled a welcome from his chicken-wire cage perched on a shelf next to the door. Valentine tossed him the dandelion.

"They didn't hit us after all," he told Pooter.

Pooter chuckled as a length of milky dandelion stem disappeared into his fast-working jaws.

If the Kurians dusted again, Pooter would expire in a noisy

hacking fit, giving the men inside time to ring the alarm, lower the plastic curtains, and put on their gas masks and gloves.

Valentine felt tired. He'd spent the past eight hours moving across the forward posts, keyed up for a battle that never came. He was probably more tired than he would have been had there been action: The weird I'm-alive-and-I-can-do-anything exhilaration of surviving combat would have floated him back to the Razors' HQ.

In the five weeks they'd occupied the airfield, Narcisse and her staff had set up sinks and stoves, and even had a pizza oven going. Companies rotating to or from the forward positions always had a pizza party before creeping out to their strongpoints, covering the approaches to Dallas. Narcisse wore no uniform, held no rank, and wandered between the battalions' kitchens and infirmary as the mood struck her, dispensing equal helpings of cheer and food, pulled in her wheelchair by a steadfast mutt who'd wandered into camp on the Razorbacks' trip south from the Ouachitas. The men and women whose job it was to aid and comfort the frontline soldiers obeyed the old legless Haitian as though she were a visiting field marshal.

Valentine said good morning to the potato peelers, who were working under faded paint that once demarked a maintenance garage. He rinsed his hands and poured himself a mug of water from the hot pot. He plopped in one of Narcisse's herbal tea bags from a woven basket on a high shelf. He covered his brew-up with a plastic lid masquerading as a saucer and took the stairs down to the subbasement and the hooches.

He smelled the steeping tea on the way down the stairs. It tasted faintly of oranges—God only knew how Narcisse came up with orange peel—and seemed to go to whatever part of the body most needed a fix. If you were constipated, it loosened you; if you were squirting, it plugged you. It took away headache and woke you up in the morning and calmed the jitters that came during a long spell of shellfire.

Valentine had a room to himself down among the old plumbing fixtures and electrical junction boxes. In the distance a generator clattered, steadily supplying juice but sounding as though it were unhappy with the routine. A little nearer down the hall Colonel Meadows occupied an old security office, but Valentine didn't see light creeping out from under the door, so he turned and moved aside the bedsheet curtaining off his quarters.

Even before his eyes picked out the L-shaped hammock in his wire-frame bed, his nose told him that someone lay in his room. A pale leg ending in a callused hammertoed foot emerged from the wooly army blanket, and a knife-cut shock of short red hair could just be distinguished at the other end.

Alessa Duvalier was back from the heart of Dallas.

Valentine examined the foot. Some people showed experiences of a hard life through their eyes, others in their rough hands; a few, like Narcisse, were bodily crippled. While the rest of Duvalier was rather severely pretty, even exquisite when mood or necessity struck, Duvalier's feet manifested everything bad the Cat had been through. Dark, with filth between the toes, hard-heeled, toes twisted, and dirt-crusted nails chipped, scabbed at the ankle, callused, and scarred from endless miles on worn-through socks—her feet alone told a gruesome tale.

A pair of utility sinks held her gear, reeking of camphor from its smell in the decontamination barrel, her sword-concealing walking stick lying atop more mundane boots and socks.

"Val, that you?" she said sleepily from under the blanket, voice muffled, a fistful of wool over her mouth and nose to keep out the basement chill. She shifted, and he caught a flash of upper thigh. She'd fallen into his bed wearing only a slop shirt. They'd never been lovers, but were as comfortable around each other as a married couple.

"Yeah."

"Room for two."

Not really; it was a small bed. "Shower first. Then I want to hear—"

"One more hour. I got in at oh-four."

"I was out at the forward posts. Pickets didn't report you—"

She snorted. Valentine heard Hank's quick step on the stairs he'd just come down.

He looked at his self-winding watch, a gift from Meadows

when the colonel assumed command of the Razorbacks. The engraved inscription on the back proclaimed forty-eight-year-old eternal love between a set of initials both ending in C. "One more hour, then. Breakfast?"

"Anything."

Valentine took a reviving spout-shower that kept Hank busy bearing hot water down from the kitchen.

"Haven't seen Ahn-Kha this morning, have you?"

"No, sir," Hank said, reverting to military expression with the ease of long practice.

Valentine hadn't smelled the Grog's presence at headquarters, but Ahn-Kha kept to himself in a partially blocked stairwell when he was at the headquarters. Ahn-Kha was evaluating and drilling some of the newer Razorbacks, mostly Texan volunteers who'd been funneled to them through Southern Command's haphazard field personnel depot north of the city. Southern Command tended to get recruits the all-Texan units didn't want, and Ahn-Kha knew how to turn lemons into lemonade. The first thing Valentine wanted recruits to learn was to respect Grogs, whether they were friends or enemies.

Way too many lives had been lost thanks to mistakes in the past.

Valentine asked Hank to go fill a tray, saw that the light was on in Meadows' office, and poked his head in to see if his superior had anything new on the rumored attack.

"Forward posts all quiet, sir," Valentine reported. "Anything happen here?"

Meadows was closing his shirt, his missing-fingered hand working the buttons up the seam like a busy insect. "Not even the usual harassing fire. They're finally running out of shells. Big Wings overhead in the night."

Big Wings were the larger, gargoylelike flyers the Kurians kept in the taller towers of Dallas. Both smarter and rarer than the Harpies Valentine had encountered, they tended to stay above, out of rifleshot, in the dark. Some weeks ago Valentine had seen a dead one that had been brought down by chance. It had been wearing a pair of binoculars and carrying an aerial photograph. Grease-penciled icons squiggled all over the photo marking the besieging army's current positions.

"Could come at dusk, sir," Valentine said, and regretted it before his tongue stilled. Meadows was smart enough that he didn't need to be told the obvious.

"Our sources could be wrong. Again," Meadows said, glancing at the flimsy basket next to his door. Messages that came in overnight but were not important enough to require the CO to be awakened rested there. The belief that an attack was due had been based on Valentine's intelligence—everything from deserter interrogations to vague murmurs from Dallas Operations that the heart of the city was abuzz with activity. There was no hit of reprimand, nor peevishness, in his tone. Meadows knew war was guesswork, and frequently the guesses were wrong.

"Sir, Smoke came in while I was out," Valentine said. "I just saw her; she would have told me if she'd seen anything critical. I'll debrief her over breakfast."

"How are the men up the boulevard doing?"

"The boulevard" was a wide east-west street that marked the forward edge of the Razors' positions. Snipers and machine gunners warred from blasted storefronts over five lanes of a former Texas state route.

"Unhappy about being on the line, sir. They only got three days at the airfield." Comparatively fresh companies had been moved up from the relative quiet of the old field in anticipation of the attack.

"Let's rotate them out if nothing happens by tomorrow morning."

"Will do, sir. I'll see to Smoke now."

"Thank her for me, Major. Eat hearty yourself—and then hit your bunk." Meadows tended to keep his orders brief and simple. Sometimes they were also pleasant. Meadows picked up the flimsies from his basket, glanced at them, and passed them to Valentine.

Valentine read them on the way back to the galley—or kitchen, he mentally corrected. Shipboard slang still worked itself into his thoughts, a leftover from his yearlong spell posing in the enemy's uniform as a Coastal Marine, and then living in the *Thunderbolt* after taking her from the Kurians.

01:30 POTABLE WATER LINE REESTABLISHED TO FORWARD POSITIONS

02:28 OP3 OP11 ARTILLERY FIRE FLASHES AND SOUNDS FROM OTHER SIDE OF CITY

03:55 OP3 BARRAGE CEASED

04:10 OP12 REPORTS TRAIN HEARD NORTH TOWARD CITY

The OP notation was for field phone–equipped forward observation posts. Valentine had heard the barrage and seen the flashes on the north side of the city as well. Glimpsed from between the tall buildings, they made the structures stand out against the night like gravestones to a dead city.

The only suspicious one was of the train. The lines into Dallas had been cut, torn up, mined, plowed under, or otherwise blocked very early in the siege. Readying or moving a train made little sense—unless the Kurians were merely shuffling troops within the city.

Valentine loaded up a tray, employed Hank as coffee bearer, and returned to his room. Duvalier twitched at his entry, then relaxed. Her eyes opened.

"Food," she said. Perhaps she'd half slept through their conversation earlier.

"And coffee," Valentine said. After checking to make sure she was decent, he brought Hank in. The teenager being a teenager, he'd waited in the spot with the best viewing angle of the room and bed.

"What's the latest from Big D?" Valentine asked, setting the tray briefly on the bed before pulling his makeshift desk up so that she'd have an eating surface.

"No sign of an assault. I saw some extra gun crews and battle police, but no troops have been brought up."

Hank hung up Duvalier's gear to dry. Valentine saw the boy clip off a yawn.

"The Quislings?"

"Most units been on half rations for over a month now. Internal security and battle police excepted, of course. And some of the higher officers, looks like they're as fat as ever. I heard some men talking: No one dares report sick. Rumor has it the Kurians are running short on aura, and the sick list is the first place they look."

"Morale?"

"Horrible," she reported between bites. "They're losing and they know it. Deserters aren't being disposed of quietly anymore. Every night just before they shut down power, they assemble representatives from all the Quisling brigades and have public executions. I put on a nurse's shawl and hat and watched one. NCOs kept offering me a bottle or cigarettes, but I couldn't take my eyes off the stage."

The incidental noises from Hank working behind him ceased.

"They make the deserters stand in these big plastic garbage cans, the ones with little arrows running around in a circle, handcuffed in front. Then a Reaper comes up from behind and tears open their shirts. They keep the poor bastards facing the ranks the whole time so they can see the expression on their faces. They're gagged, of course: The Reapers don't want any last words. The Reaper clamps its jaws somewhere between the shoulder blades and starts squeezing their arms into the ribcage. You hear the bones breaking, see the shoulders pop out as they dislocate.

"Then they just tip up the garbage can and wheel the body away. Blood and piss leaking out the bottom, usually. Then a political officer steps up and reads the dead man's confession, and his CO verifies his mark or signature. Then they wheel out the next one. Sometimes six or seven a night. They want the men to go to bed with something to think about.

"I've seen some godawful stuff, but that poor bastard . . . I had a dream about him."

"They never run out of Reapers, do they?" Hank put in.

"Seems not," Duvalier said.

Valentine decided to change the subject. "Okay, they're not massing for an attack. Maybe they're trying a breakout?"

"No, all the rolling motor stock is dispersed," she said, slurp-

ing coffee. "Unless it's hidden. I saw a few entrances to underground garages that were guarded with armored cars and lots of
wire and kneecappers."

The latter was a nasty little mine the Kurians were fond of.
When triggered, it launched itself twenty inches into the air like
a startled frog and exploded, sending fléchettes out horizontally
that literally cut a man off at the knees.

"I don't suppose you saw any draft articles of surrender crumpled up in the wastebaskets, did you?"

She made a noise that sent a remnants of a last mouthful of
masticated egg flying. "Na-ah."

"Now," Valentine said. "If you'll get out of my bed—"

"I need a real bath. Those basins are big enough to sit in. How
about your waterboy—"

Hank perked up at the potential for *that* duty.

Valentine hated to ruin the boy's morning. "You can use the
women's. There's piping and a tub."

Such gallantry as still existed between the sexes in the Razors
mostly involved the men working madly to provide the women
with a few homey comforts wherever the regiment moved. The
badly outnumbered women had to do little in return—the occasional smile, a few soft words, or an earthy joke reminded their
fellow soldiers of mothers, sweethearts, sisters, or wives.

"Killjoy," Duvalier said, winking at Hank.

The alarms brought Valentine out of his dreams and to his
feet. For one awful moment he hung on a mental precipice between reality and his vaguely pleasant dream—something to do
with a boat and bougainvillea—while his brain caught up to his
body and oriented itself.

Alarms. Basement in Texas. Dallas siege. The Razors.

Alarms?

Two alarms, his brain noted as full consciousness returned.
Whistle after whistle, blown from a dozen mouths like referees
trying to stop a football brawl, indicated an attack—all men to
grab whatever would shoot and get to their shooting stations,
plus the wail of an air alert siren.

But no gongs. If the Kurians had dusted again, every man who could find a piece of hollow metal to bang, tin cans to wheel rims, should be setting up as loud a clamor as possible. No one wanted to be a weak link in another Fort Worth massacre that caused comrades to "choke out."

Valentine forced himself to pull on socks and tie his boots. He grabbed the bag containing his gas mask, scarves, and gloves anyway and buckled his pistol belt. Hank had cleaned and hung up his cut-down battle rifle. Valentine checked it over as he hurried through men running every which way, or looking to their disheveled Operations officer for direction, and headed for the stairs to the control tower, the field's tactical command post. He took seemingly endless switchbacks of stairs two at a time to the "top deck"—the Razors' shorthand for the tallest point of Love Field.

He felt, then a second later heard, explosions. Worse than mortars, worse than artillery, and going off so close together he wondered if the Kurians had been keeping rocket artillery in reserve for a crisis. The old stairs rattled and dropped dirt as though shaking in fear.

"Would you look at those bastards!" he heard someone shout from the control tower.

"Send to headquarters: 'Rancid,' " Valentine heard Meadows shout. "Rancid. Rancid. Rancid."

Another explosion erupted in black-orange menace: the parking garage—the biggest structure on the field.

Valentine followed a private's eyes up and looked out on a sky filled with whirling planes.